I0741531

THE CONVENIENT

Albert Marsolais

Bettyanne Twigg

COPYRIGHT

This novel is a work of fiction. The names, characters and incidents portrayed in it are the work of the author's imagination. Any resemblance to actual persons, living or dead, events or localities is entirely coincidental.

Copyright © 2017 Albert Anthony Marsolais and Bettyanne Bethea Twigg

All Rights Reserved.

This book or any portion thereof may not be reproduced or used in any manner whatsoever without the express written permission of the publisher except for the use of brief quotations in a book review.

Trade Paperback ISBN: 978-1-7751061-1-1
Independently published

Visit the website at: www.theconvenient.net

DEDICATION

This book is dedicated to those who sacrificed their lives in the pursuit of improved medical treatments for the benefit of all.

TABLE OF CONTENTS

PREFACE

The Convenient is a medical adventure and mystery set in the early part of the 18th century in Scotland. It is told by from the point of view of two characters, Elspeth MacLeod, a healer from the Isle of Skye, and Malcolm Forrester, a physician from Edinburgh. They both end up working in a small town called Torrport located near Edinburgh.

In 1705, Scotland was in many ways not so much different than today. Worries about politics and war were common, with religion and disease thrown in the mix. Queen Anne was on the throne of both England and Scotland. There was a unified monarchy but separate parliaments and laws. England wanted unification and Scotland wasn't sure, and the Jacobite supporters of the exiled James, Prince of Wales, were always a threat. Meanwhile the major powers were fighting the War of the Spanish Succession on the continent, considered to be the first world war of modern times.

But for most, making a living and caring for one's family were paramount, and disease, poverty and misadventure always a possibility. For the elite, power, wealth and prestige were prime motivators driving history.

Follow The Convenient:
Facebook: https://www.facebook.com/theconvenientbook/
Twitter: https://twitter.com/theconvenientbk
Website: https://theconvenient.net

EPIGRAPH

Convenient, mistress, whore (B.E.) Cant expression of standard meaning, favorable to one's comfort. In Etherege, *Man of Mode* (1676) III.iii.234, a man sees 'Dorimant's convenient, Madame Loveit' on the street and makes lewd comments about her.

"All substances are poisonous, there is none that is not a poison; the right dose
differentiates a poison from a remedy."

(Philippus Aureolus Paracelsus - 1493-1541)

PART ONE

Two Small Issues

ONE

Malcolm – Confrontation

Edinburgh, Scotland, Spring 1705.

I'd come the short way, the one through the rough patches from Torrport to Edinburgh and we were held up as they righted an overturned carriage to the sounds of cursing coachmen and frightened horses. The spring rains had predictably turned roads to mud, but it was better than the wet snow and chill winds we had last month. All I could do was sit and wait til the road was cleared and hope I could get there in time. Then another delay at the ferry across the Firth of Forth had me on edge even before I'd set foot in the city.

Edinburgh was wearing its usual soot-stained gray with that pervasive smell of horse dung and humanity. At least Beaton met me at the step, as I hadn't been to Liddell's infirmary before and this was urgent. They wouldn't have called me back so soon and I knew it had to be important. The coachman tossed my leather bag down, hitting stinking slop instead of step.

"Is this all you've got?"

"Aye, didn't have time to pack much."

Beaton and I were at medical school together at Leiden a few years ago, and I touted him for the position here with Young. It was always good to see him, like meeting a ruddy Scots cherub, always a smile and kind word, poles apart from me, obviously. But we made an effective duo as our friendship grew. Beaton picked up my bag and I decided not to tip the careless coachman.

"This way Forrester, they're waiting for us, but the patient died."

I didn't want to hear that of course. Live ones are more useful, but we'll take what we get. He led me up the worn stone steps into a large wood paneled room then down the stairs on the right to the cellar. It was stone, dirt floor, a few torches in wall sconces for light, the sickly-sweet odour of death competing with the astringent smell of vinegar disinfectant. I saw them as soon as I entered the large central room at the bottom. There was Liddell and Young and two others I didn't know.

"We need a decision soon." It was Young.

The body was on a metal table at the far end of the room, everyone staying as far as...well, you know. We were all scared of this. Beaton introduced me to the two new men: "This is McLean, Surgeon, and you may already know Cameron, Advocate."

McLean was short, dark-haired, serious. "Malcolm Forrester of Torrport, pleased to meet you." I offered to shake hands, but he declined. Understandable considering, but still.

"That's your practice two streets over, McLean?"

"Aye."

He was making me nervous. Not sure why he was here, physicians and surgeons were at each other's throats lately over that rushed *Pharmacopeia* publication by the College a few years ago.

"We can use your perspective and skills, McLean. This affects us all."

He grunted and looked away. Getting nothing further from McLean, I tried Cameron.

"I hope we don't need your services, but after that debacle last fall, I can see why Beaton and Young wanted you here."

Cameron was one of those all too calm types that don't seem to understand risk, and there was plenty in this room. Touch the wrong thing, breathe the wrong way and you're dead. We knew contact with infected humans or materials was key but not exactly how it worked.

"I've dealt with the College before in cases, so if there's any trouble, carefully record everything and contact me immediately."

He was at least trying to be helpful in his precise reassuring way. I decided to fill him in on the basics.

"You see Lister published a report in the Royal Society Proceedings a few years ago that suggested a method to induce immunity to smallpox. The English ignored it, came from India, not much credibility. We know from experience that those who survive smallpox seldom get it again. This new method may work. We tried it last fall, but in the middle of an outbreak. It didn't go well but we want to try it again, this time under more controlled conditions." I let him think about it.

"I remember well. Several died, we heard something happened at the College. Many are still grieving for the sick and dead." Cameron forced a smile, but his eyes betrayed him.

"My sister Agnes was one," he said calmly.

I listened feeling his sorrow as he told us about her and how she died. Smallpox is not a kind way to go.

Cameron retrieved a large white handkerchief and wiped his nose, then offered. "I will help you, wouldn't think otherwise if this has any chance of ending smallpox, and gratis, of course."

"Appreciated Cameron." I extended my hand and he shook it warmly.

"Beaton will be your contact, and you will be pleased to know he keeps copious notes."

I gave a sharp laugh that startled everyone. I was remembering Beaton's notes, he recorded everything like his physician father taught him. My father is a Lord and Judge. They record everything too. But unlike Beaton, I failed to learn that useful habit, preferring to get on to solving the next problem.

"Now let's get down to it fellows," I ordered.

We needed to move this along quickly now. We only had hours and a lot to do or it would be a repeat of the first time we tried this last year.

"When did he die?" I asked Young. He was the most respected and experienced of us. Had a good practice among the gentry.

"Less than an hour?"

"The usual symptoms?"

"Most of them, he went fast though," Beaton interjected.

"Who was attending? Who touched him?"

"That would be me." Liddell raised his hand tentatively. He looked terrified, we all were, all but Cameron and he didn't fully know yet.

"Liddell, I see he's still clothed. Did you check him over thoroughly?"

"Forrester, he was covered in rash. Seen it before, you know." Liddell blurted in exasperation.

Liddell was too frightened to be of much use in making a proper diagnosis.

"I want him out of here. You know what this will do to my practice if word gets out?"

"Aye Liddell, I well understand."

We needed a plan before Liddell ruined our chance.

"I assume none of us here has been infected previously." No one disagreed, so I continued.

"This one is fresh, looks usable. We need someone to fetch McLaren. He survived the last epidemic and can safely do the autopsy and collect samples. Young, can you find him?"

"I will try." Young turned to go.

"Liddell as soon as McLaren has his samples, you can dispose of the body. Do you have the patient's name and background?"

"I don't have much, they just brought him here because I was closest. Two men from the Sand Bar Pub at Leith brought him. I think they said he was French."

Liddell should have questioned them more, but didn't want the patient, prayed this problem would just disappear. Can't blame him, he's a wife and family, the rest of us are young with no dependents, expendable. Beaton was busy making notes as Young left.

"Alright Liddell, you know what must be done, keep this room sealed until McLaren arrives. Call the undertaker and have them ready to remove the body after he's finished." Liddell looked very unhappy and obviously didn't like me commanding him in his own practice, but I couldn't leave anything to chance this time.

"Beaton, we need to get to the pub before all traces...then we can visit Turnbull."

Beaton's head snapped up with a look of alarm on his angelic face. "Turnbull! Oh, Forrester! You know how that will end."

Beaton hated conflict and Sir Robert Turnbull is the Head of the College of Physicians and opposed to modern sciences. I had become the unofficial leader of this group mainly because I could stand up to Turnbull. Sometimes family connections are useful.

"We need his support, if possible. Don't want him complaining we're sneaking around behind his back, do we? I'll deal with him, Beaton; need you with me old chum, but bring your notes this time, for God's sake! We want Turnbull to authorize the quarantine as well. Come on Beaton, we have much to do. Gentlemen, leave a note at the College main desk if you want to contact me."

I pushed Beaton up the stairs and he started telling me something about a cousin visiting from Skye and he had to help her, and would I mind. But my thoughts were racing, prioritizing tasks, considering options, mitigating risk. Beaton had his carriage waiting on the side-street. He told the coachman to take us home. I assumed I would stay in his extra room as usual.

"John, once we dump my stuff at your place we'll go straight to the Sand Bar. I'll question the staff and you can inspect the room. Bring your bag, masks, gloves, sample jars...anything else?" Beaton gave me that look. I know he finds me a frustration sometimes.

"I already told you my cousin Elspeth is here and using that room. You'll have to look after the pub investigation yourself. Elspeth is not a bad cook, when she's not trying to poison, so you're welcome to come for supper."

"Ah yes, I did hear you, but you know how my mind works. Well, drop me at the College then. I need to make an appointment with the old man for tomorrow morning. You'd better make that one or I'll be in a tough spot. Turnbull won't accept my version alone."

"Aye, I can be there after eleven and with my notes this time." His glance warned me he didn't appreciate my dig about forgetting his notes. Beaton seldom slips up and absolutely hates when I tease him about it.

The coach pulled up to the main entrance at the College. I got down with my bag, turned and waved. "John, I truly appreciate your friendship. I'll try to make supper, but you know how these things can go. Will it be around seven?" I needed to mend some fences with him. I can be very abrasive in a crisis. He knows it, but it's still hard to swallow.

"Seven will be fine, Mal, and good luck today. I have some patients and Elspeth waiting. Farewell til tonight." He shouted for the coachman to continue. The cold rain was starting to let up and a scattering of blue filtered through the grey-white clouds. Edinburgh was that awkward mix of wealth and poverty living too close. One had always to be on guard; there were many ways to fall and few to rise.

* * *

The Royal College of Physicians was established almost twenty-five years ago by Royal Charter for the purpose of making medicine a more reputable profession and for better serving the needs of the poor. Medicine was and still is provided by a range of well and not-so-well qualified practitioners. The College was trying to professionalize medicine, and there was considerable opposition from those who did not fit College standards.

Fellows of the College had been taking turns hosting meetings, lectures, and housing the rapidly growing library, but that obviously had limited appeal, so a property was purchased the previous year and construction started on a building. Meanwhile, Turnbull's home was the current temporary headquarters, since he recently had been appointed senior physician and first lecturer. It was one of those newer stone buildings that looked like it was designed to house the Greek gods.

The main door was open, and his aide Fraser met me at the desk in the foyer. He was one of those sour types that seemed to derive no pleasure in life. "Forrester, you again?" He turned his black-coated back to me and pretended to look for something on the cabinet. He was particularly good at being subtly rude and certainly knew his boss and I were at odds. To call yourself a physician in Scotland, you needed to be a Fellow of the College. To be a Fellow, you must be accepted by Turnbull. Acceptance was based on training and, well, other factors. Turnbull was rapidly becoming the prime gatekeeper, and I was not among his favourites.

I leaned over the desk. "I need an appointment for tomorrow, just past eleven."

He glanced back at me, then dropped a book, bent to retrieve it, showing me his too ample bottom. "You know Sir Robert is a busy man, perhaps next month, Forrester." He was enjoying this too much, but I had no time for it. Some days I will spar with minions, but not today.

"Then put me down for next month, subject: smallpox epidemic started last month. But we aren't going to wait, Fraser." I pushed the desk at him forcefully and turned abruptly to leave then heard him scream as I took the first step.

"Wait! One second Forrester, I may have a cancellation for you." He ran his trembling finger down the appointment book. "Yes, here is one you can have at eleven-fifteen. I will re-schedule him." Fraser knew what shite he would be in with Turnbull had he turned me away. Of course, I could be bluffing, but was it worth the chance?

"I'll be here with John Beaton. Make sure Turnbull knows," I commanded, then left mumbling about rude servants just loud enough so he would hear. The clamour of the street quickly brought me back to purpose and I was reminded of how little time I had to sort this, and with Beaton busy I decided to call on McLaren to hear about the diagnosis before visiting the pub.

* * *

Angus McLaren's place was an older beam and stucco sagging building with dormers dropped at odd places on the roof. Most of us single men buy or rent a home and use the lower floor for our practice and upper floors for living. His was spacious enough, but had those annoyingly low ceilings from back in the days of the little people. He met me at the door with his off-kilter grin and hearty hand shake. McLaren would be scary had he not been wearing fine clothes. He was tall and thin, bent to the right side and pock-marked everywhere. He survived the last round of smallpox, but just – most of his family didn't. He was one of the nicest of men, but women didn't want him because of his looks.

"Come on in, Mal. You must be here for the autopsy results." He brought me into his tidy study, on one side, rows of books neatly stacked on an old chest, on the other, a small laboratory bench with vials, microscope, cabinets and surgery tools. The place smelled of cleaners and herbs. He offered me the best chair then sat on the one with the uncertain leg and opened his worn leather notebook. I wasn't sure what result I wanted to hear.

"There were pustules on the palms of his hands and bottom of his feet, and they were of uniform size. I did a quick autopsy. Couldn't see any other cause of death. It likely was smallpox that killed him." He looked at me with a flat, serious expression. We both knew what was coming next.

"And you took some samples?" McLaren was highly professional, but I had to check.

"Aye, Mal, they're in the metal cabinet on the bench. Got them from pustules on the face. Assumed they would be the oldest ones, have them labelled and stored in sealed glass. I understand we have to wait several days for them to age before use."

I nodded then took out my quill pen, ink, and paper. "We don't exactly know how long, but based on Lister's report, perhaps up to two weeks."

We reviewed the next steps we needed to take. The procedure was simple. It amounted to drying the smallpox pustules and grinding them in a mortar. Then the powder was packed in a small cloth and put in a pipe and lit. The smoke was puffed into the patient's nostril. It was reported that patients receiving this treatment would become immune to smallpox. Problem was that the details were sketchy. Did it depend on the age of the patient, should we use a pustule or a later-stage scab, how long should it be dried? There were many variables and if it all went sideways, they would be blaming us again.

"I think we'll be ready this time Angus. Will you be our physician again, and do you have room for us all here?"

"My pleasure, Mal. We may have to use some storerooms on the upper floors, but I think it will be sufficient to needs."

"So, we have Beaton, Young and me as patients, and Young said he may have four others. We need at least ten for our trial. I know everyone was in high panic last time and we rushed it. This time it will be tightly controlled. Five of us will get the smoke with ground pustules, five will get smoke with no pustules. I'll set it up, but you and Cameron will be the ones to record everything." He nodded in agreement and made a few notes. What we both didn't want to discuss yet was how to decide who got what. Smallpox kills one in three, so best case even if the new treatment works is that one or a few of us will die and many will be damaged for life, and that assumes McLaren can contain the spread of it while we are under quarantine. Worst case, well I don't want to think about it. Father was right, I should have gone into law. We'd finished and sat quietly for a time while Angus flipped through his notes to make sure we'd missed nothing.

"Beaton and I have an appointment with Turnbull tomorrow. Watch for an explosion coming from that direction." We both liked to joke about the current situation, but it was serious business and many lives were at stake.

"Well don't punch him, Mal, remember he's an old man." Angus grinned, perhaps trying to place that possibility in my mind.

"I know, but he can punch back in other ways, can't he." Turnbull could remove us from the College, unlikely in my case mind you, but others were not so well-protected. I rose to go then remembered. "Angus, do you have a spare room for the night?"

He laughed. "If you don't mind sleeping on an infirmary bed, you're always welcome here."

"Better than many places I've found myself!" I chortled, the tension of our meeting escaping.

"Beaton has invited me for supper and to meet his cousin. Last time he tried to line me up with one of his family, it took a month to get rid of her. Well at least I hope she knows how to cook, haven't had more than a crust since morning."

"Being fed and courted is highly unreasonable, I agree." McLaren looked away and I knew I'd been insensitive.

"I've some time to drop by that pub before I go to Beaton's, see who's around who can remember anything." I squeezed his shoulder to reassure him...well, that I cared.

"If you need anything, I'll be here. Use this key to get in the back door, and good luck at the pub and with that woman." We both chuckled at the last part.

* * *

It was getting dark when I left McLaren's house, so I caught the carriage to Leith. It gave me time to think and settle. We don't have enough physicians as is, and some of us may die in this experiment and we could cause an epidemic if it got out. Maybe Turnbull was right, and the risks were too high. The status quo usually is safe and secure, and taking risks often ends badly. Maybe God does intend for us to die this horrible way as just reward, but why is it the poor are the ones who tend to suffer and die; does God hate them more than the rich? I shook my head and realized too much time to think may not be good for me, so I sang a happy song as the carriage rolled along.

"There was twa sisters in a bowr,
Edinburgh, Edinburgh
There was twa sisters in a bowr,
Stirling for ay
There was twa sisters in a bowr,
There came a knight to be their wooer."

Reverie soon enough was drawn back to reality as I entered the docklands.

Edinburgh is located on the south shore of the estuary of the River Forth, that narrow waist of Scotland with Edinburgh on the east side facing the continent and Glasgow on the west. The Glasgow Road united the two cities, and many found it easier to offload passengers and cargo at Edinburgh and transport them overland to Glasgow than make the hazardous trip by sea around the north of Scotland. The port was located at that part of Edinburgh known locally as Leith, and the Sand Bar Pub was a block south of the docks. It wasn't hard to find this time of night with music and light blasting out the open door. I always travel armed with dagger and flintlock pistol, both hidden in my waistcoat. They aren't much good for anything but last resort defense. I tend to rely more on a sharp tongue, hard fists, and quick feet to keep me out of harm's way.

The pub was small, dark, low, lit mostly by the open fireplace. A ramshackle assortment of stained tables and chairs was set too close together on the littered stone floor. Wood and tobacco smoke, ale, whisky, puke, urine, combined to create that typical pub smell, and that's just what battered one of my senses.

I entered with confidence, always best in these circumstances. Project authority and most cooperate, and from my clothes they could easily see I was high born. I dress simply but with the best fabrics and cut. The barman saw me instantly and came out from the back to greet.

"How may I help you, sir?" He bowed slightly while wiping wet hands on apron.

"Surely you know? The man with the rash, three days-ago? Who are you and tell me what you know?" I was stern and direct, offering no friendly chatter.

"Aye, I knew someone would come. My name is Calum Duncan, owner of the Sand Bar. The Frenchman was fevered but we gave him a room anyway, said he'd just arrived and had nowhere else to go."

"I am Malcolm Forrester, Physician. Did you get his name and ship?"

The pub gradually went quiet. Eyes turned our way. Everyone wanted to hear.

"That will be in the register." He called to the woman behind the bar and she brought it. He flipped back a few days and looked up. "His name is Jean Tremblay from Rouen and he came in on the *Chantilly*."

"And how did he get to Doctor Liddell's?"

"I'd seen that rash before. In this business, you see it all. He came down to breakfast and I knew at once, so we took him immediately."

"Who took him?"

"Me and John Thompson. He's my brother-in-law and works the docks."

Smallpox is not infectious until the rash appears, and it takes about twelve days for that, so even if these two were infected, they were no danger to anyone...yet. We needed to contain this fast and that meant locating everyone who could have been infected by Tremblay.

"What about Tremblay's bedding and clothing?"

"We burned the bedding and gave Liddell's man his bag." Duncan seemed to be playing it straight with me, knew it was in his best interests. Hiding or obstructing something like this could bring serious charges.

"You and Thompson stay put. The authorities may have to quarantine this place and anyone who was in contact with Tremblay."

"I was worried it would come to this. Damn my bloody luck to hell! Och, I've just paid off the last of the fire repairs. Aye, sir, I'll tell John in the morning. Another thing, sir: There was another man sharing that room for a night, a John Smith, off the same ship, had an English accent, but couldn't quite place it."

"What happened to him?"

"He had a visitor, big man, older, well-dressed, then Smith left. Didn't say where he was going."

That's how it always happens. It starts with one, then two, then... So now we have at least two more who could be infected. Only one day in and already it felt like it was spiraling out of control. Several possibly infected by Tremblay and too many variables at play. Last thing we needed was trying to conduct an experiment in the middle of an epidemic with all fingers pointing at us.

Looking quite glum, Duncan removed his apron and went back to the bar to replace the register. I had enough to go on for now, so I said to everyone loudly: "A Frenchman named Jean Tremblay was here a few days ago, with smallpox rash. If you were in contact with him, go see a physician as soon as possible."

I didn't like having to do this, rumors spread, and people panic, but McLaren was certain, and we had to act. I left, hearing the room erupt in conversation. It was too late to look for the *Chantilly*, so I headed back to Beaton's before curfew started and hoped supper was at least edible.

* * *

Beaton was excessively cheerful that evening and the meal of roast duck and turnip served with a rich French wine sauce was beyond delicious. It was the company that turned out to be challenging. Beaton had spent the day helping Elspeth shop for medical supplies. I was not surprised to hear that she was in medicine. Their family seems to be well endowed in that regard. It was where she practiced and why she ended up there that was the shocker. The evening started slowly with me bringing Beaton up to date on what I'd found at the pub. Elspeth served us and listened quietly. But when I came to the part about Duncan burning Tremblay's bedding, she interjected: "Did you check the room?"

I wasn't sure what she meant. "Why?"

"Maybe there were other things in the room that could have been contaminated, like for instance, towels and rugs."

"Ah, no I didn't look."

"You should have." She sat, hands folded primly on her lap.

She was right, I'd been sloppy and that's why I'd wanted Beaton there; it was hard to think of everything yourself. "You seem well-informed about smallpox."

"I am. Skye was infected eight years ago, and as you can see I didn't escape." She was petite with sea-blue eyes and auburn hair, pretty in that immature girlish way, but for the few pock marks on the left side of her face; but then many had them and no one took much notice nowadays. Last thing I needed was a woman in my life right now, if that was Beaton's plan, but I was becoming more curious about her especially after she challenged me.

"Will you be returning to Skye soon, then?"

"No, obviously not!" She looked at Beaton quizzically.

"Mal, I did tell you. She's been working at Torrport for two months. Set up shop as a healer. Thought you could keep an eye on her." Beaton must have told me, but honestly, I didn't remember, but I did recall hearing something about a healer from the locals.

Elspeth flushed. "John, I know you mean well, but I don't need anyone keeping an eye on me. I have Cawdie and Janet and enough money from mother to keep us going. Sir Malcolm would be better off keeping his eyes on his patients than me."

This had become confusing, especially her insinuation at the end. "Alright John, what's going on?"

"Long story..." he started, and Beaton loved to tell long stories. After half an hour, I understood that Elspeth had fled Skye because of some problems with the Laird, and unsubstantiated witchcraft charges. She'd come to Edinburgh and Beaton helped her find a home at Torrport. Edinburgh was awash with healers and I was alone at Torrport and he thought...well maybe he hoped. That was two months-ago.

"I am seeing a lot of your former patients. They say you don't have time for them." She was chiding me, and I didn't much like it.

"That's fine, you can have the ones who aren't really sick and the ones with women's complaints." I pushed back, but it was true I didn't have much patience for the time-wasters even if they could afford to pay. "If you get anyone who *is* sick, please send them to a proper physician." I was becoming irritable, then Beaton deftly changed the subject.

We ended the evening chatting amiably about poetry and the latest city gossip. I wasn't sure what to make of Elspeth. She certainly wasn't shy about speaking her mind, and Torrport could use more medical care, I welcomed that so long as our relationship didn't become toxic. But I trusted Beaton and his good sense, except when it came to matchmaking.

* * *

I awoke early at McLaren's still thinking about last night with Beaton and Elspeth, and conversations ran through my head as I dressed quickly. I needed to get back to the docks before the *Chantilly* sailed, so I left a note for McLaren in case he wondered, and caught an early carriage to the port master's office. He'd just arrived. I asked about the *Chantilly*, found she'd already sailed, bound for Amsterdam. Tremblay may not have infected anyone while onboard, the rash only coming after, but better to be safe. I quickly scrawled a letter for the Amsterdam port master informing him the *Chantilly* may have carried smallpox. They'd know what to do. The letter was to be sent out later, on another ship. With some luck, it would get there in time. There was a growing trade between Edinburgh and the continent, ships coming and going at all hours. That's all I could do at this end and I needed to prepare for my meeting with Turnbull.

* * *

McLaren was seeing patients when I got back. I stuck my head in and waved, said we'd catch up later. I had to record all that had transpired so far. I know I'm truly bad at that, needed to make more of an effort to be organized. Using McLaren's office, I wrote a concise letter to Young, describing everything including the names of those possibly infected: Liddell, Duncan, Thompson, Smith, and the unknown man who visited Smith. I made a copy of the letter for McLaren too and one to give to Turnbull and one to keep. My hand was cramping at the end. I'd already told Beaton last night and he made volumes of notes, of course.

It was past ten and I made my way to Beaton's. We needed time to plan. "Mal, I hope you will be more moderate in speech this time." He got right to the point.

"I just wasn't expecting to be attacked for trying to solve our biggest medical problem. Just caught me off-guard and I reacted."

"I shouldn't have to remind you we don't need a war with Turnbull. Maybe you don't care Mal, but it reflects badly on the rest of us." Beaton was right of course, it had almost ended in blows last time and once people start fighting, reason is the first casualty. But in my defense, no one else would have taken him on.

"This time we'll keep him fully informed, but I'll not bow to reactionaries who think progress ended with the Romans. But yes, we'll try harder to be more diplomatic and you can impress him with your notes of recent cases."

We went over the main points we wanted to cover. Beaton was good at keeping me on track.

"So long as we project a united front we'll be fine. I prefer his backing, but we need to be prepared to do this without it. There will be some opposition. We just have to deal with it."

"Well let's get over there Mal, you have my full support, but why do I feel like I am going to my execution?"

"You worry too much, John; all will be well." I didn't believe that of course, but no point sharing my true feelings with him. I needed his stability much more than he

18

knew. I took his arm and we headed out. The streets were clogged, and the carriage ride took forever as we sat in the silence of condemned men. I went over it in my mind one last time and was ready for Turnbull and would not lose temper and harm Beaton. Fraser met us at the desk. We were a few minutes late. Apologies not accepted. Turnbull was ready. We thought we were.

"Come in and have some tea and shortbread." Turnbull walked toward us, radiant smile locked on as he offered his hand. I took it and looked him in the eye, wondering what was up. He isn't normally so welcoming.

"And you, Beaton, how is your dear father? Haven't seen him in ages." Beaton hadn't either, but we exchanged greetings and stood awkwardly until Turnbull offered us the brocade settee beside the white marble fireplace. The room was done in that new style with floral wallpaper and polished light wood floors. He served us tea, then sat opposite on a high-backed leather chair. We sipped quietly and waited an unnerving few minutes.

"I am so glad to see you both. Now what brings you two gifted physicians to my humble home today? Something to do with smallpox again, is it?" He beamed, clear blue eyes full of love. I was ready for war and now this? Next, he will be giving hugs. He always seemed to know how to keep me off-balance, and I resented it.

"Sir, we have two related concerns and yes, it is about smallpox again. We may be having another outbreak at the port." I handed my letter to him and went over it. He had a few questions, mostly about who had been told and who knew what. Turnbull is very good at controlling information.

"Forrester, you know perfectly well smallpox is with us at all times in the lowlands. Cases are reported routinely, and it has been years since we've had an epidemic."

"That's quite true, but usually it's the children of the poor infected. Accepting that is bad enough, but we know that the most serious epidemics of the past included healthy adults. Now these new cases are adults and started with a foreigner, an even greater cause of concern."

"Then what do you suggest I do? Our physicians are quite capable of treating smallpox."

I looked at Beaton. He was silent, eyes half shut, looking like he was praying.

"Sir, with the utmost respect, our physicians are not capable of stopping an epidemic and successfully treating patients." He knew I was coming to that. I assumed he was ready for me, but with what?

"Alright Forrester, I will recommend to the Magistrate that the Sand Bar pub be quarantined for forty days, and have the Town Guard locate and quarantine everyone on your list. But you must not go around disrespecting your fellow physicians by suggesting our treatments are ineffective. I know how you feel about this already. I expect your compliance, and I won't have you bringing ill-repute on our profession as you did last fall." His smile had vanished, and loving eyes replaced by blue steel. Now we were down to it, the real reason why we were here. I resolved to remain rational, despite his provocations.

"Beaton and I have been collecting cases. We interviewed physicians throughout the city, asked them about treatments and outcomes. What do you think we found?"

Turnbull looked startled. Evidently his spies hadn't reported this. "I know our physicians give the best treatments available, but I can see you are determined to tell me, so get on with it."

"John, give him the short version, please." Beaton's eyes snapped open. He was prepared and in a few minutes explained that treatments varied greatly, and yet the outcomes were about the same as no treatment.

I added, "So we have a situation where some physicians use heat, some cold, some purging, some blood-letting, some secret medications, all with no standardization, and yet we seem to be dealing with one disease. So how is it we can have dozens of appropriate treatments for one disease?" That was the main issue and he bloody well knew it.

"Forrester, we have our accepted theories that have stood us well for centuries and you know that the role of the physician is to consider each patient as an individual and devise a treatment plan tailored for that person. Are you suggesting we throw out everything we know about medicine? I cannot support that and nor should you, and Beaton you should know better." He glared at us both, temper on the half-boil.

I waited a minute to let the silence between us settle, then responded with carefully rehearsed words. "Sir Turnbull, all we are saying is that we should look at the evidence objectively and not accept what we think we know as truth without sufficient proof. The evidence clearly suggests we are doing a poor job of treating the most important disease that affects our community. My question to you is why are you and so many others willing to accept so much suffering and death as normal?" I wanted to put him and his reactionary friends on the defensive. I may have gone too far. He almost stood up, face filling with rage.

"We do not accept this! All of us work each day to alleviate sickness and many of our ranks have perished. Get off your high horse, Forrester! We just don't agree with your methods. Can't you see that?"

I didn't respond immediately. Glanced at Beaton. He looked ready to bolt. "Sir Turnbull, we will be doing an experiment with that inoculation method described by Lister. Our overall goal is to begin studies on smallpox from a scientific perspective to see if we can find an effective treatment. We wanted you to know and respectfully seek your support."

"Who's involved?"

I told him. No point hiding it. He would find out soon enough anyway. He had sources, so did we.

Turnbull answered with tense restraint and he obviously had prepared this. "You do not have my support. I will never agree to experiment on patients and risk starting an epidemic. I have done my best to protect you and your followers. You must know there are powerful forces in play and if you proceed with this irresponsible experiment, I will not be held responsible for what happens. Beaton, I've come to expect this kind of behavior from Forrester, but you, you should be ashamed. This so-called *method* is nothing more than a random report of barbarian folk medicine from Asia of all places! Beaton, do you really intend to risk harming your patients on Forrester's say-so?"

I knew that must have cut Beaton deeply, he was no lackey but a great team player. All he could do was grimly hold silence.

"Both of you, make note of my decision and pass it to the others. If you proceed, you will regret it and your families will not be able to protect you this time. I am afraid I must inform your fathers, perhaps they can make you adopt a more prudent path."

There was nothing further to say. He rose and called Fraser. "Show these gentlemen out."

We were both shaking by the time we reached the street. "I'm sorry Beaton. We did our best, but I think the results were predetermined."

"Mal, you did not have to antagonize him like that!" Beaton looked like an over-ripe cherry.

"Perhaps, but we seem to always be the ones being attacked and on the defensive. And I am fed up with being a punching bag. If they want war, we'll give it to them."

Beaton sighed, and as we got in the carriage filled my ears with the many reasons war would be a very bad idea. We were both right. Beaton dropped me back at McLaren's. I told Angus all while sharing Elspeth's leftovers and fresh bread with tea. McLaren sided with Beaton and advised caution. He knew I could be a hot-head. I needed to see Father before Turnbull's letter arrived, so I changed to a fresh shirt and headed home on foot.

* * *

Father is a Judge of the Court of Session and High Court of Justiciary, the highest courts in Scotland, and he bought a home near the courts after selling the family estate at Corstorphine after Mother's death. The area around the courts was devastated in 1700 by a great fire that left hundreds homeless. Many of the buildings were repaired, while others still showed the effects. Between that and the famine in the northern highlands that drove thousands to the cities, Edinburgh was over-crowded and expensive, the refugee camps only recently having been dispersed.

Father's servant announced me at the door to the study. It was in old-style dark wood paneling, but with modern plush furniture in earthy tones. Father was as usual at his desk, head buried in a raft of legal papers. He smiled as he saw me, and I came over and gave a warm hug, then sat in the chair beside him. I love my father. He was always there for my older brother George and me, even when he disagreed with our choices. "Father, another case? What is it about this time?"

He was discreet of course but loved talking about his cases. "Well this is a good one, a test of our new law concerning *Habeas Corpus.* The defendant claims he was unlawfully imprisoned for seven months, with no trial. It will be up to us to determine if he has a legitimate case, and as usual there are mitigating circumstances." He gave his usual wry chuckle.

Father loved the law and wanted me to follow in his footsteps. My first choice was the military, but George took that, and I hated the idea of reading books my whole life, so I disappointed everyone by going into medicine.

"Well that does sound to me like a long time to be rotting in a jail. What was the hold-up?" I was genuinely curious.

Sir William was in his element now and described what had taken place. Seems a few on both sides had been withholding evidence, and a key witness had mysteriously disappeared.

"I am sure you will parse this well, Father." He had a supremely sharp intellect and could be very intimidating in debate, but was always fair-minded, even when it meant taking a loss. But now I needed his help with Turnbull. "Father, there has been a new case of smallpox at the docks, a foreigner. This could be trouble if we can't contain it. Turnbull will be seeking quarantine from the Magistrate." I stopped to let him think.

"And you want what from me?" He knew I must be coming to that.

"And, umm, you remember last fall, the little problem I had over an experiment?"

He nodded. "Aye, Turnbull was very displeased with you. What is it this time?"

Father didn't like the medical profession. Said it was mostly made up of over-paid frauds, and he'd seen far too many cases through the courts.

"We want to try that smallpox experiment again. Turnbull is still against it and may contact you."

He reached out and touched my hand. "I stood up for you last time when Turnbull and others were saying you started an outbreak that cost lives. They wanted you charged. You know that, but there wasn't sufficient probable cause and intent. But what if there had been? Are you willing to risk all for this? Is there not a better way that's acceptable to Turnbull and the others?"

He was being reasonable, damn him. Yes, maybe if I was more political about this I wouldn't have raised the ire of so many, but what is past is past and I doubt I could turn the clock back at this point. "Father the reactionaries don't like our scientific approach. They are true believers in the status quo, in the will of God, you know what I mean. You're right, medicine is filled with quackery. Why? Because there have been few proper studies to determine best treatments. We are still largely using Roman medicine! I know I can be abrasive, but damn it all, I'm so tired of watching patients die when we use *approved* methods that simply don't work!" That had been wanting to come out for days. It was so frustrating! We were accused of being reckless and anti-religious, when all we wanted was better results for our patients.

"Son, I will deal with Turnbull. He has other issues too." Father winked, then went on. "I want you to get a good advocate. Include him at every step and for God's sake, pay heed to advice. He will tell you to document everything, consider every possible outcome, mitigate risk for your patients and community. Be prudent and professional. I know you want to improve the lot of the sick. I trust you, but I also know what and who you are up against. Never underestimate your opponents."

We ended with Father telling me about brother George and his recent exploits with the Duke of Marlborough on the continent. He understandably was very proud of George. I wished he felt the same about me. I left Father's content the situation was manageable, and so long as the quarantine was effective, we could do our work without much turmoil. I walked back to McLaren's and intended to stay the night before traveling home. I'd been away two days and my patients needed me. McLaren wasn't there so I wrote him a note and one for Beaton too, sharing Father's advice and encouraging Beaton to continue gathering cases to publish. I knew they would do their part and when I came back in several days, all would be ready. It had been a stressful few days. I washed and retired early.

* * *

The sound of metal clanging off the stone floor woke me. It was dark but there seemed to be light coming from the study. I rose up on one elbow to see better, and whispered, "Angus, is that you?"

I heard muffled speech. Someone said "McLaren". I slid my legs to the floor as a large shadow came toward me.

"Angus?'

Then he hit me with it and I was out.

TWO

Elspeth – Birth

Torrport, Scotland, Spring 1705.

Scathach made a low sound deep in her throat, lifted her head, and stared at the door. The knock came just as I had begun to pour the measured poisonous tincture into the smaller container. After carefully completing the transfer, I placed both bottles cautiously on the table, corked them securely, and turned toward the door. It was late; rain pattered softly on the thatch roof. The hour meant I would probably be stitching up a knife cut or applying a poultice to an eye.

The soft leather of my shoes makes little sound, but Scathach's nails clicked comfortingly beside me on the wooden planks. I unbolted the heavy oak door and pulled it open. Cold wet air greedily sucked warmth from the room and fat drops splashed on the floor. A woman stood framed there, the night and dark cloak clutched about her accentuated the extreme pallor of her face.

I knew her at once. Lady Julianne had come to the castle only a few months earlier. She was introduced as the Laird's kinswoman, who had just been widowed and left with child, and thus was one of his dependents. That was the outwardly accepted tale, although no one believed it for a moment. She was deemed the Laird's convenient, and had been, perhaps for longer than he had been married to Lady Margaret. The fragile perfection of her face and figure made an indelible impression on both male and female, and she was generally more pitied than censured.

Scathach sniffed once, whined softly, her wolf gold eyes watchful.

"You are the healer?" Her voice was barely audible, soft and strained. One hand slipped from the cloak and grasped the heavy oak door frame. "Help me," she said faintly. The movement dislodged her cloak and it dropped open, revealing the mound of her belly tight against a gown of pale blue silk. Dark discolorations stained the material from below the waist to the hem, and the distinctive iron and copper odor of blood was strong against the smell of wet wool. She had fallen at least once, for her hands and dress were muddy as well. I reached for her and pulled her into the cottage, out of the rain. She stood there, absorbing the warmth, shuddered and began to crumple. My arms caught her and eased her gently down. Janet, roused by the commotion, hurried in from the bedroom, drawing her arisaid over her linen shift.

The calm that I had been taught to use when I was with a patient filled me. I could hear my master saying: "Empty your mind of all except the present."

Janet moved to help me. "Blankets, and we need Cawdie to get her into the bed." She nodded, hurried to the old chest by the door and removed several woolen blankets. Kneeling, she unfolded one on the floor. Together we managed to get it beneath the woman. I removed her sodden cloak and wrapped her warmly in another blanket. Taking one too slender wrist in my hand, I felt the pulse beating frantically under my fingers.

Janet stood, belted the arisaid at her waist, tugged the top edge over her head and still barefoot, walked swiftly outside to the attached shed where Cawdie slept.

I have no memory of a time when Janet has not been part of my life. On the day my mother died, giving me birth, Janet's entire family had been killed in a raid. The Laird gave me into her hands. She was very young and grieving. My need for her overcame her sorrow. It was the saving of us both, for neither my father nor my sister ever truly forgave me for being the cause of my mother's death.

Within moments they returned, Cawdie bending his huge warrior's body to enter the door. His scarred face was remarkably devoid of emotion beneath the tumbled mass of his dark auburn hair. He had been sent by the Laird to protect me when I traveled from Skye to Edinburgh, and much to my relief, stayed. I presumed it might have as much to do with a long but frustrated attachment to Janet as loyalty to our Laird or me.

I looked up at him. "I need her on the bed, please, Cawdie. Then find out how she got here, although I suspect she walked, from the condition of her clothing."

He knelt and lifted the swathed body from the floor and placed it gently on the bed, keeping the blanket gathered around her.

Without comment, Janet moved to assemble what we would need: basins, cloths, lavender, salves, scalpels, scissors, thread, needles, the accouterments of birth. Cawdie checked the iron pot of water hanging over the fire, gave Scathach's haunch a rough scratch in passing, and left to see what he could discover about the woman's journey here. I doubted he would find anything. She had obviously made her way here unattended. I poured water into a washbasin, and scrubbed my hands and short-pared nails well to remove any remaining trace of the mixture I had just made. Ever practical, Janet removed the woman's muddy shoes and stockings, and chaffed her feet before covering them with a pair of her own clean woolen socks.

I dried my hands and moved to the bed, folding back the blanket to the woman's waist, then lifted her wet skirts to reveal her belly. As I touched it, a contraction began, and I noted the time. Janet and I removed her skirts, and lifted her enough to place several heavy layers of clean cloths beneath her. We worked quickly and efficiently together with the ease of long practice. The woman was younger than my twenty-two years, and reminded me of a broken butterfly, her fair hair, dulled by the rain, curled in ropy tendrils around her still face.

Janet poured clean tepid water into a basin, added a bit of tincture of lavender, and handed me a fresh cloth, dampened in the mixture. I began to clean the woman's bloody thighs. Another spasm racked her, and the pink tinged flood of her waters coursed onto the padding.

She opened her eyes and tried to focus on my face. "Too soon," she whispered, "the lights keep floating," her voice railed away, "and there is a...unicorn in the cup with the eagle, two heads...the eagle has two heads you know..." I could smell the sour stench of vomit on her breath as she spoke, and a strong odor as of garlic. She closed her eyes and slipped back into whatever place offered her shelter from the pain.

Janet placed a pillow under the woman's head, wiped the beaded moisture from her face, and towel dried the tangle of hair. She looked at me questioningly. I made a small sad gesture of assent. It was far too soon. Not yet eight months gone, if I guessed rightly. All I could do now is what had to be done. I lifted the woman's legs and pulled them apart. Gripping her ankles, I set her feet back toward her buttocks, exposing her secrets. Blood pulsed through her privy parts, and flooded the padding again. I could see that the baby was already well on its way; she contracted again, and a small circle of dark curls was visible in the orifice for a moment then retreated into the passage. She was losing the baby, and I could do nothing to prevent it. Birthing, once gone this far, cannot be delayed by any method that I know. Had I but seen her sooner I might have tried to prevent her labor with the juice of sage mixed with honey and enforced rest, but it was too late now for such feeble things.

She grunted, and the top of the baby's head appeared again, then once again retreated. During the next contraction, the baby crowned, and the top of the head remained visible.

"Janet, put a warmed towel on her belly. The baby is coming..."

Another involuntary push from the semi-conscious woman, and it emerged, the tiny ears appearing as the babe turned. I placed both hands on the sides of the undersized head and waited for the next push to expel the child. When it came, the baby slithered into my hands. I grasped the slippery little body firmly. My first concern was to see that the naval-string was not entangled about the neck or other part. Such might strangle the baby or cause the after burden to be pulled too violently from the womb and lead to excessive bleeding.

The child, a boy, was scarcely larger than my hand. To my surprise, he moved strongly, the wee maw opening and closing as he struggled to breathe. I put my little finger in his mouth, finding a plug of mucus, and turned the head downward while I patted the tiny back. He inhaled shallowly, and made an almost inaudible sound but did not cry as he should have. I knew he would die, but evidently, he did not yet agree, for he immediately began a labored attempt to take in air; the almost imperceptible gasps twisting my heart. I laid him very gently on the warmed cloth on the woman's belly, covered him with another cloth heated by the fire, and watched the naval string as it continued to throb.

When the pulsing ceased, I took a piece of coarse thread and tied it about five finger-widths from the miniscule abdomen. I did not do this because I believed in the old tale that the length left on the string would affect the size of the penis. By that same account midwives must cut the female's naval string shorter than they do the male's, for boy's privy parts must be longer than the female's. When cords on females are cut shorter, it is believed that it will make them modest and their secrets narrower. In my opinion, such a thing would cause a long and difficult birthing, if true. During my apprenticeship in Italy, I was taught to cut the cord to an equal length for both sexes. I looked down at the baby. His tiny penis was scarcely visible.

He would not live, but I would not stint his care. My fingers stripped the blood from about eight inches of the cord below the first string, to keep it from dripping when it was cut, and tied it off again. Then I cut the cord cleanly between the ties to release the child from its mother.

I picked him up carefully and examined him, holding him in my palm. He was a perfect small male. I put my little finger in his tiny mouth again, and rubbed his soft gums with honey, cleansed the fragile body with salt and oil of roses, and applied a salve of honey and garlic to the end of the cord. All of this I did while expecting that wee chest to cease to move at any moment. But he would not surrender. After wrapping a clean strip of cloth around his belly to hold the cord in place, I swaddled him and handed the small bundle to Janet.

"Line a basket with soft warmed cloths and put him in it. Keep it near the fire but not in the light. Poor little one. We can at least keep him comfortable while he is with us."

The mother had been unusually silent during the birth; even her pains had not elicited the normal cries or screams of a woman in labor. I tried to organize my impressions as I kneaded her belly to bring forth the after burden. She was not bleeding badly but seemed far too pale and torpid. The contractions began again, and I placed a clean basin between her legs. The liver-colored mass slid smoothly out at the end of a convulsion and I caught it in the basin, turning it over to make certain it was intact, and nothing remained inside the womb. Janet took the basin while I cleaned the body fluids and more bloody flux than was usual at birthing from the woman. Her secrets were intact and required no stitching. The babe had been so small she had accommodated it without tearing.

I washed her privates with a concoction of chervil with honey of roses added for inflammation, and placed a thick linen clout between her legs to absorb the slow but steady trickle of blood. Her clothing was likely ruined, discolored beyond reclaiming, with dirt, blood, sweat, feces, and dark urine. I would take it to the village laundry, and let Aggie decide. After we removed it all, we dressed her in one of my shifts, rolled her to the sides, replaced the soiled bedding and covered her warmly. She seemed to have slipped into a coma and I was not certain she was aware of what was happening. We settled in to wait. There was nothing more we could do except pray.

A half an hour later she was still sweating heavily, and I wiped her with a scented cloth. Leaning over, I smelled her breath again. The odor of vomit and garlic was still strong, and she was showing no sign of awakening. It was not as it should be. I checked for excessive bleeding, but it was no more than usual. I nibbled at my lip as my thoughts churned.

Looking down I realized Janet's feet were still bare on the cold floor and I was immediately contrite. "Oh, Janet, forgive me. Thank you. Please get dressed. I will watch over her."

I wiped the perspiration from the flawless face with a fresh cloth from the pile. My left hand went self-consciously to the pox marks on my own face. Oddly, it had left scars only on the left side. This woman had never had smallpox, that was obvious. As I worked, I deliberately made my mind go over what needed to be done next. The soiled linens should be gathered and taken to Aggie. They would need boiling. Should I have Reverend Robertson attend the mother and baby lest they die unshriven? Where would they bury the child? My patient seemed to be sleeping now, so I folded the cloth and placed it on the edge of the basin. The babe was probably dead by now. I walked over and looked in the basket by the hearth wondering if Father Robertson would consent to bury him in the church graveyard. My heart gave a queer lurch as two slate blue eyes stared back at me. He did not cry, but his small legs moved beneath the swaddling. That was uncommon. Children born before their time seldom move much. I put my finger tentatively on the miniature chin, and the tiny mouth opened. "You are hungry?" I was astonished... "What a brave little one you are."

Everything I had learned told me he would die. What could I do? Yet my mind refused to face the inevitable and searched for a solution. His mother was in no condition to feed him, and even if she had been, he was yet too small to suck.

It reminded me of something, and I wondered if Janet remembered the kitten.

When I was about nine years of age, I found a bag filled with rocks and three newborn kittens someone had thrown into the Loch. The bag had caught on a log instead of sinking. One of the kittens was still alive and I kept it warm, fed it drops of milk from a spoon, crooned encouragement in no sensible language, and it had survived! Might that work for this babe?

"All right, wee one. Let us try. It can do no harm." I put a bit of milk into a pan and warmed it by the fire. Dipping my finger into it, I lifted his head a little and placed one drop on his tongue. He rolled it about and then somehow it vanished. I carefully gave him another few dribs and fed him in this manner, very slowly, until his eyes closed. His breaths were shallow but regular as he slept. I covered him and replaced his makeshift bed by the hearth.

Scathach peered down at the wee bairn in the basket, then at me. She laid down, pressed herself as closely to the basket as possible, put her massive head on her paws, gave an almost human sigh and closed her own eyes.

I began to gather up the dirty clothes and linens. Scathach suddenly rose to her feet, fangs bared and fur bristling.

The door slammed abruptly open, and a large furious male stormed into the room with Cawdie following close behind. His eyes went immediately to the motionless figure on the bed and in the next moment he was crouching over her, voice shaking.

"Julianne." He looked at me wildly. "Is she dead?

I made the hand signal to Scathach that meant friend, and she settled unhurriedly back into place by the hearth, not taking her eyes from the man. I shook my head. "No, but the baby..." He was no longer listening. His body shook in great shudders of relief as he laid his head next to hers and wrapped his arm across her still body. I waited patiently until he gathered himself and thought more of him for his show. Scots have no qualms about displaying emotions. I smiled reassuringly. "Cawdie, get the Laird a wee dram of whisky."

The Laird knelt by the bed a few moments, watching the sleeping girl, then stood slowly. He lowered himself onto the rather small chair near the bed, and Cawdie placed a cup in his hand. I had never seen the Laird this close before. He was a bonny man; quite tall, with the muscled body of a warrior and eyes that looked like winter ice in the firelight. His hair was as black as the Earl of Hell's Waistcoat and curled wildly from the rain. A very wet belted plaid covered him from neck to knee except for his right arm. Beneath it I could see the fabric of his shirt which was of the same length as the drape of the plaid and equally drenched. Both were of exceptionally fine fabric. Stockings of the same quality and well-made leather brocks showed beneath the covering of muck.

Janet returned. She had put on her own soft leather shoes and laced them over her stockings. Both men and women used their long plaids as cloaks over shirts and skirts. Hers was an arisaid of white with small black and red stripes that fell to her heels. It was caught before her chest with a large buckle of engraved silver centered with a large piece of crystal. The stone threw sparks of light fitfully around the room. The remaining material had been pleated, and was held in place at her waist with a leather belt decorated with silver plates, chain and red coral. She had not put on her kerchief and her red braid fell well below her waist and shone in the fire light, little tendrils escaping in wayward curls around her face and neck. She was tall, an impressive and beautiful woman although just past her thirtieth year, and I saw Cawdie drink in the sight of her like a draught of fine wine. The Laird regarded her appreciatively as well, earning a scowl from Cawdie. I am but five feet tall and beside her I was a small unkempt female of no consequence. I brushed ineffectively at the brown wool of my dress, removed my bloody apron and turned away to wash my hands. There was a short silence as everyone gathered their thoughts after the excitement.

Cawdie had given the Laird his dram in our best cup, a wooden quaich banded in silver. He looked at Janet over the rim of it, then at me.

"Which of you is the healer?"

"I am, my Laird," I said quietly. "Lady Julianne, your...kinswoman, is still alive, although I am much worried. The babe came easily, for it was much too soon and it is very small. I am more concerned that she has not yet awakened. Can you tell me what happened? She has some symptoms unrelated to the birth that concern me. It would help greatly if you can give me some idea of why she came here alone. Did you not know she was ill?"

I could almost see his hackles rise. Like most men, he was defensive when criticized and looked at me stonily. "She was well this afternoon. I saw her but three hours ago, and she showed no signs of illness."

"Has she been ill? Is your household well? Do you know of anything that might have happened to bring the child too soon? She is quite unwell and has several signs that might mean she is sickening from a disease or that she ate or drank something that caused this." I took a deep breath, and said quickly, before I could lose courage, "If you have no other illness at the castle, she is either in the throes of getting one, or...she may have eaten something poisonous."

He sat up, some of the whisky from the cup spilling over the carpet. "That is impossible! No one would dare..." The words suddenly stopped, and he looked down at the now almost empty *quaich*. He placed it with great precision on the table.

"Are you quite certain?" His voice had an edge that told me he might know something of it.

"No, my Laird. As I said, some things might also be caused by other maladies, perhaps from dysentery or cholera, or tainted food. But not all, and not in the combination I am seeing. She spoke little, but mentioned a unicorn and a two-headed eagle in her meanderings. Does that have any meaning to you? Forgive me for asking such questions but I cannot in good faith rule out the possibility of poison."

At the mention of a unicorn or two-headed eagle his eyes flew to mine, then he recovered. "No," he said flatly. He got up and walked to Lady Julianne, and placed his large hand on her cheek. Her skin was still waxen and sheened with moisture, her lips slightly parted as she breathed shallowly. Scathach watched him closely but made no move.

"Will she live?" He did not ask about the child, so I did not tell him. The basket was well hidden in the shadows of the hearth behind Scathach.

"I am not certain my Laird, but we will care for her until the fates decide. We often tend patients here and it would be unwise to move her. We will send you word if there is a change. There is naught you can do now, but if you find that anyone else is ill and question those who saw her last, it might be helpful."

He nodded, and walked toward the door, hesitating, he spoke without looking back at us. "The baby, what was it?"

"A boy, my Laird." I should have told him more, perhaps, but the baby was not likely to live and there was no reason to cause further pain.

His shoulders slumped... "I thank you. I will return in the morning...unless you send word."

I made a small movement of my head at Cawdie, and he followed the Laird into the dark and rain.

Going to the hearth, and peering down into the basket, I was surprised to find the baby awake. I picked him up and his swaddling was damp! He had passed water! I unwrapped him and cleaned him with oil of roses then put him in fresh cloths and fed him more droplets of milk. I stroked his wee belly down from navel to groin as I had done to make the kitten's bowels move and gazed at his perfect miniature form until he slept again. Scathach shifted a little as I returned the sleeping babe to the basket, then resumed her guard.

Janet tidied up the room while I studied the woman. There was now a soft tinge of color in her lips. She opened her eyes and awareness slowly replaced confusion as she looked around. Tears gathered and slid from the corners of her eyes. I called Janet and we lifted her head and coaxed her to drink a julep of distilled peppermint water and syrup of black cherry until she sank into a seemingly natural slumber.

I sat for a while watching her sleep and thinking, then followed Janet into our bedroom and tried to rest. But not for long as Scathach nosed me into wakefulness each time the baby moved, and I spent the remaining hours of darkness feeding the child droplets of milk every hour or two, stroking his belly and changing his soggy and soiled wrappings. At first light Janet rose as I stumbled back into our room. She pushed me into my box bed and firmly closed the doors. I knew nothing more until well after midday.

I awakened refreshed, my mind sifting through the events of the night before as I washed in the basin of cold water and braided my wayward dark auburn hair and coiled it tightly around my head, pinning it ruthlessly into submission. Janet had laid out fresh clothing and I dressed quickly, anxious to see my patients.

Janet looked up and smiled as I entered the room and went directly to the basket by the fire. Scathach rumbled as I pulled back the warm covers to see if the baby still lived. I was incredulous to see his tiny chest rise and fall in slumber. Across the room his mother slept as well, her cheeks now a soft pink against the whiteness of her skin.

The room had been neatened; the screen placed between the bed and the door to allow some privacy. Cawdie had taken the pile of soiled linens and sheets to Aggie, the laundress and daughter of the tavern keeper. Aggie had a fine hand with removing stains, but she would find the ones we had sent today a challenge. I had given her the recipe for a soap made from the *Saponaria*, which grows commonly about. If you crush the plant and roots and boil and strain them, it makes a lathery liquid that is good for removing stains and grease. I add a bit of peppermint to mine for its medical effects and use it to wash bandages and clouts, as well as patients.

When Cawdie returned from his errand I had a list of things for him to get at the port. There was a soft knock and Janet opened the door. The Laird's wife stood there, a guard at a respectful distance behind her.

Janet bowed her head to the woman. "Good morning. May I help you, my Lady?"

Lady Margaret was more than ten years older than the Laird. Theirs had been a melding of two families for mutual benefit. She was not as tall as Janet but heavier with flesh, the rings on her small hands embedded in the white skin. The pale globes of her breasts were well displayed over the top of her bodice. Still a handsome woman, she dressed in the English manner with rich fabrics, embroidered and laced. A small covered basket was clasped in one hand.

"I have been told that my husband's...cousin...was taken ill here and have come to see how she fares..." She offered Janet the basket. "And to bring her some sweet honey cakes."

I stepped forward. "Come in, my Lady. My patient is still sleeping but you are welcome to our home. I moved aside, and a low growl came from Scathach. I made the hand signal for friend, but she remained alert, unblinking eyes steady on Lady Margaret. "Cawdie, help me move the screen." I wanted it in front of the fireplace, where it more effectively concealed the baby. I knew no sound would betray its presence.

Lady Margaret walked carefully around the dog and looked down at the sleeping woman. The blanket lay flat over her stomach. "She had the child, I see." She turned to me. "What was it?"

"A son." I replied. Her eyes filled with a flash of fury so quickly quenched I was not certain I had seen it.

"How very sad that it was too soon, but then had it lived, it would have had no future. She has no husband and a child would be but another impediment to any hope of another alliance." So, I thought...you do know Lady Julianne is his mistress. I did not tell her the babe lived, it likely would not survive long.

Our voices must have awakened Lady Julianne, for she turned slowly and opened her eyes. When she saw Lady Margaret they went wide with emotion and she began to convulse. A low keening came from her throat and her body stiffened and thrashed about. "Cawdie, help me." We moved quickly to control her movements before she hurt herself and she fought us like a madwoman, tearing at anything she could reach and leaving a bloody scratch on his hand.

"Move back a little and let me try with this." I took a blanket and wrapped it around her flailing arms, murmuring softly to her as I laid my body across hers. "It is alright, you are safe. We have you." I kept repeating it over and over.

Lady Margaret stood as if rooted to the floor, clutching the holy medal around her neck. "She is possessed of a demon! I warned him that she was evil! I shall call at the church to have the fiend cast out." Her eyes glittered with malice as we struggled to calm the woman, and she came toward us.

Scathach moved for the first time, snarling, fangs bared and fur bristling; she placed herself between us and Lady Margaret. The Laird's wife stopped, turned on her heel and fled, slamming the door behind her.

The loud crack of the door seemed to penetrate the consciousness of the woman and her struggles began to abate although she was still weeping and moaning. I loosened the blanket and chafed her hands as she shivered. "It's all right Lady Julianne, there is nothing to fear, we'll take care of you." After a moment, she relaxed and lay back on the bed.

There was another knock on the door and I felt the girl stiffen again. "See who it is, Cawdie," I told him.

THREE

Malcolm – Community

E dinburgh and Torrport, Scotland, Spring, 1705.
The morning rain had stopped a while ago, but the drips were still running down her window. She sighed, and I looked back at her; she'd opened her kohl-smudged eyes.

"You alright?" she asked.

"Aye, but my jaw is aching."

McLaren found me a few minutes after I'd been whacked. Nothing broken but our project. They'd taken the smallpox samples from his cabinet. I never imagined they'd go this far.

She smiled and stretched naked on the bed running hands through her curly red hair. I'd needed her after all that. "You're quiet."

"I was thinking...about what happened." I said.

Her name was Gwen, a decade older than me, a widow. Her husband had been Captain of the Edinburgh Town Guard, and she still had a lot of connections. I needed her mostly for that. In the last two days, I'd risked my life with exposure to smallpox, been accused of all manner of irresponsible behavior, been assaulted and robbed, and I needed some answers.

She patted the bed and grinned.

"Again?"

"Always." She made a kissy face. Women like her seldom remarried. They had an inheritance and children to protect. No sense risking it marrying again. They made willing lovers for young men like me, not wanting more than a night's pleasure. It was convenient. Served us equally well, at least that's what I told myself to sleep soundly.

I joined her again in bed. "You'll ask around about my problem?" I hated linking sex with business, but she needed to know it was important.

"Mal, I would never let anyone get away with beating-up my favorite lover." She tickled me and laughed.

"Be careful with these people, they're well-connected. I just need information. Leave the vengeance to me."

"Alright Mal." Her mind was on other things. I pushed her back forcefully on the bed and kissed her as she liked in the new way.

* * *

She'd arranged for her coach to take me back to Torrport. I'd left letters for Father and Beaton letting them know about the assault and theft. I was happy to be leaving Edinburgh, but hated being bested and abused like that. I didn't know who was responsible. Turnbull wanted us stopped and knew how to do it; but would he have risked his illustrious career over this? Not likely. And what about the others? Was there a traitor in our group or did an enemy find out what we were up to? It was all just speculation for now. I needed evidence and hoped Gwen, or Father could provide some.

Was it proper to try to find a radical cure for smallpox? Perhaps the religious types were right, and it was part of God's plan and we were foolishly interfering at best and at worst working with the Devil. My gut still said we were right, but so far God seemed to be on their side. I wrapped the wool plaid around me and sank into a tired stupor as the carriage rattled along the rutted road. I'd taken a small draught of laudanum for the pain in my jaw and slowly fell asleep.

* * *

Mrs. Simpson took me well in hand when I arrived at home. Usually I found her fussing annoying, but it was welcome this time. She was my housekeeper and helper, a plump, active woman who usually had a joke or bit of gossip to share. I was lucky to have her, she endured my erratic lifestyle with good cheer.

"Doctor Forrester, you have many requests from patients. I'll fix you some lunch while you read these." She shook the sheaf of note papers in my face in case I failed to notice. The work had piled up.

"Aye Mrs. Simpson, I'm glad to be home, please find me a bottle of single malt to go with lunch." I dropped my bag by the door and bent to give Henry a good ruffling as he waggled around at my feet.

She scowled with disapproval. Men should not drink before supper. That was her rule and she aimed to enforce it.

"My jaw is killing me, so it's either the whisky or more laudanum to get me through."

"Nay, a man can endure a bit of pain, and it will be evening soon enough." She was determined to have her way and more laudanum would render me useless, so I gave in. I know when I've been beaten.

"Alright, Mrs. Simpson, but I want a double measure of single malt after supper. Now give me some peace, will you, I need to prepare my rounds." She smiled having won that little contest of wills and scurried off to make lunch.

I went upstairs and settled into my favorite armchair and started reading. I had a small infirmary on the main floor of my home at the town docks. It was two stories, Tudor style, the exterior was supposed to be white with exposed beams, but now was a soot-stained mottled grey, not having been white-washed in decades. The interior at least was renewed before I moved in last year. The floors and paneling had been re-stained and there was even some of the new wallpaper, although I thought it was overly feminine. The second floor had my living and study room, bedroom and bath, and in the back, a kitchen with living quarters for Mrs. Simpson. My rooms were usually a mess of books and papers everywhere. I tended to use the floor to organize my studies, much to Mrs. Simpson's annoyance and Henry's pleasure.

Most patients expected a visit in their home, but an increasing number used the infirmary on the main floor. I usually kept an hour free at the beginning and end of the day for infirmary patients. Clientele primarily were the middle and upper classes, those who could afford to pay, but I would treat anyone without means, free of charge. Sadly, the poor tended to be too proud and would rather suffer or sort it themselves than ask for charity. I only seemed to see them as a last resort. Not my choice, theirs. That was the problem with our system, or lack thereof. Some received excellent care, others none, and to compound the problem, few physicians wanted to live in small towns.

Torrport was around a thousand souls, although with the normal flux of immigration, it could be considerably more at times. I was the only physician, there was no surgeon and the apothecary recently closed. So, I was free to do it all: from classical medicine to minor surgery to preparing my own medicines and even caring for the occasional animal. There was such entertaining variety and no one scolding me about professional boundaries. In Scotland, physicians were professional gentlemen schooled at universities, whereas surgeons and pharmacists were tradesmen who'd served an apprenticeship, and village healers were beyond serious consideration. Well that's how most of us physicians saw it anyway. I certainly didn't, but medicine is very class-oriented. That's why I moved here. I just wanted to be left alone to heal patients by whatever means I could. I used what worked and didn't care a bit for theories sans practical application.

* * *

After lunch and a change of clothes, I decided to look in on a few nearby patients. I restocked my bag with medicines and supplies and headed out after informing Mrs. Simpson. My first stop was to see James Allen, a wool merchant experiencing painful urination. He had a shop on the other end of the docks and could often be found there with his son.

Torrport was on a hilly peninsula that stuck out on the north side of the Firth of Forth about two and a half hours by carriage from Edinburgh. The wealthier part of Torrport was on the west side of the peninsula and included the U-shaped main docks. The less reputable section was on the other side of the peninsula by the fishing village. On the hill, in between, was Castle Carraig. It wasn't much of a castle, really, more of a stronghold for the local Laird and his men. Beside the castle on the hill was St. Ninian's Church of the Episcopal persuasion, complete with handsome stained windows depicting the lives of saints.

The port was used for shipping to the inland regions to the north and as an overflow when Edinburgh was too busy. Ships could unload here and transport to the city overland by wagon. There also was another reason for the brisk traffic at Torrport. Edinburgh was heavily regulated, the out-ports not so much, and increasingly taxes on imports and exports were driving trade to the rougher edges.

Rough or not, it was agreeable to be back home, and despite my sore jaw I was happy to stroll along the dock greeting friends and patients. I saw the wool merchant's son as soon as I entered the shop. Couldn't quite remember his name but I nodded in recognition. "Here to see your father."

"This way Doctor Forrester." He knew me of course as most here, and as he led me up the wooden stairway alongside the rough stone shop, he turned back and said in a whisper, "Thank God you're here. He's been aggravated for weeks over this. None of us can get much sleep and mother's worried sick."

Many merchants live in apartments over their shops. This one was spacious, taking the entire second floor of the building, he owned. The main floor had his wool shop and stalls he'd rented to others. I found him at his desk, back propped at an odd angle with pillows. He looked overheated, overweight and very uncomfortable, not good for a man of his age. I set my bag down, went to his side and offered my hand. He took it weakly and I could feel his hand was very moist.

"Good of you to come, Doctor Forrester."

"James, tell me about your problem." I wasted no time, nor did he.

37

He was having severe pains on his left side and back below the ribs, very painful scanty urination, and feeling like he needed to go often, and the urine was reddish brown. He'd been to Edinburgh on business and dropped in to an apothecary. The pharmacist thought he might have a kidney stone and sold him a course of limewater and soap as treatment. Pharmacists could diagnose but not charge for it. They made their money selling medicines.

He explained. "I tried it for a month. It provided some relief and now I've run out. I hope you can do something, business has been bad enough with all the smuggling and now I can't even get out."

"It does sound like you have a stone, but let's have a closer look, and I need a urine sample too." I suggested he go to his bedroom and strip off after filling my sample bottle with urine. I met him there a few minutes later. He looked very unfit, a trend among the merchant and professional classes. I felt his forehead and noted his temperature was elevated, then used my glass lens to look in his eyes, ears and mouth. Then I had him lie on his sides while palpating his kidneys. He winced when I squeezed the left side. The urine sample was very obviously colored, as he had previously mentioned.

"You may get dressed now." I sat on the chair beside the bed and made some notes. He slowly dressed then sat on the bed waiting.

"I concur with the diagnosis of the pharmacist, but you need much more effective medicine and a change in diet and exercise. Ask the missus to join us, I want her to hear this too."

When she arrived, I reviewed the results then started to explain that I would be giving him a monthly course of *Caustic Lixivium* in broth to soften and loosen the stones, and opium to lessen the pain. I suggested taking a common laxative should the opium cause constipation.

"James, it may take a few courses of *Caustic Lixivium* to resolve this, and in between the courses I want you to take garlic for its diuretic effect and overall health promoting qualities. You can take some cooling baths to reduce the fever and inflammation, but I think the fever will abate as the stones are expelled. These treatments should serve you well but must be combined with a proper exercise regimen." They listened carefully. I intended not only to cure his immediate problem but show him how to live a somewhat healthier life. It would be a start, if he did it, anyway. Compliance is a perennial problem and patients often lie about it too. I was very specific.

"In diet, you must avoid fish and all fat and heavy meats and especially abstain from salted meats. Fill your dish instead with all sorts of garden seeds and vegetables. Take spices sparingly, except mustard, and entirely avoid pickles. For drink take only fresh water. Avoid all forms of liquors and spirits except a little red port wine with a meal." I was dead serious, and he obviously didn't like what he was hearing.

"Now listen carefully. Nothing is more important at your age than gentle exercise. It should be frequent but gentle. The best is going on horseback in the mornings and having a walk after dinner. Don't push yourself to fatigue, but be regular in this habit." He didn't seem to mind this part and the thought of being ordered to get away from his business each day seemed to please him. I rose and handed his wife the medications from my bag, enough to get him through the month, then reminded her how and when to give them.

"If there are any changes, please call me. I'll drop back in a month to see how it's going, but don't expect rapid improvements. This will take time." I bowed as she handed me the agreed payment, then left. As I passed the wool shop I was stopped by the son.

"Will Father recover?"

"I think so, but it will take time. What you can do is encourage him to get more exercise, and I don't mean lifting pints at the tavern. Go for a horseback ride in the mornings with him. I'm sure he'd like that."

The son smiled, relieved that was all expected of him. "I love riding too and business is slow early."

"Just curious...he mentioned something about wool smuggling." I'd been in Torrport less than a year and still learning about local goings on.

He nodded and spat some tobacco juice before explaining. "Aye, that bloody Wool Act the English passed a few years ago has been giving us fits. Doesn't seem to pay to be honest nowadays. We can't get wool from the Americas or England anymore. These trade restrictions benefit only the English, and do nothing good here but encourage smuggling. Business is slow, but we'll survive."

I'd heard many rumors about smuggling in these parts and that the fishing village on the other side of the peninsula was often used for that purpose. I had few patients over there of course.

* * *

I made several more stops that day dealing with angina, stomach cramps, a cut leg and finally a pregnancy. The last reminded me to contact Elspeth soon and refer some of these women's issues to her. I was over-booked already, and she could help with those. On my way home, I dropped in at the local tavern at the dock. It was always busy with locals and seafarers. The owner had recently added a kitchen that could supply a decent meal too, if you didn't mind the tavern smells. I didn't much like the tobacco smoke, so got my ale at the counter and sat at the front by an open window next to a few gentlemen discussing local politics. I lifted my ale in toast. "Great health and every good blessing to you gentlemen."

The younger man with white wig and freckles replied, "Och, Doctor Forrester, the same to you and trust your business in Edinburgh concluded well."

This was an opening to tell them. I often sidestepped, but this time I needed the help of friendly locals. "Nay, I was assaulted and had some valuable medical samples stolen. You can see what they did to my face." I chuckled, then got to the point.

"If you see any suspicious looking men hanging about my infirmary, I would appreciate it if you would notify Laird MacDuff."

The other fellow said: "Why in God's name would anyone attack you and take only samples? Were they not after coin?"

"It seems not," I responded.

The first one smiled then offered. "We'll spread the word and keep an eye on you. Don't want to lose another good doctor."

I extended my sincere thanks and we discussed the pros and cons of our relationship with England. It was on everyone's mind lately. In my view, Scotland was too small to go it alone, but I knew many in the tavern disagreed, especially it seems an overly large highlander sitting a few tables to the left.

I finished the ale and said my goodbyes. These were good people and looked after each other, at least that was what I hoped.

* * *

Mrs. Simpson met me with a letter from Beaton. The news was not good. He'd been robbed too, and his smallpox case notes were gone. Fortunately, he'd already given Young a report of the results. No one had been hurt, but months of careful collection and collation were lost. Beaton also mentioned that they'd found Smith, the fellow who'd shared a room with Tremblay. So far Smith had no symptoms but wasn't being very helpful. The letter ended with an exhortation to welcome Elspeth properly this time. She'd be arriving tomorrow.

I slumped in my chair, they had our smallpox samples and case notes and I could still hear Turnbull threatening: *If you proceed, you will regret it and your families will not be able to protect you this time.* He'd been spot on so far and I the fool who truly didn't seem to know what or who I was dealing with. But if anything, I'm a persistent bugger, and have some resources too. However, I knew I needed to be better prepared before blundering around in Edinburgh again. Meanwhile I had to serve my patients here.

* * *

Overnight I'd resolved to see the two most influential men in Torrport, the Laird and the Reverend. They were both my patients and could use a follow-up visit as well. The day was clear, and the sun was shining off the wave ripples in the harbor. It was one of those rare spring days when spirits are lifted without liquid assistance. After a filling breakfast of oatmeal, eggs and tea, I dressed for comfort in dark brown silk breeches with white hose, a brown silk brocade waistcoat with white linen shirt underneath, and a brown knee-length wool coat, the one with the buttons from the waist up and flared bottom, perfect for riding. I finished with a simple white linen cravat, blue silk ribbon in back to keep my hair tidy, and a dark-brown felt tricorn hat in case of rain. I usually wore shoes with this outfit, but today I'd be riding, so pulled on a pair of knee-length polished black leather boots, the ones with the flared tops that are currently in fashion. One check in the mirror and I was off.

The blacksmith stables are two short blocks behind my home. I needed a horse and sometimes a carriage for my work and his rates were reasonable. "Good morning Daniel, I'll be having a horse for my rounds this morning."

"Aye, Good morning Doctor Forrester, I have that gray mare Gracie you rode last week. She's fed, groomed and ready to saddle." Daniel was the blacksmith's apprentice, a wiry dark-haired boy of seventeen, and growing fast. I watched as he saddled and led her out. Gracie knew me and seemed unconcerned. All I wanted was a horse for conveyance and she was it, knew her way around town too.

"I'll have her back at noon. Going up to the castle and back is all." I mounted, and he lifted my physician's bag and placed it behind me, tying it to the loops on both sides of the saddle.

"Alright Gracie, let's have a relaxing day in the sun." I tipped my hat to Daniel and turned Gracie in the direction of the castle, along the rutted dirt track leading up the hill. She would continue clopping along in that direction until the first turn. My first stop would be to see the Reverend Hammet Robertson at his cottage beside St. Ninian's.

The dirt road became paved stone as we left the flats and passed the terraces behind the port. The first level was shops and businesses, the second homes. Above that was a steep section with cliffs and a cut through them leading up to the castle. At the top of the cliff, I turned Gracie right and followed the road leading to the kirk. The Reverent Hammet Robertson was outside, bent over in the garden.

"Mal, come look at these tulips!" He rose with a wave. Hammet was is his early sixties, longish grey hair, thin build, and in love...with his flowers. I jumped off Gracie and tied her to a bush.

"Father, I am so pleased to see you out enjoying this fine day. How have you been?" I listened carefully to his breathing as he spoke. Hammet had asthma and moved from the city for his health.

"Oh, I am quite fine. But look at this red and white striped one with the curled petals. Is it not divine!" He could go on for hours about flowers.

"Oh, yes Father, it is perfection. Now tell me truthfully, how is your asthma?"

"Well Mal, you know how it is, some good days, some not. The worst is when it happens on Sunday, for obvious reasons. But your suggestion to use ivy tea in the evening has been most helpful." I could hear a slight wheezing as he spoke, but not much worse than usual and he'd been exerting himself.

"If you are in difficulty use a dose of laudanum. But be careful, it can be addictive. And you know how I feel about tobacco."

"I've only had to use the laudanum twice this month and I promise Mal I will be careful with it. My morning Ceylon tea and evening ivy tea, and the good air of our blessed Torrport, is all I need right now. Now why have you really come to see your old priest?"

My family were supporters of the monarchy going back to William the Conqueror, and loyal to the Episcopal Church in Scotland through all her trials. I care not for religion, try to stay neutral in these conflicts while siding with family and traditions. Not always easy.

"Ah Father, am I so shallow and easy to fathom?   Well you're partly right. I do need your wise counsel today, but I do care about you as well." I didn't want him to think I was that selfish.

"Then come for tea. My back has had enough for one day anyway." He muttered something about weeds and led me into his modest stone cottage.

It took a while, back and forth, about my family and his, how were they, so forth, til he got to the point. "I heard you had some difficulties in Edinburgh. Someone beat you and stole samples?"

I gave him the short version, leaving out the medical details and most of the names. We needed his help but didn't want him in the middle. "The thing is Father, I have no idea who could have done this. I know some in my profession are against us, and I've heard some in the religious community as well, and that's why I need you. Who in the Church would want to stop us and why?" We sipped our tea while he carefully considered the question.

"Mal there are factions in every faith, you know that, and those in positions of responsibility cannot always control members of their community." He got up and retrieved a tattered notebook, then looked for a section.

"Please know there are differences of opinion on these issues. I think most in our faith believe that God created everything including sickness and health. Many believe that disasters are punishments from God. I do not concur. Disasters in some places are a regular occurrence. So, should we believe that people who live in places with frequent storms are hated by God? Surely not! Many of our revered Saints came from such places. How could smallpox be a punishment when most of us will get it at some point in our lifetime? Is it not just another natural hurdle in life? I do not agree with those who see it as a punishment from God, but I know a minority still cling to this view." His answer was too logical, and faith is at the other end.

"And what about this minority? Why do they believe this?"

"Mal it has to do with the age-old debate about free-will and predestination. Some believe that our life and what happens to us is completely controlled by God, others believe we can choose our own path and destiny. I prefer to believe the truth lies somewhere in the middle, but that's just me, the moderate old fool speaking." He grinned and turned the page in the notebook. He was starting to look chilled, so I brought him a blanket and wrapped it over his shoulders, then poured more tea.

He continued after thanking me. "And in this case, those who may wish you ill fail to remember Our Lord and Savior on many occasions healed the sick. Remember this quote?" He ran his finger to the spot in his notebook, then spoke with that sweet smile when he read the scriptures.

"Jesus went to every town and village. He taught in their meeting places and preached the good news about God's kingdom. Jesus also healed every kind of disease and sickness. Matthew 9:35."

"Thank you for reminding me, Father." In fact, it was quotes like this that influenced my decision those years ago, when Father wanted me to be a lawyer. I looked Hammet in the eye. "Am I doing the right thing, Father, in trying to find a cure for smallpox? Do I have your blessing?"

"Aye, young Mal, you are a fine doctor and mean well, you have my blessing, but practice prudence and kindness, will you, even to your enemies?"

"I will try, Father, I will try. If you hear anything that could help, I hope you will consider passing it along."

"Och, Malcolm, I am not much for gossip, you know that, but if I can protect you, I most certainly will. Now I feel in need of a nap and you should visit some real patients."

I rose to go and as I was leaving heard him say: "And be sure to say your prayers to the Saints, young Malcolm, especially to Saint Gwen, lest you too must flee your homeland." His laugh followed me out the door and I shook my head in amazement. Seems everyone knew my business...but me.

Gracie was lost in horse reverie when I found her. Our next stop was Castle Carraig and Laird Douglas MacDuff. I'd just mounted Gracie when I remembered my lessons and that Saint Gwen had fled to Brittany to escape the barbarians in England. I laughed loudly. That old priest! I must remember never to underestimate him. As Gracie and I plodded along, I felt satisfied knowing I had some personal support, and the Church, while not officially against us, was having to deal with its many factions. It could have been worse.

* * *

The castle was one of those massive limestone fortresses built in the thirteenth century to control the port and area. It had high thick walls, few windows, and an interior bailey. Not the most comfortable of places, but home to the Laird and a garrison of forty or so. The main entrance was a large double oak door facing the port. Two men stood watch there, kitted out in the MacDuff belted plaid, sword and modern flintlock muskets. They were very young.

"Doctor Forrester, here to see the Laird and any men who might need me." I smiled down at them.

"Aye, Doctor, the Laird is in and I think a few of us may need you." He nodded to the other young man who opened the doors to let me in.

In Scotland, the clans had their own militias recruited from within the clans by the clan Chieftains, the Lairds. This ancient system was a sore spot with the English. They'd as soon have the clans de-clawed.

I thanked them and walked Gracie through the tunnel leading to the interior gate. They closed the outer gate behind me. This part of the castle spooked me. It was designed as a death trap with slits in the wall on one side and through the ceiling. Once you were in, you were stuck, and they could shoot at you from the side or pour boiling oil from above. There had been attempts to breach this tunnel in the past. None had succeeded. They made me wait a few minutes, no doubt having fun and seeing if I'd sweat. I certainly did, then thankfully the inner doors opened, and I entered the bailey. It was mud, hay, horses, chickens, men milling about, and the deep water well around which the fortress was built. I dismounted and tied Gracie to a post by the main hall.

"The Laird is in his quarters." It was Captain John Spence, the Laird's Second, a taciturn raw-boned man sporting a pair of silver-plated pistols stuck in his belt. "You know the way?" he asked.

"I do, and ask any men who wish to see me to wait in the infirmary. I'll be there after I see the Laird."

"Aye, Doctor." He turned and left, shouting abuse at a recruit who'd dropped his musket.

The Laird had taken up quarters in the apartment formerly used for visiting Royals. It was the only part of the castle well-appointed and suitable for an upper-class woman. The bottom floor of that wing housed the kitchen serving the castle. The second and third floors were the Royal apartment. He was at his desk writing.

"Doctor Forrester, please come in." He glanced back, then put down his pen, folded the paper then rose to meet me. The Laird was taller and more muscular than me, and with one of those angular faces that make women swoon. He was young too, my age, and had that air of easy command that often comes with position.

"I hope you are well on this fine spring day, Laird MacDuff." I smiled broadly, trying to re-start a relationship gone sour last time out. His name wasn't Douglas MacDuff. That was an affectation he'd adopted. The MacDuff line had died out long ago, but he was rightful heir and decided to adopt the name. Some made the mistake of mocking this, I was one, and later in retaliation he'd made a point of mentioning my family's shortcomings in front of several men. I took it with as much grace as I could swallow. Now he was wearing the MacDuff tartan kilt. Very strange for a lowlander. I didn't quite know what he was up to beyond strutting foolery.

"*I'm huir uv a weel, an' mah elbaw problem ye saw lest time has vanished. Nae doobt due tae inherited strang constitution.*" He'd switched into a fake highland accent that almost made me burst out laughing.

"No doubt." I agreed, and remembered there wasn't much wrong with him that a few days of rest wouldn't fix.

"*Next time thocht ah won't push 'at cuddie tae jump mair than she wants. Horses ur loch kimmers aren't they? Try tae force them an' they buck ye aff!*" He laughed at his own joke comparing horses and women.

I'd heard rumors but decided to change the subject. "I'm glad the problem is resolved and ended well. If you have no further medical complaints, I can see some of your men, at your leave, of course." One had always to ask permission from these people or they took exception.

"*Ah, indeed thaur ur puckle it thaur, but afair ye gang.*" He stopped and looked away, wanted me to stay about something else. I waited silently.

"Doctor, it is well-known in these parts that we have been married these three years and no heirs have been produced." He thankfully switched back to lowland Scots English.

"It is known, of course. The birth of an heir would be most welcome." The Laird was still young, but life is tenuous at best. People were still whispering about his father who'd died falling off the castle roof the winter before last.

"My wife insists it is my fault! Can you believe it? I am with her often, and still nothing. How can it be my fault?"

I wasn't sure what he wanted to hear. This just came at me. I had my issue to discuss with him, now this.   "Sir, it is well-known in medicine that there are many reasons for infertility and it is unwise and unwarranted to point the finger of blame unless there is solid proof." I hoped that mollified him somewhat. "I would be happy to consult with your wife on this issue, if you wish."

"Can you not prove I am not to blame?"

"Sir Douglas, it is not possible to prove that. It has only been discovered a few decades ago that semen has spermatozoa. They look like tadpoles swimming around and we think the spermatozoa have something to do with reproduction but don't know the exact mechanism. Can I ask a few personal questions?"

"Aye, go ahead." He was looking disappointed and I had to tread carefully.

"Do you have problems maintaining an erection? Are you able to ejaculate in her? Lastly, how often do you copulate?"

He laughed, I suppose at the directness of my questions. "I have no problems with any of those I assure you, and we copulate, or as we say hereabouts, _fack_, a few times a week."

"Then, barring any problems with the spermatozoa, I would hazard a guess that you are likely not the problem." I tried to give him what he wanted to hear while leaving ample tadpole wiggle room. I had my agenda to work too.

"I knew I couldn't be the problem. Now I want you to tell her."

I agreed to see her. He was pleased, then I asked, "Laird MacDuff, you may've heard I had a problem in Edinburgh and I'm concerned about my safety." He listened and understood at once I needed something too. I explained it in brief as I'd done with the Reverend. He looked at me and took a step closer, extended his hand and grasped my wrist in that way that means fealty. I let him.

"Forrester, you are our Doctor and under my protection. Any that offends you, offends me. You have need of me and I of you. Let us help each other. I may have another problem you can help with too. But enough for now. Tend to my men and leave your bill for payment. Have a good day."

I had been dismissed. He returned to his desk and I left wondering what the other problem might be and what I'd agreed to do. Didn't much like this, but I needed a haven, and he was it and knew it.

I returned to Gracie and pulled down my bag. The patients were in a room at the back of the armory just off the bailey. My mind was on the Laird when it hit me as soon as I walked in. There were five of them, but one was serious. It was palpable, I could sense the pain. He was on the near bed lying down, two men by him.

"What happened to him?" I needed to know fast. He had bandages covered in blood and was semi-conscious.

"It was no one's fault, sir. We were cleaning our muskets last night and it went off. Poor Ronald took one in the back." It was the man next to me. The other nodded.

"Then roll him over and take off these bandages. Why wasn't he brought to me last night?" It was appalling how poorly these boys were treated.

"We were told to wait and see. He didn't look good, and..." His voice trailed off. So, they were too cheap to spend some money on him, but he was still alive, and I never give up on a patient.

While they were removing the bandages, I took out my surgery kit. It was just the basics wrapped in a pouch for travel. I found the cauterizing tool and placed it in the nearby brazier then returned and knelt beside him to have a closer look.

"Looks like the ball went in his lower back here just above his lowest rib. I don't see an exit, so it must still be in there. I want you two to hold him still while I work on him." They each took a side while I selected the long forceps. I didn't want to risk using opium because he was half dead already and I didn't want to slow his breathing any further. There was just a slow leakage of blood from the wound. "Alright boys, hang-on while I try to find it."

"Aye, Doctor," they both bleated.

I decided to go in the entry hole with the long forceps to see if I could find the musket ball. If it went straight in and not too far, I might be able to get it without cutting him. He was starting to moan and move. "Give him a leather to bite on and keep him still, damn-it!" One slip and I could puncture something, and I didn't need that. I was annoyed enough as it was with everything.

"There it is lads. I think I can feel it." I inserted a spreader in the hole, so I could see better, then locked it. "He's lucky it didn't get in his organs." I carefully reinserted the forceps and tried to grab it. Took a few tries, but I got it. I held the ball up to show them, then dropped it. "I'll let him bleed a bit to clean it out." I looked at the entry site. There may be some rib splinters inside, but they're too hard to retrieve.

"Bring me the cauterizing tool." One of them handed it to me. It was just an iron rod with tapered tip and wooden handle. "Now keep him still while I staunch the blood." I wiped away the blood and quickly dabbed with the tool. I repeated a few times til the bleeding had stopped. He flinched, but I was quick. The sickening smell of burning human flesh filled our noses.

"The worst is over lads, just need to tidy up a bit and we're done." I soaked a cloth in turpentine and pressed it into the wound for a few minutes, repeated with a fresh cloth, then sat back, relieved.

"He's lost a lot of blood, but he should be stable now. Wrap some clean linens around him and keep him quiet. Once the bleeding has completely stopped, let the wound air for good healing. Give him a little whisky if he complains too much. Get some broth in him when he wakes, then bread soaked in milk for a few days. When his appetite comes back, he can eat what he wants." I went through my usual list, then added: "A healer may come to see him in a few days to see how he's doing and apply a poultice, if needed. If he takes a turn for the worse, come get me immediately." I stressed that last word in rebuke and they knew it.

"Alright, who's next?"

The rest had minor complaints that I dealt with quickly. I was tired and needed sustenance, but had one more stop, so I packed up, submitted my bill to the Laird and set off. Gracie was happy to go. Something about that place made us both nervous. We headed back down the hill to the town, then turned left along the lower terrace past shops on our way to Elspeth's cottage. I stopped to buy some shortbreads and a bottle of port. Didn't want to be accused of being a bad host again, didn't want to hear about it from Beaton. Gracie seemed perky, so I kicked her, and she happily broke into a gallop as we left the town.

I was hoping this visit wouldn't take long, but we did have a few professional matters to address. I was going over them in my mind just before knocking on the door, then I heard a moaning from within. I waited and heard it again, then a shuffling and low voices. I didn't want to come back later, so knocked loudly and shouted: "It's me, Forrester."

Several seconds later the door flew open and the space was filled with the dark form of a hulking highland Scot with kilt askew and shirt pulled out at one side.

"*Noo whit th' heel dae ye want?*" he growled at me menacingly.

FOUR

Elspeth - Opinions

orrport, Scotland, 1705.
"Let him in, Cawdie." I was breathing a bit hard from trying to control the woman, and had just enough vanity left to wonder why I always seemed to look my worst when I saw my cousin's friend. There was no help for it. Cawdie moved aside muttering under his breath something that sounded suspiciously like *glaikit bastart.* I wondered what Malcolm would think if he understood that Cawdie considered him a stupid bastard. I was not certain they knew each other, but they both frequented the coffeehouse in Torrport where information and ideas were dispensed in equal measure to men of every class with differing opinions often spawning fierce argument. I had treated a few of the results.

Janet looked up and spoke sharply: "*Haud yer wheesht!*" Cawdie stared at her, surprised, she seldom used that tone to him, and subsided. He tucked his shirt under his belt, wiping at the bloody scratch on his hand, and glared at our visitor.

Janet smiled at Malcolm; what woman would not? I examined him dispassionately. He was of medium height, with the slim honed body of an athlete. His face was almost classically handsome, but rather harsh, with dark brown eyes and an aquiline nose above perfectly sculptured lips. The shadow of his beard was already visible on his formerly clean-shaven face. His clothing in sober shades of brown appeared to be casual, but the fabric and cut betrayed its London origins. Threads of his un-powdered brown hair shone gold in the light. It was longer than that of most men and tied back with a ribbon. I wondered idly if it was as soft and silky as it looked, then guiltily transferred my thoughts back to the present.

Janet took the packages Malcolm proffered, and nodded in my direction, while I stood up and tried to straighten my clothing. He had not been here before. I saw him take the room in with a single assessing glance, noting the juxtaposition of rustic and sophisticated furnishings. The warm antique carpet, the paintings, a striking colorful Italian vase on wooden shelves crammed with volumes, stacked papers and the miscellany of the healer. His glance lingered, arrested on the books, reading the titles. Many were in Latin, Greek and Italian. I could almost hear his thoughts sorting and rearranging themselves.

"*Collectio video bene dixit. Numquid non legistis?*" He asked me in Latin if I'd read the books in my collection and smiled condescendingly, expecting I hadn't.

"*Equidem libenter hoc amplius habere.*" I'd read them at Padua and pointed to a copy of *Bioblioteca Anatomica* and suggested he might like it. "*Ut sicut hic homo.*"

He raked me with dark intelligent brown eyes, taking in my plain, rumpled clothing and flushed face, and inclined his head slightly. I dipped my own coolly back.

I put a comforting hand on my patient. "All is well. Tis only another physician." Then I colored, remembering that John's friend knew little about me or the extent of any training I might have. To him I was only a woman with some small skill in healing and herbs who somehow knew Latin. I turned away from Lady Julianne and walked across the room toward him.

"Welcome, Malcolm." I hesitated and thought perhaps another viewpoint would help. "Would you care for refreshment? We have an excellent mead that is much commended. Tis our own make." For some reason, I found myself babbling: "We put a quart of honey to a gallon of fair spring water, boil it well with nutmeg and bruised ginger, and scum it much while boiling. It must stand for two weeks and we just drew it off in bottles yesterday." At the end of this breathless recitation he looked at me, raised one slanted brow and nodded. I guided him to a chair by the table and poured him a cup of the mead. Taking a seat across the table from him, I rushed into speech again, keeping my voice low so that the woman on the bed could not hear me. "I need your help. My patient has some troubling symptoms that are not part of her pregnancy. You may observe things I have missed." I played shamelessly to his ego. He looked at me thoughtfully for a moment and I had the distinct feeling he knew exactly what I was doing. It made me uncomfortable to think so. In fact, Malcolm himself made me uncomfortable in a way I did not understand, and I felt my scarred face warm. But he still said nothing, just listened, finished his mead and agreed to examine her. His face melted into the impassive mask, so many male physicians affect.

"She arrived late last night," I explained, "in the rain, already in labor, bleeding badly. We delivered her child soon after she came. It was far too early. The baby, a boy, was small so the birthing went quickly. The after burden was intact and the bleeding was controlled... But..." here my voice trailed off. What if he thought me mad... Sighing, I spoke hastily again: "Malcolm, she was preternaturally pale, vomiting, delusional and mostly unaware of what was happening. Her urine is bloody, she has bloody flux, her pulse is irregular, and she is having bouts of convulsions although those are becoming fewer. Her breath smells strongly of garlic and she was sweating profusely earlier. I well know many of those things can be explained away as symptoms of cholera or dysentery or some other disease, but together they say something different to me." I took a deep breath. "I think she's been poisoned, probably arsenic, which would account for all of the symptoms including the early birth. But I must be certain. I would be in your debt if you would look at her too." He grimaced but stood.

We walked to the woman. "Will you permit him to examine you?" I asked.

She looked up at me, then at him, and finally shook her head tiredly in resignation. I turned to Malcolm.

He leaned over the bed. Taking the woman's hand gently in his own, he moved his fingers over her wrist, smiled down at her and said in his soft soothing baritone, "I am Malcolm Forrester, physician. What is your name, my Lady?" She stared at him, mesmerized. "Julianne Morrison, sir, cousin and ward of the Laird."

Her voice was hushed and unexpectedly cultured with an almost imperceptible lilt to her speech that made me wonder if English was her only tongue. I frowned to myself. Why had I expected that she would speak like some slut from the streets? She was outwardly accepted as part of the Laird's family even though it was believed in the village that she was his lover. I felt he had used her badly, for it was almost certainly his baby. Because I believed that he was employing her as his convenient I had judged her without knowing the circumstances. It made me angry with myself and I liked him less for that. But I would think about that later. Large parts of her story seemed to be missing. No one knew where she had come from, or who her parents were, only that they were related in some way. Aggie, who helped with our laundry, was one of my best sources of information. Servants always know everything about their masters and the latest gossip came, appropriately enough, with the dirty linens.

Meanwhile I watched Malcolm bend over and speak calmly to Lady Julianne in that dark treacle voice of his.

"I am grieved for your child, and your illness. Lady Elspeth," he looked at me, "wishes a second opinion. Tell me when you first fell ill? Where were you, and what were you doing when you felt your pains begin?"

Lady Julianne's smooth brow puckered as she tried to remember. "I was having tea with Lady Margaret in her chamber. She invited me to see her new tapestry cartoon, I was to help sort wools and silks for it. It was beautiful. The artist's cartoon had a forest, trees and flowers, and, and...a white unicorn...with an arrow in its flank...it was bleeding, I found the red silks..." She stopped.

"What did you eat or drink?" He continued questioning her, listening, as his hands went to her throat feeling both sides for swellings, touching her skin lightly on her forehead and then in her armpits. He bent over her looking in both of her eyes intently and then smelled her breath, his concentration fully on her. I noticed his face had relaxed and now held only interest and compassion.

"Tea, little cakes with honey, sweetmeats, some marchpane. I began to feel sick after eating and left Lady Margaret, but I shortly began vomiting and then my pains came, too soon, and I was frightened. It was raining, but I dared not ask for help in the castle. I had heard of the new healer in the cottage and came here."

Malcolm nodded and pulled the blanket down to feel her belly, deftly palpating the recently emptied womb and checking the clout I had placed on her for staining. Straightening, he covered her again, and stood looking down at her pensively. "I think Lady Elspeth has cared for you well and you will be feeling better soon," he spoke reassuringly, and turned to me.

I called to Janet. "Our patient should be a little hungry now. I think you should be able to give her some beef broth with sops dipped in milk."

I led Malcolm closer to the fire. "Well," I asked him, "tell me what you found? Am I seeing things that are not there? I'm going to have to speak to Lady Margaret. There's no way to avoid it. I know it may cause trouble, but Malcolm, I cannot in good conscience send lady Julianne back to that household without knowing."

"I think you are meddling in things you know little about."

I felt the heat rise in my face. For a moment, I could say nothing. Then I was angry. I took a deep breath. "You see nothing amiss?"

His mouth tightened, then he said in a quiet, clipped tone, "I think you are well out of your depth. All the symptoms your patient exhibits could be attributed to other causes, yet you preferred the least probable diagnosis, and one that you cannot prove or support. And by making unfounded accusations you are bringing disrepute not only to yourself, but on me and Beaton. Elspeth, stay with what you know and leave real medicine to those who are qualified."

He stood there looming over me, emotion filling the space between us, and he wasn't done. "Your patient is obviously getting better. Be content with that and control your wild imaginings before you get us all into serious trouble. Surely you know there could be nasty consequences and we may not be here to save you next time."

I was so hurt and angry I had to remember to breathe. I clinched my lips firmly shut to keep from answering unwisely while I was so enraged. After a moment, I gathered myself, raised my chin and forced myself to meet his eyes and say meekly, "I thank you for your opinion, Sir Malcolm. I shall remember your words. If you will forgive me, my poor skills are needed. I must tend the lady, empty the chamber pot, and make some simples." If my sarcasm reached him he showed no sign, but nodded at Janet and Cawdie and left, closing the door behind him with exaggerated care.

My knees trembled, and I sat, refusing to let myself cry. Janet placed a hand on my shoulder. "Why did you not tell him you are a physician?"

FIVE

Malcolm - Intrigue

I was back in Edinburgh on my way to see Beaton and Young, and had dropped my bag at Father's. They wouldn't dare attack me there. After the long carriage ride I was happy to walk the several blocks to Young's. It was in the posh area near Edinburgh Castle. Young had inherited it and he and Beaton were doing well. I saw Young as soon as I entered.

"Mal, welcome, be with you in a few minutes." Young was always concise, accurate, very well-regarded. I sat myself down. It was one of those refurbished older buildings with polished oak floors, wainscoting and cream-colored plaster with paintings of bucolic countryside, all carefully arranged to soothe. Young's practice was mostly lawyers who seemed to have all the money in this city, but suffered like the rest of us from the same complaints. There is some justice, isn't there? Except they could afford the best doctors, like Young and Beaton.

I'd received Beaton's note yesterday. He said come for lunch, we have urgent news. So here I was back in Edinburgh and already feeling the nerves after the rough ferry crossing and wondering what was up. It had been just over a week since our meeting in Liddell's cellar and I'd been back at Torrport and involved in another controversy.

"Mal, come on upstairs, Beaton will be along shortly." It was Young, and I followed him to the second-floor dining room, laid-out precisely by his girl.

"What will you have? Port, wine, whisky?" He was already pouring one for himself.

"Port will be fine."

He brought mine over. "Let's have a quiet drink by the fire before lunch. It's been chaos here today. You sure you want to stay in Torrport? We sure could use you here." He smiled but knew my mind. No need to explain, but I did.

"You know I have a love-hate relationship with Edinburgh. Grew up here and could hardly wait to get away. But I see there's a new bookstore down the street. Always something new. I'll give it that." I sipped my port and he stared into the fire, obviously wanting time just to turn off for a few moments.

Beaton has one of those distinctive walking styles and I knew it was him as soon as he started up the stairs. I got up to meet him, leaving Young to his meditation. "Elspeth sends her regards." I met him at the top. Elspeth had said nothing of the sort, but I wanted him to know I'd met her.

"She did? And what truly happened, Mal?" He'd caught me out. Guess he knew her too well. I decided to get it over with.

"Seems she's involved in something delicate. Maybe in over her head. Good thing she has that brute Cawdie to shield her."

"What kind of something?"

He wanted details and I went over what'd happened with the Laird's convenient giving birth and her unusual health issues. I ended with the part about Elspeth's unfounded suspicions and my concern that this could go very badly if she doesn't keep her mouth shut, unless she has solid proof. "Elspeth is not particularly tactful but seems competent as far as her training allows, and it goes without saying I'll back her up, but if she has to flee again, this may be why. I have plenty of work for her though, so if things settle, she'll be fine." I wanted to end on a positive note, so he wouldn't panic and interfere.

"Thanks for letting me know Mal. I was hoping that Torrport would be suitable, but maybe not. Not much call for a new healer here though." He shook his head and sighed. Beaton took everyone's problems on his shoulders. The weight could bring him to his knees one day.

Young awoke from his trance. "Beaton, you must be famished. I know I am!" We were indeed and there wasn't much conversation over the soup, bread and roast chicken.

"My appreciations to your girl. She cooks a fine meal." I dabbed my lips with the linen and leaned back in my chair waiting for the news.

Young started. "On Turnbull's request, the Magistrate dropped a quarantine on that pub and those involved. Plenty of bitching, but not much they could do with Town Guards everywhere. You heard they found John Smith too, if that's his real name. They have him in the hole at the Guard House on the High Street. He's got smallpox and McLaren's been to see him. Smith isn't talking though, so we've no idea who he's contacted so far."

"Turnbull knows?"

"Aye, I informed him," Beaton continued. "We're all keeping an eye on the dock area, but God knows where Smith went after he left the Pub."

We all knew what was coming next. "In a few days, we could collect fresh samples from him." I said it then waited for their response.

Beaton went next. "Mal, there is so much unresolved. We don't even know who attacked us the first time, or why."

Young folded his arms and leaned forward. "I will not be cowed by opposition! They are wrong, and we will prove it. We have our patients to protect too. I say we try again, this time with more security and our eyes open." Young looked at us both. He was seething. This was not just about science anymore.

"Beaton, do you agree?" I asked directly, we needed his support now. He nodded, but I could tell he didn't want to do this, not right now anyway, there was too much male ego for good sense to prevail. "Then it's settled. I'll work with McLaren to get it underway. Meanwhile, I need to visit a few friends who may have some information about who our opposition might be."

Our lunch meeting ended with a toast to good fortune. We needed it. We truly did this time.

* * *

Gwen wanted to meet at one of her friend's homes not far from Father's. I had some time to kill, so walked to McLaren's. He was seeing patients, so I left him a note about our decision to proceed, would fill him in later, best wishes, and that I'd be staying with Father this time. Thanks for the bed offer, but it was a bit uncomfortable. I chuckled as I signed it. McLaren loved a good laugh.

It was not a bad day by Edinburgh standards, clouds threatening and variable breeze, so I went shopping. Not one of my favorite pastimes, but I needed a few items and there was a medical supply house nearby. I bought a nice tooth extractor. Had to do it with brute force last time, and it was not pleasant for either of us. Got the usual bandages and ties, and had a closer look at that lovely brass microscope in the shop window. I had to have one of those, not today but soon!

Gwen's friend owned a lovely grey and white plastered stone townhouse. She was another of those *Master-less* widows the authorities are concerned about. Can't have women with money free to do as they wish. I was ushered through the sumptuous main floor to the back garden. It was terraced with outdoor seating in a partially glassed-in section. Must have cost a fortune. Gwen was there with her friend who was of a similar age, plump and well-used looking with bad teeth showing when she smiled. We weren't introduced. She left, and Gwen poured some tea and offered cakes, then looked around to make sure we were alone.

"You must not tell anyone where this came from."

I assented.

"The three who attacked you are not important. They're not from here. Just off a ship, likely gone now, but there are lots of rumours. Word got around. People brag."

She was nervously fussing with the sleeve of her dress as I reached over and touched her knee. "It's alright, just tell me and I'll deal with it."

"Lover, I think you were robbed by doctors!" She blurted it out like a shocking profanity.

"Do you have names?"

"No. My man would only say your boss was involved."

"Gwen, I don't really have a boss. Well maybe some think they are." I was making light of it but of course I was thinking of Turnbull, but wouldn't tell her. "Did your source say why?"

"No. He's a friend of the guy who found the rough men to do it. They both thought it odd a doctor would do that."

"Doctors aren't saints, Gwen. Except me, obviously." She knew that was a lie for certain, but seemed relieved I wasn't so upset with her news.

We finished our tea and she was delighted to fill me in on who of our friends were dating. She was in her element now and meant to keep it so.

"I'm so sorry, I am busy til tomorrow afternoon. Can you come around then?" She gave me that well-practiced pouty look. I knew better than to ask. She had many lovers and reasons it would not be a good idea to show-up uninvited.

"Don't know Gwen. I'll send you a note when I'm available." I didn't want her calling the tune every time. I left it at that and gave her a warm kiss, waved to her friend on the way out and headed home to Father's.

* * *

The main streets this time of day are filled and the shouts of hawkers competing with the clatter of coaches going by every few seconds. People jostling each other to stay out of the mud and manure, the din and stench at times making one want to run for the tranquility of home. Father had just arrived from the courts a few minutes earlier and was in the mood to talk.

"Come and sit with me, son. What brings you back to the city? Or perhaps I don't want to know." He laughed softly, pouring us a few drinks and returning to his favorite chair by the fire. Of course, he wanted to know, so I told him about Smith and our plans to try the experiment again. He quietly stared into the fire sipping his port.

"Son, I know that woman you see has been sniffing around the port. Better call her off. Out of her depth with that bunch. She's a respectable widow. You don't want her involved. Understand?" I didn't, but agreed to warn her off. "The men who want to stop you are in the top ranks, and no I'm not going to tell you who, suffice to say that Turnbull isn't one of them. We can control Turnbull, it's some of the others, we have no leverage, you see?" That hit me. I'd pegged Turnbull as the prime suspect and I wasn't sure who else it could be.

"Leave it with me, Malcolm. We are monitoring the situation." I wasn't sure who he meant by "we" but thanked him anyway.

"In any case we're facing much bigger problems now, what with the war in Europe bogged down and the French ready to counter-attack. George is in the thick of it, you know, with Marlborough. They retreated to the Meuse after the Germans failed to support the offensive. Damned wars, so bloody wasteful!"

"Knowing George, he'll be a credit, won't he? But I worry too. It's all so chancy." Father was almost as much against George entering the service as having me a physician. We were all he had and both at risk now.

"We must do our part, but this is just a grand chess match, isn't it? The French on one side wanting more power and to reinstall a Catholic on our throne. That'll never happen, I can tell you!" He pointed at the fire as though scolding it, then continued. "The Jacobites have some support, but not enough to matter. The Act of Settlement to exclude Catholics from regaining the throne passed in the English parliament but still doesn't apply in Scotland, and that has everyone worried, including Queen Anne. We've been giving the English a rough time of it and understandably they've retaliated a few months ago with the Alien Act that demanded we accept the Act of Settlement by the end of the year or all Scots will be considered aliens under the law and our exports banned. Of course, what they want is to force a union of England and Scotland. What turmoil!" There was a tone of anger in his voice that I seldom heard. This was upsetting him.

"How it will end, no one knows, but meanwhile we're keeping a close watch on the Lairds who are known Jacobite supporters. We don't want another Jacobite rising in the middle of all this." Father had a lot of worries in addition to his court cases. Made my problems seem insignificant. I was ashamed I'd burdened him with them.

"Father, I can take care of myself. You don't have to worry. We'll be prudent and respectful."

"I'm sure you will, Malcolm." We both laughed knowing how unlikely was that prospect.

He changed the subject. "Tell me: What do you know about your Laird at Torrport, the one who fancies himself a MacDuff?"

I shared what little I knew including the possibility of an heir being born. Father listened carefully and thanked me at the end. It wasn't much in return for his help. We sat quietly, Father looking gaunt by the firelight with eyes closed, then I heard a soft snore and knew he was asleep. I left him there, and on the way out told his servant to awaken him soon for supper. I intended to have a night out before the horrific work I knew had to be done next day.

* * *

The coffee houses in Edinburgh were the place to be. Many called them penny universities because for the price of a cup of java, one could sit for hours and listen to all manner of lectures, discussions and debates. So, that's where I headed. The one close to Father's was among the best for political gossip and argument. It was the entire first floor on a corner building built years ago as an elegant home and since redone by opening it up and adding the latest fashionable wall coverings and décor. I found myself a spot near the podium at the front, under a large window looking on the street below.   I shared a table with three others amid a heated debate on the appalling state of local roads. I dropped my penny and the boy brought me coffee, hot, black, thick and bitter, served in a shallow ceramic bowl. This coffee house served light snacks as well, so I ordered buttered bread and jelly.

I sat back and smiled at my neighbors, sipped my coffee and watched the women making the many pots of coffee, tea and chocolate in the fire. Another woman was in the back, roasting coffee beans on a large flat pan. But the conversations drowned out all cooking sounds by a wide margin. The room was filled with over thirty men, seemingly all talking at once. To make any sense, one had to focus on a few and tune out the rest, otherwise it was just noise.

I decided to catch up on the local news first. Each table was supplied with local newspapers. It didn't take long to see that Father was right, the Scots were inflamed over this new Alien Act and saw it as another example of English bullying. The man nearest could see what I was reading and commented.

"And what d'ye think of that?" he pointed at the paper.

I looked up and smiled slightly. The last thing I needed tonight was getting involved in a fracas. "I think when cooler heads prevail, we'll find a way through."

He snorted. "The English want to own us. Always have, haven't they?"

I thought he was daft. No Englishman would want to own us troublesome Scots. Like having an untrainable horse. But I said, "Perhaps some do, but they're a lot more of them than us, and we're the poor cousins, so have more to gain from cooperation, don't we?" It was the simple truth that few Scots wanted to hear.

He could see I wasn't on his side. "Any forced union without the support of the common folk is bound to fail. You'll see." Then he turned away and resumed his argument about roads. He was likely right about his last comment though, but the Scottish Parliament wasn't made up of common folk, and the clergy, nobility and burgh commissioners were not known for their willingness to listen to the lower classes. Then there was the issue of so much English money being made available to certain Members of Parliament, as speculated by many.

Coffee and bread finished, I left with ears and mind buzzing. It was still early, and I needed a quiet place to walk and think. Quiet is hard to come by in Edinburgh, but the streets in early evening when the commercial traffic has abated, can be a lovely place to stroll, and that is what many were doing this fine spring evening. Women lavishly dressed in silks, eager to be out of the house for people watching and the theatre, escorted by tired husbands and suitors placidly smoking their pipes, nodding and saying as little as possible. There were a few of us single men too and even more prostitutes standing in doorways vying for attention.

Thoughts turned reluctantly to smallpox. I'd been trying to block it for a few hours. It was my obsession and I knew instinctively it could lead to ruin, and many including Father had warned me. In the morning, I intended to go with Angus McLaren to see Smith. I'd been out of touch and wanted back in to lead the charge. But as it turned out, fate had other plans.

* * *

I heard voices as soon as I got back to Father's. It was Beaton. He was telling Father something about Torrport and the Laird. I caught bits as I flew up the stairs. It was late for a visit, must be an emergency.

"John, what is it?"

"Mal, you must come now, back to Torrport. The last ferry's in an hour. It's the Laird and Elspeth again. Come on Mal! My carriage is waiting out back."

SIX

Elspeth – Conspiracy

I picked up my bag, stepped out of the door of the cottage and walked to the stone posts that mark the boundaries of my small piece of land. The clouds had carded themselves on the hills and lay in soft stringy white sheets in the valleys below me. It had been more than two days since Lady Julianne arrived at the door. She had improved greatly and was taking care of the babe, who despite my fears was still clinging stubbornly to life. We took turns holding the wee bairn and giving him tiny droplets of milk. Even Cawdie helped and the sight of that tiny bundle in his large gentle hands is one I shall never forget. When I put my little finger into his mouth he would make his first weak attempts to suck and I encouraged Janet and Julianne to do the same. I was considering making him a sugar rag with a bit of honey inside. He seemed to be more alert although he had not gained any weight that I could discern. I had no high hopes for his survival. About one third of all babes died before their first birthday, and this one had come too early. We kept the fact that he still lived from everyone outside the cottage. Lady Julianne had begged us to do so and for reasons of my own, I acquiesced.

Lady Margaret had summoned me to the castle this morning. I had heard nothing more of her threat to inform the kirk that Lady Julianne was possessed by a demon. Poor Father Hammett, he would be torn by conflicting loyalties in these strange times. I made my way slowly down the side of the hill into the valley that lay between Torrport and the fishing village and then up the cliffs, taking a hidden path that I had discovered one day while first investigating my new home. I suspected it had been made or used by either smugglers or the sheep that were permitted to graze freely nearby. At the top, it ended in a small copse of trees at the back of the kirk. I walked across the grassy common past the vicarage where

Father Hammett's flowers bloomed brightly. The mix of rich fragrances was calming, and I decided to stop on the way back and ask Father Hammet if I might have some of the red rose petals to make a decoction of them with wine for headaches and pain. Turning again toward the castle, I went to the gated entrance which was wide enough and tall enough to permit a cart or horse and rider to pass. A burly guard, whose foul breath was a weapon itself, barred my way. One side of his face was slightly swollen, and I wondered if he had a bad tooth or something worse. He asked me gruffly what I wanted, and I told him I had been summoned by Lady Margaret. After making me show him the contents of my bag, he pulled on the bell rope.

A small panel at the top of the massive doors slid open revealing a familiar face. Two weeks ago, its owner had come to me, panic stricken, thinking he had been infected with scrofula during a drunken night at the tavern in the small fishing village west of the castle. Fortunately for him he had not. It was only a simple boil in a rather complicated and embarrassing place, and had healed well after I had lanced it and given him a jar of salve and a lecture.

"Hello Thomas. How are you feeling?" I smiled at him. "I have been bidden here by Lady Margaret. Would you please tell her I have arrived?" He opened the door and stood there looking down, face flaming. After the smallest of hesitations, he replied, "Yes, my Lady." He was not certain exactly how to address me since my social status as a healer was confusing at best, and my very personal examination of him was a mortifying memory at worst. He led me into the bailey and asked me to remain there while he told Lady Margaret I was here.

While I was waiting, a large man in military dress strutted confidently out of the armory and saluted me. "Welcome, are you the healer? Dr. Forrester said you would be here to poultice one of my men. I am John Spence, the Laird's Second. If you will come with me, I will take you to him."

At that moment, Thomas reappeared and beckoned for me to follow him. I turned to the man, "Thank you, Sir. I will see him after I speak with Lady Margaret." I inclined my head to him then trailed Thomas up the stone steps into the castle and up a second flight to Lady Margaret's solar. Inside it was warm and filled with the scent of bergamot, wool, and growing green things. I was immediately struck by the number of intricately worked tapestries and wall hangings covering every available surface, most of them portraying hunting scenes. Several had unicorns. The Lady herself was occupied with a new one, copying a painted cartoon that depicted a wounded unicorn lying in a flower filled glade.

I bowed my head. "You sent for me, Lady Margaret. How may I help you?"

She turned to me gracefully, a practiced smile on her still pretty face. Her upper incisors were slightly longer than average, but her skin was as white and perfect as a babe's. "I wish to thank you for taking care of poor Julianne. How is she? Is it not time for her to return to the castle? We would not wish to impose on you."

Her words were not what I expected given her earlier accusations of Lady Julianne and of me.

"Almost, my Lady. She has been most unwell, and we are still not certain exactly what caused it. She said she was with you when her pain began, and I was wondering if you or anyone in your family might also have eaten something, perhaps some food or drink that caused it, and been ill too?"

A dull flush suffused her face. "Indeed? I noticed nothing. No one here has shown the least sign of sickness. We all ate the same foods. Twas more like to do with her...condition."

"I don't think so, my Lady." My eyes held hers as I stepped over the precipice of common sense. "I think she was poisoned. I have gone over the symptoms carefully and concluded that she ate something deadly." I deliberately left out the fact that Malcolm had examined her too. His harsh words still hurt, and I did not want him involved if I was wrong. Blame for my words or actions would rest solely with me.

She went from flushed to quite pale, but her expression remained composed. At that moment, the door opened, and the Laird entered. Lady Margaret looked at him. "Well come, my Laird." She pointed a white, plump, beringed hand in my direction. "Here's a pretty thing! This woman has said that Lady Julianne was poisoned while she was here with us! As Laird, you must give her over to charge for lying!"

The Laird slanted a strange look at his wife, then at me. "You accused someone here of poisoning Lady Julianne?"

"I did not, my Laird. I simply asked if anyone else here has been ill. I wondered too, were there any here that might have reason to wish her harm? Perhaps it was an accident? But I do believe she may have been poisoned." He knew that all too well. I had told him so when he came to the cottage to see Lady Julianne.

Lady Margaret kept her eyes on me. "Mayhap you did it with your potions! She was possessed of a demon! We all saw it and I saw you wrestling with it." Her voice softened to silk over steel. "Or you were embracing it! Only witchcraft could account for such. I bear witness that she is a witch, my Laird. Torrport has no place for such as she!" She sank onto her chair as though exhausted, and began to sob quietly, a handkerchief hiding her tears or lack thereof. Her maid, who had been sitting in the shadows of the solar, rushed to help her mistress and glared at me. Did Lady Margaret feel threatened by Julianne? Enough to want her dead? Perhaps the birth of a child, perchance a son, was the catalyst? I stood immobile, caught in memories of another time in my past.

The Laird looked at his wife. "Calm yourself, Margaret," he said tightly. "We are indebted to Lady Elspeth. She is a healer. It is she who helped Lady Julianne, and we owe her much for that."

She turned to the Laird. "You would take the part of this, this common woman against me? She should be examined by the Church, imprisoned and tried for witchcraft! You are my husband. I demand that you have her brought before the Church and charged!"

The Laird stared at her for a moment, some private message passing unsaid between them, then he turned to me.

"Guard!" he shouted. One of his men, obviously listening outside, almost tumbled into the room and stood waiting for his orders. "Take Lady Elspeth to the...bailey and keep her under watch. She may not leave the castle without my permission. He looked at me. "Lady Elspeth, you will stay here until this situation has been settled. You are free to walk within the bailey until evening, when you will be placed in a cell in the armory." I was quivering with anger but said nothing more, simply lowered my head to him and followed the guard out of the chamber. It was Thomas. The back of his neck burned crimson with discomfort as I followed him down the steps.

We reached the bailey and he turned to me, helplessly. "Lady Elspeth, you must stay within these walls. Would you like a place to sit down?" he asked uneasily.

I put down my bag, which I had been clutching tightly the whole time, and tried to smile at him. "No, Thomas, but your Captain Spence wishes me to see a patient. Please go and tell him I am ready to look at his man. I shall do that first, and if there are others who might need me, I will see them, also."

The bailey, an open area inside the castle building, was bustling with activity. Chickens scratched underfoot, cows munched contentedly in the stalls separating them from the horses, and a sow nursed her piglets in the shade of the massive stone walls. The smell of manure, hay, baking meats and bread mingled with occasional whiffs of sweat and leather from a group of soldiers training near the armory.

Thomas returned shortly with Captain Spence. He obviously had been told of my change from guest to prisoner, and seemed uncertain how to deal with it. I hastened to reassure him. "Sir, your men will not suffer at my hands. It is your choice, but I am prepared to tend them if you wish." He nearly smiled, then beckoned me to follow him. The armory was filled with the tools of war. We passed an empty cell in one corner. Just beyond it, a turret room had been made into an infirmary scarce large enough to turn around in. There were two beds, one occupied by a large ginger-haired man lying face down. He tossed restively beneath a light blanket.

Captain Spence touched his shoulder. "Ronald, this is Lady Elspeth, the healer that Dr. Forrester told us of. She has come to tend your wound and apply a poultice."

He turned his head to the side and his eyes roved glassily over me.

"May I see to your wound, sir? I need to look at it." I waited. After a moment, he made a small movement of his chin in assent, and I placed my hand on his wrist. His pulse was a little rapid, and his skin warm and dry. "Are you in pain, sir?" He glanced briefly at his comrades, then nodded again. Malcolm had told me what happened. I folded the blanket down from his shoulders to his waist, so I could see the injury. The bandages needed changing but there was no evidence of unusual bleeding. I carefully removed the cloths and smelled the soiled areas for the odor of rot, but there was blessedly none. The wound was red and slightly swollen, as might be expected. "I will need a basin of clean water, please, Thomas."

By the time he returned with it, I had unfolded fresh bandages and cloths and placed a container holding a poultice of garlic and honey, with a little cinnamon added, on a nearby chest. I washed the wound with the water after adding a little lavender.   I gathered from the sound of several slight snickers from outside the door while doing this that he might well get some teasing about how he smelled. When I placed a white cloth over the wounds and covered it with the poultice the garlic odor was so pervasive in the close room that the laughter immediately stopped. I layered a second cloth dressing over the poultice, and the whole tied in place with long strips of cloth around his body, finished the treatment. I emptied the dirty water in the basin into a slop bucket and rinsed it out.

"All-done, sir." I secured a final knot in the last strip. "Dr. Forrester is an excellent physician. If I am not here, do you have a friend who can replace this poultice tomorrow? I will give them fresh bandages and a jar of the poultice mixture." One of the men moved forward, and I handed him a small bundle. "Just in case." I smiled at him and stood up and regarded the watchers.

"Does anyone else need looking at?" It was quiet, then a small man stepped up to me and wordlessly held out his hand. It was covered with a filthy rag, but I could see that it was badly swollen. "Come and sit here on the other cot and let me look at it." I unwrapped the cloth carefully. His hand was indeed badly inflamed, one finger twice its normal size and the nail loose and pushed away from the bed with blood streaked pus. I could smell the putrefaction. "What happened?" His hand was hot, the skin stretched taut across it.

"Twas the cannon, my Lady. I did not move me hand fast enough from the recoil."

I reached for the basin again, filled it with clean water and a packet of red pepper and cinnamon from my bag. I placed his hand in it. "Soak your hand for a while. I am afraid I must open it to let some of the infection out. I fear you may lose the nail, but that will be better than losing the finger." After a time, I pulled his hand from the water. Reaching into my bag I unrolled a cloth with my tools inside, each in a little pocket I had sewn to hold it. He blanched at the sight of them, but sat stolidly while I selected one to lance the crushed finger. A putrid stream of pus mixed with blood burst from the cut. When I had wiped it away and the wound was bleeding freely, I put his hand back into the water until it stopped. The pepper must have hurt, but he made no sound. I took his hand from the water again, dried it and applied a salve of garlic, cinnamon and honey. After wrapping his hand in a clean bandage, I gave him instructions to apply the salve every day, and to see Dr. Forrester if needed.

When I was done, Captain Spence thanked me by escorting me to the nearby cell. A meal of bread and cheese was proffered, but I was not hungry. The day already seemed too long and despite knowing I probably shared the rough sheets with several species of vermin, I fell asleep almost instantly.

SEVEN

Malcolm – Rescue

I ran to my room and threw everything in my bag and hugged Father, and as soon as we were underway started calming Beaton who was having a bossy panic fit. If anything happened to her, he'd be exiled from his clan. We tore off through the darkness with Beaton screaming out the window at the coachman and cursing the damnably slow horses. Late that night we arrived at her cottage. I let Beaton do the knocking, this time keeping back several steps out of highlander range.

Janet answered the door so quickly I thought she might have been waiting on the other side. She looked at us both with a combination of fear and relief. "She's not here. She was called to the castle early yesterday morning by Lady Margaret and has not returned."

"Where is her man...that giant highlander?" I spoke up from behind Beaton.

"I think he's at the castle, but last I heard they wouldn't let him in. Sirs, she needs someone to help her, someone with authority. Please go quickly!"

* * *

I wasn't in such a panic as Beaton because I assumed the Laird could be reasoned with. The carriage lurched to a stop. Cawdie was there just outside the castle doors hunched down and covered in his thick plaid. Beaton stopped the carriage and shouted. "Cawdie, we'll take over from here. Go back to Janet and warm up."

Cawdie rose and saluted. "Aye sir, that would be welcome."

The guard approached and recognized me. I told them we had urgent business with the Laird, and they let us in promptly.

"John, let me deal with this. I know you're upset, but it's likely just a misunderstanding. Let's see what's going on first, alright?" I needed him to give me the lead on my turf.

"I understand, but you mustn't let anyone harm her."

"You have my word, John." Not sure how much my word meant in a situation not under control, but he knew I would do my best.

Captain John Spence was there sitting on a chair propped against the wall when we disembarked in the bailey. He had a wry smile as he got up and swaggered over. "I think I can guess the reason for this late visit."

I had no time for games, so barked at him in a tone of command. "Where is Elspeth MacLeod and the Laird?"

He stood for a moment likely considering options, then Beaton broke in. "Sir, we have come in good faith, please do us the courtesy."

"The woman is in the cells in the armoury, but you can't see her without approval from the Laird, and he has retired for the night." He smirked at us smugly, having put us in check.

"Spence, the Laird will want to see me at any hour. I am his physician and have urgent news. Now take me to him immediately." I was not going to be thwarted and he could sense it now, so he turned and grumbled something under his breath and led us to the room at the top of the main building reserved for the Laird and clan leaders. It turned out the Laird hadn't retired for the night. In fact, he was amid a boisterous draughts match with a scowling opponent. There were several others standing by drinking and cheering. I walked to the side of the table facing Laird MacDuff. I was hard to avoid and his face involuntarily grimaced.

"Enough of this, boys. Looks like I have some business with the good Doctor Forrester." He rose, and the men dispersed.

"Laird MacDuff, this is my friend and colleague John Beaton of Edinburgh. He also is the cousin of Elspeth MacLeod."

The Laird nodded at Beaton then said. "Have a seat the both of you. I think we can quickly deal with this." We sat opposite, and MacDuff looked calm enough as he leaned back and finished the last of his ale.

"I have Elspeth in a comfortable cell in the armoury," he started to explain. "It is for her protection and to get her piece off the table. Understand? There were too many moving parts and I needed to calm the situation." Then he proceeded to tell us about the birth and the mother's suspicious symptoms and Elspeth making accusations of poisoning and his wife having a hysterical fit and accusing Elspeth of being a witch.

"Mind you, I don't believe in witches, but I do know my wife tends to over-react, so I had to do something, didn't I? I am not sure what is going on..." He paused and looked at John. "And sir, Elspeth MacLeod is a healer in my community and I will not harm her unless she has broken the law."

Beaton spoke for the first time. "Then release her now into my custody. She will be safe with us and I assure you she will not interfere further."

The Laird folded his arms then glanced at me, then John. "Nay, Sir Beaton, you are not of our clan or community. She needs to stay here til this matter is resolved."

I had an idea. "My Laird, with all due respect, you cannot hold her without proper charges and a trial per our new *Habeas Corpus* law. Release her into my custody and I will provide your guarantees." I didn't know what I was talking about, only just recently having learned of this new law, but I hoped the Laird knew even less than I.

He looked surprised. "A new law? Those damned English!" He stood up suddenly knocking the chess board and pieces to the floor. "Alright Forrester, you may have her, but she mustn't leave Torrport without my agreement and you must present her if she is charged in future. Also, keep her damned mouth shut while we sort this, will you?"

I readily agreed to his terms and was happy to see Beaton supress a smile.

The Laird shouted for Captain Spence. "Release Elspeth MacLeod into the custody of Doctor Forrester." He took a step closer, grabbed my arm and whispered: "I'm going to need your help with all this. Come back tomorrow morning when we're fresh."

"I will indeed, Laird MacDuff, and thank you for your kindness and understanding." I may have underestimated this man. My initial instinctive dislike may have been unwise.

Captain Spence lead us to the cage where we found Elspeth curled up on a cot under layers of blankets. She awoke, and we briefly explained the situation as she was freed. I let Beaton be the first to caution her as questions came flying at us like bees from a disturbed hive. "Elspeth, you must stay away from the castle and the Laird's family and hold your tongue! That is part of the agreement or you must go back." He enjoyed saying that. She made a token effort at protest, but I think she was just happy to be free. I smiled inwardly as peace finally settled between us.

EIGHT

Elspeth - Investigation

There is no reasoning with self righteous men, so I said nothing more on the drive home from the castle. I was too busy scratching. As I feared, the cell at the armory had been occupied by more than myself. I itched unmercifully. It had been a long day and I was tired and dirty and depressed. Neither John nor Malcolm cared a groat about what I thought or how I was feeling, so I made myself as small as possible in one corner of the carriage and tried to ignore the sensation of being eaten alive by wee creatures. We arrived at the cottage and Janet opened the door as soon as we drove up. I could see Cawdie sitting by the fire as the door opened, but he stood instantly when Malcolm helped me down from the carriage, pushed me ungently into the house, and glared at them both. "Take more care that your mistress keeps her mouth shut, stays away from the castle and invites no more trouble!" he said harshly. John had the grace to look a bit abashed at this order from his friend, an outsider, but Malcolm stood unmoving and scowled. "I have pledged my word for her behavior, so I expect her to abide by it. Her actions reflect on us all." Lady Julianne stepped from behind the screen in the corner, and he paused in his harangue. He had last seen her ill, now her beauty had returned in full measure even more refined by her ordeal, and he was momentarily silenced.

Janet ignored him and walked over and gathered me in her arms. I thrust her away. "Oh, no, please Janet, you must not touch me! I am filthy, and I fear that I have acquired fleas and perhaps lice in the guest room at the armory. I just want to take these clothes off and have them burned or washed, and I desperately need a bath."

I had no desire to speak further to either of my rescuers, but good manners meant I must, so I thanked them both in meek honey flavored words that would have fooled no one who knew me well. Had I truly the powers of a witch, as I had been accused, I would have changed both men into toads long since.

Bowing my head to them, I stalked into the bedroom and removed my grimy infested clothing. Janet put it in a closed bag to take to Aggie at the village laundry. I dared not even sit on the bed lest my scratching give any fleas or lice a new home. Instead, I lowered myself to the floor rubbing at real and imagined bites and Janet covered me with an old blanket. She went to the door and called out to Cawdie to bring the tub and hot water.

I could hear Lady Julianne speak to the men politely and offer refreshment. They both quickly refused, perhaps embarrassed before the calm fragile woman. I hoped that she had concealed the babe, if he was indeed still alive. Julianne thanked them for bringing me home and asked if there was anything more they wished, in that sweet well-bred tone which is a dismissal. They heard it clearly and left at once, Malcolm mumbling something under his breath as they did so.

Cawdie carried in the tub. Janet followed with towels and a bowl of the soft soap that we made for our own personal use and placed them neatly on the chest. Cawdie poured hot water into the tub, left two smaller buckets of water next to it, and took himself off.

I stood somewhat stiffly, added the blanket I had been wrapped in to the sack of dirty clothes, stepped into the warm water and knelt. Janet poured some oil of cedar and rosemary into the warm water to kill lice and fleas and began to un-braid my waist length hair. It had to be washed carefully to make certain I had not picked up any crawling things from the armory. It is very difficult to control fleas, lice and itchy mites, and I had no desire to add them to our household. Janet wet my hair and worked the soft soap scented with lavender and rose into it. After drying it I would take a powder of roses, nutmeg, watercress and galangal, and mixed into some rose water and combed through my hair with a lice-comb, just to be sure.

I relaxed gratefully and let Janet lave it as though I were a child. My mind was so full of what happened today that I could no longer think clearly. I had certainly overstepped. As much as it galled me to admit it, Malcolm may have been right. I had acted in haste and needed to learn patience. He thought me untrained and limited to empiric medicine. My thoughtless actions had confirmed his opinion.

I tilted my head back in the tub while Janet poured clean water over my hair, then took a cloth from the pile and scrubbed my skin to the point of redness. When I finished, I stood, and Janet poured the second bucket of water over me. I stepped out of the tub onto a cloth, and let Janet briskly rub me dry and treat my hair. The mixed scents of roses and lavender enveloped me, and by the time she was done, and I had been dressed in a clean nightdress, I was barely conscious. I made no resistance when

Janet tucked me into my bed, covered me, and firmly closed the bed doors to keep out any noise or drafts that might disturb sleep. I remember nothing more until morning.

* * *

The next day I was again my usual self and already chafing at the restrictions laid upon me by Malcolm and John. Fortunately, there was a steady stream of patients from Torrport and the fishing village, all anxious to be seen, and eager to talk about the Laird or the excitement at the castle yesterday. To my amusement, I found that my brief incarceration had earned me more respect than disapproval.

My first patient, an aged dame with fingers so curled they looked like claws, had been coming to me on a weekly basis. I prepared a basin of hot water, poured in a spoon of oil of ginger and placed it on her lap so she could soak her hands while I treated a very small boy who had fallen from an apple tree. He had a large lump on his head which had bled copiously in the manner of head wounds. I cleaned it carefully, applied cold cloths for the swelling, and gave him a sugar plum to dry his tears. I told his anxious parents to watch him and bring him back if he began to vomit, act oddly, or sleep more than usual. They were shamed to have no coin, but asked diffidently if they might bring us fresh eggs weekly as payment. I smiled at them, assured them we were greatly in need of eggs and hoped they did not see our own chickens about when they left.

Returning to the dame, I toweled her hands dry and massaged more of the oil of ginger mixed with oil of orange and a little good water firmly over her hands, kneading and straightening each finger as I went. As I worked, she sighed with relief and rambled on about the old Laird, slyly including a few wicked memories dredged up from her youth. He had been well-liked and was genuinely mourned, few believing his final step off the parapet of the castle had been an accident. The new Laird and his Lady were yet unknown and unproven and viewed with typical Scottish reserve.

My next patient, Molly MacCool, the village seamstress who suffered a loose womb and a looser tongue, made a few shrewd references to the Laird's frequent visits to the unsavory tavern in the fishing village. Since there was a brothel over the tavern, it was generally assumed that was his reason for visiting, although that made the status of Lady Julianne puzzling. Lady Margaret had made no effort to know the Laird's people and in return was simply dismissed with the casual cruelty that destroys reputations and lives. Molly was prone to miscarry, so I gave her a tonic made with Plantain Seed to drink each morning, cautioned her about lifting heavy things, and told her to return in three weeks.

By the time I had seen a dozen patients and listened to an equal number of different tales about the Laird, his wife and his convenient, I decided to call on Aggie, just to take her my infested clothing, of course. If I happened to hear a bit more gossip, twas only to be expected. Never underestimate the poison spread by "Miss Gossip and Tattle." It could be used in many ways and might help with my investigation of Julianne's poisoning. I had no intention of letting the incident pass.

* * *

After my last patient left I went to see my smallest one. Julianne sat quietly before the fire staring at him. He was still not moving much, but he was taking a bit more substance. I had made him a honey tit and he seemed to enjoy the taste of it while not actually sucking on it. The stroking of his belly had worked, and he was having regular bowel movements. For the first time, I began to think he might live. Julianne was a good mother, instantly alert to the wee bairn's every movement. They regarded each other solemnly with the same blue eyes, and the fuzz of black hair was beginning to curl around the tiny face. Scathach guarded the bairn as fiercely as though he had been her own pup and was never far from him or Julianne.

During the last few days, titles had been dispensed with and the bairn and Julianne had fit themselves neatly into our lives. She cared almost entirely for the little one, feeding him patiently, wiping him with oil, and washing his soiled linens. I do not hold with the belief that just drying the urine soaked clouts is enough and insisted that everything he soiled should be thoroughly washed. Cawdie had scythed the grass short in a sunny spot on the lawn where she could dry his things after she washed them. Both he and Janet treated her much as they treated me. She had obviously been gently reared despite her reputation as an immoral woman.

When she shyly asked permission to look at my books, I discovered she could read French as easily as English and wrote with a beautiful hand. She was eager to help, and I soon put her to transcribing my notes and labeling medications. There was no task she would not try to do, although not always with the skill she displayed as a needlewoman. She mended everything she could find with almost invisible stitches. She quilted intricate designs in soft blankets for the babe, and even in the clouts we made for our monthly flowers. Scathach shadowed her and the babe, leaving them only for short periods when she was with Cawdie. Julianne groomed the huge dog as though she was a horse, and Scathach melted at her touch.

We would soon have no excuse for her to remain here, and would need to decide what to do about the babe. My sin of omission in not saying he lived, looked as though it might well cause trouble and Malcolm would again have a real reason to be angry with me. The Laird had called daily, but Julianne resolutely refused to see him. He accepted the refusal, but always returned the next day. Lady Margaret had not repeated her visit. That had to be resolved also. How could I let Julianne and the bairn return to a place that might be dangerous for them both? As far as I could tell, Lady Margaret was still the only person that might have a reason to harm Julianne and the babe. They could not stay with us indefinitely, and I was beginning to feel guilty about not showing the babe to his father.

I wriggled uncomfortably, picked up the wee yin, laid him on the bed, and unwrapped him. The naval string was healing, and he was perfect in every way except for his size. Julianne hovered closely as I worked with him, and I said casually as I cleaned him, "Julianne, where did you live as a child?"

She handed me a clean clout for the child, and after a brief pause answered readily enough, "My family is from Scotland, but we lived at the French Court, from the time I was eight until I was twelve. We traveled a great deal and spent some years in Russia before we returned to Scotland." Her eyes became bright with unshed tears. She offered no more, and I did not pry further. I swaddled the babe again and returned him to her.

Janet had been working quietly making French mustard from a recipe Julianne had given her and the room was rather pleasantly redolent of the scent of the cinnamon and sharp seeds she was preparing. She had cleaned eight ounces of mustard seeds and stamped them in our mortar with two ounces of cinnamon. When they were powdered, she added two ounces of honey, and enough vinegar to make the mixture smooth enough to serve. It made a good mustard, not too thick, and kept well in little oyster-barrels.

She looked up as I went to the door, took my shawl from a peg, draped it over my head and wrapped and belted it around myself. "I think I will take the laundry to Aggie." I smiled at her, reached for a small firkin of hand cream from the shelf, and picked up the sack of laundry just outside the door. "You might ask Cawdie to see if he can get some fresh fish to add to our dinner. Pick some dill to go with it." I made my way carefully down the boulder strewn hillside to the rough road that led to the port.

* * *

Once I reached the waterfront, I could see as I passed the tavern, that it was already crowded. Mrs. Scrogie set an excellent table, and her ales were well known about the countryside. I slipped around the corner to the laundry behind the tavern where their daughter, Aggie, had set up her place of business. It was well done, with two large cauldrons set on iron rods over fires, several tubs and bats, shelves filled with neat rows of sorting baskets, drying racks and even a rather elegant linen press.

Aggie was elbow deep in water when I walked to the laundry area. Two women I recognized from the village looked up, nodded, and continued to beat the wet laundry with wooden bats, or beetles. The drying racks were filled, and the cauldrons boiling. The smell of lye and urine was strong. They used a mixture of both on sheets or clothing, to whiten them. Aggie was good about rinsing, so little of the odor remained most of the time. I placed the sack I had brought well away from the cleaned clothes shelved in the shed, and put the firkin down nearby.

"Aggie, I have brought you that new cream I was telling you about." I eyed her arms which were red and raw looking. "I want you, and the others to remember to rinse your arms well when you are done, and apply this when you are finished for the day. The hot water and the lye in the soap is bad for your skin. This will soothe it and help keep it soft."

She looked up and laughed merrily. "Nay, mistress, who will care about the looks of our poor hides? But I thank you and we will do as you say."

"A warning: the sack I brought is probably full of whatever lives in the armory cells, as well as my things. You might want to just put everything directly into the boiling pot. The dress is old, and has been there before."

She lifted her arms out of the water and started to wipe them on her apron. "I did hear you were kept in there. It makes nae sense. The Laird is too easily led." She frowned, her pretty face screwed into a disapproving grimace. "And that John Spence is a chancer, for sure. He spends much time and more coin in the tavern than he could be taking at the castle, and he has roamin' hands, he does. His wife is handmaid to Lady Margaret and sometimes works in the kitchen at the castle. Tis said she do work hard, and has a good hand with sweetmeats...and if I put my foot in her shoes, I would have his heid!" She spat on the stones and called to a small child who was folding napkins for the press. "Harley, Tis enough. Go tell cook to give ye the soup I promised, and go home to your ma." The little boy bobbed his head, meticulously finished the last square, placed it precisely atop the others beneath the press, then scampered off to the tavern kitchen. Aggie walked over to the press and began to turn the screw that applied pressure to the linens beneath it. "And, Lady Elspeth, I 'ave a new tub for me, my, bluing now!"

I sat down on the stool beside the door that led to the kitchen. I liked Aggie. She had no desire to work in the tavern that belonged to her parents. To her, the drudgery that turned her skin to red blisters at times was preferable to serving the men who frequented the pub. She was a comely girl, with dark honey colored hair that probably reached her buttocks when it was undone. Her face was a little freckled from the sun, but softly colored with plump lips, and her body was lithe and slender from working. She viewed the world through intelligent green eyes, and I knew she could read and write, at least enough to keep the laundry accounts.

I responded to her comment about Spence, the Laird's Second. "Oh? One must then wonder how he can afford such extravagance." Aggie looked around and then leaned toward me and lowered her voice. "Tis said his eye can be blinded by coin and if a sack of smuggled wool falls near him, he will not see it. The things he wants most are not all in our tavern, but in the one at the fishing village. 'Ware of him, Lady."

"I will heed your warning, Aggie," I smiled at her and stepped back as another customer came around the corner with an overflowing basket. "Promise me you will use that cream, starting today. Send the boy when the laundry is done, and I will have Cawdie pick it up."

She smiled at me, and half turned to go back to her washing. "I promise my Lady, as soon as I finish this batch. And...Lady, is your cousin in Torrport? I have not seen him this age." She flushed, "Mayhap he needs some laundry done?" I smiled and resolved to tell John to bring his dirt to Aggie. He could do much worse. Her father might be a tavern keeper now, but he was of good family.

On the way home, I went over the conversation in my head. Was Spence taking bribes? Aggie had insinuated such. The tavern at the fishing village was a ramshackle building on the wharf, with rooms above for the less savory activities. Three of the girls who worked there had already come to me. One for lice, one for a bad rash, and one because she was with child. I had tried to talk them into making their clients use lengths of pliable gut that fit over the man's penis and tied at one end to hold the seed, but they had laughed at my ignorance and the thought that their customers would consent to such. So, I attempted to teach them instead how to prevent pregnancy by inserting sponges soaked with vinegar and tied with a string for retrieval. There was much badly stifled giggling as I explained how to make and insert them. But if it helped only one or two, it was worth the effort.

* * *

I was restless as I walked home. I wondered if Spence and the Laird were involved with the smugglers, if the Laird had other women besides his wife and convenient, if Spence was taking bribes. I ached to go to the tavern, listen to ale-loosened talk and hear what I might, but that was not possible. Only women of the lowest sorts ventured into such a place. If I was needed there, I would take Cawdie. Being a woman meant limited choices and I sometimes hated being female. I did have an idea.

Growing up in Skye, I had borrowed boys clothing from a friend who was a stable lad, covered my hair with a cap, and tasted a bit of the freedom that males so take for granted. Because I am small, I gleefully joined the ranks of invisible children that ran wild, hung about the stables and smithy, and increased my knowledge of words that made Janet despair of me. She told Cawdie, who had come to Skye to recover from a wound, about my forays, and after that he seemed never to be far from me wherever I went. He once broke the arm of a drunken man who was beating me because I accidently stumbled into him. When I was seventeen, just before I left to study medicine in Italy, he came to me and told me he had been instructed by the Laird to go with me. I took him and Janet with me and never looked back.

Malcolm had ordered me to stay away from the castle, keep my mouth shut and stay out of trouble. I could comply with that. The tavern in the fishing village was not the castle, and I would certainly not speak. As for the trouble part, I could do that too. I would simply take Cawdie with me on my foray. The boys clothing still fit my undersized body. I smiled and increased my pace home.

NINE

Malcolm - Patients

Next day, back in Edinburgh, McLaren had left a note saying Smith looked close to death and to meet at one-o-clock in the afternoon when he checked on Smith at the Guard House. When I arrived, McLaren had that sour look that meant worry. It had been two days before Beaton and I'd returned to Edinburgh and they were very annoyed with us for leaving like that.

The Guard House was that squat stone building on High Street everyone avoided. The hole was literally that, a hole dug in the ground years ago that housed crude cells for prisoners. Smith was in the last one furthest from the entrance.

"You available now Forrester?" McLaren asked sarcastically.

"Aye, Beaton's cousin..." I could see at once he didn't want to hear the details, so I gave a friendly smile and pat on the shoulder and said: "Let's get this done."

"Aye, Mal." McLaren pulled his cloak tight around his shoulders then opened the iron-clad door to the cell and walked in cautiously holding the sputtering torch high. He set the pail of food and water on the floor, then turned back to me holding up his hand. "Don't come in. Stay out of the foul air. I'll let you know how he is." I didn't need any more encouragement, but stuck my torch in the door to see better. McLaren knelt beside the shape on the cot. He was still as death and wrapped in a stained grey blanket.

"John, are you awake?" McLaren gently touched what looked like his shoulder. There was movement, then muffled sounds. "I have some food and water. Do you need help to relieve yourself?" The shape rolled over slowly, and Angus helped him sit up, then slid the metal bucket in front of him so he could urinate. There wasn't much, but it was a good sign that he still could. Many die from dehydration, the pustules in their mouths so painful that drinking becomes nearly impossible.

"Take some food now. I have bread soaked in fresh milk. You need to eat more to regain your strength." Always gentle and considerate, Angus poured some into a bowl and started feeding him. The man ate slowly. My eyes were becoming adjusted to the light and I could see that his face was covered with puss-filled pocks running together to make his face swollen and grotesque.

"John, I brought another physician today, Doctor Forrester. He and I are trying to find a proper cure for smallpox and would like to take a few scabs from your face in a few days." The man grunted then looked up at me.

"Forr—esh- te?" he said slowly, having trouble speaking.

"Aye, John, I wish you well. I hope you can help us." I spoke loudly hoping for assent.

"I, I, said no...thin." It came out of him as a hoarse whisper. Angus looked back at me. I shrugged and decided it was too difficult and McLaren should just finish his tasks.

"It's alright, John, we'll leave it for another time. Have some water." He gave Smith a few gulps then placed the large mug by the bed. "Would you like a bit more laudanum for the pain?" Smith nodded. They almost always do. McLaren gave him a draught then rose to leave, gathering buckets and bowls. "I'll be back tomorrow. Sleep well." The man groaned then lay back pulling the blanket over his thin shoulders.

In the hall, McLaren stopped and turned to me. "I think he's improving, might make it, but sometimes late fevers take them too. He has the typical form of smallpox. We should have usable scabs in a few days if we want to proceed."

That's why he wanted me here, to make the decision. We'd heard the best patients were the ones who lived through it, and the best stage for harvest was when the scabs are mature just before they start falling off. With luck, both would occur in a few days.

"Let's assume we shall proceed." If anything, I was decisive.

"Alright Mal, I'll try to keep him alive." He smiled slightly and led me back outside. It was good to breathe the fresh air. "One more thing, we want the surgeons involved this time. It's good politics, and McLean, that surgeon you met at Liddell's, offered to harvest the scabs and give the treatments. He's a survivor you know."

No, I didn't know, and I didn't much care for McLean either, but I could fathom the logic. "Alright, Angus, but McLean had better be good."

"One of the best in the city, and he's already recruited a few of the new surgeons as test subjects."

That's what happens when you're away, decisions are made, and you have no choice.

"It will be good to have the surgeons on board, so long as we aren't making another group of enemies." I was even more worried now. Too many cooks making the stew and with some deadly ingredients from the cupboard. "We only have a few days, let's

get started. We need to meet with Young and Beaton tonight to set plans in motion."
I tried to sound confident, but my stomach told me otherwise.

* * *

The meeting that evening at McLaren's wasn't at all what I'd expected. The room was
completely full and included all ten test subjects plus McLaren, McLean, and Cameron.
It was clear Young had taken charge and it was unsettling being pushed offstage, but
I'd been away dealing with that issue at Torrport. Young was the natural leader of this
group anyway, older than the rest of us and well-liked and respected. He looked
deceptively ineffectual, chubby with thinning sandy blond hair and that disarming
half-smile.

Young rapped the table and started. "Welcome friends and colleagues. You all
know why we are here." He grinned widely and looked around the room making sure
everyone was paying attention. "We now have a suitable donor, John Smith, likely
originally from the American colonies but recently arrived from Rouen. We think he
was infected by Jean Tremblay, a merchant from Rouen. They shared a room on the
Chantilly. You'll be glad to hear the quarantine has been effective, so far." He stopped
and asked if there were any questions. Young was far more collegial than me. One in
the group asked if there had been any reports back from Amsterdam. Young responded
that there had been two further cases, but they have it well in hand. He continued.
"We will be harvesting mature scabs from Smith in two days. McLean will do that
with McLaren assisting. The samples will be stored at McLean's apothecary. Then we
wait a week for the scabs to mature and dry. It is highly recommended that in the
next week everyone involved make whatever arrangements are necessary. That
includes requesting time off work and making sure your personal commitments are
covered. Patients will be in strict quarantine enforced by the Town Guard for at least
twenty days. Any questions?"

I didn't much like where the samples were to be stored, so I asked. "Young, what
steps are being taken to ensure the samples will not be tampered with or stolen?"

He gave me that disarming smile. "McLean has well-secured doors and is
providing guards round-the-clock at his own expense, I might add."

I still didn't trust McLean, but it seems Young did, so I decided to let it go for now.

Young continued. "One final item. There are two treatments, with and without
smallpox scab powder and we have ten volunteers as patients. Patients will be
assigned at random by drawing paper ballots out of a box. Each paper will have either
the number one or the number two written on it. There will be five of each in the box
to start. Cameron will organize this and record who got what. Then he'll flip a coin

to decide which group gets which treatment, but only he and McLean will know. The patients won't."

There was a murmur of discussion, then one spoke up. "You're saying half of us will be in quarantine for nothing?"

Young's smile left. "Yes, that is quite true. This is an experiment. We want objective proof about whether this method works or not, and to do that we need to use a proper experimental design, and that includes a group of those who haven't received the smallpox powder. It also is very important that the patients don't know which treatment they received. We've all experienced patients who only believe they are sick, haven't we?" This elicited discussion on some of the more practical issues around applying the treatments and so on. Then Young finished his explanation. "This experiment will be in two parts. The first will be a comparison of inoculated versus non-inoculated patients. We want to see what effect, if any, the inoculation has. This will be recorded in detail. The second part of the experiment will involve exposing this group of patients to live smallpox." There was an immediate outburst of concern. This was the source of the controversy last fall, and everyone knew it.

I stood and raised my arms and roared above the clamour. "Now wait, friends! This time we will not *directly* infect our test patients with live smallpox." I waited a few seconds for some calm to return. "I repeat, we will not directly infect our test patients with live smallpox, but when there is an outbreak in future, we want all ten of us to volunteer to treat infected patients. We will carefully monitor everyone to see if the inoculations are effective in providing immunity. We know this is risky and a lot to ask, and if anyone here is unable or unwilling to do this, now is the time to withdraw." The room went silent as it all sunk in. No one withdrew, at least not in public. We anticipated a few would, once things settled.

I finished on a more positive note. "Those who put themselves at risk for the benefit of others are true heroes and I trust the sacrifices we are about to make will benefit countless men, women and children through the ages. On their behalf, I sincerely thank you and know that your efforts will not be forgotten." There was tentative applause as though they weren't quite sure they wanted to be remembered for this.

Then Young concluded by outlining the schedule for the next several days. The meeting broke up as quietly as it had begun. I stuck around to have a word with Young and Beaton.   I got right to the point with Young. "I prefer to have those samples under our care. Who knows what could happen to them sitting at McLean's for a week."

"I understand your concern, but McLean comes highly recommended and we don't want this to be another irritation between us and the surgeons. They rightly claim that inoculations should be their business, not ours, and if this is successful...well, there could be a lot of money involved, you know that."

He was right, but I still didn't trust them. "Then please consider a compromise. How about having the Town Guard there as well? We could invoke concerns about public safely, and so forth."

Young thought for a moment then replied. "If it will allay suspicions, I will broach the subject with McLean."

I agreed then we said our goodbyes. Beaton offered his carriage to take me to Father's. I was glad to have some private time with him, but as soon as the carriage set off, he rounded on me. "Mal, I know you've been taking the brunt of this, but you shouldn't assume the world is against us. We have a great many supporters including all those in that room tonight. You should be thankful of McLean's support. He is one of the best surgeons in Edinburgh and we need him, and Young is superb at building alliances. Something you could learn." I sat still and heard him out. Perhaps Beaton was right, and I was being paranoid. Maybe it was because I'd been the one assaulted and robbed and condemned by Turnbull? That is what I was thinking, but held my tongue.

The carriage lurched to avoid a knot of people arguing on the street and I grabbed the handrail above the window. "John, I have many faults, but one thing life has taught me is that people often will tell you what they intend to do. If your friend brags about swindling someone, then offers you a deal you can't resist, should that not raise legitimate concern? We've had many threats. Do you honestly think it wise to be so trusting?" I was being testy, and it wasn't helping.

Beaton crossed his arms, feet bracing just in case. "I know we have some enemies, but my point Mal, is that they aren't all enemies and you need to let others lead too, especially those who are less flammable."

The image he'd conjured was amusing but this was serious. "I agree that Young is more politically adept, especially now when we need a cohesive coalition to pull this off without war breaking out. I'm happy to step aside, believe me, but you should clearly acknowledge that the forces against us are formidable and will not stop, and Young doesn't have my family protection, does he?"

"Mal, I'm not saying you aren't capable, far from it, but your style can sometimes be confrontational. Please let Young lead for a while, perhaps we can side-step these political issues this time." There was nothing more to add. Beaton was my closest friend and I believed he had a good heart and was very often the most sensible of us.

"Then I will enjoy some relaxing time in beautiful Torrport with the lovely Elspeth MacLeod and let you and Young deal with it!" Beaton gasped, then I guffawed. We parted a few minutes later with well-wishes and promises to keep each other informed.

* * *

The light was still on in Father's study and he was in his chair by the fireplace, head tilted and resting on one hand. I startled him as I pulled up the other chair.

"Good evening, Father, sorry to have awakened you." His body was slumping, but I assumed it had just been another long day.

He cleared his throat and spit some phlegm into a white handkerchief. "Ah, you are here! I was just thinking about you. Heard some rumours." He stopped and looked down then started fussing with his robe.

"Father, we are going to start that experiment again soon, in a week or so, and could use some help and protection."

He looked up then over at me. "Eh? Oh, yes, that damned experiment! There have been rumours you know."

"No doubt word is getting around by now, but what I need are some reliable Town Guards to make sure our samples don't escape again. You know they can be a public health hazard in the wrong hands." I continued giving him the details and he listened but seemed to be having trouble focusing, then he glanced away and shuddered. "Father are you alright?" He looked like he'd been drinking too much, although that was unlikely.

He said in a halting voice. "I am fine son, just tired is all. But there are these rumours."

I needed to be sure my message was getting through so repeated my request for the Town Guards.

"I heard you the first-time, Malcolm, and yes I'll see if I can arrange that with the Lord Provost." His answer was curt and perhaps I'd been too pushy.

"Thank you, Father. I knew I could count on you."

"Rumours." He mumbled again.

Then I saw his face contort as he stretched to one side and I realized he wasn't fine. "Father, what's going on? You don't seem well."

"It's nothing, perhaps a cold coming on. You know how I hate this damp spring weather."

I reached over and felt his forehead. "You don't have a fever. Please rest and drink lots of fluids and stay warm." I was beginning to feel guilty, so focused on my problems that I didn't see he was not well. "Father, I'll have your man bring you some hot tea and cakes. Would that please you?"

"Aye, and a rum would be welcome too." He tried to laugh but had a coughing spell instead as I rose to leave.

"I need to get back to McLaren's before curfew, but I'll drop by tomorrow morning." Father nodded, wiping his mouth. On my way out, I shouted for his servant and told him that Father may be getting sick and of his needs and that I'd be back next day.

* * *

Curfew had begun. McLaren's was not far but I needed to stay clear of the Town Guards. They tended to be at main intersections and patrolling streets with important buildings. Edinburgh was a maze of narrow alleys, but I'd grown up here and knew my way around. When we were young we used to enjoy a tease and chase with the guards. But tonight, I pulled up my collar and scarf and walked as quickly as I could, trying not to draw attention.

I kept close to the buildings and stopped to look both ways at every block. If they caught me out after curfew, they wouldn't hesitate to throw me in the hole for the night and it wouldn't matter how much I complained or dropped names. The temperature was falling fast, and I could see my breath in the air as I passed lit windows. Then I heard something behind me, so I pressed into a doorway to listen. It was footsteps and coming from the direction I'd been. They stopped, and I chanced to have a look. It was a large dark shape, likely male, half a block away, then a flame, maybe lighting a pipe. He looked quite heavy, with wide-brimmed hat and long dark coat. I thought I could see the glint of steel at his waist. I wasn't sure if he was following me but decided to take a detour on the left. It was a very narrow lane with tall buildings and few places to hide. I ran, then dodged behind some crates, crouching low, my back against the wall. I could just see out between the crates. He came around the corner on a half-run, looking side to side, then he went back to the intersection and shouted down the cross-street. "Can't see 'im!"

The hairs on my arms and the back of my neck bristled and I knew then he was after me and there was at least one other. The guards were just ahead on the main street. If I went forward, I'd have to finesse my way past them and I couldn't go back without confronting my two opponents. I waited and slowed my breathing and hoped they would leave.

Then I heard him slowly walking toward me, feet crunching through some twigs and bark. I had no choice. It was fight or flight and if he had a gun and I ran, it could be over for me, so I pulled the flintlock pistol out of my belt and cocked it slowly. I wouldn't shoot him cold of course, couldn't do that to anyone, but I needed to be ready. Then more footsteps behind him, running. Oh, shite! I had one shot and no time to reload. The first one was getting close. I could hear his raspy, wet breathing through the pipe clenched in his mouth. The only chance I had was to disable the first guy and use my pistol on the second. I had a dagger, but it was next to useless against a proper weapon, and I didn't know what they had.

He was coming near my crates now. At least he was on my side of the lane. I had to time it perfectly, before he could react, a few seconds too early or late and he'd have me, at this range. I waited, rehearsed the moves in my mind. Time seemed to slow, and I was ready and as soon as I saw his foot pass the bottom of the crate I leapt over and hammered him hard with my shoulder. He was heavier than I thought and staggered back only a few feet. I'd thrown all I could at him and he was still standing, so I rolled to one side and crouched into firing position on one knee. They were both there now, one behind the other. I didn't have time to analyze, only react and avoid like a predator.

"One more step and your guts will feel my lead!" I growled in as menacing a tone as I could muster. They both stopped. I'd surprised them. Neither had a weapon drawn. The tall one in the back said something like "Just trying to get home, laddie." Then he slowly reached for the pistol on his belt.

"Go ahead and pull it. Do you think I can miss at this range?" I tried to stop him while remembering my shooting lessons. *Don't try to be cute, aim at the torso and shoot first, if you can.* "Raise your hands so I can see them. On your knees!" The tall guy in back had other plans and shoved the first guy forcefully at me. I managed to roll out of the way, but not in time to prevent the guy in back from drawing his pistol.

"Stop!" I yelled. He raised and cocked it in one well-practiced move, the man in front scrambling toward me. I was still moving but couldn't wait to stabilize and fired on the tall one, the sound like an eight-pound cannon echoing down the lane. He staggered back, his pistol veered and went off, then a crack and crash as the ball blew out a nearby window. I rushed him head down, pounding him hard against the wall, then punched him in the side of his face with the butt of my pistol. I was so close I see his eyes roll up and feel his body sag, then knew I had my chance to escape, so I pushed him down then glanced back and saw the heavy guy, cutlass out coming for me, so I ran back down the lane putting as much distance as I could between us.

My body was on full rush now as I heard the alarms clanging behind me and people shouting. Last thing I needed was to explain all this, so I ran until lungs were searing and legs buckling, and I could go no further. I'd instinctively headed for some warehouses that lay on the way to McLaren's and found a loose window and slid in and onto the floor completely spent. I lay there gasping and swearing as quietly as I could. All I could feel was anger. Anger at everything and everyone. I knew this wasn't going to end well, but didn't know how to change it.

* * *

I was there over an hour waiting for the furor outside and in my body to subside. I went over it again and again. I may have killed him. Could I have done it differently? Well yes, I shouldn't have been out after curfew. Should have stayed with Father, could have run to the guard up the street, but I didn't and now there will be consequences.

It was very late when I crept into McLaren's house, but he was still up and greeted me, disheveled, spent candle in hand. One look was all he needed.

"Forrester, what in hell?"

"I know, I know, Angus." I waved my hand and fell into the nearest chair, emotionally if not physically exhausted.

"Well, are you going to tell me? You look like you've been wrestling in the street."

"Close enough. I was attacked...again!" I tried to make light of it, but we both knew it was all too serious. He wanted details, so I went through it one more time, leaving out nothing in the hope he could make more sense of it than I.

"Malcolm, you know how I feel about physicians using weapons. Are you absolutely sure they were after you?" He got to the nub of it quickly.

"Don't judge me Angus, my life is so different than yours, always has been. My family has been a target for generations, you know that, and I'll be damned if I'll allow myself or Father to be victimized without putting up a fight." I knew this was a contentious issue. There was the physician's oath that I'd sworn in public, especially that part about doing no harm, but life often is about dealing with compromises, and those nasty grey areas.

He looked at me with a pained expression. "You don't have to remind me and I'm not sure what I'd do if in your shoes, but try to think rationally, Malcolm. What evidence do you have that those two were trying to harm you? Perhaps they were just trying to get home?"

He had me on those points and he knew it. It had been just a feeling, and that heavy one saying: *Can't see 'im!* and the other one seeming to reach for his pistol, but I might have done the same facing the barrel of a flintlock. "I know Angus, but it happened so fast and reflexes take over, don't they?" It wasn't much of a rationale.

"Are you sure you killed him?"

"Just that look in his eyes. I'd seen it before, and the sudden sagging of his body, and I don't think I'd hit him hard enough to do that. But who knows? I turned and ran. Had I stopped to give him aid, the other one would have cut me to pieces."

"Are you sure?"

"No one is ever sure. The animal in us takes over, and there's no time to think." I was sure about that at least, just talk to anyone about their experience in battle.

"Are you going to turn yourself in?"

"Not yet. I need some time and to see what happens." I shrugged off my soiled jacket. "And now I need some rest, and even an infirmary bed is a welcome sight."

Angus sighed. "Go consult your father, Malcolm. If that guy is dead, I doubt this will just go away." He said goodnight then turned back to me. "Oh, and there is this note someone left today." He handed it to me and said goodnight again.

The note was from Gwen. She wanted to see me in the morning and said she had some interesting news. I didn't even undress beyond removing boots and was asleep in minutes.

* * *

Edinburgh is quite a different city by day. Gone the menacing gloom of the narrow alleys, replaced by traffic chaos and bright colours of men and women hurrying to wherever. I was glad to see Gwen again. We'd promised each other at the start always to be honest with each other and she'd been good to her word. We'd learned to trust each other. When I arrived at mid-morning she was still in bed sipping tea and reading the Edinburgh Courant newspaper. I sat on the bed and she poured me some tea.

"You look like you slept rough last night." She could readily see my rumpled, scuffed clothes and day-old beard.

"Is it that bad?" I looked down, then had to agree. "Well, parts of it were rough, but I was at McLaren's."

"And you smell. I can tell from here. Please have a bath while I get ready." I welcomed the suggestion, so she called her girl who filled the copper tub with scalding hot water scented with flowers. I am convinced the reason for Gwen's popularity had to do with this. She was always clean and smelled like fresh picked flowers, somewhat of a novelty these days. I barely fit in the tub even with knees pulled to chin, but it was a fine luxury to soak and scrub away the street smells. I dried with a fresh towel and put on a new linen shirt and underwear. She'd thought of everything. Spirits buoyed, I padded back to her bedroom in time for a nice snuggle and more.

She was chatty and I sleepy after. "Mal, I've heard some rumours. They say something is being planned, things ordered, people hired. And it has to do with you." She was resting on my chest and looked up into my eyes.

"Rumours? Father mentioned rumours too. Gwen, there are always rumours. I mostly ignore them. But we're going to start that smallpox experiment in a week or so. Maybe it has to do with that?"

Perhaps, Mal, but these are not nice people. Please promise me you will be careful?" I hadn't told her about last night, and wouldn't, it would only worry her. I pulled myself up a bit on the bed and stretched.

"I'll be very careful, Gwen. You know I never take risks." She snorted in derision. "But if you hear anything specific. I need to know who is behind these attacks."

"I will ask, but people are reticent, you know that." She rolled off me and sat up, then started brushing her unruly red hair. "I wish we could run away for a month, just get out of here. It's becoming oppressive, isn't it? Forget about this silly experiment and come with me to London. Please?" Gwen survived by avoiding problems and adapting to whatever life presented. I knew she was very worried to have suggested this.

"I wish, but you know I can't." I patted her arm. "You can help us in one very crucial way." Her eyes said it all, sadness, worry, fear, but a slight smile appeared at the thought of being involved. "We'll be in quarantine for twenty days and living on McLaren's gruel. Some of your cakes and tarts would be very welcome." I wasn't joking, and she knew it and got up and angrily threw her hairbrush at me. I batted it away but got the point and as she left I could hear her saying all too clearly, "Mary, make his Highness a fine breakfast. Seems all he cares about is my food!"

* * *

Clean and with carnal and other needs met, I left with a spring in my step and confidence restored. I knew what I had to do, and I didn't want anyone else involved. I needed to get myself out of this on my own, so I went to Father's for a fresh change of outer clothes. I knew he would be in the courts, so I quickly dressed then left him a note saying I'd been in a scuffle last night and needed to report it to the guards, love you, see you later, etc.

I was looking as good as I was going to when I arrived at the Guard House. The guards were mostly retired highlander military men, middle-aged, gruff and not inclined to put up with nonsense. I'd decided to go on the offensive, so I strode purposefully to the desk and asked to see the ranking officer on duty. The man at the desk gave me the once over and decided he'd better do as I asked, so ushered me into the office of the Captain of the Guard, who was an impressive looking man in red serge with gold-braid and a chest full of medals. I'd met him before of course, through my Father, so we shook hands and I wasted no time laying my complaint: that I'd been assaulted on the way home. I apologized for being out a bit after curfew, then he raised his hand and stopped me.

"We did get a report this morning of a man being shot and killed in that area last night. Witnesses said they saw two men leaving before the guards arrived. One was described as heavy with dark clothing, and I guess the other could have been you. The victim was a tall man shot once in the chest and found dead." He thrummed his fingers on the desk and looked me in the eyes, then said slowly. "Was that you who left after shooting the tall man?" He needed to know, of course.

"It likely was." I responded without hesitation. "I fired then ran. The other man was right behind me with his cutlass out. I didn't know if I'd actually hit or killed the tall man." I sat calmly waiting for his decision.

"Then I want you to make a written report to aid in our investigation." It didn't look like he was going to charge me at this point. There obviously hadn't been any other testimony about what'd happened, but I wasn't satisfied just to get away with it.

"Captain, I have reason to believe we are being targeted by attacks whose goal is to stop us from conducting vital research into a cure for smallpox." He didn't react. That told me a lot. "I want these people organizing and committing these crimes against us to be brought to justice."

He smiled politely, eyes fixed on mine, then leaned back and pulled his cuffs down. "We've heard things, of course, and know you and others have been sniffing around. This is getting out of hand and we want it to stop. We have some idea who is behind these so-called *attacks*, and have been advising restraint." Then he leaned forward suddenly and deepened his voice a pitch. "And I insist that you and your group back off too. If you can't work together, at least delay this experiment to let tempers settle."

I didn't agree, but I'd been duly warned, hadn't I? "I will give a written report. Am I free to go?" He nodded, then said in parting: "For the sake of your father, I don't want to see you back here again any time soon."

As I wrote my report for the guards, I thought about my next steps. I was sure the opposition were put on notice through the Captain of the Guard, but so were we. I would not be stopped, but we had to be very careful from now on. Everyone was watching, and our next mistake could be our last.

* * *

All that at the Guard House took longer than I'd expected. I hoped to see Father again before I left on the noon carriage, but there wasn't time, just enough to retrieve my bag at McLaren's and leave a note for Beaton to look in on Father. I arrived back in Torrport mid-afternoon, thoroughly sick of all the commuting and anticipating a placid week of doctoring. I had to make arrangement for my absence too and was making my mental list during one of Mrs. Simpson's most welcomed meals of roast beef and potatoes, served with a full pint of fresh ale from the tavern.

I'd lined up a young doctor to fill-in for me and needed to see Elspeth to go over some case files I thought she could handle. It was good to be home. Mrs. Simpson had the usual pile of requests for me to deal with and I sorted through them over a nice glass of port, with Henry curled at my feet.

Next morning, I set out on patient visits. The day was blustery, and it was a chore keeping hat on head while walking along the docks. The men were at work tying ships and rigging in anticipation of worse weather. One was a captain who asked me to come by. He was on the *Silver Fin*, a two-mast brigantine of recent build. I boarded her and was shown aft to the Captain's room. He was there gazing out the back window, hands on waist and in that bow-legged stance favoured by seamen.

"Captain, it's Doctor Forrester. You wished to see me?" He turned quickly, and I was surprised to see he was so young, I guessed no more than sixteen, with curly black hair loose and falling over much of his smooth face.

"Aye, Doctor, I am glad you could come. I need some advice before we set sail." He didn't introduce himself before sitting on the edge of the bunk. "Please join me." There was nowhere else, but the small chair bolted to the floor by the desk, so I sat on the bunk with my bag on one knee. "The Laird said you could be trusted."

I waited for him to continue, but he pulled a long, curved pipe out of his belt and lit it with the candle by the bunk. He affected a squint as the smoke curled up. The Captain didn't look old enough for this, but I'd seen stranger. I took out my notebook, quill pen and ink, then reassured him. "The Laird is a friend and I am the doctor here in Torrport. Whatever you tell me will be held in confidence." I assumed that was what he wanted to hear.

"He said you are one of us."

I wasn't sure what he meant or even if I wanted to know. "I am here to give medical advice and treatment. Now tell me about your problem." He looked at me intently for a few seconds, deciding perhaps if he could trust me.

"The *Fin* was father's. She isn't much but affords us a living, even with the English making it hard. We mostly ply the continent trade, but at times take a few passengers." He spoke well, obviously educated but, with a trace of accent I couldn't place. I was becoming curious. Not a wise thing these days. I entered the ship's name in my book. He continued. "Sometimes these crossing have to be done in bad weather. Don't ask why. It's not easy on our passengers." I didn't quite know where this was leading, but was beginning to have that sinking feeling in my stomach. "Doctor, we need something we can give them for sea sickness and to keep them quiet, something we can take with us in case we need it."

So, that was it. These were not your usual passengers. No one would cross on a small merchant ship in bad weather unless they wanted to evade authorities, or they perhaps they were captives. I looked down and inwardly sighed.

"Alright, I can give you some licorice root powder to take with you. Come by my infirmary and ask for it. Have your cook make it into small lozenges, with sugar and salt. I'll give you the recipe. The lozenges will help with nausea and vomiting. Serve them with weak tea or broth, both taken cooled, not warm if they are vomiting. Once the vomiting has subsided, a little mulled port wine in bed will give further relief." It was a simple enough request, but I felt like I was being drawn into something, and I didn't much like it. The boy captain thanked me and offered coin, but I graciously refused and suggested he leave two pence with Mrs. Simpson when the licorice is received.

The rest of the morning was the usual assortment of major and minor ailments. There seems to be no end to human misery, well, except death and most of us are avoiding that for some reason. By lunch I'd made my way close to Elspeth's. I needed to see her, and before leaving Edinburgh had bought a pound of the finest chocolate to be used as a bribe. Beaton had tipped me off about her greatest weakness. Most women have one or another. The beautiful ones want to be complimented on their intelligence, the intelligent ones on their beauty. For her it was chocolate, and I came prepared.

The wind was almost gale force by the time I crested the hill at her cottage. I knocked and once again, the door flew open and Janet was there holding her arisaid in place with one hand while trying to keep the door open with the other. She was quite striking in blue and green tartan framing red hair and freckled porcelain skin.

She laughed and said: "Come in will ye, before the wind carries us both away."

I strode past her closely, catching her scent. "This is for you...err, I mean for Elspeth." I'd almost forgotten why I'd come as I offered her the chocolates.

She blushed and looked away noting my mistake then took the box after closing the door firmly. "I am sure Lady Elspeth will appreciate them. She is visiting patients now."

I was surprised by my reaction to her. I'm normally not overly impressed by women, especially the ones layered in subterfuge, but this one had a natural beauty I couldn't ignore. I needed to be careful. "Please tell Lady Elspeth that she's invited to dine with me tomorrow at noon, so we can review some cases while I'm away."

"I will tell her. Thank you for visiting." She looked at me directly with a smile that suggested wanting, at least to me, but then I am often wrong about these things. We stood there looking at each other in silence for an uncomfortable few seconds, then the door burst open and the space was filled with that hulking highlander, hair and beard blowing wildly like a demon, with a distorted insane look on his face as he glanced from one to the other of us. I could see fists clench as he took a step toward me, then Janet yelled:

"Cawdie, let Sir Forrester out before the wind chills the wee bairn!"

He moved aside, hardly enough to let me pass and was glaring intensely as I came close. I hate being intimidated, so I gave him a bit of shoulder on the way out. I didn't understand the relationships here or why he seemed to resent me, but I wasn't about to take that kind of disrespect.

* * *

By next morning the storm had blown through. Even though the harbour is well-protected there was still a fair chop and I could see bits of flotsam bobbing amid rocking ships. Mrs. Simpson was in the kitchen preparing lunch and I was sorting case files. A few of the cases were worrisome and I decided to refer them to more skilled hands in the city.

Elspeth arrived just before noon and was greeted by Henry at the front door. I left my study to rescue her, but she was laughing and on one knee getting lots of doggy kisses.

"He must smell Scathach on my dress," she blurted as she saw me enter.

"That must be it, and he's overly friendly to start." I pointed to the basket. "Henry, that's enough. Go lie down."

"Och, that's alright Malcolm, I quite like dogs, better than most people!" She chuckled and blushed as she rose and faced me. She had a fresh cuteness about her, offset by those challenging, direct eyes.

"Mrs. Simpson will have something delightful for us, but we have some time to review cases. Shall we?" I extended my hand and she proceeded me into the study.

She looked about briefly then burst out laughing. "Malcolm, I didn't picture you as the messy type!" It was the papers and cases all over the floor.

"Mrs. Simpson normally keeps it under control, but I find the floor a perfect place to organize things. Come and look." I sat on the floor cross-legged beside a large pile of folders. She joined me, gathering her dress carefully.

"Are we going to have a picnic too?" I was pulling out some files when she said that. It caught me off guard and when I turned my head I could see she had that mocking look on her face.

I couldn't resist. "Only if it includes the dessert." She looked stunned for a second, then I poked her arm and laughed. Maybe I'd gone too far, but she deserved it.

Her face contorted. "Only if you like poison apples."

"Maybe some other time then!" I was glad we were on friendlier terms. "Now let's have a look at some cases." We reviewed several, mostly having to do with birthing complications and baby complaints, and I could see she was fully concentrating. She agreed at the end to take them and I called Mrs. Simpson to see if lunch was ready.

It was just leftovers, a beef pie in an ale and gravy sauce served with red wine. I ate quietly listening to the two women discussing recipes and local gossip. Dessert was apple, not the poisoned kind, but in the form of a pudding with a lattice pastry top. I complemented Mrs. Simpson on her fine meal then began to explain what was likely to come.

"I've left several pounds in my desk to buy any essentials while I'm in quarantine, and I want Elspeth to have full access to our medicines and supplies. I normally charge double the cost for these. Please keep track." I looked at them both. It was getting serious now.

I put down my spoon and turned to Mrs. Simpson. "My will has been revised so that if anything happens, this house will be yours. I'll not have you put out because of my poor choices."

"Aye, sir." She looked down and I could see a tear form in the corner of her eye.

"But I have one condition." I put on my most serious face. "You must care for Henry and give him a cuddle every day."

She laughed because we both knew he was her dog. She wouldn't give him up for the world.

"One more thing. A substitute doctor will be here two days a week. He has chosen to stay at the Inn, but I trust you both will make him welcome."

Elspeth chimed in. "I'll have Cawdie give him the express tour of Torrport." I raised my eyes hoping that wasn't true. She laughed, and Mrs. Simpson added something about it depending on how handsome he was.

We were being a bit silly when a few drop-in patients arrived to remind us it was time to get back to work. Elspeth quickly gathered her files and gave Henry a hug, then waved goodbye as I washed up and Mrs. Simpson cleared the table. The first patient was a boy with his too-young mother. She was poorly dressed in a working frock and well-stained apron. I may have seen her at the coffee house, toiling in the back, grinding beans. Today, she was hanging on fiercely to her son who was valiantly trying to escape. He was sneezing constantly with snot running down both nostrils. The boy looked to be about seven, at that age when mothers regret having boys. I laughed as she dragged him into the examination room like a wild animal on a tether. Most boys remember those days fondly, the parents not so much. He was in constant motion as I inspected him, feeling his forehead for heat and under his jaw for swelling. I ended by listening to his chest and heart as he bounced on the chair.

"When did these symptoms start?" I looked over at her.

"Umm, let me see." She looked up at the ceiling and counted on her fingers while mumbling something. "I think four or five days-ago. Will he be alright doctor?"

It was nothing serious, just the latter stages of a cold. I gave the boy a small sugar candy.

"It's good you brought him in. Best to be cautious, isn't it?" She nodded slowly in agreement and I told her that he would be back to normal in a few days but if he showed any signs of fever or chest congestion to bring him back right away. One of the first things I learned as a doctor was never to criticize a worried parent. She looked relieved and so did the boy as I recommended that he could go out and play once the weather settled.

Mrs. Simpson brought my tea. I had a few sips then stuck my head out into the waiting room to see who was next. It was Ronald, the boy who'd been shot at the castle. I waved him in and had him lay face-down on the examination table.

He turned his head toward me as I lifted his shirt. "Doctor, the Laird is sending me home, now that I can travel. He says there's not much good having me here."

"Aye, Ronald, you are better off home where your good mother can tend you. I'm going to take this bandage off to have a look. How have you been feeling?" I pulled the bandage away carefully.

"That lady came twice and put some poultice on me. She was very nice." Some men don't like being treated by a woman, but I could see young Ronald wasn't one of them. "It's not as sore as before." I could see the wound had sealed and the inflammation was going down. There might be bone splinters inside that could give him trouble, but it wasn't worth the risk of retrieving them.

"And how about your appetite, bowel movements, urination, anything else?"

"They seem fine, Doctor, but can I have a wee drink now?"

"Ronald, you are making good progress, but this could take a few months to heal completely. It's very important that you not tear it open, understand? And that means being careful about bending and carrying and anything that might rip it open. An ale or perhaps something stronger in the evening might help." He seemed pleased with that, then I teased. "But no wild sex! Not just yet anyway." We both laughed, and I replaced the old bandage with new. Sometimes it turns out well, and makes it all worthwhile.

I was cleaning the examination bed when a boy came running in with the letter. He said it was urgent and from the afternoon post. It was from Beaton. I assumed something to do with our experiment or the shooting. I ripped it open and scanned it quickly. It was about Father. He has a high fever and Beaton said don't come, nothing you can do, and there are three more smallpox cases at the port. My heart almost stopped, and I cried out: "Oh Father, no, no, please forgive me!"

PART TWO

Malady and Murder

TEN

Elspeth – Alehouses and abscesses

The chilling cold of early morning made me pull my woolen cloak more tightly around me as I stepped outside the cottage. It was still dark, but the sky had paled to a soft slate blue scattered with a few flecks of silver, and fringed with black and pink where the trees touched the dawn. It is my favorite time, and when I think most clearly. A full moon glittered the dew and my footprints left a trail of dark smudges behind me as I walked to the lean-to and the animals.

Ahern whickered and tossed his head when I filled the trough with hay for our two beasties. Coo's wavy silver coat gave her the look of a malformed unicorn, and she shifted restlessly, her swollen udders swinging as she ate. She lowed softly, and I patted her rump as I went by. Cawdie would be up soon to tend the fires and do the milking.

I took a small trug from those hanging in the shed and went into the garden to cut back the lavender and rosemary. As I started to kneel, I saw a flash of light over the water. It was repeated twice, and after a pause, blinked three times again. The source seemed to be floating over the dark sea beyond the fishing village. A ship standing off the coast? At this hour, it was impossible to see anything clearly against the shadowy cliffs across the channel.

Our cottage was atop a hill. The hills here are not as beautiful as the Black Cuillin mountains of Skye, but still imposing. The elevation provided an unobstructed view of the surrounding countryside. Curious, I turned slowly, searching, and saw it! An answering flare from the ramparts of the castle, shuttered even as I watched. Then everything was quiet again. Intrigued, I continued to watch but there was nothing more. Why would a ship be signaling to the castle? Or the castle to a ship? My desire to visit the tavern in the fishing village increased. Gossip said that more than ale and women were for purchase there and any traffic could be bought for the right price. The long light of morning began to slowly cast pale fingers across the earth. The glow at days beginning and end seems warmer to me. I unexpectedly realized I was happy here. I loved my cottage, the people of Torrport and the village. I closed my eyes, lifted my head and breathed in the cold clean air. Content, I sang softly as I cut away the wear of winter from the plants, gathering what was usable this early in spring. Boiled together they would make a useful decoction. The mints were already showing tender green leaves and delicate shoots from other wintered plants marked faint lines in the mulch.

And then there was Malcolm. He often angered me with his arrogant attitude, but meeting him had proved surprisingly pleasant. I looked forward to tending his patients, and to be perfectly honest with myself, poking among his books and folios to my mind's content. The seeming mess of his rooms had revealed a logical structure. It was a revelation I longed to sort through and understand.

Gathering my meager harvest, I stood. Whatever ship might have signaled was still lost in the forest of masts and sails now faintly discernable in the morning light. I shook out my skirts and walked back to the cottage. Janet was stirring porridge on the fire, and Julianne was patiently feeding the bairn drop by drop. He was still unable to suck, and not moving a great deal, although he seemed well enough. His mother had regained some bloom, and I noticed her breasts seemed larger.

"Julianne, do your breasts hurt?"

She turned toward me and looked down at herself. "Yes, and they have...grown. Could it be my milk coming in?" she flushed.

"Yes, so please tell me if you feel wetness and see stains." She nodded, and I stood thoughtfully for a moment before going to the book shelves to look for my copy of *De Arte Medica Infantum* by Ferrarius. If I remembered correctly, there was a drawing in it that showed a woman removing milk from her breast using a receptacle with an opening for the nipple and a long spout reaching up to the mouth. Using it the mother could suction milk from her breasts. Thus, the babe might be fed his mother's milk even though he could not suck. I had seen one used in Italy. I found the volume and the illustration, and put it in my bag so I could show the drawing to the blacksmith in Torrport, who was also reputed to be a metalworker of some skill. I reached for my cloak again, but Janet harrumphed loudly, ordering me in her own way to eat something before I left. I did.

* * *

I picked up my bag and began my rounds. The first patient this morning was Sir Ross Campbell. His servant had left word asking that I call on him as soon as possible. His house was in a charming part of Torrport. A stone fountain gurgled near his door and a container of flowers hung from the eaves. The heavy door opened quickly at my knock. The man who answered it was dressed entirely in black, taller than most men, and bearded. For some reason, I shivered. His black hair was silvered at the left temple, and tied back from a broad forehead. Flat eyes flicked over me briefly as he bowed respectfully and took me to his master. Sir Ross was standing by the fire and even from this distance the stench emanating from him was almost palpable. A man of early middle years, he was of medium stature with round blue eyes in an attractive tanned face. His sand colored hair matched a beard that turned up naturally, and gave him an oddly energetic and almost graceful look.

"Good morning, sir, your man left a message for me, how may I help you?"

He looked at me rather vulnerably and his face bloomed red. Pain tightened his lips as he bent over in a slight bow. A light sheen of sweat gleamed on his forehead. "Good morning, Lady Elspeth. I have a somewhat delicate problem. There is a...sore, on my arse, that hurts terribly. I am unable to ride or sit comfortably, and now walking is agonizing as well."

"Would you like for me to look at it, sir?" I asked, knowing well that most men refused and distrusted women healers. He surprised me by agreeing, which told me that the pain was severe enough to overcome his prejudices.

"If you would be so kind as to come this way?" I followed the two men upstairs to his bedroom. He lay on his stomach on the bed, and his man lowered his pants and soiled linen braies. His left buttock was inflamed, with a festering sore about an inch from his anus. Pus and foul dark matter oozed from it. The odor was almost overwhelming. I realized immediately what it was most likely to be, and that here, as a woman, I would not be permitted to perform the operation he needed. The procedure for closing a fistula was known, and I had even performed it once in Italy, but I had no license to perform surgery in Scotland. Until it was done, feces would continue to flow unchecked through the opening created by an infection.

"Sir Ross, I can help relieve the pain a little now, but I fear that you must see Sir Malcolm when he returns. You will need a qualified surgeon. He may know of someone. I reached into my bag and took out a small bottle. "This is a tincture of willow bark. Have your man put a tablespoon of it in a glass of water and drink it for pain before you try to sleep. You should also drink as much water and juice as you can."

I turned to his manservant. "Meanwhile, I want you to prepare a mixture of salt and warm water, and wash the sore four times a day. Between washings, take a bulb of onion and one of garlic, mash them together into a paste, and make a poultice for the abscess. Hold the poultice in place with a clean bandage for five hours. Then remove it and wash the area with salt water again. Let the sore air for an hour, and then apply the paste and fresh bandage again. Do that for one day. This will not heal it, but it should dry the wound and help the festering. I will come by again in the morning." The fetid air of the house was beginning to make me a bit lightheaded, so I took my bag and left as quickly as good manners permitted.

I continued with my calls, one pregnancy, one sprained ankle, one rash, and one lonely elder with an imaginary illness that required tender attention. My final stop was the metalsmith. Aggie had told me the owner's name was Aidan Buchanan and that he was very handsome. According to the townspeople, he had appeared shortly following the death of the former smith several months ago. No one knew much of him. He was quiet, kept to himself, and did his work quickly and unusually well. His skills were much needed, and he was a valued asset to the town. He was a fine-looking man, muscled from his work and almost as large as Cawdie. The local lassies were fascinated and even more so when they discovered he made beautiful jewelry in the little room next to the forge.

I showed him the drawing of the breast pump, and explained how it worked. He spoke little, only studying the drawing, and asking gruffly if I wanted it in copper or pewter. We decided to use copper and he made a surprisingly good copy of the drawing. As he returned the book, he looked directly at me for the first time. His green eyes were clear and intelligent. Something flickered in them...amusement? I suddenly realized what I had just done. By asking him to make the pump I told him the babe lived. There was no help for it. "Sir, I beg that you say nothing of this commission."

"You need not be concerned, you have my silence, Lady. Twould be a poor thing to discuss such things with others." His accent puzzled me. It was the common vernacular of the port, but just slightly off, more...deliberate. I felt relief and a rather pleasant frisson of interest and awareness. Shrugging my errant thoughts away, I thanked him, picked up my things and left.

* * *

On the way home, I began to plan my visit to the tavern in the fishing village. My boy's clothing remained folded at the bottom of a trunk where I kept it. I was still no taller, although I had filled out a bit, and it might need some readjusting in certain places. First, I had to convince Cawdie and Janet to help me. They both balked at first, but finally gave in, knowing I would go no matter what they said, and it was better to oversee my schemes themselves. Janet let out a few seams and altered the worn ragged clothing to fit what I thought of as my bony body. I went to the fireplace, scratched off soot from the stones, making sure it got under each nail, and applied it liberally to my face and hands. Other than a resigned grumble about no lad having a doup shaped like that, Cawdie said little. I tugged the jacket down to hide my offending doup more and smiled sweetly at him.

* * *

When it was dark, Cawdie and I walked down the uneven path to the fishing village. A few scattered lights at the base of the hill it. The moon was low, but still cast enough light to help us see the way. My fingernails and hands were as grimy as those of any other urchin. My hair was tightly braided and pushed under a faded old apprentice cap whose brim concealed much of my dirty face. The freedom of breeks instead of skirts was intoxicating, and I slipped ahead of Cawdie to sneak through the back door of the tavern while he entered by the front. We could not go into the tavern together. I was almost drunk with excitement. My heart beat quickly as I assumed a boy's jaunty step, and sauntered toward the back door.

The village is small, and I knew each evil-smelling byway from visiting patients. It is foolish of me, but I do not frighten easily. The comforting weight of the *sgian dhub* dagger belted next to my calf was reassuring, and Cawdie had made certain that both Janet and I knew how to use it.

The back door was slightly open. As I put out my blackened hand to open it, an equally grimy one grabbed my arm. "An who might ye be?" said a hoarse voice from the darkness.

I stopped and lowered my voice, then said in the patois of the villagers. "Ah be Tam Morrison. An ye?" I shook my arm free, realizing that my captor was no taller than me, and much younger. I looked closer and saw a face as dirty as my own reflected in the wavering light spilling out of the door. It was the tavern keeper's son, Jocki. I reached into my pocket, pulled out a coin, pressed it into his grubby palm and we became friends instantly. It took but a moment to come to an understanding. He jerked his head toward the door as a sign for me to follow and we crept furtively along the wall. Stopping just inside the door he pointed to a space beneath the dilapidated bar almost directly in front of us. Molly, his mother, was off serving ale so we quickly fitted ourselves between two evil smelling crates. Cracks in the rotting wood of the front of the bar permitted us to see most of what was going on in the room, including a few things that neither of us should have been watching.

The tavern was not large but warm, heated by a stone fireplace and the fusty bodies of its occupants. A mixed group of customers sat on rickety chairs, benches and barrels around tables that tended to list as drunkenly as their occupants. Soldiers from the castle drank with their backs secure against the walls. Rough fishermen shared tables and spoke in low tones to well-dressed men from town. Women moved among them, serving and soliciting under the watchful gaze of the tavern keeper and his wife. The only light came from the fireplace and tallow lamps that added another layer to the smell of malodorous bodies, urine, feces, mutton stew, ale and vomit. The floor was covered with damp musty straw that had not been changed any time recently. A man lay snoring in it beneath a table in one corner, part of his face lying in his own puke.

Sound filled the room but soon I began to hear bits of intelligible conversation here and there out of the din. A rasping voice at a nearby table murmured something about "wool walking safe past customs men with deep pockets and blind eyes," earning a laugh from his companions. A ribald comment followed about "contraband more valuable than wool and maybe warmer, waiting offshore." Someone else muttered crossly that the port was safe as a kirk for those who knew the right people. I strained to hear more but there was a sudden commotion in the room and I sought the source through my peephole in the bar.

Captain Spence was there and patently well into his cups. He had pulled one of the serving women onto his lap, and his meaty hands were roughly fondling her breasts. She flinched away from him and tried getting up. It was Gilly, who had come to me pregnant.

"Git yer stinkin' hands off me, ye blaggart!" She pushed at him with both hands and kicked back at his shin with the heel of her shoe. He twisted her breast brutally and she arched against him in pain.

"Want it rough, do ye bitch? Just havin' a bit o' fun! Ye liked it well enough before. Gettin' above yourself are ye? Me coin is still good."

I watched with horror as he slapped her hard, and her head snapped back, eyes rolling up as he tightened his grip. My teeth gritted in helpless wrath, but I dared not move from my hiding place. As I watched, his drinking companion reached out and stayed his hand from a second blow. "Enough!" It was the Laird. His voice was soft, but Spence stiffened, then likely thought the better of challenging his master. Instead, he stood, dumping Gilly on the floor, and kicked her twice in the belly as she lay there half conscious. "Yer not worth me time or coin!"

I felt the blows with her and a fury born of knowing I was unable to aid her. Spence was a large man, but the Laird was even larger, and he dragged the drunken man ungently from the tavern as though he had been no more than a recalcitrant child. Gilly lay quite still for a few moments, then dragged herself into a sitting position. I saw her pale and bend over and retch into the pest infested straw on the floor. Others in the room looked away from the sight, and talk stuttered and then began again, as though nothing untoward had happened.

Cawdie was sitting with his back to the wall watching it all, a large tankard of ale gripped tightly in one white-knuckled hand. I whispered a message for Cawdie into Jocki's ear and pushed another coin into his hand. He slithered out the end of the bar avoiding his mother who still seemed frozen in place, picked up a stained cloth and strolled casually toward Cawdie. As he passed the massive highlander he dropped the cloth, paused briefly to pick it up and after a slow tour of the room stopping once to wipe a table, returned to the bar. Cawdie did not so much as glance at the boy but I knew he had heard Jocki speak as he picked up the cloth.

He immediately stood, and moved his large bulk in front of Gilly, shielding her. The tavern keeper's wife finally seemed to regain her senses and went to help. She spoke to Gilly softly and turned to Cawdie. I could not hear her words, but she obviously asked him to take Gilly to another place for he picked up the shaking girl and followed Molly toward the steps that led to the upper floor. During the brief commotion, I crept from my hiding place and fled out the back door.

I fell twice in my haste to get home. Janet let me in and between us we quickly transformed me from a filthy urchin into a respectable young woman. The fingernails were the hardest part. Julianne took away the basin of dirty water and my boy's clothing just as a frantic knock sounded at the door. Janet opened it to admit Jocki. Breathlessly, he looked up at her. "Me mam says ah must ask ta healer to come." His eyes searched the room, and seeing me he stared, his brows knitted, and suddenly blinked in confused recognition. I smiled at him and slowly winked. He turned a fiery red, but one corner of his mouth tipped up and he kept silent. I picked up my bag, and followed him, Janet close beside me. He was a clever lad, and I made a promise to myself to help him. Perhaps we could teach him his letters and how to read.

When we arrived back at the tavern, Gilly was settled in a shabby room above stairs. She was curled into a shivering ball on the bed, eyes closed. She had tucked her skirts between her legs, but a small patch of red had already blossomed on the coverlet. Moving to her, I placed my hand gently on her shoulder. She opened her eyes and smiled at me oddly. "My lady ah be thinking ah have rid meself of me problem. Tis for the best." She took a deep breath and closed her eyes again. "Ah feel no weel. Ye'll no leave me yet?" I touched her arm and promised I would not.

Janet and I pulled the blanket on the bed around her upper body, and removed her skirts. They were covered with dark blood and liver colored tissue. Clots of shiny dark red spilled down one side, the dark remnants of her baby. Sighing, I put the worn skirts aside to be washed. Clothing meant much to someone who had little. Gilly's stomach and side were already bruising, and I hoped Spence had not done more than make her lose her baby. Janet brought a basin of water and I washed her and applied clean folded clouts from my bag to absorb the bleeding. Janet had asked the tavern keeper's wife for more bedding, and we changed the coverlet and enfolded her in another blanket. There was nothing more we could do. I stood there, looking down at Gilly's pale face, thinking, then picked up my bag, and we walked down to the tavern. A brief lull followed our appearance, but everyone carefully avoided looking directly at us. Even such as they have at least a bit of shame. I told Molly, the tavern keeper's wife, to give Gilly some broth and bread if she asked, and gave her a small bottle of tincture and instructions on its use for pain. She tried to pay me, but I refused, and Cawdie got to his feet and took us home.

* * *

The next few days passed peacefully enough. Gilly recovered without any sign of damage except the many-colored bruises on her belly. She came to the cottage and asked meekly if I would teach her about the sponge and string again, so perhaps something good would come of the evil. Jocki came to the cottage with a small keg of ale in thanks from his mother. His face wore the bland innocent look that children have perfected for adults, and he never once showed he remembered his new friend Tam Morrison. I would ask Malcolm if he could use him in town to widen his horizons a little. I would have found work at the cottage, but Julianne and the baby were still with us.

* * *

The metalsmith sent word that he had completed my commission, so I walked down to the smithy. He had just taken a glowing clod out of the coals with tongs, and spared me no notice as he turned it under a great hammer to beat into bars. It gave me a moment to admire the perfectly muscled arms and powerful torso glistening with sweat so admired by the female inhabitants here. When he had done as much as the now blackened metal would permit, he stopped and turned to me. Wiping his face with a dirty rag, he smiled, displaying perfect white teeth. "Lady, forgive me, but the metal must rule here. Come, let me show you what I have wrought from your drawing. Tis a strange contraption and I hope it does what you wish." I noticed that his manner of speaking had become noticeably that of an educated man, and was not the same one he affected with the townspeople. It was an interesting fact to be tucked away and think about later.

He led me to a small room on the side of the building. The walls were covered with shelves and drawings. Some shelves had books, but most were filled with metal objects of every kind. A few delicately rendered necklaces and rings shone in the light from a window. An astrolabe stood next to what looked like a *Bourdaloue*, or chamber pot designed for females. The pot was oblong with the front slightly raised and higher. I wondered who would have ordered such a thing. Perhaps the Laird's wife? A table sat in the center of the room. Displayed like a jewel on the dark velvet cloth covering the table top was the breast pump. The design was exactly as the drawing except for a slightly rounded smooth lip he had added at the top of the spout. He saw me looking at it, and blushed. "I thought it would make the needed suction easier. It will be removed if you wish."

I hurried to reassure him. "Tis perfect, Sir. I am pleased beyond imaginings, and thank you." I lifted the pump. It was as carefully finished as a silver piece. He stammered his thanks as I paid him the agreed-on fee, packed it in a piece of clean burlap, and handed it to me.

"If it works, my Lady, I would like to know, and should you need other things, I will be honored to help you."

I told him that I would certainly return sometime with another book showing some metal braces that I would like to discuss with him. His face brightened, and he bowed, the polished movement incongruous with his attire. An enigma, indeed.

When I removed the breast pump from its wrappings at home, both Janet and Julianne stared at it, then at me in puzzlement. "Is it a pipe? Are you planning some of the treatments with tobacco smoke?"

I shook my head and gave the pump to Julianne explaining how it worked. "Put the end of the spout in your mouth and the opening in the large bowl end tightly over your nipple. Then keep sucking out the air. The suction should pull your breast milk into the bowl, so you can feed the bairn your own milk instead of cow's milk."

Julianne's face lit with excitement as she pulled down her gown to free her breast. We were all blushing a little and giggling like small children as we tried to help her adjust the pump. When it was positioned, Julianne began to suck on the end of the spout. At first nothing happened. Then I saw her face change. After a few more pulls on the spout, she released the bowl from her breast. A tiny bit of milk pooled at the bottom! We were all smiling, and I felt tears gather as I watched her pick up the babe from his basket, dip her finger into the bowl, and offer him the droplets. His tiny tongue licked at her finger...and I knew then he would live. Julianne looked at me, her eyes brimming with moisture and I was content.

Julianne quickly learned how to use the breast pump more easily, and we could help with feeding the bairn as usual. Cawdie hesitated slightly the first time he put his little finger into the small bowl containing Julianne's milk, but was soon comfortable with it. The babe was filling out, and his slate blue eyes seemed to be getting darker.

* * *

One day after cleaning and feeding him, she held him up to her face and said softly: "Little one, you need to be baptized. I think it is time I spoke to the priest. I shall name you Peter Alekseyevich." That seemed strange to me and I asked her why she chose a Russian name? She did not look at me as she answered, but continued to gently rock the babe. "My father had been designing ships at the Deptford Dockyard after we returned from France. When the Tsar of Russia came to England he visited the yard, even worked there as a common laborer, and persuaded many of the builders and designers to return to Russia with him. My father was one of them. I...loved Russia." She busied herself with putting the baby back into his basket, and picking up soiled cloths.

"Julianne, we cannot keep the babe a secret from his father much longer. To have him baptized is to reveal his existence."

She acknowledged my statement. "I know. I will decide this week if all goes well." Our conversation had ended.

The Laird no longer came each day, but always sent a servant to inquire about Julianne. He sent small gifts, oranges, sweets, a silk shawl, which Julianne accepted but she sent only her thanks and no messages of any kind. Of Margaret, we heard nothing.

* * *

I do not often dream, at least, I do not remember dreaming, but that night I dreamt I was alone on a cliff overlooking the ocean. It was moonlit dark, and the sea was rough, luminescent waves splintering against the black rocks below. I love storms, and leaned over the edge of the embankment to watch. From out of nowhere a huge black bird flew toward me, its wings haloed silver by the moon. It was eerily silent as it swooped down, and I crouched as it passed over me. One feathery wingtip grazed my arm, and I awoke. The sun was just rising, and I shook off the feeling of dread caused by the dream and began my day.

I had been to Malcolm's infirmary often, but had only managed to get through a small portion of his books. Each one was a treasure and I was trying to read as many as possible and make notes before he returned. I had *borrowed* his copy of *Ane Breve Description of the Pest* hoping to find some new information on the plague, but there was nothing except the usual treatments and the exhortation to pray and pray yet more.

Feeling a little guilty, I packed the book in a basket with a jar of honey of roses salve I had just made. Janet and Cawdie were going to pick up some laundry from Aggie, and I asked Janet if she would return the book to its proper place on Malcolm's shelf and leave the salve in his infirmary as a small form of payment for access to his library. I told them that on the way home they might wish to stop at the bakery to see if they had any marchpane or candied fruits.

There was a new concoction I wanted to try, so I busied myself with preparing the ingredients. A slash of terrible pain caused me to drop the cup I was holding and sent me reeling to the floor. I had not shielded myself here in my own home, so it sliced deeply. I was rapidly losing consciousness when I felt Janet lifting my head. Her face

flickered blurrily above me. "Malcolm, it is Malcolm...Oh God I need to go to him..."
Then it was blessedly dark.

ELEVEN

Malcolm - Assaulted

I went over it repeatedly in my mind, looking for alternatives, but there were only two possibilities that made sense; either I'd given Father smallpox, or somehow, he'd been in contact with Smith. The latter was highly unlikely. I was the most probable source. I was at Liddell's with Tremblay's body and next day, wearing the same clothes, visited Father and gave him a hug. I remembered all too clearly, and it was making me uneasy thinking I may have killed my Father because of my damnable obsession; but Beaton was mistaken if he thought I would sit in Torrport and do nothing. I may not be able to do much, but it would've driven me mad not having tried. I brought Mrs. Simpson and Henry with me to Edinburgh this time, and Elspeth agreed to care for our patients for a few days.

I ran up the stairs to Father's bedroom. "How is he?" I demanded.

"As well as can be expected, sir." Father's servant stood there barring the door, squat, barrel-chested, ram-rod straight, chin-high in that way they teach in the army.

"I want to see him." I was about to push the man aside when I saw him tense, readying himself. I'd never understood why Father hired him. He wasn't much of a servant, but I knew then looking in his hard eyes that I would only get in that door over his unconscious body.

"For pity's sake, I only want to see him. I know the risk, dammit!" It was exasperating being only feet away and unable to help. I tried to think of the servant's name and couldn't.

"The Magistrate has ordered quarantine and I must enforce it, sir." He said sir more like *suh*, snapping it out like they do on the infantry line.

"I understand...err. I apologize I have forgotten your name."

"It is Archibald Fowler, sir."

"Oh yes, I remember now, ex-regiment, right?" I didn't remember, but needed to know more about Father's gatekeeper.

One corner of his mouth turned up and he puffed his huge chest. "Aye, sir, the 26th Regiment of Foot, under Sir George, until Blenheim." He assumed I understood.

"Yes, George was wounded, wasn't he? Nothing serious as I recall." I tried to think if George had mentioned this man but came up with nothing.

"I'd been shot, and Sir George got a bayonet in the thigh pulling me to safety." I could see his body start to relax. I was on the right track.

"Let me guess. George sent you home to recover and Father took you on?"

"Something like that, sir." I didn't think George was that sentimental, but let it go.

"Archie, I just want to see him. I won't go in. If it was your father..."

He gave a sharp laugh. "My father beat me, but I'll open the door to let you see him. Sir, you have my solemn word I will protect your father with my life."

He opened the door part-way, his arm blocking entry. I could feel the cool-air from an open window. I nodded and stepped forward to look. The room was dark, curtains drawn and wafting. Father was sleeping on his side, turned away. I listened carefully, heard his shallow breathing; it was not laboured, thankfully.

"Is the fever down?"

"Aye, been giving him cooling baths, twice daily." At least he was doing that for him.

"And the rash?"

"It covers most of him now, poor sod." I could see the look of empathy as he said that and knew he was in good hands for now.

"Who is his doctor?"

"Twas Beaton, now McLaren. Gave him a vomit and purge yesterday. Said he would be back."

There was a sudden thud downstairs, and someone cursed. Archie closed the door and looked down the stairs quickly.

"It's Mrs. Simpson bringing our baggage." Archie looked bewildered. "She'll help here with cooking and cleaning. You can focus on Father."

"I don't need any help, sir. I'll take good care of Sir William."

I wasn't about to argue with him. "Mrs. Simpson is an excellent cook and I'm sure you'll like her roast beef. Better than your army cooking, I'll wager."

He could see I wasn't going to back down, so bowed and took a step back. "I will do as Sir William wishes."

"Fowler, you will do as I wish or be released. Is that clear?" I was on a short fuse and he needed to know his place.

He reverted to that military posture and snapped. "Sir!"

Impertinence like that is rare among military men. He seemed devoted to Father and reluctant to take orders from anyone else. I made a mental note to find out why.

"I'm going to see Doctor McLaren. Show Mrs. Simpson to the spare rooms and make her welcome." He nodded, eyes giving nothing away. On the way-out I told Mrs. Simpson about Fowler. She has a way of jollying men. We needed that on full force with this one.

* * *

McLaren had just finished lunch when I arrived. Tankard drained, he solemnly ushered me into his study. He leaned back in his chair, rubbed his eyes and sighed. "I am sorry, Malcolm."

"I know, and it's my fault too. Should have been more careful after seeing Tremblay at Liddell's."

"He mentioned Smith yesterday. Fevered, but wanting to talk as we purged him."

"What about Smith?" Now I was confused.

"We thought you might know. He said: "Get Smith", but he was delirious, not making much sense. Do you know what's going on?"

I tried to think, but there were only scraps. "The tavern-keeper at the Sand Bar, Duncan, Calum Duncan said there was a large well-dressed man to see Smith. But that could describe hundreds in this city."

"I agree Malcolm, but that doesn't rule out your father, does it? And do you remember Smith's reaction at the prison?"

"He did say something, didn't he? Has he been more forthcoming since?"

"No, but you must not rule out that your father was infected by Smith."

We sat for a few moments looking at each other, the clock ticking, a candle sputtering, the guilt and responsibility oppressive as prison chains on our necks. Then Angus blurted, spittle catching his lower lip. "Your woman was here. She's quite something, isn't she?" He smirked and wiped the spit away with his sleeve.

I wasn't sure who he meant. "Ah, what did she want?"

"She left some candies for you. Said that's all you cared about. Oh, and this message." He slid it off the desk and handed it to me. It was from Gwen. "She was just joking, Angus. You know I have many vices." That made him laugh out loud. He imagined I had many women and did nothing but party. I didn't, but wouldn't disabuse him. "Aye, she's a comely lass, is she not, with that wild red hair and sassy blue eyes?"

"She has many charms indeed!" He responded, and it was good to see Angus smiling.

"Her name is Gwen, a widow, well-to-do. I'll introduce you next time." That seemed to please him greatly and I wondered if Gwen had ignited fires here.

The door-bell rang, and a patient entered the infirmary. "Tell me about Father, what is your diagnosis." He started readying himself for the patient.

"Mal, his fever is going down, the rash has spread quickly, no hemorrhaging so far. Looks like confluent smallpox to me, but early days. We gave him a vomit and purge, just wanted to clean him out before it gets too bad." I could see it on his face, how much he hated telling me this.

Confluent pox is one of the worst types, not as bad as a few others, but still... Most people get distinct pox, the rash scatters thinly, leaving normal skin between. The great majority of those patients live, but with skin pocks as a forever reminder. With confluent pox, many die, the rash so dense that the pocks join-together covering large areas of the body, especially around the face, forearms and hands. The body swells, and it becomes difficult to eat, drink, and even breathe. Survivors are left with heavily pock-marked skin and sometimes blindness and deformities. Other types include malignant and hemorrhagic pox. They are usually a death sentence. In malignant pox the lesions are deep and flat on the surface, with the patient experiencing prolonged high fever. Hemorrhagic pox is even more horrifying, with extensive bleeding from the skin and mucous membranes. The cause of death in both types is usually due to heart failure or fluid in the lungs. It is a mercy that patients often don't live long.

Father was at the start of a very hard journey, but he's a hard man. He may not survive, but not for lack of fortitude. No one deserves smallpox, least of all Father, who dedicated his life to the service of others. My chest tightened. I felt helpless, guilt-ridden. I needed Father's calming voice and sage advice desperately.

Angus was almost out the door when I offered, "Thank you, my friend. I know this isn't easy for you either."

"Mal, I'll do my best, but it is in God's hands now." It was what most of us say when our skills are inadequate to task, it was a solace, but I knew that Angus would not stint in his care, and I was thankful for it.

"I am sorry I haven't time now, please go see Beaton and he'll fill you in on the latest. I'll drop by to see your father tomorrow around nine o'clock. Hope you can be there too." Angus waved and closed the door. I could hear him greeting his patient as though he were his favourite.

＊ ＊ ＊

I caught Beaton just as he was leaving his infirmary, medical bag in one hand, brass-tipped walking stick in the other. "Mal, please join me, I have an interesting case and we can chat on the way."

It was always surprising how fast Beaton could walk. "My father may have confluent pox." I glanced at him while dodging boys hawking oranges.

"I know Mal and I am so very sorry. McLaren will provide the best care. Leave it to him." Beaton looked calmly purposeful.

"I won't do anything stupid, if that's what you're thinking, but it may've been me that gave it to him."

"We discussed that possibility of course Mal, we need to know where he got it too. If we can find a link between your father and Smith, you're off the hook." His stick darted back and forth, clearing a path through the crowd. "If your father is able, find a safe way to communicate with him and we will continue working on Smith."

"I'll try but his man is not making it easy."

"Then have McLaren help when he visits." I nodded in agreement

"Also, Malcolm, you may not have heard but there are four new cases at the port. We are trying to contain it, working with the Magistrate, but it may already be too late." I listened as he described what they were doing about additional quarantines and tracking people down, but it was very bad news indeed.

Beaton pointed his stick to the right. "Next door on the left across the street."

We were let in by a plain-looking woman of middle age, and led to the main room on the ground floor where an elderly lady was rocking by the fire. The room was richly appointed in blood-red and gold rugs, black lacquered furniture, and painted porcelain, all in Asian style. There also was a peculiar fragrant smell, cloying, floral, woody. I sniffed and looked for the source.

"You must be smelling the incense. Unusual, isn't it? Father brought it from China. Mother says it reminds her of him. My name is Gillian." A weak smile struggled to form on her face.

"I'd heard of it, but this is a first. I'm Malcolm Forrester, pleased to meet you." She blushed and looked away.

Beaton went over and knelt beside the elderly woman. "Mrs. Findlay, it's Doctor John Beaton. How are you today?"

"Mother has been doing better since we started your diet, but her spirits are depressed, as you can plainly see, and she still complains about her stomach." Beaton looked up at Gillian using his best angelic smile.

The old woman slowly turned her head and gazed intently at Beaton. "My husband will be here soon. You are welcome to wait, young man."

Gillian cupped hand over mouth and whispered to me. "Father has been dead these past three months."

I was beginning to understand. John took her hand gently in his and said soothingly. "All will be well, dear Lady. You will see your husband soon enough."

"I should hope so. He is very late already. I've been waiting far too long!" She was still blaming him even now.

Beaton got up and joined us, so close he was almost touching Gillian. "All we can do is keep her comfortable and try to lift her spirits. Continue using that diet I gave you but add some cocoa for breakfast instead of tea, and now that it's warmer take her out in the fresh air." He smiled benignly, eyes locked on hers, then added without looking at me: "Doctor Forrester, do you have any recommendations?"

I considered the question while observing their courting ritual. "We have more patients like this now, especially older women who lose their husbands. There have been many since the war. I've used a mixture of rose water, syrup of dried rose, and oil of Vitriol added to ordinary wine to good effect in treating melancholia. I can give you the formula." They didn't seem to be paying any attention to me.

"I agree, perhaps she does need a bit more support. Lady, I'll send some of that mixture to you tomorrow." I smiled at Beaton's uncanny ability to give full attention to several at once. He presented his bill with an exaggerated bow and flourish and Gillian thanked him profusely. We were back on the street a few minutes later.

Beaton leaned in to confide. "The old woman inherited the largest shipyard in Scotland, the one at Leith, and Gillian will get it next."

"Ah, that Findlay! The name did sound familiar." I laughed out loud.

Beaton was walking quickly though the mob, dodging and skipping in that way he has. "Great fortunes have been made because of this war, and Gillian will not be able to manage alone."

His guileless sincerity always amused. "Then you must help her! It is your duty as a physician and a gentleman." Had we not been in a crowd, I'd 've had a proper go at him.

"Malcolm, you are not the only one with charms for the ladies." Beaton playfully whacked me on the shins with his stick.

"You're a crafty one, John, and I thought I was the schemer." He looked at me in astonishment, then pulled me off the road into the doorway of a coffee house.

"I wanted you to meet her, she may be very useful in future. They are one of the wealthiest families in Edinburgh. I didn't actually need your medical advice, you know." He chuckled, getting one back at me.

"I agree we need all the friends we can get, and it doesn't hurt if she pleases you as well." I loved teasing Beaton, but he ignored that one.

"Everything is ready for the experiment. McLean and McLaren took the samples. They are stored at McLean's Apothecary, guarded by two Town Guards and one hired by McLean. In five days, we can be inoculated. I have a lot to do before then, and Young too."

I listened as he went over the details again, but my mind was distracted; there was too much going on right now and my life was a bloody mess. "I'll be there, John." I was going to tell him not to worry, but it wouldn't have helped.

"I have another patient now, Mal. Please let Angus care for your father. There is little you can do here, and others need you." I assured him I would, and we embraced and wished each other well.

* * *

Highly animated voices coming from the kitchen greeted me at Father's. It was Mrs. Simpson and Archie in uproar. They seemed not to have heard me, so I walked quietly to surprise them.

"—and you know Malcolm has a lucky doll in his room? Painted and varnished and with a silk gown. Keeps it under a pillow!" They were both laughing as I walked in, then faces instantly changed from mirth to horror. I stared back with as much of a scowl as I could manage without bursting out laughing.

"That was Mother's." I started, but couldn't continue when I saw the colour drain from Mrs. Simpson's face.

"I am sorry, sir, please forgive me." She looked down. Archie was silent. I sat down with them.

"It is well you find me amusing." I reached over and patted her hand. Of course, I knew servants enjoyed having a laugh at master's expense. I'd heard a lot of it as a boy. "You don't remember my mother, and I barely do. Father only kept a few of her things. He doesn't know about the doll. It'll be our secret, alright?" I wasn't sure why I was explaining this. The anchors of my life were losing hold, and I didn't need another emotional issue to surface right now. It was becoming awkward. "How is Sir William?"

"He is still asleep, sir. But resting well, I believe." Archie responded, then folded his scarred hands on the table in a way that suggested he'd said enough.

"Then serve me supper in Father's study and we'll have an early night. It's been a trying day for all." I got up to leave. "And Archie, you said you would protect Father with your life. I am going to hold you to that." He looked up at me no doubt wondering what I'd meant.

* * *

McLaren arrived promptly at nine next morning. I'd been up for hours and took Henry for a walk, had breakfast, organized my schedule and notes, looked in on Father, fidgeted. McLaren was unusually cheerful and joked about some drunks he saw last night. One had fallen in a fresh pile of horse dung while the other was throwing him a rope like one would a drowning man. Edinburgh is never boring. I'll give it that.

"Good morning, Sir William!" McLaren felt Father's forehead. "Fever's down. Close the windows now and no more cooling baths." Archie immediately closed them and pulled the curtains aside to let in some light. I could see Father was awake, face covered in rash. McLaren pulled up the sleeves on Father's nightshirt to look at his arms and hands.

"Father, it's Malcolm! I'm here." I waved from the doorway, desperately seeking contact.

"Arms and hands completely covered now." McLaren muttered and made an entry in his notebook. I could see Father trying to speak. Angus leaned closer to hear, then turned his head to me. "I think he wants to say something to you."

"Angus, tell him I love him and I'm here for him." I stood there helpless, not knowing if he could hear. Angus repeated it to him and asked how he felt.

All I could understand as Father tried to speak was the word "Son". Angus turned back to me again. "I think he is trying to warn you about someone. I'll ask him."

The sound came out as a raspy animal–like growl, but it was clear. "Son, it's the Captain!" Father slumped back, exhausted from the effort. I wasn't sure what he meant. I knew many captains and was unsure of the context.

Angus said his goodbyes and well wishes to Father, then washed his hands in the basin before coming back to us by the door. "Fowler, continue his bland diet and make sure he drinks a lot. Keep him warm now that the fever is gone. Doctor Forrester, I am confirming the diagnosis that your father has confluent smallpox and it is progressing normally. Condolences."

I knew he was right, but it was a shock seeing and hearing it first-hand. "He's fortunate to have you as his doctor, Angus." Beaton was right, it was best leaving this in McLaren's capable hands. I was doing no one any good here. It was painful to admit that when Father needed me most, I couldn't help him. We walked to the street together in silence, Angus pulling on a fresh pair of linen gloves. They were his affectation. He didn't much like touching things with bare hands and needed to wash constantly; not a bad habit really.

He tried to smile, but it broke in the wrong direction. "May God protect you both."

"And you as well, dear friend." We embraced as brothers. "I'll see you next at the start of the experiment."

"God-willing," I replied, but honestly, I never understood what God willed.

I would try to catch the noon carriage back to Torrport and be of use there while I waited for the experiment to begin in a few days. Mrs. Simpson was helping me pack and Henry nosing around, curious as always, when the boy banged on the front door.

* * *

I got to McLean's Apothecary as soon as I could. The boy said I was urgently needed, and I didn't think McLean was the type to ask for help without good reason. The door was ajar, the floor covered in broken glass, herbs, medicines, and spatters of blood. I called out. There was a muffled response. I called out again, then carefully made my way through the debris to a side room. It was McLean. He was at his desk trying to suture his hand.

"I can do that." I pulled up a chair beside him. His face was stoical. It was a clean slice on his palm. I took the needle from him.

"You caught a blade in your hand?" It is a common wound, better than letting the blade slice your face off.

"Aye." He grunted as I inserted the needle and pulled it through. At least it wasn't bleeding too much. He gritted his teeth as I finished. Suturing wasn't commonly used, especially among physicians. We tended to bandage, and cauterize if necessary. But I'd seen a few army-trained surgeons use it, and now I was curious about McLean's background.

"That should hold it." I wiped away the excess blood with a clean towel. "Let it clot for a few minutes, then I'll bandage it." He said nothing, so we sat there looking at his hand.

Once the bleeding had stopped, he angled his head. "The bandages are in that cupboard by the sink." As I was getting them he added: "Forrester, why were the Town Guards removed last night?"

I stopped, stunned hearing it. I didn't want to say anything rash, so I gathered the bandages, returned to him, sat down and placed them between us. "Tell me what happened, and we'll see if we can figure it out." We needed each other right now and my gut told me to trust him. He went over it step-by-step as I bandaged his hand.

It was early morning and he heard a noise, came down, found two men searching the apothecary. He challenged them, the larger one pulled a cutlass, cut him on the hand with an unexpected slash, but McLean was quick and started throwing scalpels and other sharp objects at them, hitting one in the throat. That one fled leaving him facing the larger one who smelled strongly of tobacco. They fought, McLean got behind him and leapt on his back choking him, shelves breaking, glass crashing as they lurched back and forth, then the big man drove McLean against the door jamb hard enough to knock him off, then ran out the front door, leaving McLean sucking wind on the floor. It was becoming a familiar a story.

"What happened to your man, the guard you hired?" I asked.

"He was gagged and tied in back. I released him and sent him home. But Forrester, there were two Town Guards here when I went to bed, one in front and one out back. What happened to them?"

"I don't know, but I'm damned well going to find out!" McLean nodded but looked like he didn't believe me. "You have my word...err...I am sorry I don't even know your first name. Mine is Malcolm."

He extended his good hand and I took it. "I'm Alistair, former surgeon in the 26th Regiment."

"Ah," I smiled. It was starting to make sense. "Alistair, I'm so glad you're with us." I said that sincerely thinking how brave he was to have taken on two of them. "I assume the samples are safe."

He chortled. "Oh yes, they never were here, you know. I have them securely stored elsewhere. I was expecting an attack. Just not this way."

"Aren't you a sly one!" I laughed, appreciating my new friend.

"Alistair, I think you should lodge a formal complaint with the Royal College of Surgeons. These attacks must not go un-challenged. Meanwhile, I'm going to find-out why the guards were absent. Are you with me on this?"

"I am, more than you know, and please extend my regards to Sergeant Fowler too." It took me an embarrassing few seconds to remember who Fowler was, but as we parted I was more than ever eager to know more about him and this web of army connections. What I didn't tell McLean was how angry I was. I was seething inside. Our opponents seem to think they can abuse us with impunity. I'd had enough of our pacifist stance on all this. It was time to fight back and I knew where to start. McLean had called on me for good reason. I checked my dagger and pistol and set-off at a brisk pace, heart buoyed at the prospect of retribution.

* * *

I knew my way around the Guard House by now, so went straight to the Captain's office, trailing a lackey shouting at me. The Captain was alone, writing.

"I want to know what happened last night at McLean's Apothecary." I stood there, knuckles on his desk looming over him, ignoring the guardsman babbling incoherently behind me. Captain Donald Mackmain rose slowly to face me. I'll admit he was impressive in his red serge uniform trimmed with gold braid and sporting a chest full of medals. He was a few inches taller than me and heavier, with wavy silver hair. He would have been handsome, but had the look of a man past his prime and too fond of drink.

"Get out Forrester!"

I stood my ground. "The guards were ordered by the Lord Provost to protect us. Why were they not there?" I was beginning to shout now, temper rising.

"You are not in-charge here Forrester, now get out!" He had that look of hatred in his eyes.

116

"I will not until I get some satisfactory answers. A surgeon was assaulted last night, under your watch, Captain. You are responsible!" I shoved a finger in his face.

"You!" He pointed back at me, his finger shaking. "You are scum and an abomination in the eyes of God. You must be stopped!"

With that I stood there astonished. I'd assumed he was just incompetent, and now this. Then I remembered Father's words: *It's the Captain.*

"It's you! You are the one behind the attacks!"

He threw his pen down and yelled: "Guards!"

In a bloody-minded rage, I vaulted the desk and grabbed the Captain by the throat. He fell back over his chair taking me with him to the floor. I could hear cries, boots thumping. There was a scramble of fists and legs punching and kicking, sharp pains everywhere. I had the Captain by the throat pressing my fingers into the sides, our faces close, my eyes frozen on his, and I wanted to kill him in a moment of sublime clarity as I watched his face turn a bloated purple. I was squeezing as hard as I could, trying to ignore the pain from my attackers, then one bashed me in the head with the butt of his musket hard enough to loosen my grip and allow them to drag me off him.

Consciousness was fading as two grabbed me and forced me to my knees, hands behind my back, while another was behind me swearing and tying me. He smelled strongly of tobacco. It was familiar, but I couldn't remember from where. He leaned in behind me and whispered. "This is for Owen". Then stood and kicked me in the lower back near my kidney. They held me there as he continued kicking. I tried not to cry out, but body detached from mind and it came out as a pitiful wail. I heard it, not quite believing it was me. Mind knew body was going into shock and couldn't stop it, only suffer and endure, and with some luck, live. Then the kicking stopped, and I could hear him wheezing as they let me fall to the floor.

I tried to focus, get breath under control, turn off pain. I could hear them talking. I turned my head sideways to look up and hear better. There were several guardsmen in the room, no point struggling, only wit and my name could save me now. I watched them help the Captain up. He was bent over gasping and pulling on his collar, then straightened, horrid red-devil face unmasked. He tried to speak but couldn't at first, then fussed straightening his uniform and medals.

I tried to get up, made it to hands and knees. The Captain came at me suddenly. I flinched thinking he would kick me, but instead he spat in my face. He croaked a few orders to the men telling them to get back to duty. Two remained. One was the large man who'd kicked me, the other one younger, looking very frightened.

The Captain stood over me. "Your father is dying, boy. You have no one to protect you now." He turned and paced back and forth in front of me, hands clasped behind his back. "I want you out of Edinburgh...permanently, understand?"

This was becoming very dangerous now with so few witnesses, but I wanted to know more and decided to push it as far as I could. "Aye, it looks like you've won,

Captain. Your masters will be pleased." I moaned softly as the pain flowed through me.

"Boy, you don't know who you are dealing with. You were warned and didn't listen. We have been more than reasonable. You are blasphemers, hated by God and all of us who follow the true Faith." I watched him closely, trying to see if he was lying, but I think he believed what he said. I had to be very careful if I was to get out of this alive. These religious fanatics would not stop at murder if they thought they were doing God's will.

I slowly sat back, one foot under, trying to position myself to be able to rise and run if needed. "Captain, this is a misunderstanding, surely. The Church supports our work. We have documents."

That stopped him. It was a lie, well the last part anyway.

"I have not seen any document of support!" He blurted out defiantly, but I knew I'd created some doubt in his mind.

"The Royal College of Physicians has entertained our work as well."

"Turnbull?"

"Aye, the very same, and a close friend of the family." I knew I was lying, but I needed that seed of doubt to grow. Sending the other men away was an ominous signal. I feared he was setting me up to be disappeared and I needed to change these plans if I could. He said nothing for a few minutes, perhaps weighing options, risks, outcomes.

"Get him up." He motioned to the men and they dragged me off the floor. I was in such pain I couldn't have stood un‑aided, but I tried to stand tall facing him.

He came close again, looked at me thoughtfully as he pulled on a fresh pair of white gloves, then said to his men, "Get rid of him." Then he leaned in to my ear and whispered, so only I could hear. "Stay away from Gwen." I could clearly see the welts I'd left on his neck as he turned his shoulder a bit, took a step back and punched me full in the face.

* * *

It was the rattling and jarring of the wagon that woke me. I don't think I'd been out that long. I tried to get up, but they'd tied my legs. I was feeling nauseous from the beating and from bouncing upside down in the wagon. Just in time, I turned my head and spewed out the contents of my stomach that voted to live somewhere more peaceful. It wasn't long before the wagon stopped, and they pulled me out, cursing me for the mess I'd left, cut my bonds and rolled me into the ditch.

The wagon rumbled away, and I lay there disoriented, paralyzed, with nausea and sharp bolts of pain striking regularly. It was the water in the ditch that revived me.

It was too cold to stay, so I had to get out and that wasn't easy. It seemed to take hours to crawl up to the road through the long grass and rocks. I sat on the side of the road like a beggar and prayed for help. In time, a wagon stopped. The driver was hauling a load to Torrport and helped me in the back. I offered coin, but he refused, mumbling something about bad luck.

The first friendly face at Torrport was Daniel's and he helped me home from the stables, curious about my new look. I laughed through the pain and said I'd had a bad day of doctoring. It was comforting to be home but when I passed the hall mirror, I could understand his concern; there was blood everywhere, nose askew, clothes muddy, hands covered in filth. I was a sight, as the ladies say. My appearance was as nothing compared to the damage I felt inside, and when I remembered Mrs. Simpson and Henry were in Edinburgh, I fell against the wall and slid to the floor. I was broken and alone, I'd failed and let everyone down, and I may have killed my Father. Slumped there, head in hands, I tried to block those thoughts, but they pressed heavily on me and I started to feel a warm wetness on my cheeks as my body shuddered in pain and regret.

Then the front door opened suddenly, and she screamed. "God's bones! Is that you Malcolm?" It was Janet in her flowing multi-coloured arisaid looking like an angel descended as she tore off her wrap and covered me. It was warm from her body, and I sank gratefully into the welcoming darkness.

TWELVE

Elspeth – Mayhem

Torrport, Scotland.

"Take off his clothes." I concentrated on keeping the contents of my stomach exactly where they were. I hurt. Closing my eyes, I took several deep breaths, and pushed all emotion into the tiny circle of light in my mind as I had been taught. I knelt, afraid to move him until I had examined him. Malcolm was blessedly unconscious, though his breathing was labored and through his mouth. Blood trickled slowly from the swollen ruin of his nose which tilted improbably to the left. His clothing was so covered with gore, I feared he had been knifed. Both eyes were red and swollen closed; he would have two black eyes later, and he was deathly pale. Janet and I worked quickly to remove his filthy shirt and pants. The soft fabric was stiff with blood and torn in several places. His tailor would be horrified. The chest and abdomen were both a mass of angry red welts, with lesser ones on his lower limbs, but there were no open wounds. I ran my hands over the inflamed skin on his chest and sides, checking the wheals, then we rolled him gently to his side, so I could see his back. There were two especially large bruises just above the buttocks and a second about a hand's width above that. I touched that one gently and sighed. Sitting back on my heels, I reached for a blanket to cover him and called Cawdie. "Can you carry him to his bed, please, Cawdie."

He picked Malcolm's inert form up as though he weighed nothing, and carried him to his bed. I had never seen his bedroom. It said taste and money. I glanced at the painting of the beautiful unclothed woman over his bed, then turned to the equally unclothed man before me. He was beautiful too, lean and surprisingly muscular, which suggested that he was not the dilettante he seemed.

Janet prepared a basin of cool water and we washed away the blood and dirt. I applied a soothing salve to his scraped and reddened skin before covering him with more warm blankets. He was going to have an assortment of colorful bruises by tomorrow, but I was more afraid of internal injuries. His belly had already begun to bulge a little beneath two crimson streaks. A broken nose was the least of his injuries. I touched it, tracing the break and decided to try to repair it before it was even worse. I was no bonesetter, the Guild would not accept women, but I had a much-worn copy of *The Compleat Bonesetter*. Leaning over Malcolm I looked down. Even mauled he was a handsome man. I studied his nose for a few moments, and then positioned the heels of both hands on either side of it and firmly pushed. It moved back into place easily enough, but the bleeding increased. I packed his nostrils with lint, cut a square from a cloth roll in my bag, laid it over his nose and put short splints on both sides, wrapping strips to secure them around his head. Just as I tied the bandage in place, he stirred.

"Malcolm?" I reached for his arm to keep him from moving but he shook me off like a fly, and tried to sit up, a stream of obscenities hissing from his mouth between gasps.

"Are you trying to kill me? By Christ's fingernails, woman, what have you done? I can't breathe." His face contorted in pain and he moved his hand to his chest.

"Malcolm, stop, please! Be still, I think you have a broken rib. You know perfectly well that moving might cause more damage. Show me where it hurts?" I saw him twist his torso, press the red ridge on his side and flinch. He stopped moving. "Can you bear it if Cawdie helps you sit so I can wrap your chest? After a brief hesitation, he nodded, and let himself be guided to the edge of the bed and into a sitting position so I could reach him. His pallor increased but he made no sound as I wound his chest firmly with long strips of cloth, and tied them as tightly as I dared. His breath was labored, and he touched his face gingerly, testing the area of wetness beneath his nose. "No," I said hastily as he reached for a cloth on the table. "Please don't try to blow your nose yet. I have packed it to stop the bleeding. Are you seeing normally with both eyes?"

He blinked, and looked around the room. "Yes," he shuddered. "I have to pee." His voice was carefully neutral. He had finally noticed he was nude beneath the blanket and a tide of red suffused his damaged face. It is true, what they say about physicians making poor patients. I turned away to hide my smile and asked Cawdie to bring a chamber pot and help him. Janet and I pointedly began to pick up discarded clothes and busied ourselves neatening the room. When he had finished relieving himself I took the chamber pot from Cawdie and went to the window. The urine was dark with blood. I looked up and saw him watching me. He actually grinned at me a bit, and said "Yes, I know. But at least I can still pee, a good sign is it not? Now if I could only breathe." And then he sank slowly back onto the pillows, asleep almost instantly, mouth agape and snoring slightly.

There was nothing more to be done except watch and wait. I decided to go home and get more barley water and a few other things we might need. I had cherry syrup and laudanum for pain in my bag. Knowing Malcolm, I decided to bring back several kinds of tea and some of our latest batch of ale as well. Any liquids we could get him to drink would help.

* * *

Cawdie took me home. I was clearly more tired than I thought; I stumbled twice on the way and decided to send him back alone with the things for Janet. Julianne helped me pack it all in one of the willow and grapevine baskets Janet and I had made last winter. She was dressed in soft blue wool with a slightly stiffened bodice which showed her eyes and delicate complexion to advantage. I noticed that her small hands were slightly chapped from washing as they packed the basket neatly and gave it to Cawdie. I would make myself remember to give her some of the cream I made for Aggie later, but right now I needed to rest. Only for a little while, I thought dimly. I crept into my bed fully dressed except for shoes and pulled a blanket over me, leaving the door open.

* * *

It was almost dark when I awoke to the sound of someone knocking on the door. Julianne answered it. She began speaking softly, in Russian, a language I know little of. Our visitor was a man. I recognized the dark raspy voice at once; it was Gregor, Sir Campbell's manservant. Julianne inhaled sharply at something he said, and began to weep softly. By that time, I was at the door, into the other room, and reaching for Julianne. Scathach stood protectively by her side, fur bristling. Gregor watched impassively as I pulled her back and glared at him. "What is it? What do you want? Does your master need me?"

His black eyes, so dark there was no discernable pupil, remained on mine as he replied in his accented but excellent English. "My master is well. I have but brought Lady Julianne news from an...acquaintance."

She had ceased crying, and nodded to him. "Thank you, sir. It was most kind of you." Gregor looked down at Scathach, flat obsidian eyes to gold, and nodded. I fancied the two of them exchanged some message, for Scathach relaxed and regarded him stolidly. He bowed low to Julianne, accorded me a mocking and much less reverent gesture, turned gracefully for someone the size of a small mountain, and left, his feet making no sound on the path. My own cold feet found my slippers and I looked at Julianne.

"Julianne?"

She had recovered her usual tranquil demeanor, and did not look directly at me, but spoke in a clear uninflected voice. "I have been less than honest with you and repaid your kindness with deception. I must beg your forgiveness." She moved to the hearth and looked down at the bairn. "Lady Elspeth, I have let you believe that the Laird is the father of my child. He is not. Only a charitable kinsman and friend who offered to help. I was already pregnant when I arrived here from Russia. Gregor was bringing me news from..." her voice trailed off, and she took a deep breath, "his real father. It seems he may wish to visit and see his son." She looked up. Her eyes were brilliant with unshed tears.

I could feel a mixture of emotions washing from her, guilt, exaltation, fear and beneath it all, a deep sense of isolation. She bent over the basket and picked up the babe, holding him close and staring down at him. I knew she was examining his tiny face for traces of the other. I touched her arm." Sit, I will make some tea. Would you like to talk about this now?" She indicated her agreement and sat, rocking the child in that instinctive timeless way that women have.

The kettle was always left heating beside the fire. I put three large spoons of dried lemon balm into the blue ceramic teapot before pouring hot water over it. It needed to brew longer than most teas, so I filled a tray with two of the fragile blue and white bowls we used for hot brews, a container of honey, and a few small anise seed biscuits. Placing the tray on a small table between us, I filled the two bowls, sat back and began to drink mine slowly inhaling the warm lemon scented steam. Julianne picked up her bowl in one hand, and began to sip slowly, her eyes not leaving the babe cradled in her other arm. He was still quite small, seldom cried and slept a great deal now that he was getting enough breast milk from Julianne. He was not yet able to suck properly but nuzzled her breast with interest when he was put to it. I thought it would not be much longer before he learned to suckle. His survival was nothing short of a miracle.

Julianne sighed softly and began speaking "I told you I went to Russia with my father. There was to be a new ship construction yard built on the left bank of the Neva. He was, is...a designer and builder of ships. The Tsar needed his skills and offered him far more than he could ever hope to get here, riches, housing, perhaps even a title. Then, too, we are Catholic, and it was very difficult for us here. When the Queen would not assent to the Act of Security passed by the Scottish Parliament, he said we would never be free to choose our own destiny, or trade with England and the colonies. I think that was when he truly began thinking of leaving Scotland permanently. Everything we believed in and owned was being torn from us. He would never leave us behind, so we went with him to help build the Tsar's new capital, Saint Petersburg...my mother, my brothers, all of us. My father was given a free house and an exemption from all taxes for ten years." She inhaled. "The Russian people are not always happy with foreigners; they see them as having an evil influence on the Tsar. But, we were under his protection and he often worked beside his foreign craftsmen.

He has the rough hands of a working man." Her voice was dreamy, and I leaned closer to hear it, almost spilling my tea as she continued.

"Russia is a place of deep contrasts, and can be both beautiful and terrible. The winters are bitterly cold with skies alight with auroras, while the summers have almost constant daylight. There were often food shortages because of supplies delayed by snow or mud. It was an uncomfortable but not unhappy time for me."

Her voice was softer, and she moved the babe carefully to her other side. "We moved in high circles and frequently attended Court. I met a Russian nobleman there. He was a giant among large men, but oddly shy for his rank, mayhap from the illness those of his intimates sometimes witnessed that gave him...a tic, or tremors." She paused, remembering. "His face would twist into a grotesque mask with no warning. Out of deference, everyone around him would pretend that nothing was happening. If it became very bad, his servants would run for his mistress, or convenient as she was called. If she could not be found, they sought someone, anyone, whose presence he found comforting, usually a young woman. One day there was no one else about, and it was me they asked to help him. They led me to him, and said 'Sir, here is the person to whom you wished to speak.' Then left me alone with him. I was terrified, but that great giant of a man was as helpless as this babe. He was shaking, and half of his face was drawn into a frightful rictus. He motioned for me to sit next to him and looked at me searchingly a moment before he simply closed his eyes and laid his trembling head on my lap. I had seen others soothe him, so although I was shaking almost as badly as he, I tried to mimic what they had done." She was lost in the memory. "His hair was so soft...and he smelled of leather and man and some herb I could not identify. I sat, stroking his head and temples until he fell asleep. My leg became painfully numb, but I dared not move, and when he awoke some hours later, he kissed my hand and left without saying a word. Thereafter, when his mistress was not nearby, they would come for me. You may guess the rest. I soon took her place. I willingly became his convenient and loved him and every moment of it. I fear I lack the grace to be shamed, and would not change the past even if I could. Those memories are dear to me." Her voice was steady.

My tea had grown cold. "Julianne," I said carefully. "Who is this man?"

She looked up. "That I cannot tell you. I have sworn not to reveal his name, but he is important in the Russian Court. I can only say that he has been kind and generous, and has helped many of the people who left or were forced to leave Scotland because of their religious beliefs. There is even a Catholic chapel in Russia now. And, he wishes to visit me...and the babe...here. Gregor said he would come soon, by ship. He will let me know when."

Of course, I thought. I was beginning to see a faint pattern. Scotland was rife with unrest, and the Jacobites were at the center of much of it. Our fishing village offered haven or escape for the right price, and Torrport was nearby. It fit. And so, we would serve some highly placed Russian nobleman homemade brew and bannock in our small cottage on the hillside, while he became acquainted with his bastard son   I had difficulty trying to imagine it.

My mind sifted through the little information I had. In Skye, it was well known that one of the Jacobite Gordons had become a military advisor to the Tsar, and worked to enlist his support for the Jacobite cause. In this he had some success, and we heard he was permitted to build the chapel spoken of by Julianne. He had also defeated an attempt by the Streltsy troops, the hereditary guards of Moscow and the Tsar, to restore Sophia, the Tsar's sister, and former Regent of Russia, to the throne while the Tsar was traveling in Europe. Sophia had been confined to a convent thereafter, but it was commonly believed she still schemed from her cell to overthrow the Tsar. Did her influence extend this far?   Were any of the increasingly numerous Russians in Torrport involved in her plotting? Gregor came immediately to mind. How long had he been employed by Sir Campbell?   And what about Sir Campbell himself?

Our problems were bad enough! Many Scots resented the control of the English monarch and feared losing both their faith and their fortunes. In retaliation for the Act of Security passed by the Scottish Parliament, which said that Scotland would not be bound to accept the same monarch as England if they were not granted free trade, the English Parliament passed the Alien Act only a few months-ago to enforce a full union with England or face seizure of Scottish assets and end Scottish exports to England. It was a recipe for disaster, and I did not think Julianne was fully aware of the danger that threatened her.

I shook my head to clear it. "Julianne, we have to discuss this. You want to have the baby baptized. I assume that the babe's father is married, so that is going to be a problem when you speak to Father Hammet. Illegitimate children are usually recorded as such on the parish register, and someone must take responsibility for the child to prevent it being a ward of the parish or kirk." I hesitated, "And... under Scottish law, there is a possibility that you could be charged with fornication, or at the least must pay a fine of five marks for fornication or twenty marks for adultery. By law you could be imprisoned or sent to the workhouse. First, you must go to the Laird and tell him the babe lives. He can keep you safe."

A bitter little smile played about her lips. "Coin is not a problem. I have more than enough for such things. Believe me, I have been over this, many times in my thoughts. I will tell the Laird, and do what must be done. You need have no fear for the babe. He will be protected. His father will assure that he is well cared for. Be assured Elspeth, I will take care of it very soon, I promise."

"All right, then." I was quiet for a moment, then continued. "Julianne, I will help you in any way I can, but some things cannot be avoided. The priest must ask you for information about the babe, and unless there is some way to change it, the child will most likely be recorded as base born or natural, a bastard. You need to think this through carefully for the sake of the future of the babe and your family. There might be other ways. In Scotland, you can be wed by intent...perhaps we can find you a husband?" I was thinking out loud of alternatives. She did not hear me, but smiled at me again and rested her cheek gently in the babe's soft curls, already withdrawing into her own private heaven or hell.

* * *

I felt restless and reached for my cloak. I was upset and worried and wanted to check on Malcolm. I needed a walk in the fresh air. The day had turned to gold and purple twilight.

"I will stop by the vendors near Malcolm's home and bring back some honey and barley if they are still open." I touched the baby's forehead with my finger and was reaching for the knob when the pounding came from the other side of the door. I opened it to see a man standing there, a wrapped bundle cradled in his arms. It was MacTavish, the tavern keeper from the fishing village.

"Lady Elspeth, ye have to help me." His voice broke. I could feel the fear emanating from him as well as the smell of the mixture I recognized as the potent blend peculiar to the tavern. He was Jocki's father, a large lump of a man with dark pocked skin like overused leather from his years as a seaman and fists the size of beeves on his oddly short arms. His eyes were embedded in wrinkles from squinting at the sun, and red with fatigue. He held out the bundle. "Tis Leana." He peered around me trying to see if there was anyone else nearby, but Julianne had vanished behind the screen with the bairn. "Lady, she has the smallpox. Will ye help? Me wife is sore ill and fair to panic o'er this." His voice trembled as he pulled back the blanket from the little girl's face, his clumsy looking hands as deft as a woman's.

I had seen Leana several times. She was about three years old, and one of those strange things that sometimes happen in nature, a faultless flower growing in a dung heap. It seemed impossible that the fairylike creature in his arms had sprung from his union with Molly. Somewhere in their past lay beauty that had capriciously emerged in the finely boned body and perfect features of their child. Soft honey-colored curls clustered around the flushed face, marred by several blisters on the side of her cheek. The blue veined paper-thin eyelids were closed. My heart sank.

I dared not bring her into the house. I was safe from infection, the ugly scars on half my face attested to that, but Julianne and the babe were not. "Bring her this way." I went around the side of the cottage to Cawdie's room in the shed. Both he and Janet had survived smallpox in the same epidemic I had. I pushed open the door, took a clean but frayed blanket from the shelf above, and placed it over Cawdie's bedding. "Put her there and tell me when she started getting sick." I threw my cloak on a chest, rolled up my sleeves to the elbow, and bent over Leana, pulling down the blanket she was wrapped in. Her bed gown was more elaborate than I expected. Someone had painstakingly embroidered the little bodice with a tracery of blue flowers and soft green leaves. I pulled it down. There were numerous pustules on her chest but only a scattered few on her lower body.

"She were poorly, an sick fer a day or so. Naught bad. An yesterday these come on her...and today, she be even more covered." He stared at his daughter with palpable anguish.

There were a few blisters on her back in various stages. Some had already begun to crust over, while others appeared to be just forming. They resembled small liquid filled domes and sat on the surface of the skin.

Her long lashes fluttered, and the child looked up at me with eyes as blue as a summer sky in the evening. "Me bad. Me sorry."

"Shhhhh...it is all right. You are a very good girl. Do you hurt anywhere?" As I spoke I took the tiny hand in mine and turned it to look at her palms. There were no pustules there or on the soles of her feet. They were mostly on her face and torso. "Open your mouth, Leana. Let me see you stick out your tongue." The little girl obeyed, then looked up at me with feigned innocence and giggled at being told to do something she had been taught was wrong. Her mouth and throat were clear. My heart resumed its normal beat. I was reasonably certain that this was the less virulent type of smallpox. I had learned how to differentiate it in Italy. Richard Morton, a London physician, called it chickenpox, a milder form of smallpox. The blisters or pustules were patterned differently from those of the more virulent pox. Leana had relatively few on her face, more in diverse stages on her torso. Smallpox produced pustules that appeared all at once and looked the same on all parts of the body. Scabbing over did not begin for more than a week or two, and depending on the type, the pustules varied in coverage and appearance. Leana's were beginning to scab over, with a new crop just beginning to form as well. She would be contagious until all her blisters were crusted, but likely she would be more fractious than seriously ill for less than a fortnight. Perhaps we would be lucky.

"Mr. MacTavish, I am almost certain that Leana has what is sometimes called chickenpox, which is a much less dangerous form of smallpox. She will probably start to get better in a few days and have little scarring if we can keep her from scratching. Cutting her fingernails will help."

He blinked at me in astonishment, his hand fisting in the blanket. "Lady, are ye tellin' me that me bairn will nae die?"

"Yes, I believe so, but we do have a problem. How many people have been near her?" I was concerned about who else might be infected. Any pox is very contagious. MacTavish and Molly both bore the telltale marks left by smallpox, but Jocki did not. One tends to notice such things when one is also scarred.

MacTavish looked slightly sheepish. "Nary a one since she were taken sick. Me wife is o'er careful with the bairn. Watches her like a cat with one kitten. Keeps her like a princess, that one."

I thought for a moment. "All right," I said slowly. "I will give you something to help with the itching and fever, but she must be kept away from everyone else until I am certain I am right. You must boil anything she touches including your own clothing. If people know there is pox in the village, they will panic. Make sure no one sees you on the way back, and tell Molly to keep her out of sight for a while longer. No one, not even Jocki, should come near her. I will come every day, just to be sure." The little girl was quiet, watching and listening with bright intelligent eyes. I smiled at her, wrapped the blanket about her again and went into the cottage. I filled a small basket with a jar of honey, a container of salve, a bottle filled with liquid, and a bag of rolled oats. When I returned to MacTavish he was holding Leana to his chest and staring at her with a look of besotted adoration.

"Take this to Molly. Tell her to rub the honey on the pocks, leave it for about half an hour and then wash it off. Do that about four times a day. For the itching, she can put about a cup of pounded oats in a wash tub of warm water and stir until it becomes milky. Give Leana a good long bath in it just before she goes to bed. This bottle has something for the fever. She can have one teaspoon of it in the morning and in the evening. Give her all the liquid she will drink. Tea, milk, broth, anything. Will you remember all that? I will be there tomorrow. Just keep everyone away until I tell you otherwise."

His head moved in silent affirmation and he had some trouble making his voice work. "Lady Elspeth, ye dinna ken how much I owe ye, but I will make it good, I swear on me mam's grave. I be yer man, my lady, should ye ever need me."

I laughed, tucked the blanket more closely around Leana, and handed him the basket. "Mr. MacTavish, be on your way now. And, remember, tell Molly to boil any bedding or clothing that Leana has used. Do not send them to the laundry. She must do it herself."

After he left I rolled up the old blanket I had placed on the bed to be burned. I washed my hands and arms with the peppermint soap we used, carefully rolled down my sleeves and picked up my cloak. It had been a very long day, but it was still light enough to go to Torrport and see Malcolm. Knowing his vanity, I decided to bring the leech carrier. It was quite small. Just a rectangular metal box with ventilation holes on the end and rounded top, that would fit easily in a pocket. It would be amusing to see Malcolm's face when I opened it.

THIRTEEN

Malcolm - Smugglers

Torrport, Scotland.
"It's not so bad, please eat it or Elspeth will be very upset with you." Janet was enjoying teasing me about the bland oatmeal porridge she brought to go along with the jug of spring water.

It wasn't easy eating or speaking since my face was half-covered in bandages. "A juicy cut of roast beef with a double dram of whisky would be preferable." I spoke very slowly, as though the words didn't want to come out. "I suspect she is punishing me for past wrongs." My attempt to laugh was quickly stifled by a sharp pain from my broken nose.

"If that be the case Malcolm, I am sure you deserve it." I was beginning to like Janet. She has a sassy sense of humour and was certainly pleasing to the eyes, but I had to be careful of that hulking brute of a highlander hovering nearby.

"I'll be back at supper with another bowl of porridge. Now go back to bed and rest as Elspeth instructed." She was smirking knowing how much I hated porridge and how unlikely it was that I'd stay in bed. Doctors make the worst patients. "I am her obedient thrall and will do as commanded." I could hear her laughing heartily as she left, then silence filled the room to the brim and my spirits sank though the floor. I didn't want to be alone now, and to make matters worse even Henry was gone. I didn't know I would miss him so much. Henry was a constant presence of happiness and my home seemed lifeless without him. I was feeling sorry for myself, still in considerable pain and looking like a ghoul with bandages and bruises everywhere. Elspeth had done a commendable job repairing me and I wisely refrained from second guessing her. My kidney was the remaining major issue. There was blood in my urine and pain emanating from that area. I hoped it would resolve itself in a few days, but there was the risk of permanent damage and not much could be done. It was a good thing he kicked me on one side only. I must thank him one day. Elspeth's recommendation of bed rest and a bland diet free of meat and alcohol until the bleeding stopped was appropriate but hard to bear. I couldn't just sit here for days, and a wee dram to dull the pain surely wouldn't go amiss?

I rose slowly from the kitchen table and immediately remembered why I should be in bed. Fortunately, the cask of whisky was close by. I'm not much of a drinker, but at times it is a welcome friend. I poured a large mug and retreated to my study. Janet had replenished the wood in the fireplace, so it was burning cheerfully, it's warmth surrounding me as the whisky warmed my innards. It wasn't long before I was nodding in my chair and I welcomed a fitful sleep when it came.

* * *

Elspeth shook me awake. "Malcolm, have you bathed in whisky?"

I'd just been having one of those dreams about being unable to move while those around were crying for help.

"Let me up!" I thought I cried out, and for a few seconds, I was in that confusing boundary between realities.

"I think you spilled your whisky. You smell like a distillery. Wake up Malcolm!" She lifted my head to help me focus and I faced that disapproving look women give.

"I am awake, damn it!" I glanced down and could see the mug on my lap and felt the embarrassing dampness between my legs.

"I can see you are not a responsible adult and cannot be left alone." She laughed, enjoying my discomfort. "I am sorry, I just couldn't resist, but you should have gone to bed and refrained from drink."

"Aye, you have me there, but Janet was just here with her gourmet meal."

"Nay that was hours-ago. Come let me help you out of those clothes and to bed before you catch fire." She pulled me out of the chair and into my bedroom and turned her back as I undressed and put on a knee-length linen nightshirt. I settled uncomfortably in bed, pillows propped against hurting back.

She sat on the chair beside my bed and looked at me expectantly. "Shall I read a story to put you to sleep?" She must have noticed how painful it was for me to laugh, and sat there primly with the mischievous look of an apprentice torturer.

"Aye, please read the story of how Lady Elspeth, the witch of Skye, ends up burned at the stake." I may be weak, but I could still fight back...well, a little.

She choked, then laughed lightly. "Ah, now that is a good story, but for another day. I have put a draught of laudanum by your bed, should you need it. Go back to sleep now Malcolm." She hummed softly to herself as she tucked me in. I closed my eyes. I vaguely remember feeling something tumble across my cheek and Elspeth touching the flesh around my eyes. I think she rose and touched me quickly on the forehead as she murmured, "You are a very foolhardy man."

I couldn't argue with that, considering my state.

"Janet will be back with your supper, but keep your lecherous hands off her or Cawdie will finish the job of killing you." The last I heard was a mumbled complaint about being too short, as her dress caught on the door knob on the way out.

Janet did indeed bring more porridge for supper, but this time included a sliced apple coated with honey. Life wasn't all bad, and she was good company for an hour telling me about life in Skye and the friends she missed. She was one of those people who are pleasant to be with and easy on the eyes; but Elspeth was quite wrong, I had no intention of further complicating my life at this point, and the risk of being dismembered by a claymore-wielding highlander deranged by jealousy had little appeal.

* * *

I heard his steps on waking in the morning, then saw him tentatively peek into my bedroom. "Tis Jocki, sir." He chirped too happily. He was young and from the look of him could use a bath, and new clothes. I thought I'd seen him hanging around the fishing village.

"What do you want, Jocki?" I swung my legs over to get out of bed, assuming he needed medical help.

"Lady Elspeth did send me, sir...err...ta help ya."

"She did, did she?" I was feeling somewhat better after having slept most of the past day and night, but in no mood for her practical jokes, if that was her aim. "Then fetch some hot water for the basin."

"Aye, sir." The boy scampered to the basin and took the pitcher.

"There might be some warm water over by the fire. Stoke the fire up too while you're at it. Does your mother know you are here?"

"Aye, sir, and Lady Elspeth said you'd pay." He looked at me expectantly hoping it was true.

I knew there must be a catch, but in this case, didn't mind at all. "I can use the help, that's for certain, and I shall pay, but no thieving, ye ken?"

"Aye sir. I be true and honest."

"We shall see about that, won't we? Now stop staring at me like I'm a monster! Take that pile of clothes over to Aggie for repairs and cleaning when you're done with the fire, and here, buy some new clothes and wash yourself, I don't want an urchin working here." I flipped him a coin and it made me smile as a look of wonder lit his dirty face. I guess this was Elspeth's idea of helping us both, and not a bad one at that.

"You can sleep in Mrs. Simpson's bed in the attic. But keep it clean or she'll have your hide!"

"Ah weel, sir"

"One more thing, Jocki. Can you read and write?"

"Ah be learnin'. Ah kin read some."

"Then you must work on that to be useful and a proper gentleman." I smiled in encouragement. "Now off you go!"

After Jocki left I stripped nightshirt and bandages and washed as best I could. I was a wreck, but alive. There were large bruises on my lower back and likely cracked ribs and an unknown amount of kidney damage. Elspeth had wrapped my ribs well and I replaced it with fresh, but decided to do without the head bandage protecting my nose. The bleeding had stopped, and it was swollen and bruised but otherwise straight enough and I could breathe properly.

The opposition had made a major tactical error in letting me live. I suppose I'd created just enough doubt to stay their hand, but if they'd killed me, I only had an ailing father, an absent brother, and a few friends interested enough to avenge me, unlikely in any case since it had been difficult to penetrate their conspiracy. My options were limited. I could back off, but that would expose my colleagues even more. I knew Young and the rest wouldn't quit even if I pulled out. It might give them pause, but I knew they were fully committed. An alternative was to ignore their threats and proceed as planned, but that would only be inviting more abuse and it was unlikely the experiment would be completed. The only viable option I could see was to go on the offensive; push them back on their heels just enough to complete our experiment. The main risk was that it could escalate into an even bigger conflict.

I'm far from heroic and live the good life, but this was leaving me no choice. At least we had identified one of the major leaders in their group and could use that to good advantage. I still believed Turnbull must be involved somehow, but had no proof. The opposition seemed to be a coalition of religious and medical people united by common cause. All this was going through my mind as I dressed. I knew I was in no condition to take on any further conflict, and there were only a few days left before the start of the experiment to bolster our alliance. We needed more friends, especially those with power and influence, and I had to be very careful my desire for revenge didn't distract from what we'd set out to do: find a cure for smallpox.

I finished tying my hair back while looking at my ruined face in the mirror. I was dressed in a dark blue brocade waistcoat with brown silk vest and trousers, quite stylish, I'll admit. It's amazing how looking good makes one feel-good, well, a bit better anyway. I decided to start the day by renting a horse and carriage from Daniel.

I was too sore to ride or walk any distance. I quickly scrawled a note with tasks for Jocki and was happy to greet the chill salt air of dear old Torrport.

The carriage Daniel rented me was a two-wheeled gig with padded seating for two and a place for my bag on the floor, all in the open air. It was light and easy to pull, and he'd harnessed Gracie to it. She seemed to recognize me despite my altered look and gave a whinny as I stroked her side before climbing aboard.

It wasn't long before I spotted Elspeth trudging up the hill, clutching her medical bag in one hand and trying to keep her hood in place against the wind with the other.

"Fancy a lift, little girl?" I must have looked like every mother's worst nightmare.

She looked up and grimaced. "Oh, for the love of all that is holy, what are you doing out here? Do I have to tie you in bed?"

I laughed, in pain again. "Maybe next time. Get up. We need to talk." It turns out she was on the way to see a man about a delicate problem in his nether parts, and wondered if I'd like to consult.

On the way, I quickly reviewed the state of our smallpox experiment. "I could use your help in Edinburgh. McLaren may be overwhelmed. There will be ten of us. I have that new fellow coming here as locum physician in a few days, so your work will be reduced, and he hasn't experienced the pleasures of smallpox, so is of no use to us in Edinburgh." She sat quietly, listening with head tilted, hood opened on my side.

She turned to look at me. "I may have to return from time to time. Twenty days is too long to leave some of my patients." I knew she especially was referring to Julianne's bairn.

We were slowing now as Gracie struggled up the steep part of the hill. I didn't push her, we had plenty of time. "I understand and that's why I hired this horse and gig for the month. You can use it as you wish."

"That is considerate, Malcolm, thank you." She smiled then added, "And all I have to do is take care of ten sick doctors for three weeks in addition to my full schedule here?" She laughed mocking me.

"Not at all, Lady Elspeth. You must care for my father too, since that is where you will be staying in Edinburgh." I tried not to laugh along with her in deference to my aching lower back and throbbing nose.

"As you wish, Malcolm, and it will be good to go shopping in the city with Janet too."

I reined Gracie in front of the patient's home. It was one of those newer townhouses half-way up the hill behind the port.

"One more thing." She was already out of the gig, then turned back to hear. "We...err, I can really use Cawdie...in Edinburgh. I mean as a warrior." I hated asking this. It was humiliating to have to beg for protection.

"Ah, poor Malcolm, of course my warrior will defend you. Don't be afraid." She flipped her hood back regally and knocked on the door, all the while humming happily to herself. I could only sigh and endure.

A large raw-boned man opened the door. He was dressed all in black and had a long black beard turning grey around the mouth, and eyes like charcoal in snow. Elspeth said she was here with Doctor Forrester to see Sir Ross. The man said nothing but opened the door fully to let us in. Elspeth had briefed me on the way and I thought I was prepared, but the smell almost made me gag, and I'm not one to be squeamish. It was a foul combination of excrement and herbal poultice. The manservant must have been well-paid. I saw Sir Ross Campbell as we entered the salon. He was laying on his side on a chaise by the fireplace.

"Good day, Sir Ross!" Elspeth went and knelt in front of him and smiled radiantly. "I have brought Sir Malcolm, as promised."

Sir Ross lurched awake and pushed himself up off the chaise pillow. "Forgive me, Lady Elspeth, I must have fallen asleep. I don't rest well at night and when it comes, I'm grateful."

"That is understandable. Now let us help you." She took his hand in hers and guided him upright, so he was sitting but supported by pillows on one side.

"Sir Ross, I'm Malcolm Forrester, the physician here at Torrport, and Lady Elspeth has reviewed your condition with me. How are you feeling?" There were chairs on either side of the chaise and I pulled one near while observing him closely.

"My man Gregor has been applying the poultice and cleaning as ordered and he says the swelling is going down. I feel somewhat better." He smiled weakly.

"Aye, that is the first step, but you may need surgery. I would like us to have a look today, then we can decide what needs to be done. If that is acceptable, we can do it now." I trusted Elspeth's diagnosis. She seemed reasonably competent, considering, but before referring him for surgery, I had to see for myself.

"That will be fine, Sir Gregor, help me up and to my bed."

"He needs to be on his stomach with pillows under to raise his buttocks." I hoped his manservant understood my meaning, but he just gave a dour look.

"Oh, Gregor has done this, many times, doctor." He chuckled and pulled down his trousers and braies, then assumed the correct position.

I sat beside him on the bed and waved for Elspeth to join us on the other side. His bottom was typical of a man of his age and build, so it wasn't easy prying the cheeks apart to have a proper look. I glanced up at Elspeth. She was leaning in. "What do you think?"

She raised a small handkerchief to her face briefly, then must have thought better of it and replied. "The swelling and redness are reduced. I can see the fistula more clearly now. It is not as large as it seemed at first when it was so swollen."

I pointed while pulling one buttock to the side. "I can see one fistula, there on the left of his anus. The hole is about one-half inch in diameter. He will need surgery to close it. Do you agree?"

She nodded. "I do. It will not heal without it."

"I assume you have done a lot of riding, Sir Ross?" I needed more background to better help him.

"Oh indeed, it seems I have spent half my life in the saddle traveling throughout northern Russia developing my fur trade connections." He said with voice muffled by the pillow.

"I gathered as much. Once we've solved this problem we will address the issue of preventing saddle sores, so this doesn't recur."

"That will be welcome, Doctor, although the days of extended trips are past, thankfully."

I looked up at the brooding manservant standing nearby. "Dress him and bring him back to the salon."

While waiting for Sir Ross to return, I noticed a large Russian samovar on a table on the far side of the room. It was made of silver, finely engraved, ornate, and with a charcoal burner. There were also rich furs piled on another table; some were dark brown-black and others white, perhaps sable and ermine. I was intrigued. Meanwhile Elspeth was entranced with a beautifully crafted cabinet containing an extensive household of miniature furniture, complete with diminutive occupants.

"A baby-house!" she exclaimed and smiled at Sir Ross, so brilliantly that he blinked. "I did not see it when I was last here!"

"I see you have noticed my treasures." Sir Ross picked up one of the small figures to show her. Look at this workmanship. Is it not divine?"

"Oh, yes, the clothing is quite intricate, isn't it?" She smoothed an invisible wrinkle from the tiny skirt. "I have a small baby-house too, though not so grand as yours. I would enjoy showing it to you." She was admiring a doll that looked dressed for the royal court, complete with white powdered wig.

I cleared my throat. "Shall we discuss your problem, Sir Ross?"

Elspeth stared at me. "I will be pleased to come and see your collection at a more convenient time, but Doctor Forrester is right, we need to decide how we can help you."

I glared at her. "Thank you, Doctor MacLeod, but I will decide on appropriate treatments." She didn't like that. I could tell by the set in her mouth and stillness of her body that she was upset, but she was disrespecting me by assuming we were equals. She would never be accepted by the College because of her sex and needed to be reminded of her place.

"Sir Ross, I assure you that the fistula will not heal on its own, and without surgery the result will be your continued misery and an early death should it become infected.

I am sorry to have to tell you this. I believe you should see a surgeon as soon as it can be arranged. I have neither the training nor equipment to perform this surgery here. It has attendant risks, but I will find you the best surgeon in Scotland to perform it."

He had settled on his chaise and pillow again. "I was prepared for that outcome, and I have no desire to live like this anymore. Arrange it then and I will pay whatever it takes."

Elspeth was staring straight ahead, still, like a mannequin. I needed her cooperation, but without control. "Do you agree with our decision Lady Elspeth?"

"Of course, Doctor Forrester. It will be as you wish." She went over to Sir Ross and touched him gently on the arm. "Please invite me for tea. I truly would love to see your collection."

"Then do come over once I am over this dreadful surgery." The two of them inexplicably seemed to have bonded over dolls, of all things.

* * *

I met up with Elspeth outside a few minutes later after reaffirming instructions concerning the washes and poultices with Gregor. She was rubbing Gracie's nose and speaking in whispers. We got on the gig and she leaned her head close, said in a voice so soft it was like a breath, I *am* a physician, Malcolm." Then her voice took on a harder edge, "And I don't give a damn what your College thinks."

I pulled Gracie around and we set off. We said nothing to each other for several minutes, the tension palpable, even Gracie glancing back a few times, no doubt wondering.

"I must visit the Laird now, Lady Elspeth. You are not welcome there, so I must drop you somewhere." I slowed Gracie at the crossroads that lead to the castle.

"It seems I am not welcome anywhere. I will walk. Do not put yourself out on my accord." She jumped down even before we came to a full stop. I sat there for a moment wondering why Elspeth was behaving so badly, then realized that her emotional reaction was further proof that women cannot be competent physicians.

* * *

I arrived at the castle several minutes later. Captain Spence was in the bailey drilling his men. There seemed to be more of them than usual and they were equipped with gleaming new long-barrel flintlock muskets. He was putting them through the load-kneel-aim-fire drill as I tied Gracie to the post. Spence waved then pointed to the opposite corner of the bailey where I knew the armoury was located.

136

Laird MacDuff was looking in a crate being opened by two of his men.

"Be sure to count them and check each one for defects. I'll not be cheated this time." He heard me come in and smiled broadly. "Let me guess. You ran into a door?" He was referring to my ruined face.

"Something like that. More like sticking my nose where it didn't belong." I was here to ask for his help again.

"That would've been my second guess, and yes I've already heard what happened. You need to stay in Torrport where you belong." He stood there smiling condescendingly with large hands on hips.

The men were taking muskets out of the crates. They were greased and packed in straw. "Oh, I would love to stay put, but there is that smallpox experiment, remember?" I could see the markings on one of the muskets. "French?"

"Aye, the best, from Rouen, recently liberated."

I wasn't sure what he meant by *liberated*, but let it pass. "I can use some help, Sir Douglas, if you can spare some men. They may come after me and I'm in no condition to defend myself right now."

He looked straight in my eyes then, and a few moments passed in silence. "*Alrecht laddie, we will protect ye. Fear nae.*" He'd reverted to his highland accent again. What could I do but accept gracefully?

"Appreciated, my Laird."

"Spence will visit to see what you need. Meanwhile you are welcome to stay here with the men." He must have thought that amusing because he added. "But we have no soft feather beds." He had to get that in that dig, didn't he?

"A word in private." He tilted his head then went out into the bailey. I followed. On this end, it was crowded with an assortment of livestock and stacked supplies. He found a corner and leaned against the wall waiting for me.

"What of my wife?" he asked, standing there with arms crossed. A curious goat came too close and he gave it a gentle kick.

"I can meet her today, if she's available and doesn't mind my looks."

"Then do so. I want this resolved. Our marriage has chilled, and I want it warmed or finished."

I could see the look of determination was real and I had better help before it was too late. "Do you want to stay with her?"

"Aye, but she needs to be a proper wife and bear me some heirs."

"What of Lady Julianne?"

He smiled briefly then came closer and took my arm, and in a whisper said: "Malcolm, she is my kin and I am sworn to protect her. You have no idea what this is truly about, suffice to say I have never touched that girl. You have my word. I have heard the malicious rumours too and they are laughable, I assure you."

I wasn't certain what he meant, but I'd assumed the baby was his. "Did you find any evidence Lady Julianne was poisoned?"

"We have a few suspects, but no proof of any kind. I cannot tell you more."

"What of your man Spence. He arrived around the same time as Lady Julianne, did he not?"

"Aye, Malcolm, I hired him through a Jacobite friend in Russia, that is true. He came well-recommended. Do not ask more, you are well out of your depth. You must know that many of us are concerned the English want to annex Scotland. We will never allow it." He let go of my arm and stood solidly facing me and I knew then he was not playing at being a warrior chieftain. "Now go see my wife and help us."

"I will see her now, my Laird."

I bowed crisply and as I turned to go he added in a gruff commanding voice: "I want Lady Julianne back here as soon as she can travel, and what you saw in the armoury..." He made the sign of closing lips with his fingers. I got the message.

* * *

Lady Margaret lived in the castle keep on the far side of the bailey. It was three stories high with a battlement on the roof bristling with cannon. The main floor was the castle kitchen. Her apartment was reached by a stone staircase to the side leading to the second floor. On the way, I had time to think about what he'd said. I'd been running into far too many Russians and Scots Jacobites having recently arrived for it to be coincidence, and then there was the large arms shipment and many new recruits. Something was brewing. But why would the Laird confide in the son of a Lord so publicly supportive of the English? Did he want me to pass this information along to Father, or was he just naïve? I try to stay out of these political controversies, but these days it is in the air we breathe. I hated being torn between loyalties to family and my adopted town, but in truth, I would never side with the Jacobites. The idea that the English would allow a Catholic king to sit on the throne of Scotland was absurd, especially while they were at war with France and Spain. Any Jacobite military threats in Scotland would be perceived as treason and crushed mercilessly. I did not want that for Torrport, or Scotland.

Lady Margaret's handmaid let me in. The rooms were richly appointed in dark wood paneling with many colourful tapestries depicting mythical and religious scenes. Lady Margaret was at her loom and stood to greet me. She was strikingly noble in bearing and dress, tall, buxom with olive skin and lustrous raven black hair. She waited silently for me to approach.

"I was punched."

"Yes, I heard." She smiled more warmly than I expected.

"Apologies for my appearance. The Laird has asked me to see you."

"He has told me."

"He wants me to see if there is anything I can do to help you have children."

"Yes"

She wasn't being very helpful. "Can we sit by the fire and discuss this?"

"By all means. Rachel, bring us some tea and biscuits."

I waited for them to finish arranging cups and plates. "Lady Margaret, I may ask some sensitive questions. Please forgive me."

She sat calmly holding her tea cup. "I know my husband will soon put me away, and to be honest, I will be relieved. I hate it here. It is no place for a lady. God knows I've tried to make it a home, but he prefers the company of his men and whores. But...if I do not bear children, he is as much to blame."

I didn't want to get into finger pointing. "Tell me about your health. Have you been well?"

"Do I not look healthy?" I could see her back arch and chin lift as she said it.

"You are a most desirable woman, Lady Margaret, but these are questions I must ask. Have there been any changes recently?"

She blushed. "Well, yes, but it matters not. He doesn't use it anyway."

"Tell me about it, please. Your health is important regardless of his needs."

That was the key that turned the lock and she leaned back and eyes glazed. "Thank you for caring, Doctor Forrester. Um, yes my privates have been itchy lately and the smell has been a bit odd."

"How do you mean?"

"Like the smell of fresh bread. I thought at first it was the baking smells from below." She laughed nervously.

"I see. Do you bathe often?"

She looked as though I'd asked her to admit a sin. "No, of course not! Everyone knows bathing causes sickness."

"Lady Margaret, that simply is not true. Cleanliness is essential for good health and conducive to ardor too. I can tell you from personal experience that a clean, good-smelling woman is irresistible." She sat there fidgeting then looked at her handmaid for support.

"If you are sure, doctor, but are you suggesting it is my fault? If so I must tell you he spends too much time at that foul tavern and comes home smelling like a goat. If I must make sacrifices, then he must too. Is that not fair?" Her brown eyes were fiery in defiance.

I smiled in agreement. "I believe we can find a middle ground. Here is what I would like you to do. First, you need to see Lady Elspeth. She's very good with female problems. Tell her about the yeasty smell. I know you two had a falling out recently.

This is an opportunity to heal that problem as well. She's sorely needed in Torrport and you should make her welcome, so start by asking her to help you. Do you agree?"

"If you wish, doctor, but she was very unwise to have come here hurling insults and accusations. What did she expect me to do?"

"I know, and it will not happen again, I assure you." I hoped that was true and reminded myself to caution Elspeth, when we were on speaking terms again.

"That problem, if left unattended can adversely affect your health, so it must be treated regardless." She nodded, then I continued. "Once it's resolved, I want you to bathe at least every other day and before you have sex with your husband. Use clean warm water and soap, then rinse with cool water. Your handmaid should scrub you well, and be sure to include your hair and privates. When you are finished bathing, dab some perfume here and there, but not too much."

"I know how to bathe, sir, I have seen it done. I will do my best, but it frightens me."

I rose to go. "You'll enjoy the results, I assure you. You must make it, so your husband will not want to go elsewhere. Understand?" Looking down at her, I saw a vulnerable woman trying to be all the world expected of her, but fearing the worst, that she was barren and now risking illness to save her marriage.

"I'll go and speak with the Laird before I leave."

"Doctor, I do love him and will welcome him back to my bed, and he will always be my Laird." Tears were starting to well in her eyes as I reached the door and turned back.

"One more thing, Lady Margaret."

"Yes?" She was wiping her eyes with an embroidered handkerchief.

"Lady Julianne has recovered fully, so no harm done. You can tell me now: did you poison her?" I wanted to see her reaction in this moment of weakness.

"Me?" Her head jerked up. "How dare you say that! I was scared to death! I thought I was the target, and she poisoned by accident. I think we ate the same that day."

Her face told the truth and I believed her. "Then tell me who might have done it."

She turned her head away. "I do not know, but there were only a few who could have. I was feeling rejected and unloved. He was always doting on Julianne too, so I assumed the baby was his. She just turned up several months-ago, from Russia of all places. My Laird didn't explain, only that he was her ward and to make her welcome. Please try to understand how I must have felt, and hence my reaction."

"He was insensitive to your needs, I agree, but I think he is a good man, nonetheless."

"He is, but I wish he would think of me sometimes." She paused a moment. "Doctor, that man Spence came here about the same time as Julianne. He is now my handmaid's husband, but I don't trust him, he is up to something and I fear he is a bad influence, but what can I do, I am only a woman?" She lowered her eyes and I bowed.

"I bid you a good day, Lady Margaret."

I didn't believe the Laird would poison his wife to be rid of her. That was not his style. If he wanted her gone, he would just send her away and take another woman on the side, and there always was the possibility of adopting a bastard or close relative as heir. No, it wasn't him, but I could understand her paranoia and jealousy. I was worried too about the new arms and recruits. Was Spence behind this, and what if anything did it have to do with Julianne? Was it a coincidence they both arrived at about the same time from Russia?

There were too many unanswered questions and my back and nose were both pulsing with pain. I needed to get home to lay down and have some relief before I buckled over. One last stop to see the Laird before heading home with Gracie. He was back in the armoury instructing several men on how to clean the new muskets with oil and rags.

"*Dornt pit tay much gin oil oan th' rag, Jamie.*" The boy wasn't much more than seventeen, tall and lean with sunken cheeks. The highland boys are keen to join the clan militia. At least they'd have enough to eat and a warm place to sleep.

"*Push th' oiled wad doon ben th' barrel wi' th' rod, loch thes.*" I watched as he patiently showed them each step, and now I clearly understood why he used his highland accent. I could see it on their young faces. He was one of them, their Laird, handsome and strong, and they would follow him to hell if need be.

When he finished, he came over, wiping hands on a clean rag. "These boys will be effective when trained."

I decided not to ask why they were being trained. One problem at a time, if you please. "I spoke with Lady Margaret. She has agreed to certain changes I think you will appreciate." I briefly described them, and I could see a smile gradually form on his rugged face. Then he clapped me heartily on the shoulder, sending a shock through my back. "Now my Laird, there are some changes she has requested as well." He listened to them without derision or disagreement, a good sign.

"Malcolm, I will bathe as well, if it pleases her, and I seldom avail myself in the tavern, they are a last resort, at best. I am there often on business, not pleasure, and she has no reason to be jealous of Julianne. It would have been preferable had she trusted me on this. Now I suppose I must tell her. It matters not anyway since the wee bairn is dead."

Did he not know the baby was alive and thriving? I must tread carefully now.

"You must have known she assumed the baby was yours."

"Aye and I am sorry she suffered not knowing the truth. That bairn could have set us free, but alas." He looked at the ceiling, perhaps offering a prayer or a wish, and I stood there speechless.

* * *

It was a torturous trip back to the stable. His words wracking my thoughts as the gig did to my battered body. What could he have meant? Was the baby of such great importance that his existence could threaten the state? Julianne likely was in Russia when the baby was conceived, but who was the father? We needed to find out before the Laird realized he was still alive, and I had enough problems to deal with already.

I left Gracie in Daniel's care and as quickly as I could, made my way home. My mind was fixated on a jar of willow bark on the lower-right of the apothecary shelf. I needed it, and some rest desperately, but when I entered I was surprised to hear voices coming from the examination room.

"*If we confess our sins, he is faithful and just and will forgive us our sins and purify us from all unrighteousness.*" I knew the voice, it was the Reverend Robertson. I wasn't in the mood for a visit, but I did need to see him, so I grabbed the willow bark and got back in time to hear Jocki trying to repeat what he'd heard.

"Jist an' will forgife us uir sins..." He stopped as soon as I entered and quickly jumped off the examination bed.

I chuckled at the sight of them, Jocki looking like he'd been caught stealing, and the Reverend with that sweet look he has when reading the Holy Book. "That was good Jocki. Don't mind me, I just need to lay down." I stuffed some willow bark in my cheek and flopped on the examination bed on my stomach to take the stress off my lower back. "Apologies Father, but I have been having some tests from God."

He closed the Bible then placed it in an embroidered cloth. "I am not so sure your tests are from God, Malcolm. You attract them like bees to honey."

"Aye, so it seems." I didn't feel like laughing, but my life at times was as laughable to me as to others. "Jocki make us some tea and bring something to eat, if you can find anything edible back there."

"Aye, aye, sir."

"And take those filthy boots off."

He slipped them off quickly and ran to the kitchen. I rolled to my good side to face the Reverend. "I guess you heard."

He shrugged. "Everyone knows."

"I need your help Father, that goes without saying, but what should be done is the question." I raised myself on one elbow, resting my head in my hand.

"Malcolm, since we last met, I've been speaking with friends in the Church and others, to find out what's going on and what can be done to resolve this peaceably. I'm going to be forthright with you, understand?" The sweet look had been replaced by one of a stern father.

"I want a resolution too, Father, but there are limits."

"I told you before that there is a small faction of those in the Church and in your College who oppose your attempts to find a cure for smallpox. They have valid reasons, whether you agree or not."

"I know, Father, but violence is not acceptable. They have not the moral or legal authority to use force against us."

"Ah, but if it were that simple. Do you not see that these attacks have been mostly aimed at you? I believe there is more to this than your experiment. It's to do with you. It's become personal."

I guess I always knew, the way Turnbull and others spoke to me, and then there was Captain Mackmain. "What do you recommend Father?"

"I will not tell you what to do. Life is made of choices and you must make yours. If you care about finding a cure for smallpox, please consider a path that is less divisive, one that may include removing yourself as an obstacle."

"I have considered that many times. I do not lead out of choice, but necessity."

"And there is one other issue: your lover in Edinburgh."

"Aye, Gwen."   I smiled when thinking of her, then remembered Captain Mackmain's comment just before he broke my nose. *Stay away from Gwen.*

"What does Gwen have to do with this?"

"Malcolm, you know her husband died under suspicious circumstances. Captain Mackmain may have been involved and it is well-know he wanted her, but she chose freedom, and men like you instead. Then you used her to spy, then confronted him, and are astonished when you are beaten-up."

"I see. I guess I am naïve, ignorant and abrasive, and Elspeth said I was foolhardy too, so you can add that one." I sighed and laid my head back down.

"Malcolm, God uses people like you when he wants change. You are his agent. I truly believe that, but you must try to be a wise agent if you want His work to bear fruit."

"I will try, Father, I will try."

He stood slowly, arching his back, then came to me and placed his warm hand on the side of my face. "I will go to Edinburgh tomorrow to see the Bishop. He has close contacts in the other faiths too. We will try to help keep the peace as our Saviour would have."

Jocki returned with tea and some stale cakes. All I wanted was rest.

"Jocki, help me remove his boots and waistcoat and cover him with a blanket."

I lay there and let them.

"Rest now Malcolm, and Jocki, let's go finish our lesson on forgiveness."

The willow bark was having its effect and the pain was finding a new victim to torment. I was so tired I was having trouble thinking, but anxious thoughts of the Laird and baby were the last to leave.

"Father," I said in a whisper.

He was placing the blanket over me, then stopped. "Aye, Malcolm, I am here."

"Russians." I may have said more, and he may have replied, but I don't remember. I was asleep in minutes.

* * *

I knew it was early evening. The golden rays were slanting in my front window off the port waters. I heard a rustling behind me and rolled over to see her holding a small container up to my face.

"I will make you beautiful again." She was grinning and shaking the container, which I knew from its shape was full of writhing black things.

"Elspeth?" I rose to one elbow and shook the sleep from my head.

"Lay back, Malcolm, and I will put some leeches on those ugly black eyes. They will suck the pooled blood and help them heal." She placed the jar on the table beside the bed as I lay back.

This was awfully kind considering how I treated her when last, we met. I decided to try being a kinder, gentler Malcolm, as the good Reverend suggested. "Elspeth, I am sorry... for what I said."

She smiled at me while removing a leech with forceps. "No need to apologize. I know perfectly well what I am up against. Now close your eyes while I place these creatures."

"I know, but it was unkind of me nonetheless."

"It was, yes."

I felt nothing but a cool bit of slime under each eye. "Now stay there for about thirty minutes. Once they are attached, they won't slide off. I'll come back to remove them."

"Please stay. We need to talk, urgently."

"Ah, I thought there was a reason you were being nice." She smiled and shook her head. "Well what is it this time?"

I sighed. "Where do I start?"

I went over it as concisely as I could over the next half hour, my meeting with Margaret and the Laird and the Reverend. We needed to pool our knowledge. She had many questions as did I. Meanwhile, Jocki arrived to replenish the fireplaces for the night.

"I agree that the symptoms likely correspond with arsenic poisoning, but that is rare in Scotland, more a problem on the continent," I mused.

Elspeth shrugged. "It was all too common in Italy when I was there, and we know she was sick right after having tea and sweetmeats with Lady Margaret, so it was likely something she ate then. Rachel prepared the food but why would she want to harm

Julianne? Was she doing it for Lady Margaret? Now there you have a motive! She was jealous of Julianne and afraid the Laird would put her aside for someone who could give him a son.

"Good points, but I did ask Margaret about it and she denied poisoning Julianne. Unless there is solid proof, I think we can rule her out"

"Why? Just because she says so? Malcolm, that does not eliminate her."

"Perhaps not, just my opinion, but Rachel's husband Captain Spence is another matter. I don't trust him."

"Nor do I. Still, Malcolm, why would Spence want Julianne dead? Maybe Julianne repulsed him? According to Aggie, the laundress, he is a dishonest brute with wandering hands. She warned me about him and I witnessed his cruelty first-hand.

I didn't understand. "First-hand?"

She started to blush. "Well sort of. It was a close friend. Tam Morrison. He and Jocki were there with Cawdie and saw Spence striking Gilly, one of my patients. She was with child and lost the babe. Now that is cause. Mayhap not the babe, but the beating." She looked down at her hands clenched in the fabric of her skirt. "I could understand that."

"Mmm. What seems to link most of the players in this drama is Russia and the Jacobites. Julianne, Spence, Ross and Gregor, recently arrived from Russia and all know the Laird. Curious, isn't it?"

"I can see Gregor as an assassin, but I don't think Sir Ross would have the strength." Her words trailed off and I could see her piecing things together. "It may not be a coincidence, Malcolm."

"Well let's continue and see what else we can discover."

Elspeth nodded. "I will be happy to see Lady Margaret about her problem. It doesn't sound too serious and if we can mend our friendship, I would appreciate it too. There are many in the castle that need what I offer."

"Do you know what the Laird meant when he told me about the importance of the baby?"

"No, I don't, and that worries me too, Julianne intends to baptize and name the baby soon, and if she does, the results are unpredictable. I will speak to her and try to find out more. The wee bairn is growing well."

"I wonder too if this has to do with the arms build-up?"

"Perhaps, and I have direct knowledge of how easy it is to smuggle goods in and out of Torrport."

"You do?" I raised my head to look at her and realized I had little knowledge of what she was up to.

"Never mind, Malcolm." She laughed softly.

We looked at each other for a few moments, then she said. "But I think I know of a way we can find out more about the smuggling. That may be the link."

"And how do you intend to do this?" I lay there worried about what she was going to say next.

"Jocki"

"Jocki?"

"Yes, he knows everything that's going on down there. Why don't we ask him?"

I shouted for him and was pleased to see he'd removed his boots this time. He looked at me lying there with leeches on my face and grinned. Elspeth grinned too and placed a finger on her lips cautioning him.

"Here, boy, a coin for your work and advice. Now tell us what you know about smuggling."

"I ken wee, sir" He looked at Elspeth for permission.

"Tell us, Jocki, and don't worry we will not reveal our source." She smiled at him warmly and took his hand.

It turned out he knew a lot more than we did.

"All folk knows, but mammy won't let me go there. Ah only ken where the trail starts from the village to the cave."

"There is a cave at the end of a trail from the village?"

"Aye, sir."

I flew off the bed and barked at Elspeth. "Get these damned things off my face and fetch your cloak!", then I grabbed my boots and commanded: "Jocki, show us where that trail starts."

Elspeth removed her pets gently from around my eyes. A quick glance at my mirror showed that they had served their purpose. Most of the bruising was gone.

It was late, and Daniel had gone home, so we hitched Gracie to the gig ourselves. She looked surprised to be removed from whatever horses do at night, but excited about a new adventure. I had to hold her back from breaking into a trot as we sliced through the streets filled with people making their way home for supper.

Elspeth wrapped her green cloak around Jocki and pulled him close for warmth, the two of them equally matched in size, if nothing else. She'd objected to this little foray on the grounds of my injuries and foolhardy nature, but I assured her that I was well enough for a wee hike, and all we would do was have a look and no harm in that, surely. She acquiesced on the condition that Jocki not accompany us on the trail and that we would leave if threatened.

The sky was clear and the temperature dropping fast. We'd remembered to bring a few torches, although I prefer to let eyes adjust to darkness naturally. We would use the torches only if we were lost. The fishing village was a few miles from the stables, across the small peninsula that makes up Torrport, and we arrived at the outskirts as the last of the day's light was failing.

The fishing village is a major source of employment. The waters of the Firth of Forth and North Sea are rich in seafood including cod, haddock, oysters and salmon.

These were harvested seasonally and processed at the village for shipment as far away as Glasgow and the Continent. The oysters harvested in the fall were especially prized in France and had brought in a considerable amount of cash until the Royal Navy blockade put an end to it. We can't have wealthy Parisiennes enjoying themselves at our expense. Wars have unintended consequences.

The spring salmon catch was in full-swing and the village smelled of it. The fish were brought in late-afternoon and gutted and filleted by dozens of lassies working under covered sheds by the docks. The inedible parts were scraped into the harbour, to the delight of flocks of seabirds. That was the scene when we arrived and tied Gracie to a post near the tavern.

Jocki ducked in to let his mother know he was home and would be back shortly. I'd given him a coin that no doubt he'd added to the sum they lived on. Elspeth was standing surveying the village then nudged me.

"Is that Captain Spence I see over by the privy?"

"Looks to be his size and gait, but too hard to tell for certain in this light. Don't worry, we won't be going in the tavern." I smiled at her, but she was less than amused.

Jocki came back wearing a tattered cloak, then pointed down the wharf to a collection of ramshackle homes. "We ur gonnae 'at way."

We saw an old man lighting lanterns on the wharf. There was a din coming from the tavern as we passed, men happy to end the day with a pint or dram, and women trying to make a living serving their needs. The village was set on a cove with a low hill on one side and rocky shore on the other. There was a natural terrace in back, the poor with rough stone cottages on the lower level open to the sea, and those with more coin having built larger stone and stucco houses on the upper terrace. Looming over all was Castle Carraig, formidable and dark on top of the cliffs above.

We picked our way slowly over the flat rocks by the sea in front of the last of the cottages, saying nothing and allowing our eyes to adjust to the growing darkness. Beyond the last cottage was the forest, too rough for farming or building, a jumble of rocks and trees at the base of the castle cliffs.

Jocki stopped as we entered the forest. "Here is the path tae the cave. Dae ye see thes mark oan th' tree? Follaw th' path an' these marks. It isnae far."

The mark looked like a sideways V cut knee high pointing down the trail.

"Thank you Jocki, and if we don't return by tomorrow, let Reverent Robertson know, alright?"

"Ah will, sir. When ye come back, thaur is anither trail tae the reit gonnae the castle. Bide tae the left oan the way back."

"We will remember to stay left, then." I looked over at Elspeth, her face was hidden in her cloak hood. "Are you ready Lady Elspeth?"

"Aye, Malcolm and remember your promise, and Jocki, run along home now."

"Och aye Lady Elspeth. Ah wish ye weel." He vanished in the darkness like a small wraith.

We stood there a minute to get our bearings. The trees were mostly pine with a few oaks interspersed, the canopy thin due to the large rocks that looked to be the result of collapsed cliffs. We knew the shore was to our right, the castle on the left on the height above, and the cave not far ahead. How could we get lost?

"I will lead. Hold my coat-tail and stay close. If you hear or see anything, give a tug. Got it?"

"I don't like the feeling of this Malcolm. We should go back."

"Nonsense, it's only the dark. We are the scariest things out here."

"I don't think so Malcolm, please let us go home."

I sighed, "Go back and stay with Gracie then. I'll return within the hour."

"Nay Malcolm, we are in this together." I could sense the fear and frustration in her voice, but we needed to find out what was going on.

"Then let's go."

We picked our way carefully and silently along the trail. I could barely make out the tree slashes. The trail was rough but had been groomed for use, and it wasn't long before the village lights were gone, and we were alone in the dark with only the sounds of our steps and the soft rustling of trees and enhanced smells of rot and new growth.

I thought we must be getting close, so we slowed our pace even more, stopping to listen often. I was sensing nothing unusual when she tugged on my coat-tail. We stopped to listen carefully and look. Elspeth came close and whispered. "Light ahead." I could not see it. We continued forward another twenty or so steps, and there it was, through the leaves and brush. I motioned for her to crouch. It was too dark to venture off the trail and we couldn't use our torches without being seen. We had to be quiet and careful. In a few minutes, we could see two men standing there in dark relief against the light of a torch held between. Beyond them appeared to be a rise, perhaps the back of the cave. We continued ever closer, and gradually could hear them speaking. It wasn't English or Scots. We stopped, crouching, trying to hear. They seemed to be speaking French, one clearly, the other muffled, accented. We listened for several minutes, focusing completely on their words. The conversation was about a woman. She was very attractive, and it was bad luck and so forth, and they just wanted to go home. Then Elspeth tugged on my coat-tail again. I looked back just in time to hear her scream as a man grabbed her by the throat and another pointed a pistol in my face.

One shouted in French and the two we'd been watching came running.

"*Sur les genoux, les mains derrière le dos.*" I got on my knees with hands behind my back as he ordered. I couldn't see him well.

"We are lost, please don't hurt her. Just tell us how to get back to the village and we'll be on our way." It was worth a try.

The men with the torch arrived. All four were sailors, with tasseled caps, smocks and baggy trousers provided by the ship's slops. They were bare-foot and affected that rolling gait of their kind.

"*Attachez-les et amenez-les à la grotte. Le capitaine décidera.*" The one with the pistol on me seemed to be in charge. My French was poor, but I understood the last part and was relieved they weren't going to slit our throats on the spot. I looked over at Elspeth. She was being tied by a man behind her. Her eyes were full of rage. I whispered, "Sorry".

She blurted, "Oh Malcolm!"

The man smacked her on the side of the head and growled. "*Silencieux!*"

They tied my wrists and blindfolded me with a cloth that smelled of feces, then pulled me up by my hair. "*Leve toi!*" I understood and rose.

I could see the torchlight filtering through the rag and followed it, with a pistol prodding my back. We turned sharply to the left and entered a well-lit area. I could hear men around us, grunting, shuffling, breathing, dropping heavy things on the rock-strewn floor of what I assumed to be the cave. He pushed me forward then said "*Par terre*" and pushed my shoulder down. I assumed he meant to sit on the ground, so I did. A second later, I could feel Elspeth join me. My back was to a hard wall, on my left what smelled like fresh-cut pine. Elspeth scooted closer. I whispered to her. "Get behind me if you can." She pushed her way partly between me and the wall.

We sat quietly waiting. A few men were speaking French, some heavily accented. It sounded like they were going over the inventory of the cargo, so many of this, so many of that, counting what was there. Then one said "*Que ferons-nous de ces deux?*" Another grunted and said something. The first one said: "*Tu les connais?*" We may have been recognized. I could hear one walk to us, the rocks crunching under his feet, and leather creaked as he knelt near me.

There was silence for a moment and I thought I could smell garlic. Then he pulled my blindfold down and I found myself staring into eyes like charcoal in snow.

FOURTEEN

Elspeth – Caves and Caveats

The man who tied my hands behind my back had the pissing evil. I could smell it on his clothing and breath, the sickly-sweet odor of rotting fruit overpowering the stench of unwashed flesh. I wondered if he knew it yet; diabetes is not a good way to die. He took off his discoloured neckcloth and used it to blindfold my eyes. I smelled urine and something musty on it too, and I tried not to think about what other uses it might have been put to.

I was furious with Malcolm, but it had been my choice to come with him. When he apologized I limited my response to "Oh, Malcolm!" That earned me a backhanded blow from my fragrant captor which snapped my head back painfully. I saw Malcolm jerk ineffectually at his bonds as the blow landed. The man pushed me roughly in front of him and we stumbled along a path that alternated between almost level and rough rocks. I could see nothing, so I tried my other senses. Nothing registered except the dank scent of moist earth and decomposing vegetation in the damp cold sea air. After what felt like an eternity, we began descending a steep path over slippery rock. Blind, I would have fallen but for the strong hold of the man leading me. I could hear the surf pounding close enough to spray us with salty drops. We turned left, and after a few steps another change in sound told me we were in enclosed chamber. Movement and men's voices echoed off walls as they bickered among themselves. A heavy hand pushed me down to a sitting position. I could feel Malcolm next to me. He whispered for me to move closer and behind him. I did, scraping my back on the jagged edges of a stone wall. The layers of my skirts did not prevent the dampness from the ground from creeping into me. I pressed as close as I could to Malcolm as much for his warmth as for protection and buried my face in the heat of his back. He smelled of soap and man and safety.

We both kept quiet. The conversation around us became heated, one voice was familiar, and I tried to associate it with a face. Little flickers of light danced at the bottom of the blindfold, and the smell of oil from torches was strong.

Footsteps approached and stopped nearby. Someone helped Malcolm stand. I heard his sharp intake of breath and there was a peculiar lull in the conversation before he began to speak. He was attempting to offer valid reasons to someone about why we were creeping about on the side of the hills at this time of night, none of which impressed his inquisitor. Suddenly I recognised the other man's voice. It was Gregor, and he sounded well beyond annoyed.

"Cease, Forrester. I am not a fool, nor are you. You are meddling in things that do not concern you, and have put both of you in grave danger. We cannot afford to simply let you go. There are those in the village and Torrport, and even other places, who would gladly see us all dancing at the end of a rope should they discover what we are doing."

Why in the name of merciful heaven would Sir Campbell's servant be here with our kidnappers? And questioning us? He said something sharply in French, and awkward hands began to remove my blindfold. I blinked in the sudden light and looked around. Wavering torches illuminated a large cavern. Almost a third of it was filled with long wooden crates stacked neatly, while more stores of crates, kegs and boxes of musket balls were being unloaded on the sand. No wonder we were in trouble. This had to be a smuggler's landing point! I thought of the steep descent we had made earlier. There was no way the long crates could be carried up the path we had used. There must be other ways of moving them to their destinations. The local owlers, a term used for villagers or labourers who needed the illegal nocturnal work, would gladly be involved for the coin. Darkness would provide concealment for small fishing boats, or even daylight might be safe with a layer of fresh fish or sacking covering the illicit load. Stacked along one wall were bags of highland wool undoubtedly destined to be loaded and sent to Rouen, a manufacturing city in France. Next to them, piles of furs and hides, still smelling strongly of the urine used in the tanning process, waited. Since the Wool Act of 1699 had forbidden the export of Scottish wool to foreign markets, smuggling had become widespread. Scots were prevented by law from selling wool to any country but England. As the only buyer, England bought it cheaply, manufactured it and sold it abroad, thus doubling their own profits. The prices paid the Scots who produced the wool were ridiculously low, so the result of the edict was to make it contraband. Smuggling was common along the coast. Torrport was but one small part of the vicious and often bloody game played by the local gentry, magistrates and revenue officers who looked the other way for a fee. For the poor, there was often no other choice. Smuggle or starve. Even the church conveniently overlooked the practice, since every household, from the highest to the lowest, benefitted in some way.

My own personal nemesis stood nearby. I could tell he was nearing the final stages of his illness by his gauntness and the way he frequently gasped for breath. It was the beginning of what physicians called "air hunger" which marked the irrevocable end of the disease. He was extremely thin and the clothes that had been made for a much larger man now hung about him in limp folds. He retied the filthy neckcloth he had used to blindfold me on his raddled neck and moved back, not meeting my eyes. He was obviously one of the smugglers. The others were briskly unloading more boxes and small barrels. The nearby crates I could see well enough to decipher were labeled Rouen. So more than wool were exchanged with that city.

One of the men called to Gregor, gesturing to him with a piece of paper. He stood up, gave us a warning glance, and barked a question at them. They responded by opening one of the barrels...very carefully and very slowly. Packed inside it was another smaller barrel containing a cloth bag of black powder. I could see markings on the outer barrel probably giving manufacturing information and powder type. The men repacked it cautiously and opened a wooden container next. Inside it was a second case made of copper. It too held black powder. I had seen this kind before. They were a newer way of packing the volatile contents, and deemed safer for transporting black powder by ship. Gregor nodded, satisfied, and they began to close the container, again very gently, although the way they did it suggested it was a routine they had performed many times before.

My mouth went dry. All of this must be arms for the Jacobites! Surely the Russians and French were not trying to open a second front in Scotland? The tension among the smugglers was unmistakable. They had just run the English Royal Navy blockade, slipping by the Royal Mary in the dark, their black painted hull and sails invisible in the moonless night. The lights I had seen were signals of some sort. The unloading was almost complete, and many were standing about restlessly in small groups talking sullenly amongst themselves, anxious to be back to the comparative safety of their ship. France and England were enemies. What they were doing here was high treason, and punishable by death.

Two of the men nigh me were discussing smuggled goods of another sort. I had no trouble understanding their language, having learned it when I was but seven years of age, including some of the more colorful idioms. From what I could gather there had been several men and women and two children aboard the ship. The first man objected to bringing women on board. Superstitious dread of females bringing ill luck aboard a ship was still very strong among seamen. Had they not almost been intercepted by the Royal Navy when they came in? The second man retorted by taking a long swig from a flask of his belt and replying in French that "live cargo paid better than the other" and "one of the women was very beautiful even if he could only touch with his eyes." He even kissed his fingers in reverence to the lovely passenger. His disgusted companion muttered a disgruntled expletive and kicked one of the wool bags back into line with its kin. "I wish to get home. I am fatigued with this cold and misbegotten country. I want my pay, a warm bed and a warm woman." He coughed twice, hawked thick yellow phlegm into the sand, and sat down on a nearby barrel either not knowing or not caring that it was labeled black powder. His mate looked at him, raised a shaggy eyebrow and stepped outside away from the crates and kegs to light his pipe.

There was no sign of the *live cargo*, so I assumed they had been landed and sent on their way. There was little chance of knowing from where to where. French, Russian, Jacobites? It could be anyone.

A disturbance by the opening of the cave heralded the arrival of several more men. Malcolm had been silent since Gregor had left us, simply observing as I did, but now he cursed under his breath. The men were from the castle. One of them was Spence. The leader of the smugglers turned away from Gregor and pointed to us, speaking rapidly to him. Spence turned cold expressionless eyes on us and I could read malevolence in them. He made a step toward us, but a large figure blocked his way. Gregor said something in a low voice, and Spence stopped, listened for a moment then pushed by him.

"Well, well. What have we here? Making a late-night call on a patient, were ye?" Spence seemed to change his speech with his company. Now it was the coarse jargon of the smugglers. His eyes flicked from one of us to the other settling on Malcolm. "What, courage man! What thou care killed a cat, thou hast mettle enough in thee to kill care." He quoted the line from Shakespeare with malicious glee.

Malcolm looked pointedly around the cavern and returned the quote with one of his own. "And you must have the gentlemen to haul and draw with the mariner, and the mariner with the gentleman." Spence flushed at the double meaning and his hand strayed toward his sword. Gregor halted the movement with a firm grip on his wrist.

I had to say something. "You would lift your sword to a bound and unarmed man?" My words dripped with scorn. "And if you dispose of us, what will you say to your Laird when your part in this is known, and there is no one to care for his wife or his people. You would bring down the wrath of Malcolm's family? Or that of the clan MacLeod?"

Gregor added, "Nor will Sir Campbell be pleased. He has a certain fondness for the Lady." He paused and bowed to me. "As do I."

The captain of the black ship looked at them as though they had gone mad and spoke vehemently in heavily accented English. "Be ye fools? They must be silenced! Should word of this get out we will all hang together! Kill them! They will make fine food for the fishes in the middle of the sea! No one will ever know what happened to them!"

"I will." Gregor's calm words stopped the conversation.

"And I must." Spence said grudgingly. "This woman is nothing but trouble, but the man is the Laird's physician. I have orders to trust him completely but naught for her, though sadly, I fear the Laird would object to losing her, too. She needs to be taken in hand by a man who will beat her often." He sneered at me, spitting into the sand dangerously close to my hem.

"Ye take their side agin us too?" The smuggler was incredulous. "They can get us hanged or worse! I still say kill them both and let me rid us of the tangle. Tis the only way to be sure their tongues will not wag. Tis not a risk I will take! We are more than ye two can take, and I say cut their throats!"

"And I say not! You are not master here, nor are you more than I can take." A soft lazy voice came from a dark corner of the cave. A stillness fell over the torchlit scene as a slim figure stepped into the light. He was young with dark curly hair, his face smooth, but the dark eyes were old and held something that froze the men in their places. The smuggler's captain inhaled abruptly, and Spence nervously shuffled his feet like a bairn caught in the honey pot.

The man strode forward, an elegant predator, paused in front of us, bowed with an exaggerated flourish, and said in a deceptively silky tone. "William Kidd, Jr., Captain of the *Silver Fin* at your service. You must forgive us, but you will be our guests for the night." He turned to the captain of the smuggler's ship. "When your vessel has taken on the return cargo, and has had time to reach the open sea, and the Laird's Second has removed all traces of this," he waved a languid hand around the cave... "I will release them, and be responsible for their actions. Provided, of course, that they both swear on their honor to forget this little adventure." He raised an inquisitive eyebrow at us. I looked at Malcolm. He nodded, so I bowed my own head in acceptance. I could not help staring at the young man and quivering slightly. A concentrated aura of power and surety surrounded him. One errant lock fell over eyes of the deepest blue I had ever seen, standing out vividly against bronze unlined skin. A classically proportioned nose jutted above unsmiling sharply chiselled lips, fitting the severe planes of the rest of his face. He gestured to one of the crew. "Remove their bonds. I will send them dinner." He beckoned to Gregor. "And you will stay with them." He did not wait to see if his orders were followed, but simply walked to the front of the cave and vanished into the night. Two men, noticeably cleaner than their fellows, followed him.

Talk resumed slowly but subdued, as the cavern began to empty. The smugglers returned to carrying the bags of wool and bundles of hides back to their ships, while Spence's men began moving out the consignment that had been offloaded. We were studiously ignored by both groups.

Malcolm impatiently shook off the last of the bindings securing him. Taking one of my wrists in his hands he began to massage away the rope marks. If I was this tired, he must be exhausted. His bruises were now explosions of color where they were visible, and I wondered about the one over his kidney. "Malcolm, how do you feel, I mean, are you having any pain, do you need to piss?"

"God's bones, woman. Have you no modesty?" He looked around, but no one was paying us the slightest attention now. "Are you alright?" His fingers touched the red streaks on my arm, then the welt on my face. "Your skin is so...fragile," he said almost absently, then shook himself and looked around, seeking the weapons they had taken from him.

"I am good. Tis your own health that is my concern." I was angry, and jerked my arm away. "We are prisoners here overnight. Janet and Cawdie will be frantic. There must be some way to let them know we are safe." I frowned looking around. "Perhaps you could speak to Spence, and have the Laird send word we are his guests or some such? I don't want Cawdie to destroy the village looking for us, and you know full well that he will!" He scowled back at me but before he could say anything, Spence came over to us.

"You will spend the night here." The man smirked! "The accommodations will not be what you are used to, but I will have blankets brought down." He looked at me. "There will be warm water and a chamber pot brought for you, Lady Elspeth. The saints forbid you should tell the Laird that you were mistreated. I must stay also, to bear you company, but first I will go to the castle and make certain all is as it should be."

"Unless you wish to risk having Cawdie find us, while you are there it might be wise to have the Laird send word to Janet that we are staying at the castle." Malcolm's voice was grim. Spence paled, plainly appalled at the idea that the big man might find him detaining us and immediately agreed to Malcolm's request. He left two armed guards with us, one was the man whose finger I had saved. Then he departed for the castle with the last of the cargo.

After they returned with blankets and a few other things, I cleaned myself as best I could, and busied myself making up two beds in the corner farthest from the cave opening where it might be drier and warmer. No fires were lit because the smoke might give away the location of the cave. A spouted smugglers lantern stood on a ledge near the front of the cave. It was squatty, with a top that looked like a little fluted hat and a long-tapered spout, extending from the front so that the light from within would show only from the narrow opening on the end. Standing on shore, it could be aimed toward the water and be invisible from any angle except from the direction where it was pointed. By the same token, it could only be seen from shore by those it was directed toward. This undertaking had been well planned and carried out.

Spence invited himself over when he spied the huge basket that had arrived from the *Silver Fin* with Gregor and a young man dressed in clean slops. Gregor looked speculatively at Spence for a moment, then proceeded to unpack the basket and serve us. He placed a white linen cloth over a wooden crate, and arranged bowls, goblets, silverware and wine atop it. We sat on the sand to eat and it occurred to me that I was having dinner with three very different and powerful men, although Gregor did not eat with us. The food was surprisingly good. A huge pot of chicken stewed in plum sauce, leavened bread, butter, and a white pudding studded with almonds. After a while our wine-loosened tongues allowed us to engage pleasantly enough in careful dinner conversation. When we had eaten, Gregor repacked the basket and gave it to the young man who took it away. I was eased from the wine, so I excused myself and went to my makeshift pallet, removed my shoes and pulled the blankets around me. In moments I was asleep.

* * *

I woke refreshed as the sun picked its way into the cave, despite my sandy mattress. The blankets were warm...and wriggled? I sat up quickly, dislodging them. Malcolm lay with his back to me, one arm folded protectively across his belly, still fast asleep. He is one of those people who gives off body heat like a fire. The side of his face dark with two days' growth of beard but his eyes were no longer bruised. The leeches and rest had taken care of that much. I longed to lift the blanket and look at his injuries but refrained.

Instead, I stood and looked around. Gregor was standing at the entrance to the cave looking immaculate and immovable. He bowed gravely to me. I bent my own head in acknowledgement. Spence was no where in sight. Another basket had appeared. It contained bread, cheese and ale to break our fast. Malcolm had awakened and stepped outside the cave just as Spence returned. Neither of the men tried to stop him so I assumed our captivity was at an end. Gregor turned his jet eyes to Spence.

"When they have eaten, I will walk back with Sir Malcolm. You will see Lady Elspeth safely home." He placed a slight emphasis on the word "safely".

"I have my instructions from the Laird. I will take her back by way of the old path near the castle." His voice was surly.

"Then be quite certain she stays away from the edges of the cliffs there. One would not wish to see you responsible for any mishap." Gregor's voice was flat. Spence grunted something. I ate a few bites of bread and cheese and walked over to Malcolm.

"Are you still bleeding?" I whispered.

"A little. Definitely better." He smiled down at me. "Little mother."

"Hummmph." I regarded Spence. "I am ready to leave."

The path we used on our return showed signs of frequent use. It was undoubtedly the one used to move the arms and black powder to the castle. And the human cargo as well. The cliffs fell sharply away on one side of the narrow track I placed my feet warily, conscious of Spence behind me. It would not be a good place to stumble. We turned down into the valley, up again toward the cottage. Spence had been quiet, the whole time, but just as we reached the stone fence surrounding my small house, he stepped close to me and turned me viciously.

"Ye be lucky this time. Next time may not end so well. Be warned. I be watching ye!"

As he said the last words, he walked over and flung open the door to the cottage without knocking. Three surprised faces turned to him. Cawdie stood and blocked his view of the room with his huge body, but it was too late. Spence had seen Julianne and the tiny bundle she was holding.

He stared, his face turning the color of whey. "A ghalla! Bitch! The babe lives!" His voice crackled with fury. "Dinna, think he will wed ye! Ye are naught but his convenient. A thing he uses." He stepped toward her. I was not sure if the snarl came from Scathach or Cawdie. Both were planted firmly between Spence and Julianne. He stopped and glared at them, trembling from the effort he was making to control himself. "I lay this at your door, Lady Elspeth. Ye should have let them both die. But tis only a delay." He turned and stalked away.

I must have looked worse than I thought, for Janet came and put her arms about me, pulling me into the warmth of the house. "Come, little one. We will get you cleaned up and rested." I let her take care of me.

* * *

When I woke up for the second time that day, I felt much rested. I dressed quickly and braided my freshly washed hair into a long plait...winding it around my head and securing it with two hairpins Julianne had given me. They were pretty, little things, with colored carved ovals at the top, surrounded by paste brilliants. I looked at them more closely. Or perhaps not paste?

Janet was cleaning vegetables. Julianne was sitting by the fire. Scathach laying nearby. She was staring down at the baby, but glanced up as I came over and sat down next to her. "He is doing well." I smiled at her. "Julianne, you must send for the Laird. Spence has probably already reported to him that the bairn is alive. He will not be happy, nor will Lady Margaret, and you must decide what to do now that everyone realizes the babe lives. There will be much speculation and gossip. He will be justifiably angry with us both."

"I know. I think I was trying to avoid it until his father arrives." She looked up. "Gregor says that will be very soon. I will send for the Laird today." She rocked the baby. He was still so quiet that it was often difficult to tell when he was in distress. I had begun to wonder if his vocal cords were damaged. My mind worked furiously.

Whoever had poisoned Julianne would soon know there was a living child. Spence's words repeated themselves in my head.

"Julianne, do you remember who was there when you became ill? Did Lady Margaret have any other guests?" Julianne shook her head.

"Only me, and of course her maid, Rachel."

"Her maid?" My mind conjured up a figure sitting in the shadows of the solar. "Has she been with Lady Margaret long?"

"I really don't know how long. She was here when I came. Lady Margaret said she works in the kitchen part of the time because she has so little to do upstairs and has a light hand with pastry. Her husband is the Laird's Second," she said with distaste.

"Spence?" I hummed. "Did she take tea with you, or just serve? Tell me about her."

"Oh, no, Lady Margaret would never eat with a servant." She thought for a moment. "The woman is not especially comely but has the sort of pillowy body that men like. And she is an excellent pastry cook, much respected and in demand in the kitchen for her artistry. Lady Margaret has a taste for sweets and comfits except those made with almonds. She never touches anything that contains them. How can anyone dislike marchpane?   I could never understand that. Marchpane is one of my favorite sweetmeats, and Rachel often saves a few of the ones she makes for banquets for me. They are exquisite. Some are even gilded with real gold." She sighed. Before I could question her further, an imperious knocking sounded on the door. Janet answered it, the kitchen knife still in her hand. The Laird stood there. The time for dissembling was over.

He stepped inside, bending his head to get through the door, his eyes going immediately to the babe in Julianne's arms. He made no comment, just looked at her.

"I was afraid." she said in answer to his unspoken question. "And, we did not know if he would live."

"And you could not trust me to take care of you?" His voice was hoarse but level. I could hear the hurt in it. Her face paled.

"You could not. It was too much to ask." She walked to him and held up the tiny bundle. "Is he not beautiful?" Her voice broke, and he gathered her in his arms, holding them both gently.

"Forgive me," he murmured against her hair. "I have failed you. I swear I will not do so again. Is he well? And you? Does he know about the babe?"

'Yes, to both. And he is coming here to see us!"   Her eyes were brilliant with excitement. The Laird stiffened. "When? And how do you know this?" Julianne lifted her head and stared at him.

"He sent a messenger saying he would be here within a week. No more." The Laird clamped his lips shut, and turned his face to me. "You knew this? You said nothing of it to anyone? Last night?"

"Nay. Tis not my habit to let my mouth outrun my brain." Flushing, I remembered our last encounter. "At least, not when it concerns others, my Laird. It would make me a poor physician, err, healer, indeed."

He lowered his eyebrows in a fierce frown, but a telltale upturn at the corners of his mouth betrayed him. "I trust you were treated well during your visit with our...friends?"

"As well as one could expect, my Laird. Thank you for your help." Neither of us spoke of what was painfully clear now. The Laird was a Jacobite, and deeply involved with the movement here in Scotland. Arms were being landed in Torrport. The human cargo from the ship might be spies, refugees or anything in between. Both were being funneled in and out of the country from Torrport and the castle. It was high treason, and could easily end in his head being removed from his body and displayed on a pike. I felt suddenly sick.

"Have you seen Sir Malcolm?"

His shoulders relaxed a little. "Yes, he was at the castle this morning and seemed none the worse for your little adventure, as far as could be seen." He let out a long breath. "Julianne, if Lady Elspeth will permit, I think you will be safer here until after...your friend...visits. I will have guards stationed nearby but out of sight, and Cawdie alone is worth a regiment. I fear there are too many people about the stronghold who might be inquisitive." A complicit look passed between them, and I understood at once that the Laird was aware of the identity of the babe's father. Julianne nodded.

"Of course, she and the babe can stay as long as they wish." I added, "Julianne wishes to have the bairn baptized."

The Laird shifted uneasily. "I will take care of it. Father Hammet will do as I ask. I will take responsibility for the babe." I was burning with curiosity, anxious to know if the babe's father was married. If not...then in Scotland, unlike England, if the parents married, even after the bairn was born, it would make the babe legitimate. It would be a simple solution. Then I groaned. I was doing it again, making plans and decisions that were not mine to make. It was none of my concern. My head was beginning to ache again. Keeping everyone out of it did that.

"My Laird, I will leave you and Julianne to speak privately. I know you must have much to discuss." I motioned to Janet.

We left them and walked outside to the garden, my own thoughts a maelstrom of unmatched pieces. Janet went to the shed at the side of the house, and knocked on Cawdie's door. When he answered, they began to talk, and I knew she was telling him all that had occurred. I walked on quietly picking my way among the rows of herbs in the garden. Bending down I ran my hands through the mint leaves, releasing the oils, I closed my eyes and lifted my palms to my face, smelling the calming scent.

The Laird left, and we trailed back into the cottage. Julianne was quiet and thoughtful, Cawdie and Janet talked quietly, and I was exhausted beyond measure. I excused myself and sought the peace of my bed, quickly becoming oblivious to it all.

* * *

Morning brought that quick brightness I love after a good night's sleep. I dressed carefully and ate because Janet frowns when I do not. I do not really like to eat until several hours after I awaken. Cup in hand I wandered out into the garden, enjoying the sounds of birds and the sough of the wind in the trees. I often imagine they are speaking to each other in a language I can almost, but not quite, understand. I smiled at my fancy.

An unexpected scrabbling sound came from the pathway leading to Torrport, and Aggie burst into the garden through the gate. Her neat clothing looked as though she had fallen, and she was white-faced and trembling. "Lady, ye must come now! Twas in the new tub of bluing! Whatever will I do? Ruined, ruined. Me mam sent me here. Mayhap ye can save him, but I think tis far too late." She grabbed my sleeve and pulled...babbling something unintelligible about a man in one of her tubs. I did not hesitate, I picked up my skirts and let her lead, running to keep up with her as we moved down the path to the village and then behind the tavern to her laundry. We were both out of breath when we turned the corner. The laundry was in its usual orderly and spotless condition, the only thing out of place was the figure on the hard paving-stones in front of the tubs.

FIFTEEN

Malcolm - Strangled

Torrport, Scotland.

"It's a breech birth and we have to turn it, or it won't come out and they both could die." My head was turned to speak to him as I was palpating her abdomen and vagina. He'd crouched down to be close, kneeling on the straw beside me. I knew by his well-stained clothing and crumpled cap that he couldn't afford this, so I was prepared to work *pro bono*, but a loss like this could end him. He'd come at dawn to ask for my help, said he lived a short walk away in one of the farms just outside of Torrport on the road west to Edinburgh. "I can see the water sac has broken awhile ago. It should've already come out."

"Aye that was more than two hours past, and she's been fussing since." His curly dark beard was moist from exertion, and well-lined face showed every year of toil and worry.

"Get some clean water, soap, oil and cloths. I'm going to try reaching in and turn it manually, so it can come out properly." I sat back on my haunches and took a few deep breaths as he gathered the supplies. This would work provided it was done quickly and safely. I didn't want to end up injured again, so soon after...

He returned in a few minutes and I pulled up my shirt sleeves and washed hands and arms thoroughly. I'd be inserting at least one arm up to my elbow and didn't want to hurt her, so I liberally coated myself with his used cooking oil.

"I see you already have tied her legs, so if you'll secure the ropes so she doesn't kick me, I can begin." I got into position behind her, speaking to her soothingly and touching her gently on the rump. It's always best with females to work into things gradually. He was sitting on the ground now with boots braced and the rope to her legs wrapped around his wrists.

"Ready?" I asked to be certain.

"Aye, doctor." I could hear him mumbling a prayer as he leaned back adding tension to the rope.

The feet had just emerged, and the top of the calf's feet were pointed in the wrong direction. Normally they are pointed up, toward the cow's tail. But this calf was wrong side up in the birth canal and had to be turned or it wouldn't come out.

"Going in." I slid my right hand in on the top-side past the hoofs and legs til I found the head. One had to go slowly, any pain would cause her to lurch and make it worse for us both.

"I've got the head, now the other hand. Keep her steady." I looked up to assure myself he was focused because this was the critical part, getting both arms in and turning it without having my arms broken and rupturing her. I pushed my left hand in, a much tighter fit, and underneath in an awkward position. It feels incredibly vulnerable to have both arms locked in the vagina of a frightened cow who could decide to stand up or kick. It was reassuring to see the farmer straining on the ropes holding her in place, when finally, I got both hands around the calf's shoulders.

"Ready to turn." I grunted and stopped for a few deep breaths. It had to come one eighty degrees around in stages to let the back end slowly twist in place. "She's doing well, should have it out in a few minutes." He looked up and smiled slightly. I knew getting it out was no guarantee it would live, but at least we would save the mother.

"I have her, no worries." The cow gave a mournful bellow and I knew it was now or never.

I gave a series of turns and pauses that took several minutes, til eventually the calf was in the proper position to come out. "I'm going to pull it out of her. Steady now." My arms came out easily then I grasped both front legs of the calf, leaned back letting my body weight do the work. I could see it start to move slowly. "It's coming!" The farmer grinned and we both knew the cow's ordeal would be over soon.

Just as the head emerged, a boy came running in and shouted. "Doctor Forrester, please come, Lady Elspeth needs you!" It was Jocki, and he was panting heavily.

"Can't you see...!" I blurted gruffly and heard the cow let out an even louder bellow as the rest of the calf's body squirted out and landed mostly on my lap, covering me with birthing slime. I let go of the calf and fell back laughing.

＊ ＊ ＊

We ran through town, with me having trouble keeping up with little Jocki. He told me there was a body at Aggie's laundry, found with his head immersed in a tub of dirty water. It wasn't far, but my back was already starting to twinge, and I was glad we didn't have to go further as we turned the corner at the back of the tavern and I saw

Elspeth kneeling over the body, her moss green skirts forming a partial drape over the man I instantly knew.

"It is Captain Spence. We are too late." She said without emotion as she stood, brushing a strand of auburn hair out of her eyes.

I dropped my medical bag and knelt beside Spence and felt for a pulse on his neck, always best to check, sometimes they do revive. "Who found him?" I looked up at them. Aggie was there looking grim with her rough hands hidden in the folds of her apron. There were two other women there too.

"I did, sir, when I got here, first thing. He was over there, face down in that tub." Aggie pointed one reddened finger to the tub in the far corner closest to the kettles.

"Then what?" I asked and removed my fingers from his neck. It was obvious he was dead, with no pulse and his body beginning to chill.

"Then...I screamed, but I guess no one was awake but me, no one came, so I pulled him out of the tub and laid him there. I yelled for help, then mam looked out the window and said what is all the racket about? I said, someone's dead, and drowned in my tub. She said go get Lady Elspeth. So, I ran up the hill to her cottage to get her."

"Janet and I were just getting up and I came as quickly as I could. We'd better contact the Laird and Spence's family, if there are any hereabouts." Elspeth took a few steps toward me, knelt-down and whispered. "Malcolm, this is murder. He didn't just fall in the tub and drown. Look at the marks on his neck."

Spence was face-up, and it was easy to see there were bruises and abrasions on his throat, and on the side of his face. I whispered back. "It's too soon to draw that conclusion, he could have fallen on the edge of the tub, but I agree it's suspicious. We'd better get the Laird." I stood and addressed Aggie. "Keep people away from the body. No one touches him. Understand?" She nodded, then pulled up a stool and sat, ready for what had started out as a very bad day.

"Jocki, run to the castle and tell the Laird that Captain Spence is dead, and we need him. Have I forgotten anything, Elspeth?"

She rose smoothly off the ground brushing her skirts again. "Yes, a cart to transport the body, and blankets to wrap him, and a table to receive him. And Jocki..." She made that sign on her lips telling him to keep quiet about it.

"Aye, Lady" Jocki gave an exaggerated bow, trying hard to be a gentleman.

"Go now boy!" I commanded, and he took off like a shot up the ramp toward the castle. I took Elspeth by the elbow and guided her to the bench set against the tavern wall. Aggie's laundry had grown organically out behind the tavern because of the constant need for cleaning cloths and aprons. On one side was an old stable she'd converted to a room to press, fold and store, on the other side were the clothes lines for drying, and in back the fires with boiling kettles. The rinse and wring tubs were close to the boiling kettles, and Spence was found in the one nearest them.

I glanced a look at Elspeth and smiled. She could be pretty if she'd spend a little time making herself so, and even worse, her clothes were that drab olive-brown homespun or faded tartan of her homeland. She was plain and seemed to prefer it. "What are your thoughts?" I asked in a low voice.

She looked me up and down, scrunched up her nose and smiled. "I am thinking you look filthy and smell like you slept in a barn."

I laughed then poked her arm. "Well you certainly know how to change the subject! Turns out I was in a barn, but not sleeping...arms in a cow and cuddling a newborn calf."

"Ah, of course." She smiled. "Did it live?"

"I think so, but I'll check later." I leaned back against the cool stucco of the wall and felt my tension ebb. "What do you make of this?"

She sat for a moment, the fingers of one hand tapping her lower lip. "This could be very serious. First Julianne, now Spence, and then there is the smuggling and politics. We could easily get caught in the middle and I already have enough problems, as do thee." She glanced over at me and I nodded in agreement.

"I am glad about one thing." I winked at her.

"That is?" she winked back in parody.

"That you and Ross like dolls, otherwise we may've become mulch in the forest." I chuckled, but it wasn't funny. I'd been too cocksure we could get away with spying.

"Indeed," she grinned. "You should see my collection, they are quite lovely...and in this case...useful." She was referring to the fact that it was Gregor who'd saved us from the French smugglers because he knew his boss was fond of Elspeth and their shared hobby of baby-doll collecting.

"I would be delighted to see them."

"No, you wouldn't!" she laughed out loud.

"Well I would pretend."

"You are not good at that either. Now getting back to this." She tilted her chin in the direction of the late Captain Spence. "Who do you think killed him and why?"

"I know little of him. We can offer to do an autopsy and see what else the Laird wants done."

"I have some information about him and I agree about the autopsy. We should be able to establish how he died and when. That should narrow the list of suspects."

"Elspeth, I have that experiment in a few days. I can help here only til then."

"I know." She sat upright with that determined look. This was a woman not to be under-estimated.

* * *

Half an hour later, the Laird and his men arrived and parted the small crowd of merchants and dock workers that had gathered around the body. He went straight to Spence, looked down then said something under his breath that sounded like a curse. He pulled his broad shoulders back and spun slowly to look at the scene then announced. "If anyone has any information about this heinous crime, come forward now!" The crowd held their breath waiting. "I will pay well...and punish anyone aiding the murderer." At that point, a rotund middle-aged man put up his hand. The Laird pointed at him. "You! What can you tell us?"

The man pushed his way through the crowd until he was before the Laird, then leaned in and said in a low voice. "My Laird, as you may know I am a wool merchant and have the warehouse over there just past the ship loading area. We live above the warehouse."

"Yes, yes, Allen get on with it for God's sake!"

"I...err...have been having some upsets with my kidneys, trying to pass a stone and Doctor Forrester has helped me greatly..."

The Laird cut him off abruptly. "I don't give a damn about that Allen. Do you have information about this murder, or not?"

"Apologies my Laird, yes I believe I heard something last night. You see I cannot sleep well and I'm taking my medicines as directed..."

The Laird grabbed Allen by the collar and pulled him close enough, so he could feel the Laird's spit spray on his forehead. "What did you hear? Tell me now or be off! I've no time to hear of your ailments."

I had to intercede. I knew the Laird had a temper and this interaction with the wool merchant was spinning out of control. "Let me handle this, my Laird. He is my patient and I'll find out what he knows while you and your men load Captain Spence.

The Laird released his grip and gave Allen a gentle push back. "Very well, Forrester. Give him a crown if he has anything of value to say."

I put my arm around James Allen's shoulder and walked him to Elspeth. "Thank you for coming forward, sir. It will be greatly appreciated if you can help us. Please forgive the Laird, the murdered man was his Second and he is very upset."

Elspeth smiled at Allen warmly then asked. "You can tell us, sir. We are here to help."

Allen pulled his waistcoat down and lifted his chin, no doubt trying to shake off the humiliation of being treated roughly in front of his friends. "I heard voices coming from behind the tavern. It was the middle of the night, maybe four-o-clock, hard to be sure. It was very dark. I opened my curtains to look. There was a light back there. The voices didn't sound friendly either, like a heated argument."

"How many were there? Two, more? Did they sound like men or women?" I needed to get to the heart of it now.

"At least two, perhaps three, one had a very deep distinct voice, the other lower like growling. There may have been a third with a lighter voice like a woman, but it could have been echoes too. Not sure."

"What did you see, Sir Allen?" Elspeth touched his hand to calm him.

"Oh, yes, I saw shadows coming from the light, but I can't see much back there from my window."

"Did you hear any unusual sounds...like banging or sounds of a fight?"

"There was one...it sounded like *Uh!* then a thud...that is all."

"Thank you, Sir Allen. For all your help." I took out a crown and pressed it into his palm then whispered to Elspeth. "Let's go speak to the Laird about the autopsy."

Sir Allen slipped the crown into his waistcoat pocket and turned to go, then stopped. "Oh, one more thing."

I looked back at him. "Aye?"

"I was curious and opened our side door a crack to look, when I saw someone run by, going toward the castle."

"What did he look like?"

"Not sure it was a he...slight, medium height, wore a dark cloak. Didn't see the face."

I nodded and sighed as I saw Elspeth grinning from under her hood and heard her mutter, "Catch more flies with honey..."

"A few flakes of gold in the honey doesn't hurt either." I added and we both laughed.

Then a horrible thought emerged from threads new and old and I stopped and grabbed her arm. "Where was Julianne last night?"

She opened her mouth and gasped, wide-eyed. "I don't know for certain, I sleep soundly."

* * *

Several minutes later we'd caught up to the Laird, the pair of us having considered scenarios along the way. Could it have been Julianne that Allen saw running past his warehouse, or Gilly, or perhaps one of the abused boys from the castle? This was becoming too complex, so we decided to simplify and proceed one step at a time. First, determine cause of death and find any clues that may lead to the murderer, then establish the whereabouts of likely suspects.

They'd rolled Spence in some blankets and loaded him on a cart drawn by a swayback mare. The Laird looked like he'd put on his belted plaid in the dark. It wasn't tucked and fitted properly, but matched well the sour expression on his unshaven face. "We got some useful bits from Allen." I was walking beside him with

Elspeth on my left, half a step behind. It had just started to sprinkle rain and the wind had freshened from the west.

He squinted through the raindrops. "This will not go unpunished, Forrester. You can bet on it. I've had enough of this."

"Nor should it, and we can help if it is your wish."

"Help? How?" He sneered. He had a right to be skeptical considering our recent history of ineptitude.

"For a start, we can perform an autopsy, examine him inside and out to determine cause of death and with any luck find clues that lead to the killer." I went on to explain that it would be done in private and respectfully and be well documented for use in court, if needed.

The Laird listened carefully then decided. "You may do your autopsy, and I doubt Spence would care what happens to his carcass. He's like me...was like me, would demand bloody revenge, swift and brutal. I'll have the man who did this gutted in the town square and show those who dare challenge me their fate." I believed him, and any man who didn't was a fool. There would be blood to pay for this.

"Once we have completed the autopsy we can begin our investigation. Elspeth and I are well suited to assist. We know many here and have their trust. Those who may be reluctant to speak with your men, may confide in us." I was fully soaked with rain by then and wished I'd worn one of those practical belted plaids made of natural wool and more waterproof than my refined garb.

The Laird looked at us in amusement. "Alright, your help is welcome, but keep a tight leash on that one. She's trouble. Trust me." Elspeth pretended she didn't hear but I could see the telltale tightening of her mouth and knew I'd have to deal with her later.

"I will...err...protect her, my Laird. One favour, if I might?"

"Aye?"

"I would ask that anyone who comes forward to assist in this investigation be treated with kindness and respect." I cleared my throat and waited for his push-back, but I had to say it.

"Do you mean Allen? He's been a pain in the arse for some time, always nagging about wool smuggling and such. I've no time for him anymore. He needs to accept reality. The Wool Act will not be repealed anytime soon. Perhaps I was a bit harsh, but he can try one's patience, can't he?" He shrugged then added. "What do you need for this autopsy?"

"I have surgery tools with me, but this is more like butchery, so we'll need a sturdy table in the infirmary, and tools like a bone saw, butcher knife, shears, cleaver, and some trays for the body parts, and aprons and towels of course. Anything to add, Elspeth?" She said we needed a table for the trays and tools and paper and pen and ink for notes and drawings. "Aye that should do it, and we need this done quickly before the body starts to decompose."

"The butcher tools we can get in town, the rest we should have, and it will be done today. I'll send some lads ahead to prepare." He lengthened his stride and left us with a brief wave and began shouting orders in highland dialect to the men.

* * *

The castle infirmary was in chaos when we arrived, cots were being removed and mess tables from the Great Hall carried in. A few patients were standing bewildered in the adjacent armoury, so Elspeth set about to make them comfortable among the guns and powder kegs. I took charge of the young men arranging the tables and trays and asked for more candles to light the dim stone room. Elspeth requested a message be sent to Jocki to inform her patients that she would be unavailable til tomorrow. Beyond that there wasn't much we could do but wait for the equipment to arrive. We settled on some kegs to rest, knowing the day would be long and tiring: if you must stand, sit when you can, if you must sit, lie when you can, wise advice on a day like this.

I leaned closer to her. "I'll do the cutting and you the recording, and both of us observing."

She shook the dampness out of her hair. "Of course, men must always be seen to be in charge."

I sighed. "It must be so, especially in this case and you know it."

"I know my place Malcolm, but if you ever try to leash me, you will soon find out this beast has sharp teeth."

I wasn't sure if she was joking or serious, but opted for the former. "Then I'll muzzle you as well."

"You can try." I saw the hard look on her face and knew I'd chosen the wrong option.

"We must cooperate Elspeth...for our patients and our Laird."

"I will, Malcolm, but you don't understand." I guess I didn't so let it drop and we sat quietly.

The door to the infirmary was open and we could see Spence laying there wrapped in blankets. This would not be pleasant. I suppose you get used to it in time, but this was my first hands-on autopsy. I'd seen it done at school a few times, but having to do this for the first time under pressure was un-nerving and if we got it all wrong, well I didn't even want to think about it.

Elspeth turned to me and touched my hand. "I am nervous too. There is a lot at stake and we need to get it right. I will support you, Malcolm." I took her tiny hand

168

in mine, not sure why, perhaps I just needed some warm human contact. "Malcolm, how is your father?" Her blue eyes met mine and I could sense honest concern.

"I don't know. It's been a constant worry. I wrote McLaren yesterday. I guess I'll find out for certain when I return to Edinburgh in a few days, but I fear the worst."

"If he is anything like you, he will survive. He may give everyone fits of worry along the way, but he will survive, I know it." I wanted to believe her, but I'd seen too many strong men fall to smallpox. It was no respecter.

"Malcolm, I know I made light of this last time, and I apologize. I am very honoured that you consider me worthy to care for your father, and when I come to Edinburgh I most certainly will do my best to nurse him back to health."

"Thank you, Elspeth." I was truly grateful, but this was becoming too emotional, so I let her hand drop and changed the subject. "Oh, I wrote to McLean as well, about Sir Ross and his need of surgery. He will contact you soon, so you can continue working with him."

She tilted her head back rubbing her neck. "Aye, I will get him to Edinburgh and care for him when he returns."

"I am sure you will." I winked, and she blushed turning her head away, so I couldn't see, but I knew she was smiling.

A young warrior arrived with the sack of butcher's tools and aprons. Elspeth laid them out on the side table next to my surgery tools as I rolled up my sleeves, washed and put on a leather apron.

"Everyone out and close the door behind you." I watched as the remaining warriors left, then turned to Elspeth. "Ready?"

She perched on a stool beside Spence, with a board and paper in one hand and quill pen in the other. I was on the other side of the corpse. "I'm going to unwrap him. If you see anything unusual, stop me." She nodded, and I could see her start to write as I searched for the edges of the blanket.

"Let's start with what we know. His name is John Spence, Scottish born, recently arrived from Russia, in the employ of Laird MacDuff of Torrport for seven or eight months past as his Second-in-Command. Approximate age is late thirties to early forties, he's about five feet ten inches and one eighty pounds, I'd say." I folded the edge of the first blanket back as far as I could, then the one underneath as I listened to the scratching of Elspeth's pen. When she'd finished, I said. "I have to start cutting the blanket now." I had a good pair of scissors in my surgery kit and used them to cut the blanket from top to bottom down the length of his body. Then I carefully pulled back one side and the other to reveal his fully clothed body. He was still in the same bent position as we found him, and wearing a knee-length belted-plaid of the same colour as the Laird. The wool tartan cloth was a muted red with a green and blue cross weave, held in place with a wide black belt with silver buckle and a silver pin at his left shoulder. He also wore tan wool socks and garters with black leather shoes and a white linen shirt.

"His clothes are rumpled but dry and I see no signs of blood, although the tartan colour might obscure it. No evidence of dirt on the front of him, but the paving stones at Aggie's are washed clean each day. I'll turn him over to look at the back and remove the blankets." I slid him to one side of the table, then rolled-up the blankets on the other side so that when I flipped him, I could pull the blankets from under him. "He's stiff, *rigor mortis* has set in. The tips of his fingers and lips and ear lobes have a bluish tinge indicating a lack of air in the lungs before he died. It usually takes a few hours for rigor mortis to begin. The time of death would be sometime last night. He's quite stiff, so I would think at least four hours ago." Elspeth nodded.

I pulled him over with purchase on his belt and clothing. "Nothing unusual back here. I'll look at the back of his head before I turn him over."

"Feel the back of his neck too." She pointed with her pen.

"Good idea." I threw the blankets in a pile on the floor and moved to the end of the table. His head was turned to the side. "He has sandy brown hair down to his shoulders, thinning on the crown. His head and face are damp." I leaned in closer to smell. "Smells like soap. I'm going to inspect his scalp and the back of his neck now." It was plain to see there were no obvious contusions on this side, so I turned the body, so the head was resting flat on the forehead, then parted the hair at the base of his scalp.

"I see no ligature marks in the back of the neck, but there is some bruising." I pressed my fingers into the flesh along the spine, feeling for anything out of place. "His spine seems normal." I turned the body, so his head was facing the other way and inspected the other side of his scalp. "Nothing of note here, but once we have it narrowed down, I want you to look too." She smiled briefly but continued writing.

"Alright, I'll turn him back over and remove his clothing." While I did that, Elspeth cleaned her pen and had a stretch. I removed his belt and pin and began unwrapping the plaid. It is one piece of cloth, usually four to five yards long and fifty to sixty inches wide. I started at the top where the ends are pinned and pulled the top parts off his shoulders, then moved to the lower section that was wrapped in pleats with loops sewn on the inside at the waist for the cord used to secure it. I tugged until it was all removed. Then I removed his shirt, shoes, garters and socks. He lay there naked on the table, arms and knees still bent. I walked all the way around one way then the other for perspective. He looked fit and muscular. His body was unnaturally pale, the blood having already gravitated to the side nearest the ground.

"I'll start at the head and work my way down," I muttered to myself, "and I need more candles close-by." I looked down at his face. His eyes were open, staring into mine. I didn't know him well and felt no connection, he was just an object to be studied, the life that quickened him gone to...wherever. I held a candle close to his face. "He has brown eyes, and a contusion around his left cheek bone. We'll need to look at that more closely later. There appears to be reddish-purple spots in the whites. Come have a look Elspeth. Looks like burst capillaries."

She looked down. "Aye, and the right eye has some redness too, but that could be from other causes."

"Please make a drawing of his eyes." She set to work sketching as I examined both ears and nostrils. Nothing unusual. His mouth was slightly open. I could see the teeth and gums, and immediately noticed something. It was white, solid but amorphous, surrounded by what looked like a slimy ooze. "There is something in his mouth."

"I see it too. Can you open it more?"

The rigor mortis made it difficult to pry his mouth open without doing damage, but I got it open enough to see that his throat was blocked by what seemed to be a piece of soap. I smelled my fingers to confirm. "Looks and smells like soap. Do you agree?" I lifted my finger to her nose.

"In another context, it would not be unpleasant." She scrunched up her face. "Thank you, Malcolm." She said with a tinge of sarcasm. "We should take a sample. One second." She rummaged in her medical bag and retrieved a salve jar and cork. "Can you get the rest out of his mouth? We can put it in here and compare it to Aggie's laundry soap later."

I used a steel depressor to tease it out, and got most of it into the jar. "His tongue is red and swollen and pushed back, blocking the airway. It's unlikely the killer could have done that to him while he was conscious. Why would he bother doing this as well as throttling and drowning him in the laundry tub? Seems excessive."

"Rope and belt." She replied.

"How do you mean?"

"That's why our highland men seldom reveal themselves inadvertently. The rope on the inside of the plaid through the sewn-in loops and the belt without, make it well nigh impossible for it to fall off by accident. Perhaps the killer wanted to make Spence's death certain, with no chance he could survive by accident."

"You could be right, but there are other ways even more foolproof. This was an odd way to do it, don't you think? Perhaps it was a message, or revenge of some sort. Also, I see no evidence that a weapon was used. Alright, let's move on to the neck." I leaned toward the body and began describing the pattern of contusions and abrasions on the front of the neck near the windpipe and what felt like a thumb-sized depression. "We'll need to open this up."

The rest of his body from neck down looked normal except that the knuckles on his right hand were abraded and bruised. I turned him on his side to look from top to bottom again, noted those bruises on the back of his neck, but nothing else. When I rolled him again to his front, the skin on his face, hands and lower legs had the typical patterning and purple hue of blood pooling. I leaned against the table and waited as Elspeth completed her notes.

"Well, Elspeth, what do you think?"

"He was a bonny man, but I think a disagreeable disposition may have lead to this. Sad, is it not? The choices we make."

"It's not all down to choices. Much of life is forced on us. We don't know what brought him to this end, do we? Was it bad choices, bad luck, necessity?" I was becoming too philosophical, but she was kind enough not to point it out.

"Where are we? It looks like he was struck on the side of the face, throttled, choked with a bar of soap, then drowned in a laundry tub. We don't know in what order or the precise cause of death yet. Did he die of strangulation or drowning? It's unlikely the soap killed him, but it could have contributed. Did I miss anything?"

"Yes, the abrasions on his hand may have indicated there was a fight. We should look under his fingernails for blood and skin to see if he scratched the assailant while fighting back."

"I knew I should have bought that microscope I saw in Edinburgh. Aye, please take some samples while I prepare to cut him open. We need to have an internal look at his lungs, throat and that contusion on his cheek, agreed?"

She nodded and was already preparing jars for samples from under his nails. She's efficient, I'll give her that.

I cleaned my hands again and selected a scalpel. "I'll start with the cheek. Just to confirm. If this had been a serious blow, enough to drop him, I think we'd have seen other bruises where his body hit the ground, and there were none." I sliced through the epidermis and dermis on the cheekbone. He had little fat, so the hypodermis was primarily connective tissue. My incisions were in the form of an X, so I could pull back the skin in sections to look at the underlying muscles and bone. "There is little damage beyond the skin, slight discolouration in a small part of the muscle." I'd seen the effects of many a fight and this kind of damage may have lead to the victim being momentarily stunned but seldom rendered unconscious. "No major dislocations of the cheekbone or jaw." I wiped the scalpel on a towel. "And now for the interesting part, let's open him up."

It took some time to cut through the skin and muscle on his chest to expose the bones. There was no blood pressure and most of the blood already had settled, so I just had to dab here and there with a towel to keep it clean. I made a T-shaped cut from shoulder to shoulder then down the center to the pubic bone, then I pulled back the layers a few inches away from the center-line, so I could access the rib cage. I also extended the cut up the center of the throat to just under the jawbone.

"Elspeth, can you hold the tissue back, so I can cut the ribs?" I smiled slightly seeing her take firm hold of the flap of skin and muscle, with no sign of squeamishness. "I'm going to use the shears to cut through the ribs." It made a gruesome crunching sound as each rib gave way from bottom to top, ending in the collar bone. I'd already sliced through the muscle of the abdomen, and so it was a simple matter to pull the rib cage open. This also exposed the throat. The damp meat and blood smell had become pervasive now, like that of a butchery.

"I need another pair of eyes, and my back needs a rest. Let's start at the throat." I stood up straight, arching my back to relieve the tension as she slid off her stool. We positioned ourselves on either side, me with scalpel and her with pen. "I'll tease back the tissues. I see extensive bruising." There is little muscle and connective tissue in the front of the throat, so it didn't take long to reveal the underlying structure.

"Stop!" she said suddenly. "Look!" She pointed down at the ring-shaped cartilage I'd just uncovered. "It looks deformed."

I brought the candle in and looked more closely. She was right; one side was depressed and twisted. I reached in and wiggled it with a finger and it felt broken on the right side.

"That is the cricoid. It anchors a lot of the tissues around the voice box." She started sketching, then without looking up, added. "It is seldom broken except by strangulation."

I vaguely remembered that from anatomy class. It was one of those parts rarely mentioned. "I'm glad one of us is an expert on strangulation. I see nothing else broken here. It must have taken considerable strength to break that cartilage and choke him for the two or three minutes necessary to kill him."

"A sharp blow could have done it too, but the cricoid fracture is a telltale for strangulation, especially when combined with that pattern of bruising on the neck."

"I agree. Make note of that. Let's finish with the lungs. If we find waterlogged or frothy lungs, it may complicate things." Finding out was a simple matter of slicing into the lung tissue. There was no sign the victim had drowned. "So, he wasn't breathing when the killer stuck his head in the water." I picked up a fresh towel and cleaned the scalpel, then my hands.

"There is dry drowning, when the larynx closes on contact with water and doesn't re-open," she replied.

"Aye, but that usually takes place later. It's not instantaneous, and Spence was found with his head in the water. I concede it's possible, but not likely."

"I know, Malcolm, but we must consider all possibilities."

"I believe there was an argument, a fight, and they traded blows, then he was throttled to death, all that makes sense. Then for some reason soap was jammed in his mouth and his head stuck in the bucket of water. Why the killer did that is unclear."

"Perhaps there was more than one and they had different motives? The first wanted him dead, the second to humiliate him." She tapped her pen on the page to make the point.

"I've had enough for one morning. If you can help me sew him up, it would be appreciated." It turned out predictably that she was far more adept at stitching than me and we were packed and done just before noon. It was time to return to the world of sunlight and spring flowers, if only for a few hours.

Elspeth looked pointedly at my hands, and poured water into a basin and gave it to me. I was glad to wash away the effluvia of the procedure. She did the same.

"We'd better see the Laird before we go. He'll want to know." We snuffed out the last candle and I strode out into the fresh air as Elspeth stopped to console a few of the patients.

"Come on, Elspeth, no dawdling, we need to get this over with, so I can get some rest."

"Coming Malcolm, those poor boys..." She jogged a few steps to catch up and we reached the Laird's room on the top floor in a few minutes. He was alone, writing, with his left hand holding up a very weary head.

"We've finished the autopsy. Would you like our report?" I held out my hand and Elspeth gave it to me with a look of female resignation.

"Give me the short version and without the Latin nonsense." He turned in his chair to face us. I went over the main points and conclusions. He asked a few pertinent questions. Could he have been killed somewhere else and brought there? Yes. Are you sure of the time of death? Reasonably certain, likely around four-o-clock in the morning, so forth. Then he stood and approached us.

"Now what about suspects? Who should we be looking for?"

"Perhaps someone with a grudge, or who'd made threats, or..." I started ticking them off my fingers, when he threw his head back and guffawed.

"That would include half the men in Torrport. You'll have to do better than that, doctor." He put the emphasis on my title, in a mocking tone. "Why don't we start with those he's had a conflict with recently, like you and the lady here?" He folded his arms and with a bemused look waited for my response.

"If you mean the night before last when we were lost, aye we were with Captain Spence for a time." Elspeth poked me with her elbow and gave a questioning look. I wished she would remember that I'm injured.

"Nonsense, Forrester! You two were snooping and got caught, plain and simple, and you're lucky those Frenchmen didn't slit your throats. It would have been well-deserved, I assure you."

Elspeth took a half-step toward the Laird, confronting him squarely. "I make no apologies for our actions my Laird. We have a responsibility to see to the well-being of our community and that includes even the roughest sorts among us. Had we uncovered a threat to you, sir, we would have reported it." She stood, tiny slipper to massive boot, in front of him. It would have been comical considering their size difference, had the issues not been so serious. They stared at each other for a moment, neither willing to give way, so I interjected.

"My Laird, nothing happened between Spence and us that night. He left one of his men to guard us while the arms were hauled away. By dawn, the ship was gone, and we were released."

He dropped his hands to his belt and strangely gave Elspeth a friendly wink. "I am well-informed of you both. Do you think I would share my secrets otherwise? I know for example, the true reason you came to Torrport, Lady Elspeth."

I looked at her and her face flushed, but she said nothing.

"I've been in contact with her Laird in Skye. He is a family friend and fellow supporter of the Cause. Did you not know?" Elspeth glanced up and I could see the surprise register fleetingly on her face. "And as for you Doctor Forrester, I am well-aware you are the youngest son of the great and powerful Lord William Forrester, entrusted with spying on us for Queen Anne." I stood in shock, as my life was once again unwillingly immersed in the chill waters of political intrigue. I tried to say something in defense, but nothing came.

"That is why I've opened my home and confidence to you, Forrester. I expected you would inform your father. I wanted it. I need him to know we loyal Scots will not tolerate further abuse or slavery by the English, and yes, we will fight to the death to protect our independence. Go and tell your father, when he recovers, and I pray he does. I've heard he is a good man, beyond his misplaced allegiances." There it was, in the open. I suppose I always felt it. Now it was confirmed. I had to respond, on behalf of myself, my family, and perhaps all of us.

"We have political differences, my Laird. There is no avoiding it. They are real, have been for centuries, and may remain forever, but we share this sacred isle and must find a way to live together in peace. Shall we not find a method, a formula, a compromise, that will allow us to do so? There are enough threats without, we need not create our own at home." He listened patiently, then I added: "That is my opinion and I believe those of my father and most of the English and we Scots."

He nodded and clapped a hand on my shoulder. "Then tell him they must not push us too far. Now let us find the murderer of my Second, the late Captain Spence."

We discussed a few men in the ranks that could be suspects, but I don't think any of us took them seriously. While we were discussing this, in the back of my mind I couldn't let go of the idea that the Laird had set me up to transmit information to my father. Did the Jacobites want backdoor access to the powers-that-be in Britain? If the Laird was an official spokesman, it certainly seemed so, but I hated being the one in the middle, not knowing what was true or false. I'd been manipulated and resented it, but decided that if I could play a useful part I would, regardless of personal consequences. A war with England would not go well for Scotland, no matter how much the Scots wished otherwise. The English commanded far more resources, people, money and weapons to make it a close contest. All the Scots had was the choice to fight and die or flee and hide in the rough wastes of the highlands.

Elspeth cleared her throat to call attention. "And what of the girl Gilly down at the fishing village? Could it have been another of her lovers or family that sought revenge?" I knew she'd treated Gilly and it must have been difficult pointing the finger, but murder is serious business, especially when it involves one of high rank.

The Laird snorted in derision. "She is nothing! Spence was rough with her a few days ago, but it was her fault. When you pay a woman and she gets pregnant, you expect her to take care of it, not bring the problem back and dump it on your lap in front of your friends. Pregnancy was a risk she took, part of her business. But to your point, I doubt any of her lovers would care enough for that slut to risk their lives, and as for family, I cannot say, but she is low born." The Laird thought for a moment. "This had to be a man, and a strong one to have subdued Spence like that. He was a warrior, for God's sake, and could out-fight most any man here."

"I could have taken him." Elspeth said coolly.

We both looked at her with incredulity. "Tell us Elspeth," I said, suppressing a laugh.

She gracefully faced me and assumed a half crouch, with arms extended in front of her face, hands open as though she was about to slap me. I was wondering what she intended as I watched her take a breath, then it happened so fast I couldn't react.

Her small body shifted and one of her hands, fingers extended, came slashing out and stopped an inch from my throat. "Like that," she said calmly, resuming her posture as a demure lady.

"What the...!" the Laird blurted. "You near cleaved his head!"

Her demeanour suggested she took no small pleasure in shocking us like that and she said. "My Laird, even a mere woman like me, if properly trained can render a man sufficiently unconscious to strangle him. Killing someone by strangulation is not difficult, provided the victim is unable to resist." She stood there with the hint of a smile on her face, and I hoped there were no further surprises from her like that.

The Laird sighed loudly. "Forrester, our women are one-part sweet, soft heather and another part stinging deadly adder, and one never knows which a man will experience on any given day. She has earned her reputation, that is clear. Elspeth, I forbid you teaching that to other women here." He chuckled while involuntarily covering his neck with a hand.

"Then I suppose we should not rule out Gilly, and other women. At least questioning them may lead to other information." I looked to the others for agreement.

Elspeth nodded, and the Laird said. "It will be done."

"And what of this Russian connection? He'd come recently from that land. How does it fit, or does it?" We had to be open with each other now, but I wasn't sure how much the Laird was willing to reveal.

"I needed a Second and asked around. He came highly recommended by Patrick Gordon, General to Tsar Peter of Russia. Spence wanted to return to Scotland, so I hired him. He was tough but competent, just what we needed. We worked well together, but never would have been close. Perhaps it was less a love of Scotland than a desire for something else that impelled his return. There was something about him, an anger or sadness, a darkness in his soul. He never discussed it and I never asked." Laird MacDuff was far more perceptive and thoughtful than I'd imagined but a few days ago.

"Was there a link between him and Lady Julianne?" I hated changing the subject like this, but he seemed in a mood to talk.

He looked at me intently. "I don't know. They arrived about the same time, but they would have traveled in different circles, she in the Royal Court, he in the military. They may have crossed paths, but never acknowledged so here, at least not in my presence."

I didn't see a connection either, then offered: "There are other Russians and Scots with Russian connections in Torrport too, Gregor and Sir Ross Campbell, for example. Do you know of others?"

"Aye, a few, I will give you their names, but I am not sure they have any connection to Spence, and then there is our new blacksmith. I've heard he is widely traveled too." He paused. "I think we have enough to start the investigation now. My men will be conducting inquiries among the ranks. You can pay Gilly and the others a visit. I have other business, excuse me." He bowed to Elspeth and rose to leave us, then stopped. "Something has been bothering my mind. The murder scene. Where are Captain Spence's brace of silver pistols? He goes nowhere without them, and those pistols are valuable. His murder could have been nothing more than a robbery gone wrong."

"How likely was that? Most everyone knew him, and he was skilled."

"Unless he was quite drunk or knew his assailant, he wouldn't have been caught off-guard."

The Laird was right of course, and we'd missed that in our observations. Spence was unarmed when we found him. Strange indeed! Elspeth and I looked at each other and I shrugged. We were both tired and I in pain. That was obvious. "I desperately need a lay down." I pressed my lower back for comfort.

"You look it, Malcolm. You are starting to tilt. Please go home and take some willow bark and have a rest." She was beginning to act like my doctor. "I have other patients, but will send Janet to look in on you and bring some food."

"I will most certainly enjoy seeing her." We both chuckled.

It was an agonizing walk home, and I fell, listless on my bed and was instantly asleep expecting to be pleasantly awoken in a few hours by a buxom red-head bearing a loaf of fresh bread and steaming bowl of beef stew. That is not exactly how it turned out, much like my life.

* * *

I felt someone touching me and my consciousness rose out of that grave of blissful near-death, then there was the scent of fresh bread and gravy, and my soul smiled. "You've come just in time, my beauty." I mumbled, lips hardly open. Then I heard a low growl, like Henry would issue when he sensed someone outside at night. I pushed that thought away and said as I opened one eye, "I'm uncommonly athirst and long to drink in your sweet visage." Something was not right. Instead of that smiling soft face ringed with red waves, my bleary eyes beheld the angry expression of that damned bearded highlander!

He threw the bread at me and swore something in Gaelic that sounded ominously like "I'll kill you. Stupid arse!" I sat up with a gasp, heart trying to catch up.

"Cawdie, come back! I was having a dream of Gwen, my woman in Edinburgh." It was a lie of course, but I didn't need anymore trouble in my life. He returned slowly, leaning on the door jamb, massive arms crossed, scowling at me, then he said slowly and clearly so it would not be misunderstood.

"*Ye'll nae tooch mah Janet.*"

I looked him in the eye and said: "No Cawdie. She's a fine woman and all yours, believe me. I am sure she loves you very much. Now what have you brought for my supper besides this ruined bread on the floor." I bent over to pick up the damaged loaf.

"*A pot ay stew an' a jug ay ale.*"

I immediately thought how much I could use that ale right now. "Thank you Cawdie, you may return to your women."

"*Whit abit 'at guard?*"

"What guard?

"*Th' a body ah hud tae tie up ootwith.*"

"You tied someone up?" I asked to be sure.

"Aye."

I placed the bread on my bedside table and went downstairs and out the front door to the dock and there he was, a young lad, gagged and bound to a dock post. I knelt beside him and smiled reassuringly. "You made the mistake of trying to stop that hairy mountain, didn't you?" He nodded as I untied his gag. "Well done, boy, at least you tried. I'll send a letter of commendation to the Laird."

They are so young now. Days long past, a warrior needed to be strong enough to wield the mighty broadsword or pull the longbow to be of any use in the clan militia. Now all one needs are the ability to lift a flintlock and stand resolute amid chaos. These young ones today are more easily lead and have little care for health and safety, the perfect warrior for our new world. "Let Cawdie in next time. He's a friend, and protector of Lady Elspeth and her companion Lady Janet." The boy stood up and straightened his clothes. "A word of advice. Never let anyone take that flintlock from you while you're alive." I smiled and patted him on the shoulder and returned, anticipating supper.

Cawdie was still there and hovered nearby while I quickly ate. "You must be getting soft from spending too much time with women. The younger Cawdie would have hurled that boy in the drink, would he not?" I glanced up at him in time to see the beginnings of a smile under his shaggy beard. He must have thought better of it and merely gave a shrug. "Tell Elspeth, I shall leave tomorrow on the morning carriage and can see Julianne and the bairn before I leave, if she wishes." I pushed the empty stew pot and ale jug away. He collected them in his sack and was to the door when I remembered. "Cawdie." I took a folded paper out of my waistcoat pocket, rose and offered it to him. "It's a map. In case of trouble, I want you to get the women out of Torrport. That will take you to an old croft we own on a stream in Fordell Glen to the north-west that we use for fishing." He opened the map and nodded as I continued. "It has good water and forage and enough supplies til winter."

"Ah can fin' it." He glanced up.

"Good. Beside the door, you'll see our family crest with the hound on it. I know it fits." I grinned at him and was surprised, when he responded in-kind. "I've also put down a deposit on a gig and mare called Gracie at the stable. Elspeth can use it anytime, and for as long as she wants. She knows the boy Daniel there." He nodded again. "Godspeed Cawdie. I wish us all the best."

He merely said "Aye", and left.

I returned to my bedroom and lay back on the bed staring at the ceiling. I needed to be ready to leave and arrive prepared to deal with Edinburgh and the tasks at hand. It would be best if I didn't draw attention. Many knew me, and word would soon get around if I was recognized by certain people. It wouldn't do to sneak about in disguise, but changing my look might work almost as well. I went to my wardrobe and pulled out the black, wool cape I sometimes used for rough travel, then matched it with a well-worn black waistcoat, and trousers. Combined with a simple linen shirt, stockings, black shoes, and lack of adornment, I would blend in with the masses of merchants and junior bankers that filled the streets. I put them on and looked in the mirror. I looked scruffy, having not shaved for a few days. My beard is thick and black and comes in curly, quite unlike my brown hair that has only a bit of natural wave. I rummaged in the wardrobe drawer and found the old pipe given in thanks by a patient.

He didn't know I hated tobacco smoke. Now it might be of use to change the aspect of my face. I stood there with the pipe hanging out one corner of my mouth and imagining the fuller black beard that would appear quickly, and I knew it could work.

There was one more thing I had to change my style, and I might need it too. A sword. Of course, I'd be wearing my pistol and small dagger, but they are subtle, hidden. I needed to make a statement, that I would not be trifled with. I was prepared to fight. I had two swords, one a delicate rapier from Father, given on my coming of age. It was precious and inappropriate. The other was an abused cutlass, of the short kind favoured by merchant seamen and pirates, perfect for hack and slash melees. I'd reluctantly obtained it in exchange for some laudanum from a dying sailor. It was there at the back under a pile of old boots and belts. I put it on and adjusted the belt and scabbard, pulled the blade and knew it must be sharpened in the morning. My transformation was complete, from upper class doctor to a man of the masses. I took out my travel bag and filled it with the basics, fresh shirts, hose, underwear, nightshirt, toiletries. I'd be away for three weeks or so, but there wouldn't be any need for visiting or formal attire. Next was my medical bag. I went through it carefully, supplementing where needed. McLaren would have everything, but it was best to be prepared. I was ready. My replacement should have arrived on the afternoon carriage and would report for duty in the morning, as arranged. I felt that calm resignation of the warrior on the eve of battle, and sat down at my desk and wrote a note to Elspeth and instructions to the new man in case I should not return.

* * *

It was getting late but the murder of Spence and possible link with Julianne was going around in my mind, so I decided to pay a visit before bed. I fetched and saddled Gracie and we set off through town on the way to Elspeth's cottage. It was a pleasant fair eve, and I'd be leaving on the morrow, and when one considers it could be a last time, senses are more alert. I was noticing things I hadn't before, like the meats hanging in the butcher's window, so many shapes and hues arranged like an artist's tableau, or the new fashion in women's bonnets with the frilly bits and bows in the front.

Janet let me in with a radiant smile. "I apologize for the hour, but I will be leaving soon, and we need to speak."

"You are always welcome here, sir." She stepped aside, and I could see Elspeth sitting with Julianne and the babe. Lady Julianne turned slightly and pulled her shawl forward over her breasts and the baby.

"Please join us for tea, Malcolm." Elspeth rose to greet me and arranged another chair close to them.

I settled in and at once could see that the babe was trying to suckle. "Is he doing well, Lady Julianne?"

"He is, Sir Malcolm, no small thanks to Lady Elspeth and our talented blacksmith."

"He made a device to allow her to express milk for the babe," Elspeth said when she saw my quizzical look.

"Ah, how clever. Lady Julianne, a few things have been bothering me about the murder of Captain Spence."

She looked up from the babe. "I am sure there are many such things."

"Please forgive me, but we must ask everyone. Were you here all last evening?" I said it in as friendly a manner as I could.

She laughed. "No, I was not."

I wasn't quite expecting that. "Can you please explain?"

"I can see you have not cared for a babe. He fusses at night and wants to be fed, so I must care for him, and that night I went out for a while to walk and rock him in my arms. It was a lovely warm night, was it not?"

"But too wet for some." I tried to jest but it was in bad taste, I know, yet Elspeth grinned.

"The victim had come from Russia at the same time as you. Did you know him there?"

Julianne looked up for a moment, then back at me. "No, but I'd heard of him, he was a fellow Scot and many of us knew each other, but I believe he was with Sophia at the Novodevichy Convent in Moscow, perhaps guarding her. I am not sure. It would be better to ask Laird MacDuff. He hired him."

I didn't quite understand the connections, but let it be.

"Russian politics are very confusing, even for one born there." She smiled then lifted the babe and kissed him on the forehead and placed him in his basket. "I am sorry, I must prepare some milk for this eve."

That didn't help her alibi, but I could hardly imagine her being able to murder someone, unless in self defense. "Good evening, Lady Julianne." I watched her go behind the screen to the bed, then Janet returned with my tea and took Julianne's place by the fire.

"I spoke with Cawdie today." I looked at them both to see if they understood my meaning.

"Aye, we know. Thank you, Malcolm. We will follow Cawdie's lead in times of danger." Elspeth reached one hand down and stroked the babe's head.

Janet leaned over to me and whispered. "Thank you also for mending fences with him."

"A misunderstanding, is all." Well, not quite. She's a stunning woman. Perhaps in another time and place...

Her face reddened. "I hope it wasn't just that."

Elspeth looked at us both and interrupted with: "Alright you two, we have enough trouble as is."

The word "trouble" brought me back and I remembered the note I'd written for Elspeth. I took it out and handed it to her. "A list of my patients, diagnoses, treatments, etc. I made a similar list for my locum. His name is Andrew Mitchell, by the way. I know nothing of him beyond being well regarded by Young. He is a recent graduate. I trust you will make him welcome."

"I will, Malcolm. I will give him all the women's problems and difficult births."

"You will not!" I burst out laughing, while worrying she might do exactly that.

I rose to go. "It's late and I have a long day ahead."

"Malcolm, I know it will do no good to say this, but I wish you would not participate in this experiment. You are in no condition to do so, and you well know it."

"I am needed Elspeth, and trust me I'm fine."

I was about to leave when Elspeth ran to me, tried to put her small arms around my waist, then said in a voice muffled by my waistcoat. "Farewell, my friend. We will come if you need us."

* * *

I awoke early next morning thinking of all I must do in my remaining hours in Torrport. I was dressing when a knock came on the door and a cheery "hello" echoed up the stairs. It was Andrew Mitchell, precisely on time. He is thin, blond, with a vestigial mustache and a languorous slouch as he draped himself on my sofa as we went over the same list I'd given Elspeth. I told him they'd have to decide between them who would do what and warned him to demean her at his peril. She was not your typical village healer. He chuckled slowly, but I don't think he fully understood and I decided to let him find out for himself.

I had to hurry to catch the morning carriage, so we said our goodbyes and I grabbed my bags and was there just in time to throw them up to the coachman. As I climbed aboard I could hear the horses snorting and shuffling, ready for the day's work. In a few minutes, we were off, clattering along the rutted road leading out of town. I looked out the window, back toward town and saw the last of the docks, then turned my head just in time to see a farmer throwing hay down from the mow to a cow and her suckling calf. I grinned, and the farmer lifted his pitchfork in salute. I waved back and wished a fond farewell to my beloved Torrport and prayed we would meet again.

SIXTEEN

Elspeth – Handfasting

It was a relief to be back at the cottage after the autopsy and meeting with the Laird. Janet and Julianne both eyed me thoughtfully, sniffed, and immediately set about preparing a bath. My clothes were malodorous, rumpled and covered with dark splotches that did not bear identifying. My hair smelled and felt foul. I sat in the warmed water and scrubbed myself repeatedly until I realized I had made my skin raw. Memories of the morning were not going to be scoured away no matter how hard I washed. Janet toweled my hair but seeing my impatience to go out again, braided it again while it was still slightly damp.

"At least eat a bit before you go." Janet was mothering me again, so I forced down coffee and a bite of bread and cheese to please her. I picked up my bag and the sack containing my filthy clothes to take to Aggie. "I will be fine, I need to see Aggie and Molly's girl Leana," I said, and left.

So much had happened since my last trip down this path, and it seemed longer ago than just this morning. The port was bustling. The tavern was noisy and filled, patrons spilling out onto the docks. When they saw me, there was a hush; I nodded tranquilly at them as I passed. Several women were gathered at the entrance to the laundry area, but were stopped there by a rope someone had tied across the entrance opening. They fell silent as I came toward them. I pushed my way to the front and called out to Aggie who was sitting dejectedly on the bench by the back door of the tavern.

"Aggie," I said gently. She looked up at once and sprang to her feet, coming toward me hastily.

"Lady Elspeth! What did you find? Sir Malcolm told me not to move anything til he said, so I am waiting. Tis very late, mayhap I could work now?"

I ducked under the rope and handed her my laundry, knowing that anyone looking on would report that I did so. Murder is not good for business and I wanted to show my support of Aggie. I looked around. Everything was exactly as it had been. The bluing in the tub where Spence had been kneeling looked clean and placid. I shuddered. "Did someone come and look at everything? They should have told you it was all right."

"Yes, um. They come and went. Do you think it would be all right if I cleaned the place and got back to work?

"I am sure it would, Aggie." I studied the space again but could see nothing further that would be of interest in any investigation. "I have to see Lady Margaret this afternoon, and I will tell the Laird. I am certain it was just an oversight. I will tell them I gave you leave." She brightened immediately, and motioned to the women who helped her. They slipped under the rope and when I left they were lifting the heavy tubs to empty and scrub them and the paving stones free of imagined horrors.

I walked along the alley leading to the castle steps, retracing the path the killer might have taken. The stalls were mostly untended as the vendors gathered in small clusters, exchanging rumors and hearsay. I stopped at the first group, in front of the flower stall. "I wish you all a good day." I mustered my most charming smile for them. Two had been my patients, so they greeted me cordially enough. "I am sure that you have all heard about the death at Aggie's laundry, and that the Laird has ordered an enquiry? He would be most grateful for your help with this." Remembering the Laird's less than gracious behavior earlier this morning, I crossed my fingers mentally. "Were any of you here, or did you notice anything unusual when you came in?"

They looked at one another, then one that I recognized as the mercer spoke hesitantly.   "Aye,

lady. I slept with me cloth last night." He flushed. "I stayed a wee bit too long at the tavern, and me guidwife locked the door, so I curled up in that red blanket behind me stand to sleep." A few snorts from his fellows told me that this was a commonplace happening. He ignored them. "I waked to footsteps and some rough talk, but then they moved on down the alley. There were two of 'em, I think, but could not swear to it. Me old bones do not take to sleeping on the ground, so I soon tried me door again, to find the lock undone. I slipped into me bed and slept until only an hour ago, and missed the doings this morning." He sounded aggrieved to have missed the excitement.

"Did you hear sounds of a struggle? What makes you think there were two?" I focused on the mercer. He was dark of skin and short, a paunch hanging over his belt. His round childlike face shone beneath a bald pate partially hidden beneath a crimson knitted cap. A neatly groomed beard almost reached his belt, an obvious effort to draw attention away from the lack of hair on his head. He looked much like an elderly elf.

"I...be not sure, lady. Twas late, and I were very...err, sleepy. There may have been a bit of that. Twas the voices that made me think two. One were deep, but I thought the other were a boy or mayhap a woman." He looked around at his fellows, who nodded at me as though to confirm his tale. Then he closed his lips firmly, saying no more.

"That is of interest, sir. Did any of you notice anything else?" I moved slowly down the alley, but there were no more disclosures. The vendor's tale only confirmed what we already heard from James Allen, the wool merchant. But the mercer had heard only two? The wool merchant had said he heard three voices, so someone else must have joined them. Just as I reached the little park at the end of the alley, the mercer broke away from the group again, hurried toward me and spoke nervously.

"One last thing." He sounded apologetic and glanced back at the merchants who were openly curious. "What did wake me first were footsteps, fast ones, like running almost. When I saw out, someone went by. Methought I were dreaming for I saw fairy gold sparkles trailing them in the torchlight and one fell on the cobblestones nearby. But it were real enough. I picked it up and kept it in this. It may be naught, but tis strange to see such in these parts. Tis more a craftsman's like." He took a square of white linen from his pouch and handed it to me. I opened it cautiously. A long thin fragment of something metallic glittered in the sunlight. Gold leaf! It was used by many craftsmen, framers, metalsmiths, illuminators, even cooks. My hands shook slightly as I folded the fabric carefully back over the fragile stuff.

"May I keep this, sir?" He bobbed his head. I tucked it carefully into my bag, and turned to him. "Well done! I cannot thank you enough, sir. I will tell the Laird of your service. We will need to speak with you again, but this may well be of great assistance." He beamed, and I left him puffing out his chest with new importance as he strutted back to the others.

* * *

The guard at the castle door recognized me this time, and called for someone to escort me to Lady Margaret. She was in her solar, silks spilled in a kaleidoscope of color around her feet, with her maid helping sort them. When I was announced, she pushed them aside and greeted me, a slight blush rising to her cheeks. "Lady Elspeth. Sir Malcolm told me you would attend me. I am grateful to you for coming. It seems we should be friends. I ask your forgiveness. Shall we begin again?"

"Indeed so, Lady Margaret. Tis my wish as well. Sir Malcolm said you wish to speak to me?" My eyes flicked toward the maid, who did not look up, but continued to work on the threads tangled on the floor. Lady Margaret noticed my glance.

"You may be excused, Rachel. She is overset. Spence was her husband, you know. We were just discussing what she wishes to do in future. Of course, she may remain with us." She smiled kindly at the girl, who stood and looked at us, eyes red with weeping and lack of sleep. She curtsied and left the room. Lady Margaret gestured to a beautifully carved couch next to a table laid with tea things and small cakes. "Please join me. Would you like something?"

"I thank you, but I fear I have no appetite. Please tell me how I can help you."

"I want a baby." She blurted it out. Her voice was almost pleading. "Is there a way to make me more receptive to my husband's seed? Sir Malcolm gave me some instructions about bathing, but said that you were more familiar with the plaints of women?"

I examined her with my eyes. She was a handsome woman, not yet too old to bear children, nor sickly looking. There were no outward signs of illness. "If you will permit me to examine you, I may be able to help. Please sit on the couch and lift your skirts. Tell me about your courses. Are they regular?"

"Oh, yes. My flowers have not abated although..." She paused. "There is more of an odor to them." She sat, pulled her skirts to her waist, and opened her legs.

"Do you have any pain or discharge between your flowers?"

She colored, and looked down at her twisting hands and moved uncomfortably a moment before she answered. "I have an unpleasant itch and burning in my secrets and it hurts to pass

water...and to...to be with my husband. Sometimes there is a thick white substance that passes...and it has an unpleasant smell." She had just described a common woman's complaint which my scrutiny confirmed. Her privy parts were swollen, and a rash extended down her legs between her thighs. I sat back and reached for my bag.

"The first thing we must do is make you more comfortable. Malcolm spoke to you about bathing? I will add to that." I opened my bag and pulled out several small cloth sacks of powdered oats mixed with mint. "I want you to put one of these in your bathwater, and soak for a half hour in it each time you bathe. Next, please send your maid for plain yogurt from the castle kitchen. Dry yourself carefully after your soak, then apply two or three tablespoons of the yogurt to your secrets and your rash. Leave it on for an hour and then wipe it off with a damp cloth. Do it three times each day, or even overnight if possible. You will find it most soothing.

I wish for you to eat a half cup of plain yogurt each time, too. Put on a clean chemise each day. When you are better, I will make you a special syrup of arrach herb and honey that will help you conceive."

She looked at me and I was startled to see tears running down her cheeks. "I shall do everything you have told me. All...faithfully, anything! If this gives me a child, I shall be forever in your debt. Forever..."

"Let us both pray for that outcome then, Lady Margaret. Shall I tell your maid to come to you?" She nodded. I closed my bag and left her dreaming of a future filled with childish laughter amid the colorful tapestries she had created, many of which depicted unicorns.

* * *

I started back toward Torrport, but changed my mind and direction and went on toward the smithy. The fragment of gold leaf burned in my bag. I wanted to see Aidan's workshop again...and Aidan. The carriage for Edinburgh was loading in front of the square by the smithy. A neatly dressed elderly couple were climbing inside, assisted by a manservant almost as old as they, and a middle-aged woman carrying a covered basket of enraged felines protesting piercingly. The manservant closed the carriage door with obvious relief, jumped onto the empty seat next to the driver, and they were away.

Aidan was speaking with someone inside the smithy. He moved his big body slightly, and I saw it was Gregor. I wondered what business Gregor or Sir Ross had with the smith. Their conversation ceased as I approached, and they bowed politely enough, although obviously wishing me at the devil. I gave them honeyed greetings then threw caution to the winds. "Ah, the murder seems to be the favorite topic everywhere today. Is there news?" Both retained faultless expressions of polite disinterest at my question and did not immediately respond.

"No?" I reached into my bag, took out the cloth the mercer had given me and unfolded it to reveal the contents. "This was found nearby. Do either of you know who in Torrport might have use for it?" They looked down and the metal winked in the sun.

Aidan said, "I beat gold and have such in my workshop, Lady Elspeth. I use it for numerous things as well as provide it for the castle kitchen and others who might have need it. There is no jeweler in Torrport...except for my own modest work, and goldbeating is a specialized skill." His clear eyes held mine and I felt a bit sick at the idea he might have killed Spence.

"And I, also," Gregor interjected, with his scarcely perceptible Russian accent. "The flakes were prescribed by an Edinburgh physician for Sir Ross, to be added to his liquors for pain."

I turned to Gregor. That was true, I used it myself. So much for eliminating suspects. Now I must add two more to the list. I refolded the cloth and replaced it in my bag.

"How fares Lady Julianne? She has not been seen in many days. My family inquired of me about her." I was bewildered by Aidan's query. Their families knew each other?

"She is in health, sir. You know Lady Julianne well?"

"Since the day she pushed me into the loch after I put a caterpillar on her arm." He laughed. "She was six and I was eight. We were neighbors in Deptford. Her father was a shipbuilder, mine was a watchmaker and jeweler who made tools for navigation. When the Tsar was staying there, he asked both our families to come to Russia, so we are of long acquaintance. In Russia, I apprenticed as a metalsmith." He flushed and stopped speaking, his eyes wary. I wondered why. Another little piece of information to mull over.

I returned to the subject of gold leaf. "Sir, might you give me a list of those in Torrport who have purchased gold leaf from you?"

"I would be happy to be of service, lady. There are only a few." His voice held a trace of amusement, but he stepped into his workshop and prepared a list of four names written in an elegant hand. I read it. Sir Ross and I were both on it, as well as Rachel Spence and a frame maker I had not met. Smiths did not often know how to write, nor was their manner refined. Aidan fascinated me. I thanked him, nodded to Gregor, and left them both staring after me.

* * *

The path down the hill toward the fishing village was uneven and treacherous even in the light of day. From a distance, the village looked appealingly picturesque against the backdrop of cerulean water, and mottled hills. The air held the indescribable tang that so affects those who love the sea. I inhaled deeply, knowing it would soon be mixed with the odors of rotting fish and human waste. Unlike Torrport, the fishing dock was almost deserted. I soon discovered why.

The ale pole hung over the tavern door and the tavern was filled. Conversation died as I entered, then resumed as I walked up the stairs. My knock on the door brought an eye to study me through a small hole. Molly opened the door. She is a large sturdy woman, not yet gone to ruin. Her face was drawn, but lightened when she saw me. "Lady Elspeth! Glad I am to see you. The oat baths did help her, but the wee thing is covered with even more pox today!"

I put down my bag and walked over to the child. The room was a revelation, spotlessly clean, with whitewashed walls, and fresh curtains at the windows. An undersized bed stood in one corner, dressed in fresh linens. A coverlet lovingly embroidered with twining flowers and leaves lay over its small occupant. I smiled down at Leana and lowered her gown, noting that her hands were free of spots although new ones had appeared on her chest and at the hairline. She still had a slight fever but let me examine her without protest, watching me with curiosity rather than fear, obediently opening her mouth when I asked. The sores in her throat must have hurt. A twisted paper filled with lemon honey drops appeared from the depths of my bag. "These are for you, Leana, because you are such a good wee bairn. Your mother will give you one after each bath, and before you go to sleep." I handed the twist to Molly. "She will be fine. Just keep doing as I told you. New spots may keep coming for a day or so, but that will stop soon. You can let Jocki play with her when all the spots are crusted over, but not before. Keep everyone away until they are gone. Use the salve to help prevent scarring."

Molly made a low snarling sound deep in her throat. "I keep my bairn away from them all below stairs, lady. No one sees to her but me and my man and Jocki. No one!"

I touched the fairy-like creature on the bed, again marveling that such beauty could spring up in unexpected places. "I will return in a few days, but send for me if you need me." I looked around the room again seeing the difference between this and the rooms below. A wee dress lay unfinished on a nearby table. The soft fabric in the process of being embellished with beautiful stitched silk embroidery. Molly picked it up defensively. "Tis but a way to pass the time, and the child do look bonny in such."

"Indeed, she will, Molly, I have a piece of wool that I will send you. Tis too little to use for me but might be fashioned into something for your bairn." I touched the red, work-roughened hands that could create such delicate work for love of her child, and left.

At the foot of the steps I saw Gilly. "How fare you? Are you well now?" She stopped, and shifted the empty tray to her other side. "I am, Lady Elspeth. Come to see the wee rose upstairs, have you?

"Indeed, Gilly. Do you have a moment?" She looked about, then nodded, and we walked out of the foul room to the slightly less noisome air outside the tavern.

"How kin I help ye, lady?"

"Gilly, I am sure you already know that the Laird has asked Sir Malcolm and me to gather information about Spence, so we can bring his murderer to justice. Is there anything you can tell me about him that might help?"

Gilly looked at me pityingly. "Lady Elspeth. Ah ken naught, but whoever did it, has me thanks. He were an evil man an reaped what he sowed. Ye be a good woman, but ye dinna ken real wickedness. Some here breathe easier now that he does not." She sighed heavily and thought for a moment. "Ah canna help ye much. That night he were here. Sportin' them silver pistols he wore and dressed to kill." She flushed, look at me and continued. "Flashin' coin for ale for all an sundry. He took the new lass upstairs, but he were sae drunk ah doubt he did much. I dinna see him later." I thanked her and left.

At home Janet and Julianne were eating and entertaining the baby who was observing them both solemnly from his basket which had been placed on the table. I decided to say nothing to Julianne about Aidan yet. I was too exhausted to think clearly so bid them both goodnight and was asleep in my bed before darkness had fully fallen.

I awoke to the smell of breakfast, and dressed more carefully than usual. Sir Ross was my first patient today. Janet grinned at the sight of my second-best dress but wisely kept her thoughts to herself. I ate what she put in front of me and spent a few moments checking and replacing things in my bag. I leaned over the bairn and kissed his wee head and left to see my patients.

* * *

My first impression upon being admitted to Sir Ross's house was that it smelled better. The odor of unwashed putrid flesh and feces was no longer pervasive. Now garlic and lavender prevailed, mixed with the warm scent of spice cake. Gregor, ever playing the perfect servant, took me to his master, and left us.

"Sir Ross. I need not ask if you are feeling better. You are visibly so!"

"My dear lady. "He bent over my hand and kissed the air above it. holding it a few seconds too long before he straightened. He had taken some pains with his toilet. A cascade of fine ruffled lace fell from his neckcloth over the front of his fashionably shorter red coat. The wide skirts of the coat were plaited into the side seams, and the sleeves were loosely fitted with wide cuffs. More lace fell below the cuffs, covering his wrists and almost obscuring the sparkle of gems on his fingers. His matching red britches were visible below the fashionable coat and white hose encased his legs ending in fine leather shoes. I felt decidedly dowdy.

I removed my hand gently from his and smiled. "You have heard from the surgeon in Edinburgh? How are you feeling?"

"Sir Malcolm has made arrangements for me. I am most grateful. Your treatment has helped greatly. I am sleeping and moving well, although I look forward to getting the surgery over, so I can get back to riding. Tis a very confining problem." He stopped, embarrassed, coughed, and continued. "But come, I wish to show you my latest French baby. Tis a shame they have little of the same for men." He led me toward one of the cabinets of curiosities in the sitting room. I was struck again by the riches he surrounded himself with. Shelves of books lined two walls, opulent silks and velvets covered windows and furniture, paintings hung stacked to the ceiling above intricately crafted chests and cabinets. An exquisite ivory box, with a carved panel featuring the Imperial two headed eagle of Russia sat on a nearby table. Central to the eye, was a carved cabinet. He opened its doors and I saw that it contained nine enchanting miniature rooms, completely furnished in lavish detail. I knelt in awe before a series of apartments far better fitted than their full-sized counterparts. The dining room displayed plates and silver placed for a meal. A tiny silver teapot sat ready to pour into miniscule bowls, and wee foods were being prepared in the kitchen. On the second floor or shelf, mimicking the first floor of a house, were three beautifully dressed French babies. Sir Ross picked up one and held it out to me. "She came just this morning, I picked her up at the port."

The doll was about ten inches tall and made of wood with a painted face. Dark glass eyes glinted beneath her elaborately fashioned wool hair. This one was dressed "en grand toilette" with strands of miniature beads and much jewelry. I was charmed, and looked at Sir Ross and smiled. "With her own inviolable passport, no doubt?" Such dolls were exempt from the

embargo on enemy imports even at the height of the war. In an exceptional display of gallantry, the mannequins had been granted a special pass by both governments that guaranteed they would not be molested during their travels. The dolls were attired in the latest and most elegant designs and women demanded them despite the games men played. It was said that fashion takes precedence over everything, even religion.

I touched the tiny painted "gallant" patch on the doll's right cheek. Patches were often used to hide pox marks as well as to send messages of one's availability. It occurred to me to wonder what the dolls themselves could hide. This wee woman wore a sumptuous train and many layers of clothing that might easily conceal papers or other communications. With a last envious touch to the silky skirts, I gave the doll back to Sir Ross.

"Exquisite, Sir. My collection quiet pales. Where did you find such a splendid baby house?"

"In Holland. They are much collected there by both ladies and gentlemen. There are craftsmen who specialize only in such. The Tsar was much taken with them." He abruptly stopped speaking, turned, and carefully replaced the doll in the cabinet, exchanging it for a miniscule silver cup which he placed in my palm.

"This was made by Aidan. Are you aware that he is a highly talented craftsman? His father was a gifted goldsmith."

"Tis fit for a fae queen." I lifted the precious thing to better see the delicate leaves and flowers chased on it. It was a perfect replica. "I must ask him to make some plate for my cabinet." I hesitated, then went on, "I would be pleased to have you come and see my own collection. Tis small, but there are several wee Italian paintings that might be of interest." I smiled at him, and he glowed.

"I am honored, Lady Elspeth. I will give myself the pleasure of calling on you when you will permit." I assured him I would let him know when it was convenient, and left him gazing after me. He looked both wistful and slightly apprehensive. I wondered what I had done to cause him concern?

* * *

Cawdie met me at the gate to the cottage. *"Tis guests ye hae, quine, an' best Ah warn ye tae be wary. quine Julianne has a visitur. himself cam wi' tois Ah am keepin' it haur."* He gestured toward the shed where two large men stood drinking and looking at the garden. They wore slops, jackets and the warm Monmouth caps favored by seamen. The caps were made of wool, fulled by hand and foot beating, and perhaps even knit by their own hands. Many sailors whiled away the time at sea knitting, and sold their work in port. These two, however, carried themselves more like warriors than seamen.

"Methinks tis the bairn's sire, lady."

"Thank you, Cawdie." He was scowling, and I touched his arm. "It will be well." I walked quickly to the house, curious to see the "nobleman" who had ruined Julianne and let her bear his child alone. Opening the door, I stepped inside. The man who turned toward me was a giant! Taller than Cawdie who was well over six feet, he was slender but well-muscled. Heavy dark chestnut hair, escaping from beneath another Monmouth cap, curled about his handsome face. Dense black brows over large hooded and heavily fringed black eyes stared back at me above a classic nose and well-shaped lips. He was dressed simply, in a coat of salmon and white stripes, over a white shirt, and brown britches, which detracted not at all from the palpable aura of power surrounding him. He was quite imposing...and knew it. He was holding the bairn gently in improbably undersized hands. Scathach watched him closely, but she did not object to his presence. There was a short silence while we inspected each other. Julianne burst into speech.

"Sir, may I present Lady Elspeth, who has cared for us in her home. Lady Elspeth, this is Sir Peter. She added no family name. For some reason, I bowed my head and curtsied to him.

When I looked up he was smiling and said in accented but excellent English, "I have come to see my child."

"We are to be handfasted, then the babe can be christened." Julianne sounded relieved and oddly anxious. "Please? We wish for you to be godmother to him. Will you go at once to see Father Hammet with us? It must be a simple thing, for Sir Peter cannot stay long." She looked at me imploringly, more than a hint of desperation in her voice.

"I would be honored, Lady Julianne, Sir Peter." Everything was happening at an accelerated pace. I sent for Cawdie and had him go to the kirk to see if Father Hammet was there and warn him of what was wanted. Janet and I began to plan food and drink for the celebration. Sir Peter patted Julianne's shoulder in an indulgent manner and went to inform his men of the plans, and Julianne checked the bairn for dampness while he focused his own dark eyes on her face.

"Julianne, shall I send for the Laird? I asked. Her hands paused in their work, then she nodded.

Cawdie returned to say that Father Hammet would meet us at the kirk. I sent him out again to find the Laird.

We waited, chatting about nothings until Cawdie returned with the Laird and Lady Margaret. Julianne hurried to them, and they spoke quietly for a few moments. The Laird looked over Julianne's head to the large man, and a silent message seemed to pass between them. Sir Peter nodded at the Laird as Julianne returned to his side and he leaned down to whisper something in her ear that made her blush. He laughed, and turned to Cawdie. "My gratitude for your service to my lady, sir." Cawdie looked up at him, something that he had done to no man before, grunted a barely civil response, and the strange assemblage began the unplanned journey to the kirk.

* * *

The kirk sits near the castle, on the top of the hill between Torrport and the fishing village. The living includes a cottage with a bit of land nearby. Father Hammet can be found most often in the garden he planted there. The plot was deserted today, but the fragrance of early flowers drifted on the wind. Sunlight lay in bright patches on the smooth grass of the common in front of the kirk where a tethered white goat grazed content to keep it so.

The interior of the kirk was cool and ablaze with color from the stained-glass windows. Father Hammet was waiting, his white cravat crisp against the black fabric of his clothing. He had been told that this was to be a simple handfasting, followed immediately by a christening. A faint line of concern creased his forehead, but after looking at the Laird who nodded imperceptibly, he said nothing. By Scottish law, as soon as a couple made their vows to each other they were validly married, and a child born to them before the handfasting was considered legitimate. Father Hammet could then baptize the babe accordingly.

We gathered in the aisle. Julianne put the bairn in my arms and turned to Father Hammet, her face pale. "Father, this is Sir Peter Alekseyevich Romanov. We wish to make our vows before witnesses, to have you baptize our bairn, and to have Lady Elspeth and Laird MacDuff as godparents." Her voice trembled only a little.

Father Hammet nodded. "I understand your wishes, Lady Julianne, but I must ask if you are quite certain that you wish to do this? He looked inquiringly at the extraordinary tall man standing next to her. "And you, sir?"

"I do, sir." His words were delivered clearly, and he held out his large calloused hand to Julianne.

"Then I will execute the office of handfasting between...Sir Peter Alekseyevich Romanov...to Lady Julianne Morrison." He held up a length of ribbon before them.

Julianne straightened and took Sir Peter's hand firmly in hers as Sir Hammet bound their two hands together and began speaking. "Say after me:

I, Peter Alekseyevich Romanov, take thou, Julianne Morrison as my espoused wife, and thereto I plight my troth."

There was the briefest of hesitations before Sir Peter echoed the words, but he responded in a strong voice. I saw Julianne exhale, and they both recited the rest of the ceremony in accord. At the end, Sir Peter removed a thick golden ring from his jacket and placed it on Julianne's finger. It was too large, so he closed her hand, so it would not fall off, and patted it. She looked up at him. Both relief and gratitude momentarily showed in her face, and it was done.

Julianne turned and walked determinedly to the baptismal font, the rest of us in train to see the rite. I held the wee one close, enjoying the clean baby smell and feeling a tug in my womb. As his godparents and guardians, the Laird and I spoke for him, accepting good and rejecting evil in his name, while praying devoutly for the health of his parents. When Father Hammet asked the name for the child, Sir Peter looked at Julianne, then said, "Peter Gordon Alekseyevich." We signed the church register, and it was done. All I could think of was that Julianne and the baby were safe from censure. I let out a breath I had not realized I was holding, and pulled Julianne and the babe into my arms. She was trembling violently, so I simply stood there, willing strength into her until she calmed.

Cawdie and Janet invited everyone back to the cottage for a wee celebration. The cottage was crowded, and the *wee celebration* overflowed into the yard and garden. Lady Margaret had stayed quietly in the background, but now she approached Julianne and asked humbly to hold the bairn. Her eyes were moist as she cradled him. She looked happier, glancing often to the Laird, who was speaking inaudibly with Sir Peter. There was none of the Laird's usual arrogance in his stance, and he showed a deference to his new kinsman that I found strange. The celebration was becoming quieter. I was wondering about sleeping arrangements for the newly handfasted pair, and considering asking the Laird's help, when Julianne and Sir Peter drew me aside. He bowed courteously over my hand, acknowledging all I had done for the mother of his child, and explained that unfortunately he must leave at once on urgent business. The Laird and he had agreed that Julianne and the baby would return to the castle in the morning. Two of his men would be staying to act as her personal servants and guards while he was away. He looked at Cawdie almost apologetically. "I know your allegiance belongs here, sir." He glanced across the room at his son, sleeping contentedly in Lady Margaret's arms, and took Julianne's hand, as they walked together to the end of the path. He spoke to her at some length. She nodded her head once and bowed to him. He studied her a moment, kissed her forehead and hands and walked away, his tall shadow erasing the color from the stones behind him. His two companions followed.

After everyone left, we cleaned up the detritus of the celebration. Julianne did not seem too distressed that her new spouse had left, and was humming softly to the bairn. I could feel the relief emanating from her. She offered her breast to the babe as usual, even though he still did not suckle. He nuzzled it, causing her milk to let down, a drop appeared on her nipple, and suddenly he found the source and took it in his mouth. Julianne gasped, and we watched him as he moved his little head, seeking purchase and finally began to suck. There were tears in her eyes as she looked him, and in mine also.

* * *

The next day was trying. Julianne had become part of our household and it would be hard to lose her. Scathach, in the way of animals, knew there was something amiss. She prowled restlessly around as we gathered up Julianne's things, and packed them to take to the castle. When the guards came with the carriage, Julianne knelt by Scathach and pulled her great head into a tight embrace. "Promise me we can have one of her pups?" she asked. I assured her that we would, and that our cottage was always open to her. We said our goodbyes and even Cawdie gave her a rough embarrassed embrace. Scathach followed her and the babe as they left. I watched with some trepidation as the carriage rolled away, but Scathach turned back to the cottage, nudged my leg as she passed, and settled herself before the fire, staring at me with her golden eyes one enigmatic moment before she closed them and fell asleep.

The house was too quiet. I was restless and bothered by the events of the last few days. There were overmany questions and I wanted to see Malcolm. Finally, I settled for the company of Sir Ross, and sent Cawdie to invite him to have tea with us. I would question him discreetly about some of the things I had discovered.

* * *

Sir Ross arrived later in the day with Gregor, carrying a small basket. Gregor attended him but politely refused to join us for tea, so Sir Ross told him to return in one hour. He bowed to us, giving Janet an appraising glance that brought color to her face and growl from Cawdie, and strode away in that silent predator's glide that marked his walk.

195

Sir Ross was all mysterious smiles, and presented the basket to me with a flourish. I opened it to find a beautifully modeled golden bird atop a black velvet cushion. It glimmered in the light as I lifted it from its nest, the lifelike gilded feathers moving slightly as I placed it on the table.

"It is exquisite. The workmanship is magnificent." A little jeweled knob extended from its right side and I touched it tentatively, starting when the tiny thing spread its wings, took several steps, and stopped to peck at an invisible bit of something on the table. Sir Ross burst into delighted laughter at my reaction.

"Tis a clockwork bird. One of Aidan's pieces." He smiled. "One of his uses for gold leaf, as you see. Lady Elspeth, it would please me greatly to have you accept it as a gift for your kindness." He looked around the room, taking in the overflowing bookcases and the closed cabinets. "May I see your collection?" He deftly turned the subject before I could reply, and we spent a comfortable half hour discussing the contents of my baby house, especially the tiny framed paintings and the artists' vanity piece, an even tinier "cabinet of curiosities" inside the baby house. Much of the collection had been made in Italy, which interested him. When I closed the doors of the cabinet he asked if he might examine my books, and I was delighted to share them with someone who would enjoy them. He seemed impressed and commented on the ones in Latin and Italian. "Amazing, my lady. And you are fluent in both? Like most men, he believed most women incapable of rational thought.

"Indeed, sir. My study in Italy made it a necessity."

"And what did you study, Lady Elspeth?" He was watching me intently. I lifted my chin.

"Medicine, sir. I am a woman of Salerno. In Italy, I would be called a *Salernitana*."

He shook his head slowly. "That explains much. Why then are you here in this forgotten place, Lady Elspeth? Should you not be in a larger city that would offer more opportunity for you to practice your skills?" I had underestimated him and had become the questioned one.

"I am but a woman, sir. In my own country, I am not permitted to be a physician." I tried to hide the bitterness in my voice.

Sir Ross gazed at me thoughtfully. "And what do you seek from me, my lady? I fear tis not just my company you desired."

I would not dissemble with this man. "I want to know about Sir Spence. Did you know him well?"

He made a motion like one shaking off a bothersome fly. "The man was scum. His death is no loss to anyone except his convenient, and mayhap his wife. Who can say? He was unworthy of trust. I knew him for several years, but he was never a friend. Our tastes ran in different directions. Is there more you wish to ask? Ah, the gold leaf. I do use it on the advice of a physician from Edinburgh."

"What of Julianne? She has handfasted, christened her babe, and been left alone again by her new husband. He is Russian, do you know him?   Is he one of the smugglers? He seems to know the Laird very well."

"You have been honest with me, Lady Elspeth. I will answer what I can. I do know Sir Peter. You have heard of the Great Embassy?" I had, and suddenly several pieces moved into place. No wonder the Laird was so involved and anxious for the bairn. Sir Peter was the Tsar of Russia! He had even used his full name for the handfasting, and given the bairn part of his own. Julianne had been the Tsar of Russia's convenient and was now handfasted to him! The babe's father was royalty. I sat back, stunned. I could not make sense of it. My first thought was that I had to tell Malcolm. The second was concern for Julianne and the babe.

"But, Sir Ross. Is he mad? How can he wed a commoner?   Tis beyond understanding. Why would he consent to handfast with Julianne?"

Sir Ross leaned back in his chair and exhaled wearily. "He cares for Lady Julianne, but no more than he does for a dozen others, I think. He agreed to handfast with her to make the bairn acceptable here in Scotland. You should be aware that in Russia, the Tsar has recently made the custom of handfasting non-binding. Either one of the couple is free to leave at any time. Sir Peter will provide generously for the bairn, so you see, she and the babe are now secure. He will eventually invalidate the handfasting when he returns to Russia. They are agreed on this, and she is not unhappy about it. The royal courts of Russia are a seductive and vivid fairy tale, and she was temporarily lost in its dreams but completely unfit for the harsh reality of it. Is there more you would ask?"

I shook my head. When I lifted my eyes to Sir Ross I saw sympathy and sadness in his own. I touched his arm. "Thank you, sir. And, I shall accept your precious gift with pleasure. It will have a place of honor in my cabinets."

His face lightened, and he took my hand in his. "Please know that I am, and will always be, your servant, Lady Elspeth." He bowed and left with Gregor who had been standing silently outside the door, waiting. It was suddenly very quiet.

Cawdie came in with a load of wood for the hearth. Janet moved the iron stew pot along the crane, closer to the flames. Scathach stood up and pushed her cold nose into my hand. I was home. Tonight, I would rest, and tomorrow would be what it would be.

SEVENTEEN

Malcolm – Experiment

Edinburgh, Scotland.

"Malcolm! Why are you here? You look like a highwayman." Gwen examined me with a look of distaste as I came to her for a greeting kiss. She pushed me away with a hand on my chest. "You shouldn't be here. Surely you know?"

I'd arrived before noon and she was still in her morning clothes, removing tangles from her wild red hair when I barged in. I'd wanted to see Gwen first. She knew all the gossip and had helped me before. I needed her now, perhaps more than ever. "I've returned to participate in our smallpox experiment. Do you not like this latest style from London?"

She giggled. "That hasn't been in style for decades, except perhaps in unsavoury places like Torrport, and surely not London, silly man."

I watched her expressions looking for clues. "In any case, at least I am clean." I knew she hated unexpected visitors, but I could not extend such courtesies this time.

"You may be clean, but unwanted, except by Mackmain. He's ordered your arrest on sight." The smile had faded, and I thought her porcelain and rouge face had acquired a few more lines.

"He cannot do that without just cause."

"Malcolm, your family has not the influence it once had, and I am truly sorry for your dear father." She took a step back. "You should leave Edinburgh. Mackmain will kill you next time. Forget this foolish experiment. Go to London. Enjoy life while you can."

I bowed my head slightly then looked in her sincere blue eyes. "You know I'll not leave. I'll not be run out of my home town by the likes of him." I gave her a warm smile and opened my arms. "Will you not greet me properly with a kiss?"

"Malcolm, I cannot be seen with you. It is too dangerous, especially for my son. We had a lovely time, thee and me, but..." Her eyes were pleading, and I did understand, but had to know the truth of where our love lay.

She'd clutched her arms fast in front. I reached out and touched her gently. "Then I will leave you in peace, but one favour, if I may?"

She sighed. "Yes?"

"Can you support our efforts in some way, for example, by organizing the ladies to bring food and beverages to McLaren's infirmary? It would be well appreciated. Otherwise, I fear we will be forced to subsist on gruel." It was little enough to ask. I could have hired people to do this but wanted her support and involvement.

"Oh Malcolm." She sighed again. "I am sorry. I cannot risk all for you. The pox is spreading, and everyone is worried and making plans."

"What are your plans then?"

She lifted her chin looking as resolute as one can in morning clothes. "I have a friend. He has offered us refuge on his estate in the south."

"A wise choice, no doubt. When do you leave?"

"Everyone who can will leave soon. My son will miss his studies, so I will stay here as long as it is safe."

She had thought it all through. I hoped the fates were kind.

I bowed to her out of respect and love. "Farewell, then. May God protect you, and your son."

As I left I heard her whisper. "I wish you well, love." I wished her well too. I truly did.

On the day after our fortuitous escape from the French smugglers I had a chance to pen many letters. Two were to Gwen. The first was the one I hoped to give her, the other was the one I left on the silver tray on the gilt table in the foyer. Goodbye Gwen.

My spirits had sunk by the time I reached the street. I knew our relationship was just one of mutual need and convenience, but I suppose I'd deluded myself into thinking there was more. I know I'd taken advantage. She found herself unwillingly embroiled in my risky projects, and needed to protect herself and her son. It was logical and proper. I should have expected it, but the heart deceives. Was this the end? Likely. I had become a liability she could not afford to bear.

I hardly noticed the bustle and throng as I pushed my way through the streets to McLaren's infirmary, awareness deep, churning through emotions and schemes. The door to the infirmary was open and a few men were standing outside looking in the door. I was expecting to see a few arriving with their belongings, ready for an extended stay. Instead what confronted me was the sound and feel of conflict. I eased my way in and could see McLaren on the far side of the room standing with hands open, pleading. In front of me and facing him were several men. One of them was speaking. He sounded like Turnbull. His voice was threatening. I could see McLaren try to speak but he could only stammer, his gaunt face red as he twitched and tilted. I knew at once I had to act. I dropped my bags, lowered my head and with left elbow out and right hand gripping my pistol, I bowled my way through the crowd sending men lurching into each other. I quickly reached the front and stood in front of McLaren, pistol out and shouting. "Now what is this about, gentlemen?"

It was Turnbull in the lead with Fraser on his right, flanked by a coterie of physicians and functionaries. "Forrester! How dare you?" Turnbull was one that I'd made a point of pushing on the way through.

"Yes, I dare. What do you want Turnbull?" I took a step toward him, pistol pointing at his forehead.

"You will regret threatening me, Forrester. The guards are looking for you as we speak and Mackmain will teach you another lesson in short order."

"If Mackmain tries, he will have the Lord Provost and Magistrate to answer to. Do you think I would return without protections? Mackmain is rogue and you have allied yourself with him. Beware, Turnbull! Fear less my bullet than the Queen's noose." I almost spat out his name as I let my fury vent. Now it was his turn to tremble in rage, caught off-guard.

"We shall see about this, Forrester. Come men, we will leave these irresponsible blasphemers to their folly for now." They made a hasty retreat, no doubt relieved it didn't end in blood.

I lowered my pistol. It wasn't loaded. Next time it would be. I embraced McLaren. "Thank you, my friend. I can only imagine how hard this must be."

"It has been tense, I'll admit, and friends have suggested there will be trouble." He gave a slight shrug.

"There likely will be. But we will deal with it professionally, won't we?"

He chuckled. "Like pulling a weapon on them?"

"I don't often do that, call it what you will, it can be effective." I could see the hint of a smile on his pock-marked face. "Now tell me what Turnbull wanted."

Mercifully, McLaren was concise. Turnbull was there to announce that the infirmary was to be quarantined for the duration of the experiment and perhaps beyond, and that he would ensure it was rigorously enforced. No one who has not previously contracted smallpox will be allowed to leave once they have entered, while the quarantine is in effect.

"He also mentioned that he didn't appreciate having us go over his head to the Magistrate. He seemed especially enraged over that."

"I suppose he meant me. I wrote the Lord Provost and Magistrate, explained all and asked for protection."

"Ah, that might be it. Young did as well, but I suspect it was your appeal that inflamed him the more." McLaren almost crumpled into a waiting-room chair.

"Well it worked. Those who think my family is finished, underestimate us. We have hundreds of years of favours to call in, and I will unabashedly use them to see this through." That was an exaggeration. People tend to forget obligations when it is in their self-interest, but I wanted to instill confidence in our small group. I knew our opponents wanted to stop us. They could bully everyone but me, and that is why they needed me removed.

"I have faith, Malcolm. I am with you, and I hope the others are as well. It starts tomorrow. We shall soon realize the truth."

"I've several visits this afternoon, starting with my father. Do I get first choice of available luxury accommodation?"

"Aye, choose any cot, but if I were you, I'd pick one furthest from the toilet." It was good to see that through all this we could find some mirth. I dropped my bags on the cot beside the toilet and heard Angus barking out his silly laugh as I left the infirmary.

* * *

I wasn't looking forward to seeing Father. It's hard watching a loved one suffer like that even when you know what to expect. But tomorrow I would be locked in quarantine for weeks and this could be our last meeting and I needed to make it count. I could hear Henry barking as I took the few steps from the street to the black lacquered front door. He seemed to sense my presence because he was all a-wiggle around my feet as soon as I entered. I knelt and gave him a big hug that was returned with copious slobbery kisses. We needn't seek the angels around us. We have them in our well-loved pets. Mrs. Simpson came out of the kitchen wiping wet hands on her apron. I gave her a wave and well-wishes as I ran up the stairs, Henry close behind.

"How is he?" I could see that I'd interrupted Archibald amid his nap. He sat bolt upright, blinked a few times, then stood, snapped to attention and saluted. Old habits...

"Sir Malcolm! Err...your father is as well as can be expected."

"At ease, Archibald. I would like to see him. Is he awake?"

"Aye, he often is during the day since the fever subsided." Archibald knocked on the door and we heard a muffled *Yes* from within. "It is your son Malcolm, sir. He wishes to see you."

"Thank the Lord. Send him in, Archie." His voice sounded hoarse but strong.

Archibald whispered as he opened the door. "Remember to stay well clear of him and make it short."

There was a cadaverous stench filling the room and the sight of Father filled my heart with sorrow. The pocks on his face had begun to burst, releasing an oozing yellow puss. His face was covered in them to the extent that they seemed to merge into one swollen mass.

"Father?" I didn't know where to start.

He was looking at the ceiling. It must be painful to turn his head. He spoke like every syllable was agony. "The fever has not returned. Doctor McLaren says that is a good thing." His mouth was but a slit in that grotesque mask.

"Indeed, that is a good sign, Father. I want to tell you..."

He interrupted. "Malcolm listen, I have written letters for you. Archie has them."

"Umm, yes of course. I'll read them. Father...I..."

"Read them! Now!" Even half dead he could be domineering.

"Yes, Father, God speed."

"Yes, yes."

I backed out of the room trying to control my emotions.

Archibald handed me two letters. "Better do as the old man says."

I lit a few candles and sat in Father's chair in the study. All I could think of was this may be my last opportunity to tell Father how I felt about him and our past and find some small measure of peace. He never wanted to discuss it. Perhaps it was for the best. I broke the seal on the first letter and unfolded it. It was written on several pages in a large, unsteady script.

"To My Son Malcolm,

My remaining days may be short. George will inherit all if he survives me and will be the next Lord Forrester. You will receive a generous yearly allowance. This is by unbroken custom. George is solid and true, while you are the brave rebel. We need both in our family. Support each other, work together for the common good. Take a wife and have many healthy children. That would please me more than anything else. Know that George and I love you and believe in your work.

William Forrester"

My eyes were glistening as I read, and I wished I could have shared my feelings too. The second letter had a much different tone.

"In strictest confidence. Burn after reading. I may not be able to protect you much longer. Use this wisely. I have requested that your brother be returned from the Continent and have instructed Archie to help you if you need him. John Smith is our confidential agent in Rouen and may have given me the pox. Captain Mackmain caused the death of his predecessor. The Lord Provost and Magistrate will act to remove and charge him if they have solid proof. Stay clear of the Town Guard while Mackmain is in command. Your main opposition is a small

group of radical clerics. They are tolerated but not supported by the Church. Enlist help from moderate clergy to counteract them. The other main group against you are physicians who fear change. They are lead by Turnbull. We control Turnbull because we know he is...”

On reading the last few words I dropped the letter and laughed. So, that's his secret! Naughty boy!

I picked the letter up and threw it in the fire. What did it all mean? George may be coming home. Father needs him and will be pleased. I know I haven't been much support lately. Smith was not a surprise, and I was relieved it was not me who infected Father. Guilt is an exceedingly heavy cross to bear, isn't it?

My immediate worry was the Town Guard. They could appear at any moment and arrest me on any number of spurious charges. The Lord Provost and Magistrate had been made aware of what'd transpired, but I doubted that Mackmain would follow proper legal process in my case. I would simply be disappeared. There were ways to trick Mackmain into confessing, but all involved considerable risks, and he'd proven to be both clever and ruthless. Avoidance seemed the best course for now.

The last part about Turnbull, while highly amusing, had to be played with a deft hand. I wasn't sure Father was right about Turnbull, he could do a lot of damage, and it remained to be seen that he could be effectively controlled. In any case, he was married with children and the Church had little tolerance for this kind of sexual misconduct. It would be a major public scandal and could harm the College of Physicians if it wasn't handled wisely. If I was the one to expose him, my career could be over too, as well as his. Who would trust me?

My heart and mind were in turmoil about Father. I could do little to help him. He'd given me everything, and I, so very little in return. I felt the opportunities to connect with him were slipping away. I went to his desk and started to write and soon found myself pouring out long suppressed emotions about the loss of Mother, our ancestral home and the distance I felt between the three of us. I sat back, read it, then crumpled it up and threw it in the fire. I would not burden him so.

I went to his room, Archibald was awake this time. “I wish to say farewell.” He opened the door and I said in a loud voice. “Father, it's Malcolm. I must go now. Thank you for the letters. I'll return in a few weeks. I love you.”

I waved and waited for a response. “God speed my son. I...love you.” With that Archibald closed the door and I wondered if I would ever see my father again.

“Sir William told me to help you.”

My mind was still filled with Father, so his assertion confused me at first, then I remembered the letter. “Aye Archie. How can you help?”

“I assume Sir William meant my *specials skills*.

“And they are?”

"I was used in the 26th to remedy certain situations that required stealth and quiet weapons. Do ye ken?"

"You were an assassin?" I asked with incredulity.

"Nay, sir...well only if required, if there was no other way." Archie held me with that cold eye and now I knew why Father had this unlikely servant in his employ. He had that non-descript look of a man you wouldn't notice until he slid a dagger in your ribs.

"Archie, I can use you, but I don't want anyone killed, understand?" He nodded, and I proceeded to explain my situation and our experiment.

"Our immediate problem is with the Town Guards. We need their protection, not harassment."

"The guards are mainly retired men from the 26th. I know many. Good men, mostly."

"And Mackmain?"

"He is ruthless, feared, but not liked. There is a close inner group around him going back to the regiment. The rest are there for the pay."

"Archie, can you speak to your friends in the Guards? Let them know the outbreak of pox came from Rouen, then to John Smith. It spread from there. We are trying to find a cure to benefit everyone. The pox didn't come from us."

"I will do that, sir."

"Let me know if you hear any rumours that affect us, and if you can run some non-violent interference..." I think he understood my meaning and gave a salute as I tried awkwardly to shake his hand.

"I will be at Doctor McLaren's infirmary for the duration. Take care of Father."

"With my life, sir! But one thing before you go, if you please."

"Aye, what is it Archie?"

He looked right and left and lowered his voice to a whisper. "Mrs. Simpson."

"What about her?"

"Sir, umm, would it be acceptable for me to..."

"You're interested in her?"

"She is a fine lady, is she not?"

"She is indeed Archie, and if you are asking my permission to woo her you have it, but she is a free woman with a mind of her own and it is her you must convince." I chuckled and patted his shoulder.

"Thank ye, sir. You have my word I will treat her with respect."

I laughed. "Not too much respect, Archie. Women prefer a man to take charge...well most do."

He laughed too. "I will remember that."

"I must go, farewell and good luck with our enterprises!" I left him grinning and dropped in to see Mrs. Simpson. She was rolling pastry on the table.

"All is well here, I take it?" She looked up and wiped her nose on her sleeve.

"All but your dear father, and we pray for him everyday."

"Appreciated, and Archie, are you too getting on?"

She smiled, and I could see the beginnings of a blush. "He is a fine man Malcolm, and I enjoy his company."

I was glad to hear that, of course, and gave her some money for supplies and an extra amount to purchase treats for the men at McLaren's.

"I will be away for some time. Please keep me informed about Father. Also, Lady Elspeth, Janet and Cawdie may come to help in a few weeks. They can stay here. I know it will be tight, but please welcome them."

"I will pray for your good health, Malcolm, and will be happy to host them and catch up on the latest Torrport gossip."

I'd done all I could here, and we parted with a warm hug. As I left, I knew my life hereafter would be forever changed.

* * *

It started as planned, well mostly. The men arrived throughout the morning and by noon all ten test patients were there. It was gratifying to see no one had reneged. We were all trying to be cheerful and positive, but there was a noticeable undercurrent of worry that came out in odd ways, such as in the excessive amount of hugging that went on. Were we all condemned men? It seemed so at the time. Cameron, McLean and McLaren were there too, setting up the treatment station in the adjoining room. The rest of us mostly fidgeted and wondered what would unfold in the next weeks.

It was especially good to see Beaton, and I brought him up-to-date on the adventures of his cousin at Torrport. He mostly chuckled and shook his head, then commented that she seemed to attract strangeness. I think I knew what he meant.

After lunch, Young gathered us around and we once again went through the experiment, it's goals and methods. We'd heard it all before, but this time it seemed more real and we paid much closer attention to every detail. At the end, Cameron came forward with a small wooden box. In it were ten slips of folded paper, five had *No* and five *Yes* written on them. Each of us were asked to select a paper from the box without looking at it. The paper was unfolded by Cameron and the result with our name recorded on a ledger. It took only a few minutes to seal our fates. The five of us who'd selected *Yes* would be given the inoculation including the smallpox powder, the group that had selected *No* would be given an inoculation without. Cameron handed the ledger to McLean and we were called in, one-by-one, for our inoculation.

I joked with Beaton that I hoped this would not become a regular ritual for us. He didn't seem to appreciate my sense of humour and merely said, "Good luck Mal."

"To you as well my friend. Now let us pray this works." My name was called next. Angus had me sit on the examination bed while McLean retrieved the dose from the table where he'd laid them all out, labelled with a code. Each of the ten was a simple tube with powder poured in one end and a mouthpiece from a pipe on the other. Angus checked the ledger and compared it with the label on the pipe, then nodded to McLean.

"Hold still Mal, I am just going to light this and blow the smoke up your nose. It might tickle a bit, try not to sneeze."

He inserted the tube in one nostril and gave a quick puff on the mouthpiece. That's all there was to it.

"Don't touch your nose for a while and refrain from touching the other patients too." Angus helped me off the bed and they both said good luck before calling the next man.

I didn't take long before all of us had received our inoculations. We sat joking about it, then they came out and suggested we rest a while to let things settle. No one could sleep, wondering no doubt as I was what might be going on in that nostril. It was far from settling, but by supper our baser needs had overcome fears, and the simple meal of carved beef and roast potatoes was relished by all.

The first week in quarantine was far from exciting; it was naught but unrelenting boredom, notwithstanding efforts to organize game tournaments and poetry readings. The games invariably ended in accusations of cheating and the poetry put everyone to sleep. We were a group of arrogant over-achievers, after all, and just wanted to be back at work and with our friends and families and leading a normal life. Enduring that first week already seemed to be too much of a sacrifice. Near the end, I received a short note from Archie, that Father was fevered again, and they were praying for him. He also said that something might start soon. I was expecting more than cryptic messages like this, but could do nothing about it but respond with a query for details. At least Mrs. Simpson was leaving treats and homemade food at the door on a regular basis, but one had to be quick off the mark to get a share.

The ten of us living in such close quarters like this was a trial of unwanted assaults on our senses, but gradually we settled into routines that helped us co-exist without excessive conflict. A few of the messy chaps were encouraged to free the floor of dropped food and clothes, and the noisy sleepers were re-positioned behind infirmary screens, things like that. It helped a bit, but mostly we accepted each other with a measure of tolerance and good humour.

The second week began with a bang, literally, and in the form of a rock heaved against the front door. McLaren went out to investigate and we heard a few raised voices and threats by the guardsmen stationed there. That's how it started, and we should have taken it more seriously at the time. Thereafter, each day, a small crowd gathered to hurl insults at us. Thankfully, there were no more rocks. The guardsmen kept them away, but it was becoming increasingly difficult for the physicians and our helpers to come and go without harassment. At that point, none of us had any symptoms and all we could do was wait and worry.

On the eleventh day, McLaren called a meeting. "My friends, we are entering the critical stage. In a few days, some of you may be experiencing a fever, the first stage of smallpox. Those who do will be segregated to rooms on the second and third floors. I have moved to Young's infirmary from which I will try to care for as many of the new smallpox patients as I can. You may not have heard but we have over twenty in the city now, and it has spread from the port." There was an audible gasp from a few and now the protests outside were starting to make more sense.

"Then the quarantines have not held?" I asked.

"They help Mal, but we think that Smith met many more people than we first thought. He is still not cooperating, and your father is in no condition to communicate with him directly." McLaren was beginning to look like a man realizing he was about to be thrown naked into the abyss.

"How can we help, Angus?" Beaton asked.

"We are most concerned about that mob out there that seems to be growing each day. If all of you can write to your friends and family and explain that what we do is for the common good, it might help. Also, Forrester and Young petitioned the Lord Provost and Magistrate to protect us. So far, the guardsmen have been doing a fine job, but how much abuse they are willing to take before there is violence, is unknown."

Cameron stood up next. "I'll write Captain Mackmain and remind him of his duty." Several nodded in approval, then the meeting was over. It was good to know all this, but unnerving as well.

The next day ten men were bent on writing as many letters as possible. They were piling up quickly by the door and expedited to the Royal Post by anyone leaving. My first letter was to Mrs. Simpson and Archie, my second to Elspeth. I instructed Mrs. Simpson to desist in bringing us food if there was any danger to herself, and I ordered Archie to do what needs to be done to protect us. I asked Elspeth to come to Edinburgh as soon as practicable and I ended with a plea to bring Cawdie and his weapons.

* * *

It was Beaton who was the first to show a fever, right on schedule twelve days after our inoculation. It seemed that ever-organized Beaton was determined to be sick strictly by the book. We all cheered him as he was moved upstairs. Over the next two days, five of us got a fever, and yes, I was one, but our leader Young did not. None of us was sure what would happen. Was it fortunate to have had the smallpox inoculant, or were those left on the first floor the lucky ones?

"How are you feeling Mal?" Angus leaned over my cot to feel my forehead. It had come on quickly, within an hour I went from healthy to fevered and sick.

"Not so bad yet. I've had a fever before and this one isn't that high."

"We will start the treatments today with a cooling sponge bath and a vomit and purge." He made a note on the ledger. "McLean has agreed to pitch in since I've so many new cases. I can be here for an hour a day, no more."

"I've asked Beaton's cousin to come from Torrport to help as well. She's an excellent healer, and can help with the treatments."

Angus smiled. "Then she will be very welcome, indeed."

This small room with low cobwebbed beams would be my new home for several weeks. It was the infirmary storeroom with shelving piled with bedding, blankets and medical supplies along one wall and boxes scattered everywhere. They'd just made a space big enough for my cot, chamber pot, and wash basin set atop a stack of wooden crates. At least there was a small window, one of those old-style ones with small diamond-shaped panes that refracted the light. The window was facing the street and the familiar noises of life below were comforting.

That first day my fever alternated with chills and the usual body aches and swellings under my jaw. I tried to read a bit of a book called *Don Quixote* that Angus gave me as he helped me settle in, but my mind couldn't concentrate, and I accepted fitful sleep as it came and went. Around noon, my boring agony was relieved by the sight of two angels and one demon. The demon entered first, in the form of that massive bearded highlander with claymore glinting on his back. He looked around the room quickly then stood aside to let the ladies in. I could not have been happier as they knelt beside my cot and pampered me with cool cloths and candies to suck on.

"We came straight here Malcolm, I can see there is much to do. Cawdie, please have a look at the security here, and Janet, please find fresh water and towels so we can start cleaning and cooling the men."

I let out a sigh and lay back, glad they were here to organize and help. God knows we needed them. "Thank you for coming, Elspeth. Angus will be relieved. He is overwhelmed by new cases of smallpox in the city as well as looking after us."

"We will do our best. When did your fever start?" She held her palm on my forehead.

"Last evening. I think five of us have it. We are all on the second floor. John is down the hall."

"Oh? Have there been any unusual symptoms?" She looked in my eyes then felt my wrist pulse.

"The fever hasn't been as high as I've seen reported, but it has just started. Angus McLaren will be here each day to monitor us. He's already given us a vomit and purge. You can compare notes with him."

"I will and yes we could smell that treatment when we arrived. I have so much to tell you. You will not believe the half of it. I wanted to see your face when I told you." I cringed. She had that look and we didn't need anymore bad news.

"What have you done now?"

"Me?" She blinked those innocent eyes and I shuddered.

"Not me, Julianne. She has handfasted with the Tsar of Russia!"

"What!" I sat up too quickly and instantly a bout of dizziness reminded me that was unwise. "Elspeth, have you been drinking?"

"Nay, nay... Tis true." She fluffed my pillow and fussed about with the sheets. Her brow creased. "He acknowledges the babe is his, and will care for them both. But he will break the handfast soon, for Julianne cannot marry him because she is not Russian and only a commoner. It does not matter; she and the bairn are safe." Her words tumbled over each other. I just stared at her, thoughts crashing on one another as waves on the rocks.

"What the devil is the Tsar doing in Scotland?"

"He is here to see his wee bairn and meet with the Jacobite Lairds. Did you not know?"

"Bloody hell!" I sunk into protective inertness as she explained the rest. I knew I should tell Father, but was in no condition to deal with anymore. To my discredit, I decided to ignore it all for now.

"I should go see John now. Do you mind if Janet gives you a sponge bath?" She grinned knowing full well my response.

I gave up and just groaned. "Not at all and I'm in no condition for play, you needn't worry."

She laughed then rose. "I will be back shortly. I have given you my news. Is there anything else I need to know about here?"

I thought a moment. "There have been protests. We can discuss it later, but be careful outside."

She nodded and left, brushing Janet returning with a bucket of water, towels and sponges.

If you must be sick, do so with an attentive, attractive female tending all your needs. Janet was surprisingly cheerful considering the difficult situation she'd been dropped in, and happily related the latest gossip from Torrport as she cooled me. I absorbed it all like the sponge she was lovingly stroking down my chest. My moment of bliss soon ended though as she was called by Elspeth to help with another of the men. I wrapped myself in the musty blanket and listened as the women went from room to room, treating, serving and cleaning.

* * *

"George, damn you! Get out of the way!" She slurred, and her pale head lolled from side to side. She was layered in iridescent raven feathers, and around her the dark sky was a fearful murk. Her mount, a wide-eyed black mare snorted steam, then reared. I was on the ground naked, looking up at George, he in red serge and gold braid, his blond hair luminous as he thrust the wooden sword in the mare's face. I tried to move, but could only watch as the horse reared again, and Mother tumbled off the back and landed with a cracking thud on the cobblestones. She was splayed there a few feet from me, feathered hand outstretched. "Help me, Malcolm." She begged pitifully while looking through me with flat glazed eyes. I tried to move again. My skin painfully tore on the stones, but I could not come closer. My heart was breaking anew as I could see the lifeblood flow out into a red halo around her head. I called for George, for Father, but there was only me and Mother now, and I wept.

Then I heard a strange voice from above, and Mother's face became Elspeth's. I could sense myself breathing fast and I was confused as images and sounds merged and overlapped. Where was I? The dark sky became dusty beams, the black horse, wooden crates. "Malcolm, you were crying out. Are you alright?" Elspeth was looking down at me, a strand of hair caressing my fevered face.

"Oh...ah...a dream." I suddenly realized it and rolled to my side and coughed. I was soaked in sweat and disoriented. "I am fine, just a dream."

"It must have upset you."

"It was of my mother. I...I often have... It's fine."

"It is not fine if it gives you nightmares. What of your mother, Malcolm? Would you like to share?" She placed a cool hand on my forehead. "Your temperature is higher too."

"My mother fell off a horse and died when I was a boy." I was shivering now. "Can I have another blanket?"

"Oh Malcolm, that is tragic!" She got another blanket from the shelf and tucked it around me. "Were you involved somehow?"

"No, but yes, maybe, I don't know. She left me. I miss her." I pulled the blankets closer and lay my head down.

"But you were just a boy, were you not?"

"Aye."

"Then it was just an accident?"

"Aye, sort of."

She sat with me quietly wiping my face. "Would you like some willow bark tea?"

"Aye."

"I will make some for all the men before I go. We must get to your father's home before curfew."

"Aye, be careful of curfew. They would be delighted to catch our people in breach."

She brought us our tea a few minutes later and we said goodnight, Cawdie at the door ready to escort the women. I sipped my tea and silently wished them well.

Later, a large mob gathered in front of the infirmary. There were shouts of "Blasphemers!", "You are Responsible!", "Stop the Pox!", echoing up the walls to my room. I could see the distorted reflections of torches in the diamond pane window, and hoped that they would not use them to set us on fire.

* * *

Early in the morning, I heard them consulting just outside my door, Elspeth and Angus. They were discussing us, the ones who'd been inoculated with smallpox. It was the second full day of my fever and it wasn't getting better. Elspeth was insisting that sanitation was poor, and we were facing disaster. I could hear Angus weakly mumble something under her onslaught. I laughed, poor Angus, meet Elspeth MacLeod. She went on to say that the gruel was only fit for livestock and we needed more vegetables, meats and broths. I cleared my throat loudly. It's strange how one becomes invisible as a patient. They both looked in, and I waved weakly.

"I vote for roast chicken and ale, and have Janet serve the men. That will heal us instantly."

They both laughed.

"I am glad to see you back to your old rascally self, sir." Elspeth came and knelt and felt my forehead. "You still have a fever. How are your aches and pains?"

"Not as bad." I replied. "How are the others."

Angus leaned on the door jamb, arms folded. "As expected, Mal. Symptoms milder than normal. The wider issues are more worrisome."

"Such as?" I looked up at him.

"We have thirty cases in the city now and they are considering closing the port. I don't have to tell you how unpopular and damaging that would be; and then there are the growing protests, especially here at night."

I listened carefully as he further described the opinions of the other physicians in the city and how the treatments and quarantines were going. The news was bad, and the city physicians split. I spoke after he'd finished. "We must believe in our cause and stay the course. There is no other way now. The results so far are heartening. I suggest you subtly spread rumours of positive results. It may protect us."

"I will not lie, Mal, but yes, the results so far have been gratifying, but perhaps premature. I cannot risk my reputation...yet."

It was a wise choice for him.

"I must see the other men before I go. Farewell, Mal. I'll be back tomorrow morning."

I lifted my hand as he turned to go. "May God protect you, Angus." I felt so powerless that all I could offer was that.

Elspeth took my hand. "How are you, my friend?"

Her sea-blue eyes were scanning my face. "I wish I had run away to London with Gwen." I chuckled.

"You do not!"

"In moments of weakness." I smiled at her. "I am not made of steel and stone, as many may think."

"I know. None of us are."

"I am glad you are here Elspeth, and Janet and Cawdie too. Our weaknesses are becoming evident, aren't they?"

"I was speaking to Angus about us staying here at night." I raised my eyebrow. "There were only two guards on duty last night, one in front and one at the back door. Cawdie asked them what happened to the others. They said Mackmain ordered them all back to the Guard House. But a few refused. They were relieved of duty. Our guardsmen have lost their jobs."

I sighed. "Oh God."

She nodded then continued. "We can stay here at night, but the sanitation is not suitable for ladies." She smiled.

"And my Father?"

"I can go during the day with Cawdie to help Archie with your father. His second fever has broken.

She smiled and patted my hand. "Have faith, Malcolm. Meanwhile, McLaren is inundated. We can take over caring for your father, and I have offered to help with other patients in the city too. He says most physicians refuse to treat them."

"Aye they are upper class and have fled the city in previous outbreaks, my family included."

"And Angus said many physicians are leaving now as well. Janet can look after the cooking and cleaning here while we are away. We just need to be back well before the troublemakers gather."

"That sounds like a reasonable plan, but with Mackmain showing his hand again, you must stay away from the Town Guards, even during the day. Understand?"

"Aye, Malcolm, we will creep around the back alleys like thieves." She winked and got up straightening her arisaid. "Rest now. I need to see the other men before I go to Young's infirmary. Angus said he would leave a list of patients for me there."

"God bless you, Elspeth."

"Och, you are getting soft, Malcolm," she teased, then left with a swish of her skirts.

The rest of the day was as tedious as the first, relieved only by the lovely Janet making her rounds of cooling baths, food and drink, but she had little time now for idle chat, being the only one here to stave off misery and chaos.

* * *

"You cannot leave Cawdie out there by himself. They will kill him." It was early evening and the mob had gathered on schedule, now more than before. "Our one remaining guardsman is on the back door. He has a family. We cannot ask him to sacrifice his life for us." Elspeth's brow was knit, and the corners of her mouth turned down as she spoke. I lay there on my cot. Thankfully, my fever had come down through the day. We could hear the shouts from the street. They seemed to be angrier now, calling for blood and revenge.

"I'm calling a war council for the morning when we are all here. Spread the word. Tonight, we can do nothing but pray."

"Alright Malcolm, Janet and I will stand inside the door for Cawdie with whoever wants to join us."

"Elspeth, if they attack, you must run. Let Cawdie do his duty to protect you." She looked at me askance but didn't argue.

"I will let everyone know of our meeting. I hope to God you have a plan that is better than sacrificing Cawdie."

"I do. Be assured, my friend."

She touched me gently on the cheek, then drew her dagger and made her way to the front door, calling Janet to help. This had reached a crisis point. We couldn't just wait and do nothing, or we would soon be crushed by the opposition. It was time this fever broke too.

* * *

Those of us with smallpox gathered on the lower stairs. Below were the rest, a safe distance away. McLaren and McLean were there and even our solicitor Cameron. Janet was distributing tea to the uninfected patients while Elspeth conferred with McLaren. We had made it through the night...just. A window was smashed, a torch thrown ineffectually against the side of the infirmary, and our guardsman Thomas had to scare away a few drunks trying to sneak in the back door. Cawdie looked exhausted and was barely awake on a cot below. We could not withstand another frightening night like that. Few of us had any sleep and we were all raw with anxiety.

I rose to speak. My voice crackled, the rash having spread in my mouth, throat and lips.

"My friends. It is time we put an end to these attacks." I looked around the room. There was silence now. "I have a plan, both to stop the attacks and destroy our enemies. I am sorry it has come to this."

"Keep us not in suspense, Mal." It was Young, and he was smiling.

"Then hear me out. Cawdie, what weapons do we have?"

He grunted and sat up rubbing his eyes. "*We hae, a muskit, tois pistols, tree swords an' cupple daggers.*"

"And Cawdie, is that sufficient to defend against one hundred men?"

Cawdie laughed in derision and shook his shaggy head.

"Now Cawdie, you are a very experienced warrior. What will happen if that mob gets past you?"

He looked first at Janet, then back to me. "*Thaur will be bluid, th' kimmers raped an' lae killed. Ah hae sen it wi' mah een.*"

I pointed at the tired warrior. "So only one proud warrior stands between the mob and our women being raped and the rest of us killed. That is if we do nothing." I let it sink in. "This is what we must do to prevent this atrocity from happening." I outlined my plan simply and directly. The room erupted in discussion.

"Nay, I will not leave my Cawdie." It was Janet's shrill voice from the back.

Cawdie was stunned, and I saw something I never imagined could happen. Tears formed in the corner of his eyes and rolled down into his wild beard, and I heard him whisper. "*Ach, mah hen.*"

"If Janet stays, I will not leave her." Elspeth took the few steps to Janet and clasped her around the waist.

I sighed but knew them well enough not to argue the point. "Very well, but the rest of you must follow the plan. Once you are safely at my father's, you can scatter to the protection of your families. We hope and pray it doesn't come to this but now we are prepared. I firmly believe our actions will frighten the mob and break the opposition. Meanwhile, I can assure you that the leaders of the opposition will soon feel the hard edge of my family's wrath. Let us now take heart and be assured that God is on the side of those who strive to alleviate suffering, as did our Saviour Jesus Christ so long ago." The meeting ended with that. Those with misgivings could see we had little choice, and all hoped beyond hope that sanity would prevail.

I sat on the stairs with my head in my hands, imagining I could feel the pox spreading relentlessly. Beaton sat beside me and put his arm around my shoulder. I looked over at him. His rash was further along and sprinkled over his face, but thinly...a good sign. "Thank you, Mal. We may meet an ignominious death, but I am proud we tried."

"I am not going to die, nor you. You can't get rid of me that easily." I hugged him back as Elspeth and Janet arrived.

"Och, you two becoming lovers now?" Janet giggled and Elspeth grinned.

I chuckled. "John would be a most attentive lover. Now if he were equipped differently..."

"Oh, you two. Can you not be serious, even now?" Beaton pretended to be peeved.

"We are deadly serious, aren't we Elspeth?"

She knew I was referring to the goings on at Torrport and responded quickly. "I will tell all later Mal...when this has calmed."

"And if it hasn't it won't matter anyway. Oh, that reminds me. I have some letters for you to deliver this morning. Come up to my room and I will explain." Elspeth nodded then told Janet to prepare a large batch of oatmeal salve for the men with smallpox rash.

It was but the three of us. Beaton, Elspeth and I in the cramped storeroom I called home. "This is for the Lord Provost letting him know Mackmain had withdrawn the guards and left us defenceless." She took it from me and stuffed it in her bag. "This for the Magistrate detailing the threats, harassment and damage to the infirmary and who did what." She took it and nodded. "This last to Turnbull at the College."

Elspeth looked up to Beaton who was leaning on the door in agony as the rash relentlessly spread. "Malcolm, what is it about? Please don't make it worse, especially for the rest of them. For you and me, it may not matter, but..." Elspeth pleaded.

I cut her off. "If I live, he will be gone, and it will be for the best, I am certain of it." I closed my eyes as she stared at me. "The letter is a threat that I hope will deter further attacks, but in truth if he is clever, he will kill me before I destroy him utterly."

"Oh Malcolm!" she glowered at me.

I responded. "I want this to remain between him and me, to either draw his fire or send him fleeing. You must trust me on this Elspeth."

"Do you not remember the last time I trusted you? I ended the day tied up in a cave full of French smugglers." She said with a wry smile.

"I thought you enjoyed that." I rubbed an itchy eye.

She sighed. "I will do as you wish, and God help us all."

"I second that," mumbled Beaton. "Now can I get some bloody sleep?"

* * *

The day went by as expected. Each hour seemed like two. We wanted it over, but the time-gods demanded their tick and tock of torment. I wrote a few letters to some friends, saying goodbye and wishing them well, in my own way for each. The letters sounded a touch maudlin on second reading and I hoped I would be alive in the morning to burn them.

I had become resigned to death, and I think the rest of us had as well. There was a quiet gentleness that pervaded our little group. We'd bonded in a way, through

215

common cause and proximity and now perhaps a shared end, although I prayed that my plan would permit at least some to survive. I kept my gloomy thoughts to myself as I visited the other infected ones throughout the day and enjoyed some last hours with Janet and Elspeth. Beaton was beginning to look especially sick. It was an unwelcome portent.

* * *

The light was beginning to fail, and the darkness would soon bring forth the stench of misdeeds fortified by strong drink. Cawdie had stationed himself without and we sick ones sat inside awaiting our fate. We were stripped to the waist and each shrouded with a smallpox-tainted blanket. My pistol and cutlass were concealed. The women were behind us, daggers drawn and holding each other close. Young and the rest were by the back door with our loyal guardsman Thomas. We listened attentively as the crowd grew and threats escalated. It was becoming obvious, our letters had little effect. A thud was heard, then another on the side of the building as the rocks found home. We sucked a collective breath. It had begun. Janet whispered "Oh Cawdie" and covered her face in those gentle hands to hide her tears. Then a minute later some malicious fool threw a torch. It crashed on the door, and we could smell the smoke seeping in, before Cawdie stamped it out.

Elspeth pulled on my arm. "We cannot leave him out there much longer."

I replied. "Calm yourself. He will be fine."

Then there was a shout, "Kill him!" and Elspeth cried, "If you men have not the courage to face that mob, then Janet and I will!"

I pushed her back gently. "Wait til I decide." She glowered at me again, her little hand white knuckling her dagger. "Wait!" I shook my finger in her face. This needed to be done at the right moment of tension and pitch, and I would not be pushed into it prematurely. Several minutes passed, more threats, more rocks, from a much larger crowd than last night. I turned, raised my arm signaling Young. He waved, and I could see the group with him rise and ready themselves. "It is time gentlemen, and ladies. Follow the plan." I looked from one to the other. They nodded, and I said. "May God protect us." I heard a murmur of prayers behind me as I flung open the door.

The street-filled mob hushed when they saw us. I stood beside Cawdie, he with claymore raised, ready to cleave anyone who dared enter. There was blood on his cheek and he grinned with a crazed look and muttered: "*Ah loove thes. It is loch tae auld days oan Skye!*"

We must have looked like the mad monk and nuns from hell. Even more frightening is what we saw and heard. Torches were blazing and reflecting off the windows beyond and a few hundred angry faces and yet more fists in the air, many holding weapons, and a cacophony of cries for blood. Nary a smile or warm greeting, our countrymen whipped to a frenzy of hatred fueled by fear of the pox. My plan was simple, identify the leaders and split the mob. A crowd like this has few working minds, most have surrendered theirs to the few manipulators. I could see one, Turnbull with his lackey Fraser, behind a group of young physicians on our right, while on my left were men of the clergy shouting the kind of vile threats that would make Jesus weep.

I raised my arm and shouted. "Citizens, listen to me. We are men and women like you. We wish the best for our city." I was interrupted by a roar of protests. I waited a few minutes, but it became obvious that reason would not prevail this day. We had to enact the plan. I glanced over at the others and nodded. All five of us dropped our shrouds and stood before them, faces speckled in rash. There began screaming and clamour and people jostling to flee.

"Look at us! Aye, we have smallpox! We did not cause this epidemic. It came from France. We are using this opportunity to find a cure so that others may not suffer. We have sacrificed ourselves that you and your children might live!" I stood challenging them, hoping fear or reason would encourage many to leave.

Then a loud voice broke from the right. "We are not afraid of you, Forrester. We too have immunity." The voice was from one of the young physicians in front of Turnbull.

I turned my full attention on them and pointed at Turnbull. "Physicians, this man you call leader will soon step down in disgrace. He is unfit to lead. He would have our citizens die so that he and others of like ilk may profit from their suffering; and yet worse he corrupts our women for foul purpose. Come forth and dispute those charges if you dare, Turnbull, you coward."

Turnbull glared then replied loudly. "It is you who is unworthy Forrester, with your reckless, irresponsible attempts to replace the wisdom of centuries. I am here solely to protect our citizens from the likes of you!"

I had no intention of letting him argue the merits of our experiment in front of this ignorant mob. Our cause would be lost if I gave him opportunity. Instead, I intended to make it personal and assail his weakness. "Protect them? You lead them to slaughter. Shall I reveal your true nature in all its corruption for our good citizens to hear?" I'd warned him in my letter, and yes, I'd disagreed with Father, Turnbull could not be controlled. He must go.

With that accusation, all eyes turned to Turnbull. "Get thee to hell, Forrester! I shall no longer tolerate your abuse and lies. Come men, we will leave him to his well-deserved destruction." Turnbull shoved his way past Fraser and tried to leave quickly.

"You see, the depraved coward flees. He will not argue, because he knows what I say is true." I wanted him to stay, so I could humiliate him further. I'd just begun and relished the prospect, after all he'd done.

Then Beaton poked me and said. "Let him go Mal. You've won. Think of the College, for Heaven's sake." He was right of course, but I knew I'd have to deal with Turnbull sooner or later, in private with the gloves of civility off.

I smiled radiantly, watching Turnbull leave with some of his followers, then I said. "Physicians, friends, do not follow him. Join us instead in our efforts to defeat this dreadful disease. We can do it together for the benefit of all and through the Grace of Almighty God." The mob had become quiet, intent on listening to our dramatic exchange.

Then among the clergy, one spoke up. "We care not of your College of Physicians and its petty politics. This issue goes well beyond. You dare to interfere with the Divine Will. It is blasphemy and we will not let it stand!"

I returned his scowl with a warm smile. "My friend, let us consider this using the Holy Book as touchstone, shall we? You say we interfere with the Divine Will. Do you truly believe our loving God wishes our innocent children tormented, malformed, blind, and even killed? I for one do not believe in that God, and does it not say in the Book of Jeremiah that *"I have for you," declares the LORD, "plans to prosper you and not to harm you, plans to give you hope and a future."* How many of us here believe that God is cruel?" I surveyed the crowd. I saw none who would openly admit what is often in their hearts. "Nay, I believe that God wishes no harm to come to us."

"Sir, it is the natural order created by God, and you wish to pervert it with your Satanic rituals." There was an outburst of support from his group.

"Aye it is natural, but that does not mean that we must not change it. In the book of Genesis, it says *"Be fruitful, and multiply, and replenish the earth, and subdue it, and have dominion over the fish of the sea, and over the fowl of the air, and over every living thing that moveth upon the earth."* Do you not agree that God has given man dominion over the earth? We have used that dominion to fashion all we see around us including your clothing. Are you suggesting we abandon our civilization and return to a life of naked savagery?" Many laughed at that one, but I didn't want this to become street theatre.

"Your clever mocking, shows you know nothing of what you speak. There are limits set by Our Lord that we must not o'er step. Calamity and disease have always been a way that God chastises the wicked." I could see the stubborn look on his face. I was running out of memorized quotes and felt I may not convince him this day. I tried one last time.

"Do we not make our homes strong to ward off the winter winds? Do we not fashion weapons that others will not harm us? We are simply trying to find a way to ward off this disease and prevent harm. I humbly ask for your support and the support of our community." It was all I could do.

"You are bringing harm to the souls of men and warding off the grace of God offered to the afflicted. If you had true insight, you would see that these afflictions bring men closer to God. I will not give my support, and demand you stop this irresponsible behaviour." He had said it all too, and we stood facing each other. Neither of us would yield.

Then one of them shouted, "Burn these sons of Satan!", then a torch came flying, then another came close to striking Beaton. I could see the crowd parting and feared the worst, but there emerged several clergy led by Father Robertson and the Bishop of Edinburgh. They were accompanied by the Moderator of the Church of Scotland, in a gratifying but all too rare display of Christian unity. I acknowledged them and silently mouthed a thank you to God.

The Bishop held up his arm. "I know many are upset and afraid and blame these physicians. I have it on good authority that they did not cause this outbreak of smallpox."

The clergyman I'd been debating interjected. "It does not matter. They blaspheme God by their attempts to interfere with the order He created, and they lead our good people to Satan."

The Bishop walked over to him. "I agree these are contentious religious matters. I know we are not of like mind, but I promise we will institute a council to fully discuss these issues. I invite you, my good friends, to attend and fully express your opinions." There was widespread clapping. The Bishop had managed to keep the peace once again in an otherwise fractious community. I was pleased...well more than pleased. I was ecstatic!

Beaton poked me again and whispered. "We have won! Well done, Mal."

I beamed inside. "Aye, it looks like we have." I watched the mob begin to disburse as the Bishop held private conversation with the dissenting clergy. My body began to sag. I was sick; it hadn't been easy doing this. I looked over at Cawdie. He'd turned his sword point to his boot and was leaning on the pommel, looking almost ready to collapse. It had been a long day.

Just then, Cawdie's head snapped up and he growled, then drove his shoulder into mine, almost knocking me off my feet. Out of the corner of my eye, I saw a muzzle raised, then heard a loud crack, then the sound of something hard smacking into Cawdie. He slumped back into the doorway, knocking a few startled patients out of the way. I regained my balance and saw a group of men emerge from the thinning crowd, the one in front was heavy with a curved pipe clenched between his teeth. I recognized most at once, they were Mackmain's men, but in plain clothes and with weapons drawn. I took a step back, straddling Cawdie's legs, looked back, caught Young's eyes and shouted, "Run!" I turned to the front and quickly fired my pistol, one dropped. My rusty cutlass seemed a toy against so many, so I passed it to a man who'd emerged beside me. It was McLean.

The big man leading them was on me so fast I hardly had time to reach down and pick up Cawdie's double-handed claymore. He'd the look of murder in his eyes as I came up from the ground and caught his downward blow on my sword guard. Then I spun sideways and caught him on the jaw with the pommel. He was stunned when I swung back hard and sliced him on the neck. I was so close I could see his neck gape and lol sideways, and blood spurted from his jugular into my face and down my chest, the disgusting smell of stale tobacco commingling with blood. He dropped to my side in a heap. The taste of blood was on my lips now and I could barely see, but I had to keep swinging that mighty sword to buy time for others to escape. I could sense McLean to my right dancing quickly, hacking and slashing with the cutlass. Another shot went off, a scream, the sounds of boots thumping. I could hear Janet behind me crying "Cawdie! Cawdie!" and Elspeth say "He can't breathe. Get some bandages, John!"

There were several men attacking and I knew it would soon be over for us. I looked back quickly. Cawdie looked close to death. I yelled at them. "Get out now!"

Elspeth was pressing her skirt into Cawdie's chest wound, the blood oozing between her tiny fingers. "Nay," she said without looking up.

I was tiring quickly, that big sword felt like an anvil now. I'd blinked the blood from my eyes and was fending off three on me now. McLean was fighting furiously against another two, the bodies piling at his feet. Then on my left, our guardsman Thomas suddenly appeared and fired his musket, dropping one man in front of me, then others appeared including Young and McLaren, each using whatever they could find to fight, chair legs, kitchen knives, fireplace pokers. Some from the mob had joined Mackmain's men, but more joined our group, and now we outnumbered them. Several shots were fired. Men fell, the sounds of agony pervasive. The melee grew rapidly, and like the pox, rapidly degenerated into a mass of bloody, swearing, human pustules, as we pressed forward pushing them back a yard, then another. I was re-energized by the arrival of so many to our side. I'd meant our men to escape, but they chose to risk death. One mightier surge, and we can break them. I yelled. "Physicians, attack now! We have them!" I pushed forward filled with pain and rage, finishing a man in front with a brutal slash to his arm.

Then I saw a flicker of red in front, then more. I thought it blood, perhaps my own. Was it death coming? One's body fills with pain and the eyes with blood til you are no more. My arms were aching and knees beginning to buckle. I could swing that hefty sword no more. The flicker of red became a line beyond the melee, then I heard an ear shattering blast. It stunned us all and most knew it's dreadful origin. People shrieked and looked for somewhere, anywhere, to hide. There were men in red serge everywhere, muskets pointed at us. They'd filled the other side of the street and blocked both ends. There was nowhere to hide, they'd bottled us well. The smell of black powder smoke filled the street, and everyone knew we were at the mercy of men who wouldn't hesitate to fire on friends and family.

One emerged slowly from the smoke, on a horse, and in a frighteningly calm baritone said "Drop your weapons! Everyone down! The next round will not be in the air." I knew him at once. His engraved sabre was drawn and held high and he was flanked by two men with pistols drawn, the one on his right was Archie, now in uniform. One of Mackmain's men reloaded his pistol and raised it toward me. Archie coolly shot him in the back, as brother George repeated his commands, the infantry line with muskets ready behind him convincing the mob to obey. I stood there speechless, dripping blood, tired, and lost.

George rode toward me, looking like a serene god, perfectly dressed astride a well-groomed roan with immaculate polished tack, all this amid the blood and shite of us mortals. One side of his mouth tilted up in a wry smile and he said, "Brother" in a low voice as if he was ashamed to admit it.

I nodded and looked at his handsome face glowing by torchlight, then dropped Cawdie's claymore, turned and stepped over Elspeth, who was packing bandages in Cawdie's wound, while Janet sobbed, and Beaton readied for surgery. All I could do was walk away. A few steps, then one final look back at my friends. Elspeth, auburn hair astray and hands covered to the wrists in Cawdie's blood, looked up at me leaving and said, "Malcolm?"

PART THREE

Death and Discovery

EIGHTEEN

Elspeth – Pox and Pain

He left me there with Cawdie dying. Why? I know he was weak from illness and near collapse after the fight, but how could he just walk away from us? It was useless to conjecture. I had no time to think about Malcolm with Cawdie's blood drenching my hands, his life slipping through my fingers. The sucking sound coming from the wound terrified me when I lifted my hand. The left side of his barrel chest was already noticeably flatter than the right. His lung must be collapsed. Janet was weeping silently over him, her body rocking aimlessly back and forth. "Janet, I need your help!" I made my voice commanding and sharp. The tone reached her, for the movement stopped and her head snapped up. She looked at me as though she could not remember who I was, then her eyes cleared, and she leaned in to help me. With some effort, the two of us managed to roll and lift him a little. I pushed my left hand beneath him feeling for the wetness of an exit wound, but his back was dry. The bullet had not gone through his massive body. John emerged like a mirage from the drifting smoke of the rifles and scattered fires, and ran toward us with his medical bag.

"Go! Get a bed ready for him in the infirmary." Janet jumped to obey while I pressed my hands harder against Cawdie's chest and concentrated entirely on him. He was still in there, although I could feel him weakening. No! I focused my mind, reached for him and tugged. "Cawdie. Listen to me, ye great gowk! We have you. You will be fine. Stay with us. Janet and I need you. You are not to leave us! Do you hear me, Cawdie? You may not leave us unprotected! You have to take care of us." I looked down, and his eyes opened.

"Nay, nay, lassie... I ken." His breathing was labored. He coughed and bloody phlegm stained his lips and beard. John knelt beside me and was opening his bag.

"John, there is no exit wound. The ball is still in him; it needs to be removed. He is having trouble breathing. Help me bandage the wound, then find McLean." He responded with a muffled curse, but accustomed to my bossy ways since childhood, set to work. Together we removed Cawdie's shirt and applied a tight bandage to the wound, so he could be moved. It would be a Herculean task. The man was a mountain! John stood and went to find McLean, while I looked around for someone to help carry Cawdie into the infirmary. George Forrester was standing immobile in the middle of the carnage, looking at Malcolm as he walked away. He looked serene and unruffled, as if he were standing in a ballroom, his good-looking face unreadable. He turned toward the infirmary and began to move toward us. I raised my voice. "Sir, come no closer unless you have had smallpox." He stopped immediately, and backed away. "I need some of your men who have had smallpox to help me get my clansman into the infirmary." He stared at me considering for a long moment, then called to one of his sergeants.

It took four soldiers to lift the huge warrior. They were breathing hard by the time they got him onto the bed Janet had commandeered. The activity had centered her, and she stood quietly waiting for whatever would come, her eyes never leaving Cawdie's face. He lay unmoving. I was not sure if he was conscious or not. She had reverted to her normal self and set out basins, clean water, cloths, a small array of instruments and threaded needles. After washing my hands, I filled another basin with water, added some peppermint oil and began to wipe away the blood from his chest and beard. When I loosened the bandage, the wound began to bleed again, but more sluggishly, a froth of bubbles emerging with each exhalation. I replaced the blood-soaked bindings with clean ones and stood back, thinking. By the laws of Scotland, I was only a woman, even if I was a healer, and there was nothing further I was legally permitted to do. But if McLean did not come soon, I would act, regardless of the consequences. Fortunately, McLean arrived within minutes. He did not even spare me a look although he glanced at our preparations, then bent over Cawdie, pulled away the dressing carefully and examined him. He was very thorough. I watched him and kept my often-unruly mouth tightly closed. After all, he was supposed to be the best surgeon in Edinburgh. His voice was gravelly when he spoke, as though he seldom used it, but even and confident.

"I need to get the ball out. It may have hit a rib. He looked at the table Janet had set up. Get more clean water, towels, bandages. Make a mixture of half alcohol and half vinegar to wash the wound." He reached into his bag and pulled out a rolled cloth cylinder. Unrolled, it revealed a line of pockets, each one holding a different surgical implement. He removed one I recognised, a long slender bullet drawer called *Rostrum Lacerti*, or lizard's beak because of the shape of the head. The opposing jaws were controlled by turning the vise handle, and was often used for bullets lodged in bone.

Some of my anxiety left me and in relief I spoke without thinking. "Yes, the beak should work." My words caused him to look at me and raise one dark brow. Was he wondering how such as I knew of a specialized surgical instrument? There was no time for speculation. I hurried away to do his bidding.

McLean watched me remove the bandages and cleanse the area around the wound with a cloth damped with the alcohol mixture. Each time Cawdie exhaled it left a line of froth. When the wound was clean, he inserted the metal bullet drawer into Cawdie's chest. It slid deeper than I had expected before it stopped. I winced. Sweat gleamed on McLean's forehead. He closed his eyes, feeling for the edges of the ball through the slight contact vibration of the bullet drawer and the lead ball. His expression changed when the instrument hit metal and he carefully adjusted the jaws around the bullet by touch. His long slender fingers deftly turned the top of the instrument, causing the vise inside to close its teeth around the bullet. McLean slowly pulled the apparatus straight up, and it emerged clamped around a misshapen lump of bloody lead with a small wad of rag adhering to it. He dropped both on the table, and switched to forceps to remove two more pieces of rag carried in by the shot. When no more emerged, he inserted his forefinger into the wound, moved it around searching for more rag or bone splinters, and found none. There was a surge of blood from the hole following the procedure. He held up his hand. "Let it bleed a bit, then irrigate it with the vinegar and alcohol."

Under his watchful eye I did as directed, then waited for further orders, wondering what treatment he preferred, open or closed, but he said only "Pour some of the alcohol and vinegar mix into the wound, wipe it, cover it with a thick cloth dipped in the solution and bandage it. No stitches until it stops draining. Get him into a sitting position so that he can breathe more easily. Later I will return to see how he fares." I set about following his directives, and noticed that he washed the bullet drawer in the basin and dried it well before returning it to its pocket. Many surgeons did not wash their tools, the rationale being that it rusted them. I had been taught to wash mine. He watched while I finished dressing Cawdie's wound, then put his roll of instruments back in his bag and moved toward the door. There, he paused, turned back and said brusquely, "You did well". Then he left.

Cawdie had made no sound or movement so I assumed he was unconscious. Janet and I pulled the blanket up around him and tucked it in. Now we would wait. My hand on his forehead found it damp with sweat but cool. It was too soon for fever. I wiped away the sweat and kissed him gently, then slid boneless with fatigue down to the floor in a crumpled heap. My pallet was a thin blanket, my head pillowed on my arms, it was so good to rest. I closed my eyes.

* * *

Hours later, a sound from Cawdie awoke me and I floundered to my feet reaching for his face. At my touch, he opened his eyes, looked at me, and slowly and deliberately winked! My heart eased, and I leaned over and kissed his flushed cheek. It was far too hot. Janet had been keeping vigil with me.

"Janet, he has a fever. I will clean the wound and change the dressing. I want you to bathe him with cool water, and keep a cool compress on his forehead." I rummaged through my bag for the cherry syrup and looked around the room. "Open the windows and give him two, no, three tablespoons of it with water every four hours." I removed the bandages and smelled them. A faint odor of putrescence overlaid the metallic scent of blood. The edges of the wound had sealed themselves and were a swollen angry red. I washed it with the vinegar and alcohol mixture and rebandaged it, willing my fingers not to pull it open. His wound needed to drain but I dared not treat it. That was McLean's province. Janet was bending over him with fierce protectiveness. I reluctantly left him to her and sent a note to McLean telling him that Cawdie had developed an infection and asking him what he wanted done.

The five smallpox test patients needed care as well as a few others who had trickled in seeking help, and the infirmary had to be put back to rights. Volunteers had arrived to help with the nursing and cleaning. Two of them, both women, were assigned to observing and writing down the details of the progress of every volunteer in the smallpox group. I had asked George if he could send us two of his men who had already had smallpox to repair the infirmary windows and whatever broken furniture could be salvaged, and they were there and already hard at work, often casting curious glances our way as we tended patients. One of them was the regiment drummer, a sturdy lad of perhaps seventeen, who immediately developed a strong instance of hero worship while watching my cousin treat patients. He was a red Scot, his hair a bright lustrous copper against white skin that a woman would envy, with only a few pockmarks to prove that he was a survivor. Clear green eyes assessed the world, framed by a thick fringe of lashes that matched his hair. He was as tall as Cawdie, broad-shouldered with slim muscled calves, but gawky, not yet grown into his final shape. He followed John everywhere, looming over the shorter man, and quickly became adept at helping him, absorbing everything like a sponge. I carried with me the fear that the smallpox experiment may have been compromised by the riot or some unforeseen contact but there was nothing to be done except wait and see. By the time we were finished, it was late, and my legs were shaking as I climbed the wooden stairs to the storeroom on the second floor that served as Malcolm's bedroom. He was on the cot, face-down with one arm over the side, hand resting on the floor. He was quite still. I stopped at the open door and rapped on the surround. I heard a soft grunt and took it as assent.

"Malcolm?" There was no response, so I sank on the floor beside his bed and sighed heavily. "Malcolm, are you alright?" I hoped he was because I was not sure I had the energy to cope with much more today.

He turned his face toward me and opened one eye, "I will live."

At this stage of the experiment, a few pustules had begun to form at his hairline and on his cheeks. Oddly enough, I thought a few marks would only make him more attractive, even dangerous looking. His eyes were reddened and wet. Had he been weeping? "It has been a day made by the Devil himself, as my mother would say." That brought the flicker of a smile to his face, so I blathered on in like manner for a few minutes until he turned over on his side. He had a look of weary sadness I had never seen before. I took his hand.

He closed his eyes but did not take his blood-stained hand from mine. We sat for a while and I tried to send a measure of the little strength I had left in me into his soul. "Cawdie will live, I think. Janet will make it so. He would not dare leave her."

Malcolm's fingers tightened on mine. "I'm glad. He's a good man."

"As are you, Malcolm." He made a sound like a muffled snort.

"I am so tired that if I lay down, I will not get up and that will be a scandal." I laughed at the thought. "It will be better in the morning," I said brightly, supressing a yawn.

"It will not be better, Elspeth." I had become used to little reaction, so this startled me fully awake.

He was still holding my hand. Strange for one who seemed reluctant to touch. I had slouched against the side of the cot, his sad brown eyes inches from mine. I thought I felt something from him, but was unsure of exactly what. It was like a tenuous ribbon of thought fluttering between us. I decided to grasp it. "Is this about your brother George? Are you unhappy Malcolm?"

"I...I am tired, Elspeth, tired of everything. Tired of the burden. I cannot continue."

I touched his face gently with my other hand, and said, "Then put it down. We all need rest."

"No, it is more than that. I am done. I've reached my limit." He said that with such conviction, my heart sank.

"Let your friends help. We will share the weight."

"Perhaps...but they're best off with a new leader."

"Malcolm, remember what happened but a few hours past. Your friends did not flee. They risked their lives and fought beside you, and they will again."

"Hammett thinks there need not have been a fight, that it's me who incites the conflict."

"He is concerned with peace, you with healing, but in your heart, do you truly believe you are to blame for this conflict?"

"Perhaps I am. But is it acceptable that we have a College of Physicians that is against finding cures for diseases? Is it morally justifiable that our clergy espouses hatred and violence against their fellow men? And the one that galls the most is that we have a Town Guard established to protect us that has become our jailor and extortionist, all under the benevolent eyes of our City Fathers."

"Then we must right these wrongs." I could feel his outrage and anger welling up now.

"Elspeth, for pity's sake! I have been beaten almost to death, infected with a disease, lost my lover, housekeeper, and even my dog, stood against a mob, broken my Physician's Oath by killing a man, and on the very edge of victory had it snatched away by one who floats through life always seeming to be the hero despite doing nothing to earn it. I've had enough!" His voice was filled with rage now and he sat up on the cot abruptly, letting go of my hand. My head had begun to throb from the force of his emotions. I put my hands to my temples.

"Please, Malcolm, please give it time. We need you. I feel your anguish. Let it heal. Please." I was worried now he might do or say something reckless. I took his hand again. He tried to pull away, but relented. "Did I ever tell you about my sister?"

"What? Nay." He looked down at me, head tilted with a look of puzzlement. I needed to change the direction of this conversation.

"She died when we were girls when the pox came through Skye."

"I didn't know. I'm sorry." His voice was softer.

I cleared my throat. This was not going to be easy to confess. "She was a year older and beautiful, and we both loved the same boy." I hesitated. This was my deepest and most painful secret and...shame. "Malcolm, when she died, a small hidden part of me was glad. Now I could have that boy all to myself." I had finally said it aloud, and perhaps it was fatigue or old memories, but I started to cry.

Malcolm slid off the cot to hold me. "We all have those feelings."

"No, it was beyond wicked of me and I regret it to this day." I turned my head and sniffled into the sweaty linen of his shirt, feeling the comforting warmth of his body. "Malcolm, promise me you will heal the rift with your brother. Lift this heaviness from your soul."

He sighed and kissed the top of my head. "I will try, Elspeth. All I can do is try."

"Aye, it is the same with all we do in life, isn't it?" I felt embarrassed now, at my revelation and feelings. "Let us sleep now. Tomorrow will bring new promise. Goodnight Malcolm."

He helped me stand. I was a bit wobbly but left as gracefully as I could and heard him say "Thank you, my dear friend," as I closed his door.

* * *

Rats scurried away at the muffled sounds my feet made on the slimy refuse overlaying the cobblestones. Foggy damp intensified the ever-present smell of excrement, piss, vomit, dead things, and the thousand other odors that humanity harbors. Edinburgh stunk. I no longer gagged at it. One becomes accustomed to such things although my appetite grew less each day. A mottled grey and silver half-moon hung in the turquoise sky. The first birds of morning chittered on the roofs oblivious to the anguish below. It was well past dawn, but I could barely see, for the overhanging second stories, and more, of the houses blocked the early light. The old defensive walls enclosing the city made building atop and up the only solution to the burgeoning population, so necessity made neighbors of tradesmen, noblemen and professionals in the same structure. The streets were eerily deserted except for a few emaciated dogs searching the offal littering the streets. Those who could had left the city, trying to escape the specter of smallpox, some carrying it unawares to other places. The poor remained, prisoners of poverty, in the cellars and garrets of the tall ranks of flats. I walked up a narrow wynd, that ended at High Street looking for the first place on my list. A scrap of white fabric, indicating those within needed help, fluttered over the door of a stair tower that housed narrow treads leading both up and down. Inside the building a second scrap hung over uneven steps descending into blackness broken only by a faint glow at the bottom. I steadied myself with one hand on the rough damp wall and moved warily down, the fetid air thickening as I grew nearer the feeble light. Once my foot landed on a yielding wriggly mass that I refused to identify, and a soft scurry of movement increased then faded away as I passed. There was no door below. The steps ended on a packed dirt floor barely visible in the light of a single lamp perched precariously on a wooden table. Its wavering beams fell on a motionless form lying on a rude cot. The space reeked of death, and I jerked as something pulled at my skirt. Tiny hands clutched the fabric as I bent down and picked up the child. Dirty skin stretched tightly across the bones of her pustule covered face and lank hair tumbled about the filthy shirt she wore. Her body was almost weightless. Incredibly, a trace of the sweet smell that young children have still clung to her beneath the other odors. Holding her I moved to the bed and felt for a pulse in the silent figure on the bed even though I knew there would be none. The room was empty of life save what lingered in the shadows waiting patiently for me to leave. I held the child closer and left the lamp burning for as long as it might. Its light would soon be gone, and the darkness would rule again. I would inform the Town Guard to see to the body, and take the child to the infirmary to care for her. If she survived, then she would be left at the place the city provided for orphaned and poor children.

* * *

Sir William turned his head slowly toward the door as I opened it, and peered at me through the misshapen mask of smallpox. He was very ill, and looked as though he was in the final phase of the disease. Malcolm had asked me to see his father and do anything that I could to make him more comfortable, and I would try. The curtains were closed, and the room was too dark, too hot, and stinking with the sweetly putrescent odor that marked smallpox patients. His large emaciated body seemed small beneath the mound of blankets.

"There, girl, what is it you want?" Every word seemed difficult to force out of the crusty slit that was his mouth, and his oozing hands picked restlessly at the coverlet leaving streaks of pus on the fabric as he glowered at me. I knew his mouth and throat must be raw with lesions. His manservant, Archibald, had let me into the room without asking for permission that would surely have been denied.

I put on my most charming expression for him, set down my bag, stepped closer and grasped one poor seeping hand. Anger and surprise flared in his eyes, but he was too feeble to stop me, and knew it. "I am Elspeth MacLeod, sir, a healer from Torrport. Your son Malcolm sent me. With your consent, I would like to examine you and see if we can make you feel a bit better."

He exhaled slowly and closed his eyes, forcing the words out with difficulty. "Do as you wish, you will anyway." He suddenly opened his swollen eyes again and fixed them on me fiercely. "But no bleeding and no quackery! I want to die in my right mind, not in a stupor from some untrained idiot's idea of medication."

He surrendered to my examination with an exaggerated air of martyrdom as Archibald quietly moved in to help me. His pustules were clustered so closely they had become large festering eruptions in many places and he was feverish from them. We removed the heavy blankets and undressed him. It hurt him badly. I could feel the pain and despair he was holding in tight check. Archibald followed my lead and managed a small smile as we worked in tandem. I had devised my own way of treating smallpox, which as far as I knew, at least did no harm. "Get Mrs. Simpson to prepare a tub of tepid water. Line it with cloths so he can soak for a while. I have cloth bags of beaten oats that we can put in the water that will help lessen the pain and itching. And a large pitcher of any juice you can find. I want his sheets changed every day. Boil these, and dry them in the sun. Open the windows, and take away all the blankets except one. Archibald looked shocked. The common treatment for fever was to pile on blankets and to keep the room hot and dark. I believed in Sydenham's method, which contradicted the old ways, and cooled the patient to fight the fever. When everything was ready we managed to get him into the tub. He sat as one boneless, his head resting on a pillow on the edge. Archibald washed his thinning hair and face with some of the bath water, milky from the oats, and placed cloths wet with the water on his forehead and cheeks. We needed Mrs. Simpson, so Archie covered him with a large linen towel to preserve his modesty.

While he soaked, we changed the bed linens, opened the windows to let in the soft spring air, and cleaned the room thoroughly with vinegar and water. Mrs. Simpson coaxed him to drink a cup of tea with tincture of willow bark added from my bag, while he was sitting quietly. I knew every swallow must be agonizing, but he gamely managed most of it. Archibald helped him to his feet, and dried him gently. His skin seemed less flushed and some of the scabs had detached and floated on the bath water. When he was back in bed, we used a salve of honey, garlic, lavender and beeswax to lightly coat the pocks, and covered him lightly with a clean sheet and blanket. He was deeply asleep before we were done. I stared down at him and placed my hand on his forehead, willing him to live. We would repeat the same treatment morning and evening. I told Mrs. Simpson to give him a tablespoon of honey with half teaspoon of cinnamon in it every three hours as well, and that I would return later to see how he was doing. They were to send for me if there was any change.

As I was leaving I saw George in his father's office. He was sitting at Sir William's desk, rifling through the contents of the drawers. I must have made some sound, because he looked up, hesitated and stood reluctantly.

"Lady Elspeth! I was, err...checking for letters that might need my attention. What news have you of my father? I understand he is near death? You need not stand on ceremony with me. I am prepared for the worst." He bowed gracefully, regaining his poise.

"He is resting." I watched as he assumed an appropriately grave demeanor. "I would make no funeral plans just yet." I cocked my head and looked pointedly at the desk. "Tis thought that touching the belongings of a smallpox victim will spread the disease." My voice was cool and slightly acidic. He went pale in an instant and gaped at his hands. "I would wash them with vinegar, sir. It may or may not help. Tis all in God's hands," I said piously. I dipped my head regally to him and left him standing motionless with fear, his hands extended away from his body, the forgotten papers scattered at his feet.

Henry and Scathach were lying quietly in the hallway. I patted them both soothingly, certain they knew that Sir William was desperately ill in that way that dogs sense the human condition, then went back to the infirmary.

* * *

I returned to chaos. Four men were trying to hold Cawdie down as they fought to tie his hands with a rope passed beneath the bed. The left bedpost that had secured him earlier was cracked and leaning. Pieces of a broken chamber pot littered the floor over its malodorous contents. Cawdie's wrists were bleeding, white bone showing in one place where he had struggled against his bindings.

Tears streaked Janet's face as she tried to tell me what had happened. Cawdie had been thrashing about, only soothed by her voice, which calmed him for short periods, but he had finally tipped into enraged hallucinations, yelling at invisible foes, and striking out at whatever horrors his mind had conjured up. She had acquired a large purple bruise on her cheek, the beginnings of a black eye and dark finger marks on her wrist while trying to hold him. Several of the men trying to tie him would have visible mementos of the struggle as well.

I shouted across the uproar for Janet to get me a cup of water and took a bottle of syrup of poppies from my bag. Cawdie was finally subdued, but struggling, and cursing foully. I mixed a large dose of the syrup with a little water, leaned over him, braced myself, and pinched his nose shut. When he opened his mouth to breathe I poured the concoction down his throat. He went still, but ultimately had to swallow to breathe. We waited.

Finally, his body relaxed, and I could examine him. The area around his bullet wound was a hot festering red, ugly and bulging. Janet cleaned his wrists, applied salve to the raw flesh and bandaged them as well as she could. A few stitches might be needed later to pull the abraded skin together over the bone, but that was unimportant now. I stroked his brow feeling the poison growing stronger inside him. He was weakening. McLean had not come yet. I looked at Janet. "We have to do something."

"Yes," she whispered and began to assemble a tray with what would be needed. I washed my hands, turned to Cawdie, started to clean the distended flesh, and then McLean walked in. He took in the scene at once, and I lifted my chin defiantly.

"The wound needs to be drained." I was past caring what he thought.

"I see that. You are quite right," he said evenly. He removed his coat, examined the contents of the tray, murmured something, picked up a scalpel and cloth from the things Janet had arranged and simply looked at me. I moved out of his way.

He ran his fingers over the wound, chose a place and deftly sliced through the engorged flesh. A flood of evil smelling pus and dark fluid burst forth. He wiped at the mess with the cloth and dropped it into the waste bucket by the bed. I handed him clean ones until the flow stopped. He mopped up the last dribs, and considered the syringe on the tray. "Do you know how to irrigate?" I nodded in response. "Then do it. Use the alcohol and vinegar mix." He thought a moment... "Add a measure of oil of garlic and half as much oil of peppermint. When you are done, let the wound drain as it will, and irrigate again it in the morning and evening."

I saw the drummer boy, who had been watching us closely, approach hesitantly. "Sir." He spoke to McLean. "I be the Captain's personal wound sucker, but I would be willin' to do for Sir Cawdie, an it pleases you?" He spoke anxiously, eyes darting to the still figure on the bed.

McLean looked at him, then at me. "Indeed. I think that could be very helpful. Lady Elspeth, you know of this treatment? Tis mostly used in the field, but with good results. Have him suck the wound after you irrigate it now, and once each day in the morning. Use one of your honey salves to cool the edges of the wound between treatments. I will look at him again in the morning." He washed his hands, picked up his belongings and left.

We took turns watching Cawdie overnight. Even the drummer insisted on taking one. I wondered if George would be offended by our use of his man. Cawdie awoke, weak but lucid, early the next morning. The first face he saw was Janet's. Her bruised cheek and black eye were in full color and he stared at her, puzzlement following rage, then realization flickered across his features. He groaned and tried to turn away, but Janet put her hand on his cheek and kissed him softly. "*Mo chroí*, My heart." Wetness trickled from the corners of his closed eyes, while she tenderly stroked his face. Neither of them noticed when I left.

Things began to settle into some semblance of routine. The inoculated patients had passed through the first stages of aches, fever and vomiting, and the mildest forms of smallpox rash. These had begun to scab over on John and Malcolm. We made them bathe in oat water, and applied salve to the pocks when they emerged, hoping to stave off some of the scarring. A general sense of optimism replaced the anxiety, and the test volunteers who had not been inoculated began to help with patients. Young seemed to be always present, working at all hours. It worried me to see him pushing himself so, but my gentle comments were ignored. Men were too proud and stubborn to pay heed to a mere woman.

My days were filled with walking the streets of Edinburgh each morning, looking for the white cloths that indicated need, and caring for Sir William. He was still sleeping a great deal, but the weeping raw inflamed look of his pocks was markedly less, and Mrs. Simpson reported that he was eating her rich egg custards and cream soups that were easy to swallow. I felt he was recovering well, and told George and Malcolm that they would be able to visit soon. Cawdie had mended with almost miraculous rapidity and would be impossible to restrain much longer. I needed to replenish my supplies and see some of my patients in Torrport. My presence here was no longer critical.

Julianne's letters were filled with all that was taking place at home, and after consulting Malcolm I decided to go back for a few days and return with Sir Ross for his surgery. Malcolm had arranged for McLean to operate on Sir Ross's fistula and McLean had quite casually asked if I wished to observe. Of course, I said yes.

* * *

The journey home over the rutted roads was tiring. The badly sprung coach arrived in Torrport well after nightfall and I was not looking forward to the long walk home in the dark. Julianne and the baby had moved back to the castle. Janet could not leave Cawdie, and Scathach was with Sir William, so my fatigue was making me feel mawkishly despondent and sorry for myself. To my surprise, Aidan opened the coach door as I reached for it and helped me out on arrival. The driver nodded to him, handed down my one scuffed bag, then pulled the carriage away toward the barn to care for his horses. Gracie stood nearby, hitched to the cart Malcolm had rented.

Aidan smiled. "Your carriage awaits, my lady."

Evidently Malcolm had contrived to send word of my return. Warm light shone from my cottage window and smoke was curling from the chimney when we arrived. Jocki's beaming face appeared in the doorway and a waft of warm air scented with the smell of stew greeted us. Inside, the table had been set for one. A lopsided bouquet of flowers sat next to a crusty loaf of bread and a jar of berry preserves. Aidan and Jocki exchanged satisfied glances, then Aidan left after a few words of welcome. Jocki bustled about making tea, and I relaxed and let someone else care for me for the first time in many days. Our wee black cat, Isis, rubbed against my skirts, reclaiming me. It was good to be home.

* * *

The next morning broke bright and clear. In my absence, the animals had been well tended by Jocki. There were eggs and cream in the cool cellar. Someone had been caring for my garden as well, not a weed showed in the rows. A sound on the path made me look up. Gregor was striding toward me. Somehow, he reminded me of a warrior priest with his dark clothing and erect bearing. I wondered what he would look like without his beard. I usually read people well enough, but Gregor's thoughts were hidden behind a wall I could not penetrate. I tried once, when we were taken by the smugglers, but he suddenly turned his glittering black eyes on me as though he knew what I was doing. I did not try again, sensing that I might not like what I found.

Gregor did not smile, but bowed and gave me a basket of fruit and a note from Sir Ross. The note said that Malcolm had sent word that McLean scheduled Sir Ross's surgery, and we were to return to Edinburgh in two days. That barely gave me time to see anyone, but I did not intend to miss the opportunity to observe McLean work, especially since he made it a point to ask me to do so.

I thanked Gregor, and asked if he knew who had been caring for my garden. The man reddened and said that he had done a little, in payment for taking some of the garlic we grew. The daily applications of garlic paste to the fistula on Sir Ross's backside had made it needful to find more than was readily available. I assured him he was welcome to take whatever he wished from the garden. I knew that Jocki had been sharing the eggs, milk and whatever had been ready in the garden with his family too. Jocki spoke to Gregor easily, and with respect. Obviously caring for the garden and the animals together had bonded them. I found that intriguing.

I refilled the contents of my depleted bag, and walked to the castle with Jocki. Lady Margaret was glowing. Contentment can do that for a woman. I examined her and found her rash gone, and her secrets as sweet smelling as those of a young girl. Rachel served us tea and biscuits, some exquisitely decorated with gold leaf and colored glazes. I suddenly lost my appetite. I told Lady Margaret she was to let me know if she needed me and decided to look in on the castle infirmary. The Laird was in the bailey, holding Jocki enthralled with a bawdy tale, probably unfit for his ears. I inquired after his health, and he grinned wickedly but wisely said little. The infirmary was blessedly empty, so I took a reluctant Jocki and went home.

* * *

The next day was spent making salves and preparing medications to take back to Edinburgh. Sir Ross had invited me to dinner that evening, so I bathed and dressed in my best green silk gown. Of all men, he would know it was not in the latest style, but the rich Italian fabric clung in all the right places and fell in graceful folds to my matching slippers. I chose the emerald and cobwebby gold filigree necklace from the *parure* that had belonged to my mother, then added the earrings. My thick hair had been tamed into a low chignon at my neck. Two braids circled my head and ended in the chignon. I encouraged a few wisps of auburn hair to curl around my face and neck to partially obscure the ugly scars. The small mirror reflected a woman I had not seen in some time. She smiled at me.

Sir Ross sent his carriage and Gregor met me at the door. His mouth quirked slightly at the corners in recognition of my appearance, and he bowed more deeply than usual. Sir Ross appeared immediately. It was apparent that both he and the house smelled better. His eyes gleamed with appreciation, and he kissed my hand, holding it rather longer than was polite. Amid profuse compliments and the excellent dinner, he recited the latest gossip from Torrport. The English navy had added another ship to the blockade off the coast; the Laird was seeking help from Russia to free Scotland from the increasingly oppressive English rule; Lady Tenely had taken another lover; and the murder of Spence was still much spoken of. This last bit of information was imparted with the after-dinner cordial that glittered with bits of gold swirling in its rosy depths. I found myself staring at the eddying flakes and wondering again if Sir Ross was involved. We finalized our travel plans to Edinburgh for the day after next, then I was delivered safely back to my cottage.

* * *

Three days later we were back in Edinburgh and preparing for Sir Ross's surgery. It was early morning. He had leased a residence belonging to a wealthy wool merchant who had fled from the smallpox epidemic. Like most of the upper class, Sir Ross had the physician come to him, and the surgery would take place in the anteroom of his bedroom. The fistula operation was no longer uncommon, since it had been almost twenty years since it was successfully performed on King Louis XIV of France.

Several chairs had been placed around the room. A padded table was positioned with one end facing a large window. Two smaller tables sat nearby, one empty, one with basins, water, and clean cloths. McLean arrived with two apprentices. He nodded and beckoned me to attend him. The apprentices unpacked the bags he brought, and I arranged the contents on the empty table, as I knew he liked.

Gregor came in with Sir Ross, dressed only in a nightshirt, a bit ashen but composed. Gregor helped him get on the padded table and turn on his stomach. A pillow was placed beneath his belly, and one of the apprentices stood on each side of the table, lifting his nightshirt and pulling apart his thighs to expose his anus and the fistula. McLean asked Sir Ross if he was ready. He replied "yes" in a firm voice, then clamped his lips shut. I stood at McLean's right to tender him whatever he needed. He inserted a retractor into the rectum, exposing the fistula opening low in the bowel wall, and reached for the delicately curved scalpel on the table. He inserted the thin tool into the fistula until its tip emerged on the other end, made certain the razor-sharp blade faced toward him, and pulled the blade up to open the abscess along its length. It released the stink of feces, mucus, infection and the warm metallic smell of fresh blood. He was quick, skillful and precise. He pressed clean cloths along the line of the incision until the bleeding slowed, then scraped the fistula walls free of feces and pus. After flushing the wound several times, he applied a salve and bandaged it loosely. There were no stitches. To prevent a recurrence, the long gash had to remain open until it healed into a flat scar. McLean gave Gregor instructions on caring for the trenchlike cut, which were mostly about how to keep it from closing, and clean and aired. Sir Ross would not be able to travel for at least two weeks. He had grown noticeably paler but had not flinched during the entire procedure. I gently removed one of his clenched hands from the side of the bed and held it. His pulse was rapid but strong. He turned his head and smiled wryly at me, then closed his eyes and relaxed. Except for thanking McLean profusely and asking for his reckoning, his ordeal was over. Gregor helped his master carefully back to his bedroom, while I washed McLean's instruments and helped him repack them.

With Sir Ross's surgery completed, my time in Edinburgh was over. The smallpox volunteers were well past the critical stage. Cawdie was doing well, but Janet would not leave his side. Sir William was slowly regaining his strength under the loving care of Mrs. Simpson and Archibald. The pocks had left his face and hairline scarred, but not as badly as I had feared. A beard and his wig would help conceal both. Malcolm was well, and deeply involved in the after effects of the experiment, and his own life. Sir Ross was not yet able to travel, so he and Gregor were staying in Edinburgh for a while longer. One interesting thing had occurred. Following Ross's surgery, McLean had turned to me unexpectedly and asked: "Where did you study?"

I raised my eyes and looked at him directly. "At the School of Salerno." He grunted and resumed packing his bags.

Edinburgh was still very quiet. A few of the braver souls were returning but it was not yet the busy city it had been. I would try to shop for some of the wool cloth the city was famous for, visit the apothecary shops for things not available in Torrport, then take Scathach and return to my empty cottage. Suddenly I felt very much alone.

NINETEEN

Malcolm – Lure

Leith, Scotland.

"It's too early to be sure. He has a slight fever, but no other symptoms." I knelt over the gaunt sailor who'd collapsed on the floor of the Sand Bar Pub. I was muttering more to myself than to Calum Duncan, the pub owner, who was standing nearby.

"Shall I get some men to take him to the infirmary?" Duncan was a caring man, but wanted him gone. Not good for business, what little there was of it since the epidemic emptied the city.

"Not until I'm sure. Don't want him mixing with the infected ones if he has something else entirely." He didn't have a rash, but when I opened his mouth it looked inflamed, but that could be due to drinking and general abuse. "Was he drinking a lot, Calum?"

"Not especially. Had a few drams, but he was a bit unsteady when he arrived, and I think he may have complained of a sore throat." Calum no doubt regretting selling him those drams now.

"Did he say anything else of interest?"

"Nay, just bragging about exploits in the West Indies. Said the women there were hotter than the tropical sun. A few laughed at that, but most were quietly bent over a brew trying to forget the day." I knew what he meant. It had been depressing lately with so much sickness and death around, and the port had it worst.

I was suspicious about the fever and sore throat but needed him awake and sober for a proper examination. "Do you mind keeping him here til he sobers up? He may not have smallpox, but he clearly is sick. I can be back tomorrow to see him."

"All our rooms are empty, so I can keep him for a while, for you Doctor Forrester." Calum sighed and wiped his hands again on his apron.

"It is appreciated." I nodded and made a few notes about the patient.

"There are few enough doctors here anymore, and we are glad you and the others stayed. We won't forget it."

"I don't blame those who left. I stayed because...well because, and anyway I'm immune now. I must go. I have another patient..." My voice trailed off. I'd forgotten what I was about to say. It was happening often lately.

"Doctor, have you eaten? Please have some food and drink before you go."

It was late in the day and there was no end of patients and I hadn't eaten since breakfast, and the emotional fatigue of dealing with such misery, day after day, was affecting me more than I cared to admit. "Umm, surely, some bread to eat along the way would be welcome." That was more than true but I would never have asked. Calum called to the kitchen and a freckle-faced girl returned with a half-loaf of dark bread that I accepted gratefully.

"Make sure he has plenty to drink when he wakes up." I ripped off a chunk of bread to eat and stuffed the rest in my pouch. "Be back in the morning." I sputtered, mouth already full of bread.

Calum called a few men over to carry the sailor upstairs as I waved on my way out.

* * *

We'd stopped counting smallpox patients after three hundred. Several were dying every day now and the city had arranged undertakers to remove the bodies to a common grave that was spread with lye and covered each day, but it was the children that tore at one's heart. There was little we could do but offer supportive treatments and hope for the best.

I'd returned to work as soon as the few scabs I had sloughed off and I was no longer infective. My pock marks were less than I'd feared and when added to the usual scuffs, bruises and beard stubble, didn't seem to alter my look appreciably. Worse was the fatigue lingering from the ordeal of the past weeks. It was a blessing that Elspeth was there to put a stick up the back of my shirt for a few days, otherwise I'd have collapsed in a blithering heap. I was better, not yet my old self, but the doctoring work, even if emotionally trying, was better than sitting on my arse feeling sorry for myself.

It'd been a long day and I had a few more patients before taking to my cot in McLaren's infirmary. I'd moved into that storeroom I used during the experiment and the small space was cluttered with extra clothes and gear I'd shifted from Father's. My next patient wasn't far, a stone dock worker's cottage covered with moss almost to its thatched roof. I could hear a bairn crying as I knocked. An older woman opened the door. Her face was heavily lined, and on seeing me she simply pointed to the boy on a palette by the fire. I ducked my head to enter and once my eyes adjusted I could see the source of the crying was in its mother's arms in the corner, as far away from the sick boy as possible in this small space.

The mother spoke up. "We 'ave no coin, doctor, but will be forever obliged. Tis me son. He as the pox."

"Is your husband around?" I had to ask because sometimes husbands burst in unannounced ready to take my head off.

"Nay, He is off ta sea. Won't be back for weeks, an me boy needs help."

"With smallpox, there are no miracle cures. I'll do my best for him though."

"God bless you, doctor." I'd heard that phrase so many times recently that I almost believed it.

I knelt by the palette. It was just some rough crates with old blankets made of discarded plaids. The boy was naked but for a blanket, and his upper body was spotted with pustules. I felt his forehead and the fever had subsided.

"My name is Malcolm. What is yours?" I smiled at him

"I be Thomas, sir." His voice was hoarse from the pustules in his mouth and throat. I didn't have to look further.

I glanced back at his mother who was waiting patiently for the verdict. "He has distinct smallpox. That is the least worse kind and he has a good chance of surviving."

She exhaled and looked to the ceiling muttering something, then looked to me and said: "Thank ye, doctor." I could see tears welling as she bent her head.

I went over the usual treatments and care with her. I'd done this so many times in the past few days, I could do it in my sleep, and that was a good thing because I almost was. "Mam, when he no longer needs his bedding and clothes, burn them, and let your mother care for him now, don't want you giving it to your wee one." Most of the poor now understood how the pox could be spread, but I had to say it. "And if the fever returns, send for a doctor, understand?"

She nodded and said "Thank ye" repeatedly, and I smiled at the boy and assured him he would be over this soon.

On the way out, I gave the last of my bread and a jar of Elspeth's oatmeal salve to the old woman and whispered to her, "For the boy." She bowed and gave a sweet, toothless smile.

* * *

It was pitch black and the port is about two miles from the city and I was cursing the Edinburgh hills as I struggled to walk home. There were few Town Guards about anymore and the city had quickly become a lawless wasteland. There was extensive looting and little to be done about it. They'd even moved George's regiment out of the city to keep them from the pox. The worst for me was there were few carriages available now, so walking was the only option, and I wasn't getting enough to eat, so imagine how happy I was to arrive back at McLaren's to find him dining and deep in conversation with my old friend John Beaton. I dropped my bag at the door and practically fell into a chair beside them.

"Been busy, Mal?" Beaton looked as healthy and cheerful as ever. The pox experiment had little effect on him beyond gifting a few pock marks that improved his look. He was now a Scots cherub with a hint of danger. Women would be falling over him.

I sighed heavily, playing to a sympathetic crowd for a change. "Aye, saw hundreds of patients today," I exaggerated, of course.

"Then you must be making a fortune," McLaren piped up. "How about sharing?"

"I'll gladly share, if you'll share some of whatever I smell from the kitchen." It was late, but I was famished and didn't relish the thought of sleeping on an empty stomach.

"You have a deal." McLaren winked at Beaton. "I'll get you some. An ale with it?"

I was wondering what was up between them, but the thought of ale with food overrode my suspicion. "That would be grand, Angus, thank you."

As soon as McLaren left, Beaton leaned over to me and with a sly grin said, "That was your food we were eating. Thought you wouldn't mind. It was from Gwen, and she left this for you." He handed me a sealed letter. I hadn't heard from Gwen recently, so I ripped it open and read quickly. "Gwen is still in Edinburgh and wants to see me. Strange. I thought she'd left." Beaton knew little of this, so sat staring, waiting for more. "She was my...err...lover, and we split up and I thought she'd left town with the rest. I'll drop over tomorrow and see what she wants. Reminds me, how are you and Gillian getting on?"

"She is still here with her mother. They won't leave. Doing their best to help the shipyard workers." McLaren returned with a heaping plate of roast chicken, potatoes and turnip, slathered in gravy. It was a meal fit for a starving physician. "She is a fine woman, Malcolm."

"Aye, I sensed that too. You could do worse." I smiled and truly wished him happiness. "Thanks for saving some of my food," I teased Angus.

"We wouldn't let you starve," he quipped, then went to fetch the ale.

I was digging in when the ale arrived, then Beaton abruptly changed the subject. "Mal, we have bad news." I looked up with a grin, expecting a practical joke. "It is Young. He has hemorrhagic smallpox."

My stomach seized in mid swallow. "We confirmed it today. He's at home. I'll care for him, of course."

Young had been one of the five patients in our experiment who hadn't received the smallpox inoculant. One of them had fled when it came time to treat smallpox patients, but Young and three others stayed, knowing full-well the risks involved.

"But Young..." I mumbled, my thoughts shattered. He was the best of us, our mentor and leader.

"I know," said McLaren. The three of us sat there speechless. The experiment had been a success, but the gods of science had exacted a terrible price.

"I need to see him." I pushed my half-finished plate away.

"We all will...before..." Beaton clasped my shoulder and McLaren said softly, "We'll go tomorrow."

* * *

I wasn't looking forward to this day. I'd been avoiding seeing Father and George and then there was poor Young, and who knows what Gwen wanted, but I sensed none of it was good, and in my fragile state of mind... I was tempted to procrastinate but McLaren and Beaton prodded me to action and the three of us hiked as quickly as we could through the battleground of looters that had once been a wealthy neighbourhood on the way to Young's infirmary. McLaren had the sense to bring some bread that we ate along the way, and it soothed our frayed nerves, and Beaton made a silly comment about picking up some used furniture later. Young's infirmary was all too quiet when we arrived. There was only the old guard Beaton hired to deter looters, but he was asleep on one of the infirmary cots. We crept past knowing he'd likely been up all night, and headed for Young's bedroom on the second floor.

Beaton knocked, then said in a whisper. "Young, are you awake?"

The room was in semi-darkness, the curtains still closed, and there was that putrid smell of rotting flesh and blood. We all knew what to expect, but still it was hard to bear.

"Agaah," Young said weakly.

Beaton went to the chair beside his bed and I slid the curtain back enough, so we could see. "I'll make some laudanum for you. Have a sip of water first." McLaren and I helped him sit up while Beaton prepared the solution. Young was scarcely alive and leaking blood from every orifice. He reached over and gripped my hand and tried to focus his eyes on me.

"K...Keep...g...going." Those were his last words to me and I got the message as clearly as though he'd shouted them in my face.

"I will, dear friend. I promise." I held his hand as Beaton helped him drink. We all knew it wouldn't be long now. He would be hemorrhaging internally as well and

242

within hours his organs would be compromised, and it would be over. All we could do was help with the pain and be with him. No one wants to die alone.

We sat there for several minutes watching the laudanum take him to that blessed land, then Beaton said, "I will stay. You two have other duties. Thanks for coming." He was right, of course, but it felt wrong somehow to leave Young like that, so I hesitated, as did McLaren.

"Please go. He is no longer with us. I will care for him. Others need you more now."

The fresher air of the street seemed strange at first. We were no longer sharing Young's life. Angus and I stood there looking at each other, not knowing what to do next. It was Angus who spoke first. "You heard him, Mal. The torch has been passed." I was in a state of dissociative shock, and his words seemed to go through me. "You must temper bravery with wisdom. No one else can do this but you."

"But...but...I'm a wreck, Angus."

"Then get yourself together! We need you! Your patients need you!" He said it so forcefully I felt he was striking me. His eyes were ablaze with a fire I'd never seen. "We must finish this Mal...for Young...for all of us. We are counting on you!"

I spluttered something inane and we shook hands, then he strode away purposefully in that endearing lopsided gait, leaving me standing there emotionally paralyzed. I looked around to get my bearings and mind back in some semblance of order. Young was our wise statesman. He would be sorely missed, and I wasn't sure I could fill his shoes. But Angus was right, this project needed a proper conclusion and our opponents must not be allowed to win for lack of perseverance on our part. All this banged around in my mind and by the time I'd reached Father's I was determined not to allow Young's sacrifice to be for naught, and despite my current state, I would try to be a leader worthy of his memory.

* * *

Henry and Scathach met me at the door, ever cheerful and oblivious to the cares of men, and obviously getting on as good friends. On another day, I would've been happy to see them, but today I gave a cursory pat to each and called to see who was home. Mrs. Simpson came out of the kitchen radiating welcome and at once tried to ply me with food and drink. I told her I needed to see Father and to please bring tea and cakes to his room.

"Father?" The door was open and the morning sun streaming in and I saw him sitting up in bed engrossed in a sheaf of note papers. "Father?"

He looked up startled then said gruffly, "Malcolm, where in God's name have you been?"

"Well..." I started to explain, but he raised his hand.

"Never mind. I may not want to know. Come give your old man a kiss." When I came closer I could see his face was a mess of healing pocks, but he was speaking clearly and as feisty as ever. He was doing as well as one had the right to expect, all things considered.

I hugged him and kissed his cheek, and the tears, bottled up for days, poured out. "I love you, Father. I am so glad to see you well again."

"Enough, Malcolm. We have business to discuss."

I laughed and wiped my eyes, amazed at his stoicism. He was back, and our enemies had better start packing.

"George told me of that disturbance. Said you behaved badly, like a wild man, and were rude to him..." I knew I had to deal with this, so I was ready and carefully explained the background and what'd happened.

"I'm sorry, Father. It was not my intent to be rude to George, but it'd been a trying day and I was infected with smallpox and didn't want to create more problems, so I left. I will make it up to him."

Father nodded but I knew by his expression, he wasn't completely convinced. "Malcolm, this damned experiment of yours has caused a lot of problems in the city." I stopped him right there.

"No, Father. We are not the ones who caused the problems. It was our opponents, and as it turns out, our experiment was a success and may lead to the eradication of smallpox." I was exaggerating somewhat, but it was time to rally support and I knew if I could get Father on our side he could influence many.

"Is that so? Tell me more."

He listened intently as I described what we'd done, and the results. "And Father, it is well documented. It would stand up in court. Cameron has all our notes."

"Send Cameron to me with those notes."

"I will, Father." I was well pleased, knowing I'd impressed him.

"But there is still George." He wasn't going to let that go. "We will be dining tonight, and I expect you here at seven, and on your best..."

Father will never know why George and I have issues, so I had to play the good son, as always. "I will be delighted to see George again now that we are both well, and you must not worry, Father, I'll make things right with him."

Father smiled. It was so good to see that again, and he said, "You had better, or I will have you both whipped."

That made me laugh. Father had never so much as lifted a hand against us, never mind whipping us. "I must be on my best behaviour then."

"That will be a first!" He chuckled as Mrs. Simpson arrived with a tray.

I was enormously relieved that Father was clearly on his way to recovery. Smallpox never leaves its victims entirely, the experience imbedded deeper in the mind than any skin blemish. But he seemed to be coping nicely, and I could do worse than emulate his fortitude and resilience. I left his presence feeling much better and determined to make a positive contribution to family and community. I was humming a happy tune when I arrived at Gwen's.

* * *

It was unusually quiet when I entered. There were signs of minor looting on the main floor, tables tipped, paintings removed, broken pottery, that sort of thing, and no servants about. I called out to her, then slowly made my way toward her bedroom and called her name again.

"Get out! I'm armed, and men are coming." She sounded frightened.

"Gwen, it's me, Malcolm." I was very worried now. What had happened here? She was in the dressing room, the door closed. I tried to open it, but something was blocking. "Gwen, are you alright?"

I could hear scraping and grunting sounds, then the door opened a fraction and her face peered out and I knew at once she had smallpox. "Oh Gwen, not you too!" She started to cry. "Come on out, Gwen. You're safe now." My heart, singing only a few minutes before, now felt like crying with hers, but I needed to be strong for us both.

"I...I cannot shift it enough. There is a cabinet."

"Stand back, and I'll push." I put my shoulder to it and it didn't take much really. She'd barricaded herself in, and once I pushed the cabinet aside I saw her sitting on a dressing chair, sobbing, face covered in pustules. I knelt before her, taking her hands in mine. "Oh darling, I'm here now. All will be well."

I spent the next hour, cleaning and soothing and listening to her story. She'd stayed behind after sending her son to safety because a man had left a message. It was to do with her husband's death.

"He wanted to meet me at the docks at night, so he wouldn't be recognized. He said he worked for Mackmain and knew about my husband's death, so I had to meet him."

"You shouldn't have gone alone."

"He insisted. Said if he saw anyone with me, he'd leave. I had to risk it."

"I know." What I knew was that she'd loved her husband very much and he'd died under suspicious circumstances and nothing had been done about it, and I believed she would do anything to find the truth of the matter. I would have hugged her then, but for the painful pustules covering her body.

"So, I met him. He had a rash and looked very unwell. I thought as long as he didn't touch me..."

245

"It doesn't take much sometimes, a breath, a sneeze, even the message paper." I tried to console her, because I would have done the same in her situation.

"He said he was there the night my husband died, and it was Mackmain who killed him, drowned him at the docks." She covered her face with her hands and wept again. Mackmain's name brought back feelings of such intense hatred in my heart. I wanted to kill that bastard, for what he'd done to me and Gwen. I cursed him under my breath. "Malcolm, please help me bring Mackmain to justice."

"Gwen, I'll do more than that." She stared at me not quite understanding my meaning, but the look on my face was enough to convince her.

"Thank you. I knew I could depend on you." She shuddered and slumped back on the bed.

"First, you must recover. Then we'll deal with Mackmain. Who was that man you met?"

"He wouldn't give a name. I think it was guilt and perhaps he believed he was going to die. He asked for nothing."

"Then we have no proof or witness willing to testify?"

"I suppose not, but I believed him. It all made sense, somehow."

"Then we must make Mackmain confess. It's the easiest way, without credible evidence."

"Yes, but how?"

"Leave it to me, Gwen. Now what do you have left in your kitchen?"

Making tea and oatmeal gave me time to settle my mind. I knew my hatred of Mackmain was self-destructive and reminded myself to keep emotions in check. I prayed for Young to help me. I needed his wisdom and Father's resilience more than ever. I smiled when I returned with the tray for Gwen. She was trying to untangle her unruly red hair. Vanity is the last to leave.

"Gwen, you need to be under a physician's care but I'm sorry, I can't treat you."

"Malcolm, please. I need you."

"There is too much emotion between us. Physicians need to be detached when it comes to patients." She sipped her warm tea and listened. "Do you remember McLaren? He's one of the best, and I think quite taken by you, and one of the nicest men I know. You will get exemplary service from him, I'm sure." I chuckled, and she tried to as well.

"I trust your judgement, and I am deeply sorry for what happened between us." Her eyes were pleading, but there was no going back, now. We both needed to move on.

"Your pox is the common kind and you have an excellent chance of a full recovery, but for some pock marks. Your servants are gone, and it's not safe for you to stay here alone. Allow me to take you to McLaren's. I've been using an old storeroom there. It's cozy and warm and you'll be well cared for. I'll be returning to Torrport soon and

I can stay at Father's til then. McLaren's infirmary is a bit crowded, but you'll be in good company."

"Thank you for your kindness. I think I will enjoy a change of scenery."

I admired her attitude. "And you'll have a nice window to watch the goings on while you recover."

"Then let us waste no further time in this wreck of a house." I watched as she dressed, threw a few changes of clothes in a bag, and wrapped herself in her most concealing cloak. When she was ready, I took her arm. It wasn't far to McLaren's, but in her state, walking there was an ordeal.

As expected, McLaren was delighted to see her, and we got her settled in my old room. McLaren was soon fussing over her and shouting for someone to bring food and drink, and Gwen was already enjoying the attention and laughing at McLaren's silly jokes. I smiled as I gathered my clothes for burning, and left for Father's with a wave and well wishes. They hardly looked up when I left.

* * *

They'd moved Cawdie and Janet to the third floor. The space was not much more than an attic with open timbers, rough floor and a few dormers for light and fresh air. There was only one room, but it had been hastily partitioned with boards and crates and blankets hung from the rafters. It was filled with the sick and their families. "Janet?" I whispered.

"Over here Malcolm." I lifted the blanket and she was there washing a forlorn looking girl who was sitting on the edge of a cot. I couldn't blame her for being sad. I was in her situation only a few weeks back. Janet rinsed the cloth and glanced back. "Cawdie is across and down one. He would like to see you. I'll be there in a few minutes."

Watching Janet brought back memories good and bad, the pain of smallpox mixed with her loving-kindness. I smiled at her and shook away the memories. "See you in a few minutes then." I ducked out and went across and peeked in the compartment she'd mentioned. Cawdie was in a chair beside his cot, oiling his belt. He looked up and in a surly growl said, "Brother."

"You look well, Cawdie. Good to see you up." He still had a large bandage wrapped around his upper chest with a piece over one shoulder to hold it in place.

He put down the oiled rag and belt and sat back in the chair. *"I've bin better."*

Cawdie was never a man of many words, except when it had to do with Janet. I thought a moment, trying to gauge his temper. "Cawdie, that bullet was meant for me. I know that and I'm grateful for your courage and sacrifice." I wasn't entirely sure how he'd respond.

"*Noo we ur brothers.*" He said solemnly.

"I suppose so, Cawdie. I owe you my life, at the very least."

A slight smile formed on his huge face. It looked out of place somehow, like a smile that had been lost and found itself unexpectedly there. "*Brother, ah ask a favour.*"

"Anything Cawdie," I said, hoping it wasn't something completely crazy.

He looked to the opening in the blanket and said in a whisper. "*Ah want Janet as mah guidwife. Will ye help me?*"

I chuckled. "I think she's yours already. Have you asked her?"

He shook his shaggy head. "*Ah fear she will say nae.*"

"Have courage, Cawdie." I grinned understanding how even the strongest of men can wilt before the woman he loves. "I'll try to help you, but it is Elspeth you must ask too and perhaps Laird MacLeod."

"*Uir laird disnae caur.*"

The blanket opened, and Janet came in wiping her hands. She looked at us both. Cawdie immediately looked down like a boy caught in the middle of mischief, and I was smiling broadly. "You too look like you're up to something."

"Cawdie is recovering well."

"Aye, and soon will be of more help here. What is going on?" she said sternly.

I always believed a direct approach was best. "Janet, I think you should take Cawdie as your husband, before some other woman grabs him."

Janet laughed. "And why do you think I need a husband?"

"All women do." I regretted saying that as soon as it left my mouth.

She made a sound that was unmistakably derision, then looked down at Cawdie. "Cawdie, do you have something to add?"

Cawdie looked up and his face flushed and he mumbled something that made no sense.

Janet folded her arms and looked from one of us to the other, then she just said "Men!" and left.

I whispered to Cawdie "For God's sake, just take her!" He had a look of misery. For him it was worse than being shot. "I cannot do this for you, Brother. You must be her warrior." I left Cawdie with his head in his hands muttering oaths, and sought out Janet. She was readying supplies to clean another patient. I took her firmly by the elbow and pulled her to a quiet corner, and held her so close I could feel her heat and smell the lavender in her hair. She looked up, blue eyes alert, nostrils flaring, body yielding.

"He loves you, you know?"

"Aye."

"He is an honourable man of great courage."

"I agree."

"Do you not want him?"

She hesitated for a moment. "He must not ask...just take me as you have done now." She blushed and looked away.

I somehow knew she would say that. I bent forward and kissed her on her cheek. "I wish you happiness."

"And I, you." she said sincerely.

I went back to Cawdie and whispered in his ear. "Faint heart never won fair maiden. And if you don't take her now, I will!" His shaggy mop snapped up and an unholy growl erupted, then when he saw my grin, the growl became a howl of laughter that chased me out of his compartment. I was laughing heartily too, and it felt good. I hope I'd solved their problem.

* * *

I was headed to Father's but needed to make a few stops along the way. One involved planting a seed and another harvesting a reward, but first I need to check-in on the patient at the Sand Bar Pub. It was a long trek to the port, but this time I enjoyed the walk.

Calum Duncan waved and pointed. "First room at the top of the stairs."

The patient was awake, and looking hung-over. I was gratified to see a large flask of water by his bed. "I'm Doctor Forrester. I saw you last night. Feeling any better?" I noted his face had a sheen of sweat, so he likely was still fevered.

"I had one too many, what of it?" he said belligerently.

"Then if you have no further problems, I bid you a good day." I didn't need a fight with a patient, so turned to leave.

"It is me cock."

I thought as much, but I knew men didn't like to discuss this. "Would you like me to treat you?"

"Aye," he said, a look of resignation on his face.

"Then drop your trousers and I'll have a look. Is it painful to urinate?"

"Aye and there's blood."

Once he removed his clothes, I could see his penis glans and urethra were inflamed and there was a white discharge oozing from the urethra. I lifted his penis and felt his testicles. "Any pain here?"

"Nay"

"You've been visiting the wrong brothels, haven't you?"

He shook his head and cursed: "That damned woman!"

"You have the clap, but it can be treated. Here is what you must do." I went over the treatment with him, starting with mercury applied to the urethra by injection weekly, and a decoction of sarsaparilla taken orally, one pint per day for a fortnight.

"Any surgeon can give the mercury injections and an apothecary the decoction. This should resolve your problem, but if not, see a physician immediately." I wrote him a note with my diagnosis and recommended treatment and the address of McLean's apothecary and surgery.

"The sarsaparilla will give you the sweats, but that's expected." He nodded and reached under the mattress for his pouch and handed me some coins. It wasn't enough, but I knew this was going to cost the poor lad all he had, and I didn't want to tell him his prognosis was poor, so we parted with a handshake and well wishes. On the way out, I asked Calum for the name of the pub frequented by the Town Guard. It was the one near the Guard House.

* * *

It was a fair long walk and when I arrived there were only a few guardsmen, but enough to keep it open. I ordered an ale and mutton pie and settled in for an hour of gossip and bear-bating. It didn't take long, for one of the men recognized me from the disturbance.

"Good day, you the one who took down Baxter?" I didn't recognize him, but he looked a rough sort.

I smiled. "Not sure your meaning, friend."

"The scuffle at the infirmary. Baxter ad is throat cut. Was that you, who did 'im?" I tried to sense if he was going to be friend or foe knowing the truth.

"Aye that was me. He attacked first but was too slow." I waited for the place to explode, but instead there was some laughter and the man smiled.

"Had it coming, that one. He was brutal, Mackmain's enforcer. You didn't pay, and it was Baxter at your door." I could see the pub owner nodding and some of the men were swearing belated oaths.

"That's very like Mackmain to let others do his ill." The room fell silent, so I continued. "I think Mackmain's a coward and wouldn't face me, so he sent this Baxter fellow." The pub had gone silent, the sounds from the kitchen and the ticking of the clock over the fireplace suddenly noticeable.

The pub owner chipped in. "You'd best be careful with words like that. Mackmain and his men have been relieved of duties, but still around these parts, and I don't want any trouble."

I raised my voice to answer the pub owner but also because I wanted everyone to hear. "It matters not what that milksop thinks or does, I'll be back to the safety of Torrport on the morrow."

"Then we wish you safe passage." It was the first man who'd spoken, and he lifted his mug in salute. I finished my pie and ale and enjoyed some friendly banter about

250

spring rains and mud and the war in Europe and the damned English, the usual Scottish fare. I'd set my lure for Mackmain and now I needed to be sure I was ready when he came for me in Torrport.

* * *

My next and last stop was at the medical instruments shop. I was thrilled to see that beautiful microscope still in the window. I needed it for my practice. Well to be honest, I wanted it, pure and simple. I loved these new instruments, and this was top of the heap, all shiny brass and glass with gears and such. The shop owner was an elderly Jew named David Brown. He'd come from Germany several years ago and sold a variety of medical instruments for physicians, surgeons and dentists.

"I shall have that microscope." I grinned like a small boy staring at a large sack of sweets.

"It is our best, from London, made by John Marshall." He took out a cloth and flicked the dust off it. You can see all sorts of strange and wonderful things in it, like blood and cells." He had an odd accent, English, but mixed with a rare kind of German.

"You don't have to sell me. I want it and I shall have it."

"I am so happy to sell this fine instrument to such a famous....err...doctor such as yourself." He was beaming, no doubt thinking of the profit. His business was diminished lately, and it must be hard for him. "Will you need accessories?" He asked, raising his eyebrows and waiting for my response.

"Indeed, some saffron stain will complete it. I have the implements already." A few minutes later, my coin pouch all but empty, I walked the rest of the way to Father's and at his door realized I was happy and feeling energized once again. I dropped my parcel, gave Henry and Scathach well reciprocated hugs and kisses and vowed to erase all vestiges of smallpox from my body.

After a hot bath, shave and change of clothing, I was ready to see George and Father. It was mid afternoon and time for tea and I heard voices coming from Father's study. George was in Father's chair by the fire with an account book open on his lap and being served by Archie. I don't know why, but this raised my ire. Perhaps it was George in Father's chair, or snooping in his book, in a sense taking over while Father was yet alive, I'm not sure, but I had to try to control my demeanour lest we make a bad start of it.

"Join me, Malcolm." He said in his usual commanding tone. "Archibald, Malcolm will be having tea."

I choked back what came too quickly to mind and said instead. "My pleasure, George. I trust you are well, and yes I will have tea." I smiled at him, trying to break the tension. There was nothing but silence between us for several minutes while he

251

studiously ignored my presence and flipped through the account book, looking for who knows what.

Finally, I said. "Is all in order?"

"No."

"No?" Archie came with my tea, and the recent memory of him shooting that man in the back came to mind. It was done with so little emotion, like pouring tea for a master you cared naught about.

"You...There is far too much being spent recently." George pointed at a page in the account book without looking up.

"There is?" I knew why, but decided to act the fool he thought of me.

"Mrs. Simpson says she delivers food and drink daily to an infirmary."

I put on my best smile and turned to face him. "Have you failed to notice our father has been sick recently, and have you forgotten we have more staff here looking after him, and perhaps you are unaware that the physicians caring for him have not charged us even one penny for the hours of time they have spent here and the supplies they've used to bring our father through this? Providing a bit of food for other patients is little enough in return, don't you think?" I know I could have been more diplomatic, but he needed to hear it, and by his sour expression, it was not welcome.

"We are not in the business of providing for the poor, Malcolm. They can look after themselves, well enough."

"That is precisely the point, George. When people are sick, they cannot look after themselves, nor their families. Would you have them die in the streets while we look on content?"

George flushed in anger. "Then tell the physicians who treated Father to send us a bill and we will gladly pay it. As for the rest..."

I was about to respond in anger but stopped myself, realizing I was not so much angry at George but at myself for allowing this vicious cycle to continue. I was better than that, and I knew he was too. "I'm sorry George...I'll be more careful with our family expenses in future. You are quite right. I have not the authority to decide on expenditures for our family."

He looked at me in wonderment, perhaps he'd been expecting a continuation of argument. I turned my head to Archie, who was standing by the door. "Archie, thank you so much for alerting George to my problems at the infirmary. The regiment arrived in the nick of time, didn't it?" I said that in all honesty, but with a fleeting churlish thought about how nice it would have been if they'd arrived an hour earlier. Archie blinked but remained stone-faced, so I looked back at George, who'd closed the account book and was sipping his tea contentedly. "I greatly appreciate what you did that night. I owe you my life and I was rude, and I hope you can forgive me."

Then he calmly said something that stunned me. "Malcolm, you mustn't think you are the only one with a heart to be broken. I grieve for mother too."

We'd never discussed that night when Mother died, and I'd assumed he didn't fully understand or was completely insensitive to what he'd done to us, and I was afraid to raise the subject lest I destroy our remnant family, so it lay in silence all those years, alive but with her in the grave. I wanted to laugh, to cry, to know what he was thinking and feeling, but Archie was there, and no one must know, so I simply said with a quivering voice. "I know, George. Forgive me." I had to leave. It was becoming too emotional, and I didn't want a scene in front of Archie. I stood too suddenly and bumped the table and my tea cup went flying and I hastily left thinking how annoyed Mrs. Simpson would be. Minutes later in my room, I wept, for myself, for all of us. Our family had become a tragedy, and I knew there was blame enough for all to share.

* * *

Crying is a catharsis of sorts, but not that satisfying if not accompanied by resolution, and it was a few hours before dinner at seven, so I decided to get out and clear my head. I packed pistol, cutlass and coin and went to see what was about this time of day. The afternoon sun was peeking through low hanging clouds that were almost touching the castle roofs. I took a deep breath and set off at a brisk pace, going nowhere in particular. It felt good to have no goal, no destination and I imagined I was a rootless wanderer, seeing the sights with no responsibilities whatsoever. In a few minutes, I came upon a pub, door open, bawdy laughter spilling out on the street. It was just what I needed. No one took much notice as I sat in a corner booth and sipped ale and read some old issues of the *Edinburgh Courant*. I'd apparently missed a lot in recent weeks, including letters from the war in Europe, gossip about the Royal Court and numerous pages of notices about estate settlements, marriages, deaths and the like. There were also tattered pamphlets written by that troublemaker Defoe. I chuckled remembering him pilloried a few years ago. It was oddly comforting reading all this. Life goes on, with or without us. After a few or more mugs of ale, it was time to stroll home and I was thinking how fine it was to be able to walk the streets without being constantly jostled by human and animal traffic. I turned the corner to a narrow alley connecting streets, only to be confronted by a group of scruffy boys, sword playing with sticks. I thought I recognized a few as patients, so I stopped to chat, not a wise thing in my semi-inebriated state, but I felt safe enough among them. I'd helped them and their families, hadn't I, and often not been paid.

"Have you coin for us, doctor?" The boy asking was cute, as boys go, with a mop of sandy blond hair and toothy grin. The ale had done it's expected work on my inhibitions, so I foolishly pulled out my pouch and tossed him a coin.

It was all the distraction they needed and before I knew it, an older boy had appeared out of the shadow of a doorway pointing an old matchlock pistol directly at the side of my head. "We'll have the rest of it, won't we?" He had that cruel mouth and dead eyes of a boy who'd already experienced too much of life in the streets. To be quite honest, he frightened me.

The cute boy reached out and grabbed my coin pouch, while the others laughed and mocked my predicament. Guns are a great leveler, aren't they? Now even children can reign in terror. I sighed and waited for them to scurry back to their den. It wasn't much money really, worse was the humiliation of being robbed by former patients. I laughed at the irony of it all and thanked God they'd only taken my money, but I decided not to mention it to George. It would only reinforce closely held prejudices. A few minutes later I returned to the safety of home and realized it was time to dress for dinner.

* * *

"Now that was a fine goose, I must say." Mrs. Simpson beamed as Father showered praise on her and the obscenely abundant meal she'd prepared. This'd been our first formal gathering since the troubles began and it was comforting to see Father back in his magisterial black robes with starched cravat and white powdered wig. He looked not much different but for his pockmarked face. The man inside was remarkably intact.

"Let us retire to the study for a brandy, shall we?" It wasn't so much a question as a command and George and I obediently followed Father, who was steadied by the ever-present Archie. George was looking splendid in his ceremonial uniform and I had to make do with an old waistcoat I'd worn as a youth. I'd evidently lost some weight, so it fit perfectly. Once we were settled with our drinks, Father excused Archie, and I sat for a time wondering what would come next.

It was George who unexpectedly spoke first. "The damned Jacobites have been buying arms from the French, and I hear they are ending up in the clan militias." Father nodded and took a large sip of brandy. "Last thing we need is trouble here while our troops are on the Continent."

"The clans are a touchy bunch. We'd love to disarm them, but the right to form militias was ceded generations ago to secure the peace," Father replied.

George tapped his glass and added. "I know, but what can we do about it now? This cannot continue."

"I agree George, but not all Jacobite chieftains want conflict. I believe some are ready to parley. Our agents have identified a few influential ones who may be amenable to negotiation, but so far it has come to nothing of substance. If they are seen to be openly consorting with us, they will lose support. We also know the chieftains who are most likely to cause trouble."

George nodded sagely. "Aye, we have plans to move troops to those areas as soon as the war ends."

I was listening attentively, and had no idea that Father and George consulted on such things. I suppose I should've known. Then Father leaned to me. "One of the Jacobites that may be willing to deal is your Laird Douglas MacDuff."

I was not surprised but hesitant to confide, even to my father. One never knew where it would lead. But I also believed MacDuff wanted a channel, so I said, "MacDuff is a good man. He leads well and is admired by his clan. He wants what is best for them, while not wanting to be under the heel of the English."

Father agreed. "There are some like him. We need a way to negotiate with those who are amenable."

"I am willing to help, if I can, Father."

George looked surprised and jumped in. "This is not a venue for amateurs, Malcolm. Too much is at stake."

Father raised his hand. We knew that meant to be quiet. He cleared his throat and took the final draft of brandy, then said slowly, "I want to make one point simply and clearly. You two must not only pretend to get along, but learn to work together as brothers should." He looked at me then George. Not much escaped the old man. We had been properly chastised. Then he continued. "We will use whatever tools at our disposal to manage this situation, and that may include using *amateurs,* as you prefer to call them, George. I see them more as loyal volunteers, and in this case, I think your brother is a perfect example. He has the trust of both Laird MacDuff and me. Malcolm, this is what I want you to tell Laird MacDuff." Father then ticked off several points that were to be the basis for union with England, including benefits for Scotland and the clans. I wasn't sure how it would be received, but it was a start.

George was sitting there fidgeting. "Father, we need to tell them what will happen, if they don't agree."

"Not yet, George. Let us see their response, first," Father countered.

"Forcing the clans into a union will lead to blood. I beg of you to not let that happen." I glanced at George, knowing his proclivity to use force as a first choice, but I had to say it.

"Malcolm, that goes without saying, but sometimes the threat of war is enough for saner heads to prevail. The union will happen. We must make it so and with the least conflict. Understand?" Father had the last word, as always.

We both responded in unison, "Aye Father", shocking us both.

Father yawned. "It has been a long but enjoyable day, and a blessing having you both here." George put his empty glass down and rose to stretch. "George, summon Archie, I need my bath. Malcolm, stay a moment."

I could see George didn't much like being dismissed like that and I resisted the temptation to smile. "Aye, Father?"

Father leaned over toward me and lowered his voice. "Mackmain."
"Yes?" I wasn't quite sure what revelation would come next.
"He has been dismissed, and may seek vengeance."
"I know, Father."
"You must not kill him."

TWENTY

Elspeth - Heartbreak

It had been weeks since the murder of Spence, and it had lain quiescent but present in my mind while I was in Edinburgh. Now that I was seeing patients and picking up the threads of my life in Torrport again, I soon realized that in Torrport the murder was still a favorite subject of gossip. A tangle of half-truths, outright lies and fanciful conspiracies wove themselves into almost every conversation. "The smugglers did it." "His wife finally caught him cheating." "He was blackmailing an important man." He was said to be a rapist, a reiver, an assassin and more. I listened to it all and added anything of interest to my earlier notes. And it seemed that Sir Peter was still in Torrport. He was staying at the castle, but it was rumoured that he and Julianne were not sharing quarters.

There was much coming and going from the port and fishing village, some open, most hidden. Many clan Lairds had been seen meeting with the Tsar and there was much speculation about their purpose. Regardless of reasons, they, and their entourages left a trail of coinage that was as welcome as the diversion and gossip they unwittingly provided. Much to the consternation of the upper-class citizens and to the delighted amusement of the lower classes, the Tsar insisted on remaining incognito when he went out. Everyone knew exactly who the extraordinarily tall man was, but pretended not to. He laboured and sweated next to the men in the port and quickly earned their respect for his skill and hard work, as well as his ability to outdrink them all at the taverns. According to the tattle, he called on every merchant in Torrport, asking questions about their various occupations, and often worked with Aidan at the smithy, long into the night. All of this I gleaned within a day of my return, while seeing patients, shopping for supplies, and taking laundry to Aggie.

A message came from Laird MacDuff, ordering me to the castle at once. It made me search my conscience for ways I might have displeased him lately. There was no point in delaying, so I gathered things to take with me. I would call on Julianne and the baby while I was there. She had been visiting when I had come for Sir Ross, so I had not seen her or the baby since I left Torrport. Her letters reported that the babe was well, but I was anxious to see for myself. I had seen Margaret at the wool merchant's shop, and she said that the bairn was beautiful, and her wistful longing for a child of her own was palpable.

The first thing I noticed at the castle was the heightened security. I did not recognize either of the gate guards or the men who came to escort me to the Laird. The bailey was filled with sweat soaked bodies and sounds of clashing metal and blaspheming men. I ducked quickly as a sword flew over my head and landed at the feet of a cow in the bailey byre, followed closely by a sticky cursing body lunging after it. The guards pushed in front of me and scowled at the man on the ground. He grabbed his sword, stood, grinned apologetically, winked one swelling eye and dove back into the roiling melee. I edged my way around the bailey, then up a flight of stone stairs to the thick iron studded oaken door on the second floor.

I walked quickly through the Great Hall, turned and began to walk up the two flights of steps to the Laird's quarters. About halfway up the second set, a loud laugh rolled from above. I froze. I knew that laugh. Laird of the MacLeod clan, "the MacLeod", in local parlance. I stood on my toes and peeped through the bannisters. There he was. My feet wanted to remain fixed, but my head prevailed, and I stepped warily into the large room. A small group of men surrounded Laird MacDuff, half of them my kin. They turned and looked at me with expressions that quickly went from merriment to expressionless.

Laird MacLeod stopped laughing and glared at me. "Well, lass, it took you long enough to get here."

"Had I but known, sir, I would have been more punctual." I bowed my head to him. "I hope I find you well, sir?"

"You are to return home with me at once. Pack your things. We leave day after next. My business here is done for the nonce." He glanced at MacDuff, ignoring me entirely. "I will attend the meeting on the morrow, but I can make nae promises. I shall take your words to my clan. I thank you for your hospitality." He returned his hawkish gaze to me, and raised his dark brows questioningly. "I would have Lady Elspeth attend the meeting as weel." I had been a quiet presence at MacLeod clan meetings since I was but a child and once stopped an assassin because I saw and felt the anger in him. My impressions were of value to the MacLeod.

Laird MacDuff looked momentarily surprised, but agreed to my inclusion in the all-male gathering. I knew better than to argue with the MacLeod here. "Please come to my cottage, sir. Tis a baking day, and as I recall you are much taken with my pastries." His face softened at some far-off memory and he agreed, lingering to do those things men do when parting, the slapping's and well wishing's and sly jokes. I left as quickly as polite company would allow and hurried home to prepare for his visit. Julianne and the baby would have to wait. As I fled, I was interested to see the Tsar enthusiastically engaging in training in the bailey. A streak of blood bloomed on one sleeve. I did not stop to inquire if the blood was royal or commoner.

By the time the MacLeod arrived, I was ready. He brought two of his men, and they bent themselves through the door. He looked around, taking in the things I had managed to bring from Skye, and the new pieces acquired on our travels. The cabinet of curiosities drew him irresistibly, especially the cup made of a human skull inlaid with an elegantly macabre tracery of gold. The astrolabe and overflowing shelves of books and apothecary jars also gave him pause. "Elspeth, some of these things are part of the reasons you had to leave Skye. Yet you have kept them. Why?"

"Because they have meaning for me, and they are mine! You would have me deny what and where I have studied for more than three years, forsaking the knowledge I gained from my mentors? For using it to save lives?" My words were bitter with recollection. "My Laird permitted a few women in Skye, who have never set foot beyond the island, to accuse me because I have learned new ways of helping people? I kept one of ours from death because I knew how to keep him from bleeding his life away. I learned that skill in Italy! For that I am called witch?" I turned away from him, refusing to let the welling tears show. The room had become very quiet.

"Tis best you come back and face them." His voice was impatient. "Else it will spread even to here. You know that, lass. I will nae have my kin, or my clan defamed. This time ye will be well defended, ye have my word."

"Ah, so then the clan has ousted the woman who named me witch?" The words were sour on my tongue. Laird MacLeod had the grace to flush an unbecoming shade of red, but I knew I had no choice. I must return. He was my clan Laird, after all. I bowed my head in acceptance. "I will do as you wish, but I cannot leave until I complete what I have begun here. There are patients I must see and promises to be kept. I shall return as soon as may be." There was a long pause before he spoke, but he saw that I was steadfast and finally nodded. "Do it quickly then, and dinna fail to be at the meeting on the morrow." He promptly turned his attention to the food and ale, expansively thanking me for both. It was settled. I would go back to Skye as soon as I could draw things here to a close.

With all I had to do, the next morning and meeting with the Tsar came too quickly. His Highness, or however they chose to address him in Russia, sat at the right of Laird MacDuff at the head table in the Great Hall. He had forgone the plain garb he affected when he was working or roaming, and peacocked in the latest fashion. A red frock coat thickly embroidered with gold thread glittered on his preternaturally tall slim body, complete with European breeches, stockings and buckled shoes. The *palash*, a heavy Calvary sword sheathed in the ornate scabbard hanging at his waist, was not designed for display. His dark eyes roamed over the faces of the men seated at the tables in the Hall. It was crowded, but oddly quiet. The Scots are a taciturn race, and this was not a celebration. I settled quietly on a bench at the back of the room, my serviceable brown dress blending into the walls, and began to watch and listen.

* * *

The room was a contradiction; thick stone walls were softened by rugs and tapestries, glassed windows burned slashes of light on rustic benches and carved chairs alike, flashing off silvery cups and pottery mugs assigned by rank. The floors were heavily scarred and stained from use, but spotlessly clean.

Spectral fingers touched the back of my neck, and I turned my head slowly to meet Gregor's eyes. He was sitting to my right at a table near the window with Sir Ross and Aidan. The three of them directed identical expressions of polite civility at me. They bowed their heads courteously, not quite in unison. I smiled back warily, then returned to my scrutiny, but not before seeing the slight upturn of Gregor's lips, so quickly controlled I might almost have imagined it. As far as I could tell, there was no danger present, the only anomaly the usual curiously empty area around Gregor.

The Tsar rose to his impressive six feet eight-inch height and began to speak in a deep compelling voice. Julianne had told me that he could recite long passages of Holy Scripture by heart and often sang the magnificent Russian choral litany at church services. The sound washed over the hall clearly and effortlessly in an impassioned plea for the support of Scotland's clans in Russia's war against Sweden. Russia's humiliation at Narva was still raw, and the young Swedish King much admired. Since then, the Tsar had worked tirelessly to create a superbly trained force from the motley mixture he had inherited. They proved their worth with a recent victory over the Swedes near the village of Errestfer. The Russian artillery had grown significantly and the Tsar's new ironworks beyond the Urals produced metal that was now said to be better than that of Sweden. His goal in visiting Scotland appeared to be to affect a pact between Scotland and Russia. His words were met with quiet interest but no enthusiasm. The Lairds shifted restlessly in their seats. They had enough problems at home. Attempts to withdraw their clansmen from English commanders and withhold taxes had met with severe retaliation, further aggravating the fractious relationship. England was fighting on two fronts, Spain and France, and could not afford the loss of men. They answered the Scots actions with the Aliens Bill, banning imports from Scotland to England and providing for seizure of Scottish property in England.

The meeting ended with no promises beyond agreeing to carry the Tsar's request to the various clans. For similar reasons, requests for military support for the Jacobites were refused by the Tsar because of Russia's ongoing conflict with Sweden. There would be no Russian troops fighting on Scottish soil. Neither side could afford to help the other. It was an impasse. The meeting had been a great waste of time for them all. The Lairds quietly said their farewells as the Tsar stood impassive except for a swift glance at Aidan, who inclined his head fractionally in return. It was over, and I stood, shook out my skirts, bowed my head to the MacLeod and left.

Malcolm's office was next on my list. As had become usual, Andrew was not there, so I continued on my way. I would have to talk to him very soon. He made no attempt to see patients. As far as I could tell, those he did see were chosen for their ability to pay for his services rather than by need. I had treated three new patients who said that he sent them to me. A young farmer's wife having the usual problems with a first pregnancy, a man who had scrofula, and the last a soldier with an abscess on his thigh. The young woman needed only advice, an infusion of encouragement and a bottle of syrup of ginger and mint to sooth her morning sickness.

The scrofula patient, a wee Frenchman, told me had been touched by the King and could not understand why he was still ill. I could do little except give him a salve of garlic and cinnamon for the lesions and tell him to rest, drink milk, and take the medicine I gave him for the pain. The King's healing hands would not save him from the result of his excesses.

The soldier had lifted his kilt to show me an ugly sword wound festering on his thigh. I took care of it, and told him to return if it worsened. Andrew could have seen them, and they paid in coin. He simply did not wish to be bothered.

The path to the fishing village was a gauntlet of midges making a determined attack on any exposed skin, but I needed to see Leana. At the docks, I stepped cautiously over sharp fragments from a broken bottle, and the remains of someone's violently rejected meal, and went into the tavern. A man lay sprawled on the dirty floor under a table, mouth agape, snoring loudly, the familiar odors of urine, ale and stew laced the air. I lifted my skirts and went up the surprisingly clean steps to the second floor. Molly was sitting in a chair watching Leana pouring "tea" from a tiny pewter teapot into miniscule bowls for a neatly dressed cloth doll. She stood quickly as I reached the top of the stairs and curtsied.

"Lady Elspeth! Tis good to see ye. Look at me babe. Tis bloomin' she is, thanks be to ye." Leana's beautiful little face shone up at me, the pox blisters already fading from her delicate skin. She would probably have no lasting scars to mar her ethereal prettiness. I stopped my hand from reaching up to touch my own marks. She offered me tea solemnly and I accepted it with equal gravity.

"I have a wee gift for ye." Molly rummaged through a basket by the chair, and handed me a folded piece of soft cloth. It unfolded to become a white on white embroidered chemise as fine as faery wear. It must have taken her days to complete. I thanked her. Andrew could have his coin, this was of greater value. I touched the tiny stitches with my fingertips while she watched me anxiously. "Molly, tis fit for a queen. I thank you." We entertained Leana by partaking of her tea for a while, before Molly said hesitantly. "Lady Elspeth. Tis sorry I am to have to say, but more have come down with the pox. Three of Dame Richardson's bairns, and others as well. Her bairns had a fever, and a sore throat and wouldna eat. Just like Leana. I shared with her what ye did for ma bairn when the blisters started. She said her bairns are still getting new blisters, but the old ones have crusted over. I hope ye can stop by their place?"

My stomach lurched. The pox had spread. I hoped that I was right, and this would be the same sort of pox that Leana had. It was bad, but nothing like the horrors of the smallpox I had seen in Edinburgh. The Lairds were leaving soon, and I prayed they would not carry it with them. I would send Laird MacDuff a note telling him there was illness in the fishing village here, and his guests should not linger. By the time I had visited the other families it was well after dark, but I felt much better. The households I had attended all bore the signs of the lesser pox. When I returned home, Scathach met me at the door. I spent several hours making salves and tinctures, then pounded oats into powder for baths. About two in the morning I surrendered and collapsed into bed and a deep dreamless sleep.

* * *

The days ran into each other as the pox spread. The fourth morning I was awakened by a pounding on the door and opened it to find Sir Ross standing there, more agitated than I had ever seen him. "My Lady, please come at once. Tis Gregor. He is very ill. I fear he has the pox." In minutes, we were on our way. After examining him, I relaxed slightly, this was the pox that was rampant in the fishing village, and not the more-deadly form of smallpox. Unfortunately, with this sort, older men and women tended to have more severe symptoms than the children. Gregor was hot to the touch, and coughing wretchedly, the telltale red blisters thickly clustered in various stages on his face and torso. His hands and feet were clear. I was certain he was aware of me, but he had not opened his eyes or protested when I pulled back the bed covers to inspect him. He had a finely-honed warrior's body, the skin scored in numerous places by old wounds now partially obscured beneath the multiple ripening crops of pustules. Between the two of us, we managed to get him to take some honey and lemon for his throat, and washed his hot skin with cool water infused with powdered oats. Our ministrations did not seem to help, and Gregor grew more agitated, moving restlessly on the bed, and muttering disjointedly in Russian. In his delirium he abruptly switched to English, his voice harsh. "You cur, you dared to harm her and the babe? You meant to kill them both! By God, for that you die, shite!" His face beaded with sweat and he sat up violently, hands reaching up to circle Sir Ross's neck. Before I could react, Sir Ross turned his body slightly to the left, brought his forearms up between Gregor's and struck his hands apart in a smoothly trained response. I eyed him with new respect. Gregor blinked, stared at Ross, then lay back quietly. We resumed bathing him. His fever had broken. Ross looked at me enigmatically. I understood at once that I was supposed to take no note of Gregor's ravings.

* * *

The pox had spread from the fishing village to Torrport. No one had become seriously ill except Gregor, but I needed help badly and Malcolm's locum was playing least in sight. His reputation led to me to check the taverns first, so I began with them. They were very nearly empty, because ships had been turned away by the yellow flags that flew above the port denoting pox. Some supplies and food stuffs grew scarce, most noticeably French wine. The Scottish Parliament had passed the Wine Act in 1703, which in effect, allowed the Scots to legally import the wines of the enemy. The English were infuriated at having to buy their wine from the Scots. The Scots relished their vexation as well as their coin, since much of the wine, considerably increased in cost, ended up in English bellies. Those remaining in the taverns were restless men, escaping the tedium of inactivity and fear of the pox by drinking away the dual misery in their impoverished lives. I finally discovered Andrew at the coffee house, his blonde head buried in the latest newspapers from Edinburgh and London. I could tell he was not happy to be rousted from that mostly male bastion, but with a few subtle threats, a bit of name dropping and a hint that his poor performance might not serve him well with his city colleagues, and he grudgingly accompanied me back to Malcolm's office.

* * *

A small group shuffled about near the door, one woman leaning tiredly against the wall, holding two fretful children. I assured them we would be with them soon, pushed Andrew inside, closed the door, and attacked. I might not be able to defy the Laird, but Andrew was a physician. We had sworn an oath to help others. "Andrew, why are you not holding regular hours here or seeing Malcolm's patients?" He looked surprised, yanked at his cravat and avoided my eyes. "I do...have, several times. Those waiting are just village people, none of consequence, nothing important. I have seen to the Laird's men, and to his guests as well. Lady Margaret, when she cut her hand."

I stared at him. He was attractive. Not as tall as some, but with silky golden hair and a mustache curved over a well-cut mouth.

"Andrew, those people are patients, they need you, us. Are you aware we have pox victims in the fishing village, and it has spread to here? Fortunately, it is the lesser form sometimes called chickenpox, and has claimed no lives yet, but still, it needs treatment badly."

"I...heard something...but I have seen no signs of it in Torrport," he said sulkily.

"Then just look outside the door! I would wager much that least three of them have signs of it! You have been well trained in the finest schools, yet you are not making use of that training. Tell me, Andrew, why did you take the position here?" He looked at me disdainfully but finally deigned to answer.

"Malcolm hired me. His father is an important man in Edinburgh, a Lord, and I thought there would be more, more...to do. All I have found here is a backwater where you get a rabbit or a pot of jam or some such for seeing people. What am I expected to do with pots of jam or rabbits? My skills are wasted here! The only decent places are the taverns and the coffeehouse...and the castle, of course. I need better, more...suitable...company." I looked down. With my sturdy boots, woolen dress, reddened hands, and tightly bound hair, I was obviously of little consequence. He curled his lip and turned away from me.

Exhaustion and indignation tipped me over the edge. I literally spat the words at him. "You are a trained physician! Here for his people in Malcolm's stead. I am willing to help you, but I am not here to do your job. I am going to open this door. You are going help me take care of them to the best of your ability. After that we will go see those unable to get here." I looked at him steadily, then opened the door to the jumble of patients. He hated to do it, but after a brief hesitation, he did. I noticed the covered basket the first woman carried, wondered what her "payment" would be, sighed and went to work.

When we had seen everyone waiting at the office, we walked the streets of Torrport and the waterfronts looking for the scraps of cloth over the doors that signaled need. It soon became the pattern of our daily routine, tending the growing number of those with the pox. We lost only one elderly man, and the panic began to wane as life resumed its normal pace.

Andrew was a competent physician, and began to keep more regular hours. The mother of one of his little patients offered to keep the office and infirmary clean and prepare his "fees" as needed. He seemed less unhappy too, but I noticed that his patients still tended toward those more apt to pay in coin rather than in kind.

There had been no new cases of pox in the past few days. With the reduced work, more and more my thoughts turned again to the murder of Spence. I decided to write to Malcolm with the information we had collected. I sat down to do so and after a few bad beginnings that provided only twisted paper spills for lighting fires, I began again.

"My Dear Friend. Here are my thoughts about the murder of Spence. For me, it all began with the attempted poisoning of Julianne, then progressed to the murder of Spence. I beg thee read this summation and add your own thoughts. We have a need to meet and compare notes. No more unto you now, but I place you and all of yours in the blessed keeping of our Lord.
Your most humble and obedient servant, Elspeth MacLeod"

I placed it on the table to give to Jocki in the morning.

I had promised McLean that I would look at Sir Ross's fistula and report back to him. Gregor had not fully recovered, but met me at the door, surrounded as usual by that careful emptiness he wore like a cloak. Sir Ross declared himself delighted and honored by my visit and invited me to see his latest curiosity. He had lost flesh and looked, moved, and smelled much better, a faint whiff of some exotic scent clung about him. A new wooden doll stood stiffly on the mantle, her purple silk costume rich in the light. The dress style was unmistakeably French with an almost indecently low neckline. He picked her up and handed her to me. Paper crackled beneath her skirts as I took her, and then I realized that it was there to ensure that the shape of the skirts remained fixed. This doll was especially well done with a complete parure of tiny jewels that I suspected were real. Her necklace, bracelets, earrings brooch, and diadem twinkled as I turned her to see the back of her costume. There were even two tiny patches, one at the corner of her eye and one beside the mouth. I smiled. A clear message. The lady was passionate and liked to kiss. While I studied the small ambassadress of fashion, it occurred to me that the dolls would be an ingenious method of smuggling or exchanging small items, jewels or messages. The manikins, since they were exempt from the inspections of other imports, could carry secrets limited only by the size of the figure. I gave the doll back to Sir Ross. "Sir, I have promised Doctor McLean to look at your surgery"

He paused, but said, "Yes, he did tell me you would. I assure you it is fine." He looked at Gregor for affirmation, Gregor nodded in agreement. Obviously, he did not want me to examine him and continued to try to deflect me. "You do know he put me on a diet?" He grinned like a small boy. "Tis a simple one. There are only three things I cannot put in my mouth. A fork, a knife, and a spoon." He stopped when I only smiled, and looked at me. "Is it really needful?" I nodded in affirmation and he exhaled in resignation. "Very well." He went to his bedroom, Gregor following.

After a moment, Gregor came to tell me he was ready to be examined, and I followed him into the opulently appointed bedroom. Sir Ross lay supine on his bed, face buried in silk pillows, bared from the waist down. His buttocks were raised and supported by a pillow. I walked to the bed, placed my hands on his buttocks and pulled them apart. The scar from the surgery was well healed, flat and leaf shaped with a small depression in the center. I traced it with my finger feeling the scar tissue for signs of inflammation. He shuddered. "Does it hurt? Have you any other complaints?"

"No." His voice was muffled in the bedding.

"You may get up, then." When he did not move, I frowned. "Sir Ross?" I started to place my hand on his shoulder but a sound from Gregor stopped me. I turned and there was a look of unholy glee in his eyes, quickly controlled. "If you will leave, my lady, I shall help Sir Ross dress and bring you both tea." I suddenly understood and made a swift retreat.

We buried our mutual embarrassment in tea and conversation. Other than Malcolm, Sir Ross was the most interesting man in Torrport, and I found pleasure in his company. Sipping the hot liquid slowly from the fragile bowl presented to me, I looked up. "Sir Ross, I have seen you in the company of Sir Spence several times. Did you know him before you came to Torrport?"

He considered his words carefully before replying. "I did. But we did not frequent the same circles. He was a soldier assigned to the Novodevichy Convent in Moscow where the Tsar's Sister Sophia is imprisoned. You must understand that Russians are much different from the English. There is a barbaric brutality there seldom encountered elsewhere. The Tsar himself carries wounds inflicted on him by his own people when he was but a boy. He is a very intelligent and complex man attempting to drag his barbaric country into the light of the new world. But back to Sir Spence. He fit well into that cruel pack. I can assure you that no one will care that one rabid dog is gone. But enough. What can one say about a man who left no one to mourn him? Surely that is punishment enough? I neither liked him nor sought his company. He smiled at me ruefully. "Forgive my frank words. I hope that you will permit me to take you driving soon?"

I stared at him, trying to decide which of his words were important, then replied that I would always be pleased to go driving with him, and it seems we parted a bit more than casual friends.

* * *

Margaret met me at the door. She glowed, and I suspected that she had finally conceived and that was why she summoned me to the castle. A few questions and an examination confirmed my suspicions. She was radiant with joy. I cautioned her about watching what she ate, encouraged her to take long walks in the fresh air and left her dreaming of bairns and bassinettes, both resplendently covered with hand embroidered silks. I made my way back down the steps, having told my guard that I would meet him in the bailey. I was hungry. The smells of baking bread and cooking meats drew me inexorably toward the castle kitchen and tempted me to go begging.

Large barrels filled with dirt and fragrant herb plants flanked the entrance. I stood looking in the door, watching the cooks and scullery maids at their tasks. Margaret's maid, Rachel, stood at a large table kneading ground almonds, sugar and rose-water together to make a smooth doughy paste for marchpane. Her clever fingers pinched off pieces and deftly shaped them into tiny flora and fauna, dimensional pictures, knots, and other fanciful things. She laid them carefully on a wooden board to be lightly baked. Finished pieces already pleasingly painted with colored icing and gilded with delicate sheets of edible beaten gold lay waiting to be plated. Each one was a wee work of ephemeral art destined to become a fleeting pleasure for eyes and tongue as they were consumed. As I watched an errant breeze caught a stray fragment of gold leaf and wafted it gently aloft before depositing it on the stone floor. I found I was no longer hungry.

* * *

On the way home, I decided to stop and visit Aidan. My excuse was to inquire about a metal boot the two of us had designed, with much inspiration from Ambroise Pare, for one of my patients who had lost his foot. In truth, I simply wanted to see Aidan. He was in his small shop and had company. He and the Tsar were huddled intently over something on the workbench. They both started guiltily when I knocked on the open door, and I caught only a fleeting glimpse of what looked like a gun sitting on a tripod, before it was hastily covered with a cloth. The Tsar stepped in front of the worktable, wiping his hands on a grease-stained rag. His eyes glittered watchfully as he bowed slightly in my direction, while Aidan moved to intercept me.

"Lady Elspeth! I was not expecting you. Have you come to see the boot?" Aidan spoke hurriedly, trying to hold my attention as he turned to a shelf and pulled down a bundle wrapped in brown wool cloth. "Let us go where the light is better, and you can tell me what I need to change. There was a slight problem with the overlapping pieces at the ankle. The foot piece would drop and hang when the boot was lifted. I put two springs and latchets inside the bend, and now it returns to a natural position after each step." He babbled rapidly as he moved me gently away from the shop door, into the smithy, then unwrapped the boot. It gleamed in the light like a combination of some knight's discarded sabaton and greave. Indeed, it resembled both greatly, even to the leather straps to hold it on. Like all of Aidan's work, it was possessed of elegant lines and beautifully finished. I lifted it from its wrapping and placed it on the stones, tentatively walking it. It flexed noiselessly and mimicked the natural movement of the foot. My hand caressed the satiny metal as I looked up at Aidan, with inexplicable tears in my eyes. It represented a different way of life for its new owner.

"It is perfect! Thank you." My voice was filled with awe as I gazed at the boot.

"I will send the reckoning, lady, and you may not thank me as much after you receive it." He grinned, and I felt my heart flutter. Then he wrapped the boot and I carried it home like a child, imagining the satisfaction of delivering it to my patient. I did not think of the object Aidan and the Tsar had been working on again until much later when I was eating supper. Curiosity replaced euphoria. I closed my eyes and pulled the memory up. I was reasonably sure it was a Queen Anne pistol, but oddly changed. An image of the young Captain of the *Silver Fin* holding one negligently in his hand as he talked to Spence flashed into my mind, but what I had seen today was subtly different. A Queen Anne pistol had a barrel that screwed onto a breech and lock that were forged into a single piece. The design eliminated the need for a ramrod or wadding because the ball was loaded into the breech. The gun I saw today had been altered to hold what appeared to be a cylinder over the breech. There were eight or nine holes in this cylinder, each holding a bullet. It looked as though it must revolve somehow. Would that give a man the ability to shoot several times without having to stop to reload? The idea made me want to retch. It could be a weapon that might change the tide of battle and make slaughter commonplace. The Tsar wanted such a weapon. The Scots wanted such a weapon. The English would want it too. This adaptation could give tremendous advantage to whoever could fabricate it first. The Tsar was attempting to create a fearsome new firearm for his wars. He had the ingenuity and the imagination to do it, backed by the great wealth of Russia. And he had Aidan. It was a terrible thought. Tomorrow I would go to see Aidan again.

* * *

I was up with the first light, and finished caring for the animals and making two salves. One was for the stump Aidan's steel boot would fit over. I had no illusions about it working painlessly. Until my patient had used it long enough to develop a callus, it would need care. Small irritations could turn into sores and the leather straps might need daily adjustment. I packed clean cloths, tapes and salve and went to deliver the boot.

Sean Ramsey shouted his invitation to enter the cottage even before his wife could open the door after I knocked. She bobbed a curtsy, pushing two small children behind her skirts so I could pass, then bid me enter. A third child fretted half-heartedly in an exquisitely carved cradle by the fire. Sean had lost his lower leg to a cannon ball while fighting the French, and was now supporting his family by carving handsome designs in wood. He had faced the fact he was a cripple, found something he could still do well, and now had two apprentices who were learning the craft. I admired his courage and hoped the boot would give him the ability to lead a more normal life.

I set the bundle on the floor and reached into my pocket for the honey drops I always carried. The children took them and scampered away as I turned to Sean. "Good morning, sir, I have come to look at your leg." When I had first seen it, it had been streaked with infection from the swollen bloody stump. Now it was clean and pink with health. I opened the bundle, removed the boot, and handed it to him without comment. He sat for some time, turning it first this way then that, to see the various parts and mechanisms, before he spoke.

"My lady, shall we try it?" And so, we did. I showed him how to adjust the cloth padding inside and the leather straps outside, warned him about things to watch for, gave him the salve and left him standing after a few successful steps, one hand holding the fireplace mantle while he learned to move his new limb. It would take a bit of doing, but he should eventually be able to walk unaided again. I was exultant.

I wanted to tell Aidan, to share the wonder of the small miracle we had achieved together. My delight was so great that my feet fairly flew over the path to the smithy. The forge was glowing, but Aidan was nowhere to be seen. The door to the shop was closed, but I could hear voices inside from the open window. It sounded like Aidan and Julianne. I was pleased that she was here and wondered if she had the bairn with her. She must have come to get something needed at the castle, or from Aidan's shop. My hand was raised to knock, when I realized she was crying and Aidan was trying to soothe her. "Ah, my little love, it will be over soon, I promise. Then we can be together always." She murmured something in response that I could not understand. I was unable to move. Julianne and Aidan? What had happened? I finally managed to command my feet, and slipped silently away before they discovered me.

I have no memory of returning to the cottage, but found myself sitting in the chair by the fireplace, wrapped in the silence of my home. It was empty. I was empty. Something inside me had broken and drained away. I was not even certain what it was. There was just a hollow place where nothing was. I looked around. There was no one here except Scathach. I was alone except for her. She laid her great head on my foot.

A little later, I stood and walked to the bookshelves. My fingertips ran along the familiar bound paper and leather volumes to a much-used mechanical medical book by Remmelin that had been translated from German. On the pages inside, the beautifully drawn figures of a man and a woman were covered with a series of shaped overlapping paper flaps. As each flap was lifted, it revealed successive layers of the human body drawn in exquisite detail. The final fold disclosed the bones of the skeleton. There was even a layer showing a child hidden in the womb of the woman. Later pages used the same method of flaps to show even smaller layers of detail inside the eyes, and other organs. The drawings and words soothed me.

I began to lift the flaps one by one, and commit to memory each stratum as it was exposed.

TWENTY-ONE

Malcolm - Captured

I was in a panic as soon as I got back to Torrport, having poked a hornets' nest at the guards' pub and with no solid plan to deal with consequences. Laird MacDuff had provided one of his men to guard my infirmary, but he was not much more than a boy and would only slow Mackmain down a half-step and I'd grown quite fond of the lad and wouldn't have him sacrificed due to my folly. That is why I found myself early in the morning, rowing through the chop and pelting rain on my way to the *Silver Fin* which was swaying at anchor just off the fishing village.

There were several men on the top deck caulking the floor. One of them gave me a hand over the rail, and I asked, "The Captain?" He tilted his head in the direction of the hatch leading to the lower decks. The *Silver Fin* is a fourteen-gun brigantine, one of those fast ships often used by smugglers. The hull was left unpainted and she had little ornamentation, an anonymous ship for anonymous trade. I climbed down the ladder. The second deck was the living quarters for the crew with hammocks and wet clothes hanging in a maze of cloth. Nearby a few men were repairing the anchor capstan spindles. Working here was better than topside and they were happily chatting as they chiseled and sanded. One deck down was the cargo hold. It was under construction with several men building what appeared to be cabins and berths. Captain Kidd was standing in the middle, shirt-sleeves rolled to the elbow, holding a large piece of paper and speaking with the ship's carpenter.

"I want the slatted doors on these three cabins for the ladies, the others will have to make do with curtains." He pointed on the paper and the carpenter grunted. Kidd saw me and laughed. "Good Doctor Forrester! What brings you out in this nasty weather? It must be tremendously important." He was mocking me, of course, in that friendly manner that suggested friendship or how one speaks to a potential victim.

I must've looked as wet as I felt, but shrugged. "At least it's dry in here."

"Aye, we are doing a refit before heading back to the Continent. The Great Man wants the best for his guests, and for what he's paying, we can rebuild the entire ship!"

I began to understand and had a twinge of guilt since I'd failed to inform Father that the Tsar of Russia was on Scottish soil and up to who knows what.

"We are refitting my cabin for the Tsar," he continued, "and I'll be bunking with the men for the voyage. Wouldn't be the first time." He winked, and I didn't understand the context and wasn't sure I wanted to know. "Now why have you come to see me?"

"I have a wee problem."

"Someone is trying to kill you again?"

"Umm, yes."

"Of course, why not? Doctors are always getting in trouble like that, aren't they!" He roared with laughter and some of the men snickered. "Then come to my room and have a dram and we will sort it properly."

He led me through the decks, pointing out all the repairs and improvements he was making with the Tsar's money. I'd considered asking the Laird for help again, but it was awkward now due to my new role as go-between, so I opted for begging a local smuggler and hoped it wouldn't come back to bite me.

The captain's cabin was a mess of construction and he shooed the men out and found a bottle of whisky and a few mugs and patted the cushioned bench for me to join him. I'm not sure why, but I trusted him. He exuded confidence and the sense that no one would dare betray him. I certainly wouldn't.

He raised his mug and said, "Scotland forever!" and I replied, "Good health!" We touched mugs, and he sat back, sighed and said, "Now tell me what happened."

I told him everything, even the embarrassing parts. He took it all in with great interest. "We want a confession from Mackmain that will stand up in court. I admit that originally my idea was to lure him here and either get a confession or kill him, but Father doesn't want the latter and wouldn't explain why, but I will honour his wishes."

"It will not be easy getting Mackmain to confess." Kidd poured us another dram.

"I know, but I must try."

"If it is important to you. Twould be easier to kill him. Do you have a plan?"

"Not really, but I'm willing to be the tethered goat if you can spare the men to protect me when he comes."

He laughed at that. "You know what happens to those goats, don't you?"

"This goat butts hard." I grinned.

"We have a crew of forty, half are aboard working, the other half ashore with family and friends. I think I could convince some of those to spend their shore leave protecting you, with the right inducements, obviously.

I nodded.

"It will be expensive."

"It'll be worth it," I responded

"And we sail in about a week. After that you are on your own."

"Understood."

"Then we have an agreement?" He winked again and poured a third dram for another toast.

I didn't really want more, remembering I'd be tossing in the sea in a few minutes, but decided to be sociable with my new saviour. "Agreed." I nodded, and we touched mugs again.

"Now, let us plan, Sir Goat!" He laughed heartily at this and I wondered if he might have me end up the goat in more ways than one.

* * *

It was a simple plan, as these things go. I went over it in my mind as I rowed back to the fishing wharf. I was to carry on my normal activities and be secretly escorted by two of Kidd's men. We assumed that Mackmain would come with a few of his men, so if my protectors were reasonably capable and alert, the odds in a fight would be even. That was all I wanted. Also, we couldn't predict when or how Mackmain would arrive, so setting up scouts would be impractical. He would have to make the first move and we needed to be sure we were prepared to counter-attack effectively.

I paid the boat owner and walked through the sideways rain back over the trail to town. Torrport was bursting with people as the result of the smallpox epidemic in Edinburgh. It was slow going and I was thoroughly soaked for the second time as I came home to a welcoming warm house and the sounds of Jocki and Elspeth laughing in the kitchen. They each greeted me with a mouth full of pie. It was a heart-warming sight.

"Och, it is you! Join us, Malcolm."

"I will in a minute, Elspeth. I must change first. Save a big piece. I'm famished."

"I brought two pies. One for we and one for thee. Jocki will warm yours."

It was so comforting being home with friends, I thought, while changing into dry and hanging the wet ones up near the fire. In a few minutes, I returned, eager for company and good food.

"How've you been, Elspeth?"

She looked at me directly in that guileless way. "Torrport is very pleasant, especially compared with Edinburgh," she chuckled then went on, "and I think I am becoming attached to it, but..."

"But?"

"Janet and Cawdie are still in Edinburgh and Julianne and the bairn have returned to the castle. Scathach is good company, but not much for stimulating conversation." She opened her hands in resignation. "To be perfectly honest, I am lonely, especially at night."

I must have changed my expression because she quickly added, "I am not lonely in that way, Malcolm!" She tried to swat me but missed, and laughed instead. "It is just that I am not used to it. Understand?"

"I do understand. It's much the same for me. I'd offer you my bed, but I may have a few unwelcome visitors this week."

"Malcolm, you are silly. Of course, I cannot share your bed now...wait...what visitors?"

Jocki was blushing while preparing my pie and stuttered as he served. "Yer beef peh an' ale, sir."

I scowled at him. "Jocki, nothing is going on between Elspeth and me. So, don't be telling tales."

"Nay, sir." He shook his head solemnly.

"I am not in need of a man to save my reputation, Malcolm, but I thank you anyway. Now what about these unwelcome visitors?"

"I will tell all dear Elspeth, but let me finish this delicious pie first." I really was hungry and ate most of it in the few minutes it took them to clear the table and begin washing up. Jocki topped up my mug when I finished. "I have a lot to tell you both, and in the strictest confidence, and that includes you, Jocki." I smiled at him, so he'd know I wasn't angry. Over the kitchen table I explained everything that'd transpired having to do with Mackmain and my plan to get him to confess. Elspeth knew most of it already but was visibly shaken when I came to the last part.

"Oh, Malcolm!" She sighed and shook her head. "Why have you invited this evil to our home?"

Her question shocked me. I admit in my single-minded focus on Mackmain, I'd failed to consider that. "It'll be fine," I said, hoping it was true.

"You have a conveniently short memory, my friend." She said that with a half smile that suggested a bit of adventure may not be wholly unwelcome.

"In any case, it'll be over soon. You just have to stay clear of me, if you can tolerate it," I teased.

"As believes your overweening ego!" She burst out laughing. "But in truth, I shall miss you."

"Ah! Speaking of such, Cawdie should be well enough to travel now, so your lonely vigil may soon come to an end. Enjoy it while you can. And, I might add, they may have a surprise for you."

"A surprise? What kind of surprise?"

"I cannot say. Nor can I confirm that it even exists. Let us say it is a potential surprise."

"Now that is not fair to torment me so! I will be so very glad to see Janet and Cawdie again, surprise or no." The thought of it obviously pleased her greatly.

"Actually, there may be two surprises, if I am right."

"Oh Malcolm, enough! Let us go and heal some patients. Jocki, please ready Gracie and the carriage for us."

"Aye, Lady Elspeth." Jocki looked at me for permission, I nodded and added that he should go home after the carriage was prepared and stay there until it was safe to return. He agreed and was off on a run. We were alone, and Elspeth was gathering her bag and cloak.

"Elspeth, thank you for everything. Is there anything you need this week?"

She turned and smiled warmly. "Just my family back. Do you want Gracie today?"

"Nay, I have many patients to see at the port and I'll be staying close til this thing with Mackmain is resolved."

"Oh, I almost forgot!" She searched in her cloak and fished out a letter. "Here are my conclusions on the Spence murder and attempted murder of Julianne. We should go over them before we see the Laird."

This had almost left my mind. "I'm glad you did this. Next time I'll treat for lunch and we can review it."

"That sounds grand! I bid you a good day."

I returned her well-wishes and watched as she hauled her bulging medical bag out the door.

I spent the rest of the day reviewing case notes and prioritizing patients. I needed to catch up with Andrew Mitchell as well. Elspeth mentioned in passing that he was still at the Inn and didn't seem to desire a large caseload. I chuckled thinking of how attached to Torrport and her ever-growing practise she'd become.

Late afternoon two of Kidd's men arrived. I paid them in coin. They looked capable enough and were suitably armed. They would spend the nights with me as well, one on the living room sofa and the other using Mrs. Simpson's bed. We reviewed the patients I'd be seeing next day and my route, and discussed how I was to be protected at each stage. Torrport was very crowded and I'd be in public places most of the time and with guards there should be little risk, except a dagger in the back from a skilled assassin, and that didn't seem to be Mackmain's style. No plan is perfect, but I was feeling much more relaxed now.

* * *

The next day went as expected. I saw several patients including James Allen, the wool merchant. He looked considerably improved. "How is it progressing, James?" I asked as we settled into a few chairs nestled between bales of wool and rolls of tartan cloth in his warehouse.

"I am much better, thank you for asking," he beamed. "And I am back to work as you can see."

I looked at his face carefully. "Your fever has gone?"

"Aye, and I shan't need your services anymore, doctor. I am well and truly healed."

"Have you been keeping to the diet and exercise I recommended?"

"Have no further use for it. Back to my normal self, I am." He was fiddling nervously with his pocket watch, glancing down to look at it frequently.

"Am I keeping you from anything, sir?"

"Och, the times are changing aren't they. Must keep up or perish." He laughed nervously.

"Then I shall leave you to your business. James, I strongly advise maintaining that diet and exercise regime. It will serve you well."

"Aye, doctor," he said with a sigh.

I could see that that the willingness to change his ways had vanished with the pain, so I rose to leave. I was almost out the door when he asked about the Spence murder. I advised that the investigation was well in hand and the Laird would soon bring the murderer to justice. He was gratified that his testimony had been useful in solving the case. We parted on good terms with me thinking I would be seeing him again soon.

* * *

I met Elspeth at noon as arranged. I'd ordered fresh bread, cheese and beverages from the local coffee house.

"I am sorry, Malcolm. I have not much time today." She swished past me carrying a basket of the same food I'd purchased earlier. She exclaimed on seeing the table set, "Och, I can see we have enough for four! We will eat yours then. I know a few patients who will enjoy this."

I opened her letter as she cut the bread and cheese. "I read this last night. It's well reasoned, yet the results are surprising."

"Aren't they though? But what other conclusions could there be?" She looked at me like she was expecting a revelation, but I provided none.

"The science and testimony all fit, but I wonder what the Laird will do?"

"Indeed."

We sat eating a while considering the alternatives, finally I said. "We must present this to the Laird and let him decide. We...err, you have done all that could be expected."

"Then you will support this report?"

"I will. You have done well."

She smiled then said, "Thank you, Malcolm. The pox outbreak at the fishing village is spreading despite my best efforts, and recently a few adults have come down with it. Thank God it is the one called chickenpox. I'm teaching the parents how to care for the wee ones, but it takes considerable time. If you can help, it would be well-appreciated. I wish Andrew had...Oh, never mind."

"I will help if I can, and that reminds me, I had a case today that you need to know about."

She was tired, that was clear. "I am listening, but I am booked solid. Can't take on much more."

"I understand but once you hear...It's the baker's wife, Una. She delivered a boy about three months ago."

"Aye, and it was a difficult birth as I recall, and she lost a lot of weight."

"Aye, the babe was large, but now it's not thriving, and the mother continues to lose weight."

"Oh? I didn't know."

"She thirsts and urinates a lot, lacks energy and is losing weight. Sounds familiar?"

"Diabetes?"

"I think so. I checked her urine and it was sweet," I added.

"Usually women who have diabetes during pregnancy recover once the bairn arrives."

"True, but not in this case. I want to start her on a treatment of Peruvian bark. Problem is I haven't tried it on a nursing mother. I don't want to risk the bairn, so I'm going to recommend that she find a wet nurse."

"I have not used that bark either."

"It is in the London Pharmacopeia, and I bought some in Edinburgh recently. Normally, it's recommended that diabetic patients exercise and induce sweats, but she works very hard in the bakery as is. We have little with which to treat diabetes. This bark looks promising, but if it doesn't work, her prognosis is very poor, as you well know."

"I will ask around for a wet nurse. There are a few who may help. We need to make sure the bairn is saved."

"Agreed. I'll look after the mother and you the bairn."

"I will, Malcolm, but I truly wish you would stay in Torrport, at least until the smallpox refugees leave and things settle."

I patted her hand. "There are issues I must resolve, then I am all yours."

"I may die from exhaustion first!" she chuckled, "Now I am afraid I must go." I followed her to the front door. "Thank you for lunch!" She stuck her head out of the door. "Och, he is still there! Malcolm why are there some wicked looking men lurking about the infirmary? There was one at the side where I tie Gracie and another just down the dock by the lawyer's office," she said in a whisper and pointed in that direction.

I grinned. "Those are my guards...from Captain Kidd. No worries, it's well in hand."

"Mhm, alright but be careful."

"I will and safe travels, Elspeth." I waited the few seconds it took for her to turn the corner to Gracie's hitching post, then went back in to clean up.

* * *

There's a lot to be said in favour of routine and I was thoroughly enjoying immersing myself in the routine of doctoring here in our salubrious little town. Most problems could be solved easily with a measure of medicine and loving-kindness, and people were usually appreciative and willing to pay reasonable fees. Life is usually good, and Elspeth's words about inviting evil reverberated in my mind as I went about my work. Eventually I found myself near the Inn and decided to leave a note for Andrew to meet for supper tomorrow evening at the tavern on the main dock, my treat in thanks for his service as locum.

The rest of the day and next went by quickly. I'd been away too long and the requests for help went from trickle to flood, as people saw me on my way from one patient to next. It was gratifying to know I was still needed. My tandem body guards were working well too, but by the end of the day I was beginning to believe, or was it hope, that Mackmain wouldn't respond to my taunts since it was all too obviously a trap, and I should waste no more coin on paying Kidd's men for services not required. Those were my thoughts as I settled in by a tavern window facing the harbour and watched my guards take up station just before Andrew arrived. I observed with interest as Andrew glided from table to table sharing a quip, a pat on the shoulder, or a laugh about some private joke. It seems he'd become well known in this tavern rather quickly.

"Doctor Forrester!" he said in that languid slur with half-mocking smile.

"Andrew," I replied, "I'm glad you made it. I thought you could use a change from the Inn, but I see I picked the wrong place."

"My second home? Indeed, I have lifted more than a few here." He smirked and looked around, waving to some traders who'd recently entered.

"I'm pleased our townsfolk have welcomed you so. Have a seat and tell me how it's been going."

He lifted one long leg over the back of the chair then descended with a chuckle. "Malcolm, I don't know how you survive here. Half the people can't pay, and the rest want to exchange medical service for poultry. The fishing village is a dead loss."

I smiled slightly. "Aye, that is the life of a country doctor. Most of us have a family remittance to smooth the way. Do you not?"

"Of course! But why should I work for a chicken or a piece of used clothing?"

"We cannot only serve the rich, Andrew. Consider your oath. There are few enough with means in a place like Torrport. That is just the way it is."

His smile vanished, replaced with a mean scowl. "This town suits you then, but the best physicians are more appreciated in cities like Edinburgh."

I could see where this was headed, and I had no desire to provoke him. "Then you will be relieved to know you may return to Edinburgh at your convenience. I am content to serve here and barter for poultry." I laughed heartily, trying my best to lighten the mood. In fact, I'd never bartered for service here. If someone couldn't pay, I worked pro bono. It was the traditional way of the physician, in my opinion.

"Oh, but I cannot return yet, and won't give up my room at the Inn. My family has left Edinburgh for the country and there are no servants left behind, so I will stay put until they return. I'm sure you understand," he said, oblivious to his selfishness.

"I understand well. Life without servants is unbearable, isn't it? You are more than welcome to stay. Now what shall we have for supper? The mutton pie here is excellent."

"Och! I've had one too many of those, but since it is your treat, I'll have the roast beef."

The roast beef dinner was the most expensive item on the menu. It amused me to order it for him, then he stood and shouted. "A round of ale for all! My good friend Doctor Forrester has returned and will pay." An uproar of cheers and banging of mugs ensued. His impertinence was entertaining.

In the end, I did my best to keep up with his eating, drinking, and singing, but that proved impossible and after two hours I was completely engorged and drunk. Andrew turned out to be lively company and it was no wonder he'd made so many friends in these few weeks. I decided to leave before I made a complete arse of myself, so I rose and gave my protectors an exaggerated salute and tried to make my way home without falling off the dock. The guards joined me, and we made our way, arm-in-arm, laughing and singing, none of us fit for anything but sleep.

* * *

And sleep we did, until a flash of light shocked my consciousness, followed by the familiar voice of Jocki trying to wake me.

"Doctor Forrester!"

I tried to open one eye, but it was instantly dazzled by the bright candle flame. "Can it not wait til morning?" My head was throbbing, and I felt like I was going to retch. I needed to lay still. "Come get me in the morning," I whispered hoarsely.

"You must read this letter! Please Doctor!"

I could feel something being fanned in my face. "Leave me be, Jocki. Come back in morning." Was all I said before pulling the pillow over my head.

Undeterred, Jocki lifted the pillow and said one name loudly, *Mackmain!*

I was instantly awake and lifted my head so fast, I bumped his and we both cursed. My skull seemed immersed in decomposing sludge and I took some deep breaths to keep whatever was left in my stomach from exiting. "What about him?"

"He left this letter at our tavern. He is here in Torrport!"

I grabbed the letter and yelled. "Wake the men! I need more light. Make some tea." At once I regretted the noise my mouth was making, and it was all I could handle as I tried to get out of bed and have a well-needed piss. Jocki ran about and soon our rooms were lit and men were muttering and trying to dress. I sat back on my bed and tore open the letter. There were few words.

"*I have Elspeth. Meet me at Signal Hill at dawn. Mackmain.*"

"Oh God!" I muttered. What have I done? I'm such an ass. I was well into a bout of mental self-flagellation while trying to dress when I caught a big toe in one leg of my trousers and keeled over, banging my out-thrust elbow on the wooden frame of the bed. I lay there moaning and wondering if life could get any worse, when Jocki mercifully helped right me to finish dressing.

So, there we were at four-o-clock or so in the morning, still half-drunk and looking the worse for it and about to set out in the dark on a rescue mission. I tried to think positive thoughts.

"Men." I looked at the two of them standing there trying to look presentable. "Captain Mackmain has taken Lady Elspeth and we are to meet him on Signal Hill by the fishing village at dawn. I assume he wants to exchange her for me." They both looked clueless, so I added. "We must save her." That elicited a grunt that I assumed was understanding. "It'll take us an hour to walk there, then we'll have some time to reconnoitre before we climb the hill." I was trying to use what little intelligence I could muster. "Do we all have our weapons?" Sadly, the three of us had to check. "There are torches by the front door. Let's be off."

And thus, our trek in the dark started, me with trepidation that something terrible had happened to Elspeth on my account, and the men no doubt wondering if they were being paid enough. At least the weather had cleared, and the fresh air was clearing our minds as well. The forest path at night was alive with the sounds of myriad creatures deep in the throes of mating, or so I imagined, and it reminded me of how little mating was happening in my futile life.

The fishing village was still dark when we arrived, and I sent Jocki back to his family, with an extra coin, and overly profuse thanks. We extinguished our torches and sat listening and letting ale-reddened eyes adjust. By the first light of dawn, I could see the silhouette of the *Silver Fin* at anchor just off the rocky promontory hill we were about to climb. The fishing village was delimited on one side by this small promontory and on the other by a long rocky beach that culminated in a wedge-shaped area with caves and steep cliffs. The bay was the only good mooring on this side of the larger promontory that included Torrport. The village itself is just an ugly pock, smack in the middle of a truly beautiful vista, and nothing was lovelier than climbing Signal Hill on a clear Spring morning. I was almost elated when we reached the clearing at the top between some moss-covered boulders and assorted shrubs. The site was used for making signal fires to guide lost sailors, and the remnants of past fires were clearly visible. We were poking about when a shadow emerged from behind a boulder, then another, and within seconds we found ourselves surrounded by several men pointing muskets and pistols at us.

One large man stepped forward, and in the morning light he almost looked handsome, but on closer inspection it was the hated face of Mackmain, wearing a wicked sneer. He also was pointing a pair of silver pistols at me. Reflexively I tried for mine, but instantly heard several clicking sounds from the men around me and then I knew for certain I was out-gunned and out-manned. I'd expected him to bring a few, but the ten or so I saw arrayed against us was overwhelming.

"Boy, I am amazed you've lived so long." Mackmain gave a grim chuckle, then turned his head to a smaller man in a hooded dark cloak near him and said. "See, I told you he would come if there was a woman involved."

I hated the idea of proving him right, but I'd looked around and could see no one that could be Elspeth, so I had to ask. "Where is she?"

The smaller hooded man stepped forward and said. "She is likely having pleasant dreams in her bed. We will not harm dear Elspeth. She is one of us and who would be so foolish as to antagonize all those MacLeod men. She is quite safe, Malcolm."

His distinctive voice struck me like a belaying pin to the jaw. "Who..."

He flipped his hood back and out poured the luxuriant black curls of Captain Kidd! "Aye, it is me. Take him boys!"

One of Kidd's men who'd been guarding me kicked the back of my knees, sending me to the ground. The other pulled his pistol and had it fixed to my temple. I was truly dumbfounded! These were the men I'd been carousing with but a few hours previously, and commanded by a man I considered a friend.

"Disarm and tie him!" growled Kidd.

I knew it was pointless to resist. I was alone amongst enemies and had to wait for a more suitable time to escape, assuming I lived that long. I looked up at them both. One was my sworn enemy and the other a friend turned traitor, and I felt such hatred and self-loathing as I lay there powerless, that I almost wept. I rolled back onto my knees in time to receive a kick from Mackmain, then another, aimed accurately at my still-healing lower back. The sparks of pain shot through me as I heard him utter oaths and the names of the men I'd killed. I guess I'd deserved that, hadn't I? Then Kidd pulled him back and said something inaudible to me in my pain-ridden state.

A few minutes passed as Mackmain's anger subsided and Kidd assumed control. I recovered enough to look around and record in memory as best I could the faces of my tormentors. Some were hooded and masked, others in plain view, some averting their eyes when I looked at them. I vowed that some day I would get my bloody revenge, especially on Mackmain and Kidd.

I couldn't be in a worse situation with only one weapon remaining, my mind and attached tongue. "Why, Kidd? Do you not know with whom you form an alliance?"

Kidd looked down at me benevolently. "Not an alliance, Malcolm, a convenience is all. You should not have been so trusting." His men laughed as Kidd smiled at me benignly. "Did you fail to notice my name?"

I smiled up at him in defiance. "Aye, I do know your father was hanged, as you shall be for this."

"Only if they catch me and if they can prove a crime was committed, my friend. I intend neither. But why blame me, it was you who offered up this profitable opportunity? My only action was to inform a mutual friend and arrange a meeting of, shall we say...reconciliation. Surely, there is nothing amiss in that?"

"Enough of this!" snarled Mackmain, "I shall be free of this pest, once and for all!"

Mackmain lifted his pistols to fire at me, then Kidd quickly swiveled and pointed his pistol at Mackmain's head and shouted. "Stand down, sir! We have an agreement, and if you renege, your life is forfeit. Control your anger, sir!" Mackmain was flushed and shaking with rage when he spat on me then turned his back as his arms sagged.

"Forrester will be kept and ransomed as we agreed and once we split the gold you can have him, not before."

Mackmain looked over at Kidd and took a deep breath. "Aye, then I shall kill him."

Kidd shrugged. "If that is your wish. Now let us take him to the hold of the *Silver Fin* before we attract attention."

With that, the two men who were my former guards, dragged me up off the ground and pointed to the trail that lead to the *Silver Fin*. As Kidd passed, he winked, seeming to enjoy my discomfit.

It took two trips to ferry everyone from shore to ship. I was in the first with Kidd and Mackmain, well-tied and pinned by two muskets.

"I would like to be there when you finish with Forrester." It was Kidd speaking privately with Mackmain seated near the prow.

"Why?"

"The Forrester's have been our enemy for generations and it would give me great pleasure to bring them down a notch."

"Aye," replied Mackmain. "We shall have our gold and blood." He said that, accentuating the blood part and I knew there would be no possibility of reconciliation.

"What will you do with your share, sir? Methinks I shall buy another ship, a fast sloop perhaps for the coastal trade..." I could sense a direction in Kidd's conversation, but wasn't sure where he was going with it.

Mackmain scowled. "Och. I will sail to America and start a new life. It is all I can do now. Time to start afresh." They both sat there thoughtfully as the men grappled the *Silver Fin* and a rope ladder was rolled down. I was still tied, so they threw a rope loop down and dragged me up unceremoniously, banging my shoulder and head on the gunwale and landing me in a heap on the deck.

"Take him to our new guest quarters," Kidd ordered.

My guards guided me to the hatch I'd used earlier, with Mackmain and Kidd following. One of the guest rooms in the hold was finished with a fitted door and a steel hasp and loop for a lock. They pushed me inside and jammed a wooden peg in the loop. The room was small but well-appointed with a double bed against the bulkhead, an armoire, and a folding table with chair. I stood quietly beside the door, so I could hear. Kidd was explaining to Mackmain that he may have to leave in a week, so this business must be concluded before then. Mackmain replied that he needed to get back to Edinburgh straight away with a ransom note and evidence of my capture. More was discussed that I failed to hear, then the door was unlocked, and two armed men entered, followed by Kidd.

"Malcolm, we need a gift for your dear father. Would you be so kind?"

"What do you mean?"

"Your hair Malcolm. I know you are vain, but you'll survive its loss." He sniggered then motioned for the men to hold me while Kidd sliced off my braided pony-tail. "This will do nicely to convince your father. If not, we will offer to send the rest of your head." He laughed again, evidently enjoying his vile game. The door was relocked, and I stood there consumed by feelings of helplessness and righteous anger. I felt behind my head. At least he hadn't made a complete mess of it.

"Here is your proof of capture, Mackmain. Use it wisely. Sir William has one week to deliver the gold to Signal Hill, or he will not see his son again. Understood?"

"Aye, the old bugger will do it. You will see. There is naught else he can do."

"Then come let us have a wee dram before you are off. Malcolm told me what a corrupt old coward you are, maybe you'd like to set the record straight?"

I heard Mackmain snarl as they were leaving then raise his voice, perhaps so I could hear. "I can tell you a tale or two about those damned Forresters too."

It was quiet. I tried to peek through the slats and could only see part of a boot near my door. They likely would leave two guards, since this cell wasn't very secure. I could kick the door in within seconds, but it wouldn't do much good with hands tied and facing two armed men. For a time, I just sat on the edge of the bunk and brooded, thoughts of revenge filling my mind. I soon realized that brooding would not free me, so I set my mind on the task at hand.

* * *

It seemed at least an hour passed by the time I managed to wriggle my way out of the ropes on my wrists. I was better able now to plan an escape. I considered several possibilities including bribing the guards, and forcing the door at night and sneaking out. In the end, the only one that appealed was to leave like a true Forrester, out the front door and into the teeth of the enemy. I had to risk it. I would not wait here meekly waiting for my execution, nor would I beg for mercy. It was settled in my mind and all that remained was an opportunity...and that came very quickly.

"You should have seen his face..." It was Kidd. He was coming down the ladder with a few others and having a laugh, I assumed at my expense. I peered through the door slats and listened. There seemed to be three of them in addition to Kidd. It would not be easy, but surprise was on my side and if I could over-power Kidd and secure a weapon, the odds would be evened substantially. I took two steps back and braced one foot against the leg of the bed and crouched, muscles tensed and ready to launch against the door. I took some deep breaths and stilled my mind. This would be over in seconds, one way or the other. My eyes were fixed on the door, waiting for the slightest movement. I heard someone pull the pin from the loop and the door inched open. I flew forward hitting it with my shoulder, smashing it into the man on the other side. He tumbled back onto the floor, blood gushing from his nose. I was out!

"What the..." someone said as I punched the closest sailor viciously on the temple. He slumped in front of the hooded man behind him, then I went for Kidd. I had no time to think. I drove into him head-down like a bull, pinning him against the wall. He tried to push me away, but I was much too strong. He knew it was over and had that look of sheer terror that instantly turned to agony as my fists pounded his sides.

Once his shoulders rolled forward, I pulled back slightly and finished him with a right uppercut that almost lifted him off his feet. I grabbed his pistol with my left hand as he slid unconscious to the floor. There was only the hooded man left and I spun and flung myself at him, all spit and snarl, and found myself in mid-strike inches from the face of Father Hammett!

"Oh God! Malcolm, stop! This is all a mistake!" He was backing away quickly to avoid my fist, arms raised to protect his face.

I stopped in the nick of time.

"Please, Malcom. Mackmain is gone. We were coming to release you."

I was completely unhinged, rage and confusion built on deep layers of betrayal. "You are in this too, Father?" Was he really one of them, a party to all this?

"Listen! This was a ruse to get Mackmain to confess, and it worked!"

I heard the men I'd dropped begin to stir behind me. I had a choice, and only seconds to decide. Should I believe Father Hammett and stay, or flee and save myself. I took a deep breath, trying to control my emotions.

"Father, I place myself in your hands. May God curse you if you betray me." My voice was shaking when I said that. It had felt so good to fight back, but now rational mind was willing rage-filled body to desist, and it took all the fortitude I had.

He came toward me with outstretched arms. I pushed him away. I was in no mood for clerical affection. I could hear Kidd stirring. He was holding his sore jaw and mumbling curses. I loomed over him, pointed the pistol in his face and spit out venomously. "You...you cut my hair. God damn you!" It is strange what comes to mind in times of stress.

In a few minutes, the men were back on their feet, but keeping a respectful distance. I was prowling the small space, ready to punch or shoot anything that got in my way. I could hardly think clearly, bloodlust still surging through my veins. Meanwhile, Father Hammett tried his best to calm everyone. I did manage to restrain my mouth, knowing it likely would end in even more conflict and regret.

The explanation gradually came out that Kidd had set up Mackmain, and Father Hammett, in disguise, had witnessed and recorded his confession, along with several of Kidd's men who were prepared to testify. Mackmain had murdered Gwen's husband because he'd been caught extorting merchants. It was that simple. I listened to it with the last of the anger flowing to ground, but it still hurt...a lot. I'd been made a pawn in my own game and it was humiliating.

"Could you not have included me, sought my permission?" I asked angrily.

"You have your confession, Malcolm. It is what you wanted. Had you known of our plan would you have played your part as well?" Kidd was speaking slowly, holding his jaw that thankfully I hadn't broken.

I suppose he had me there. "At least Gwen will see justice done." I looked in Kidd's eyes, but I would neither thank him nor apologize. He was lucky I hadn't killed him, and I'm not sure we could ever again be close friends.

"I need a drink. Anyone care to join me?" Kidd tried to clap me on the shoulder, but I brusquely pushed his hand away. "Malcolm, we did this for you," he pleaded.

"And you let Mackmain get away too."

"You did not ask me to capture him, and even made a point of telling me he was not to be killed."

Father Hammett stepped between us. "Try to see this fairly. Mackmain will be brought to justice, and no one was seriously hurt. I am sorry you were treated roughly Malcolm, but surely you can find sufficient grace in your heart to admit that Kidd's plan was brilliant, and it worked."

He was right of course, and I should be grateful that my friends helped me. "Aye, Father, you're right. I'm being churlish, and my ego is bruised. Forgive me." I extended a hand to Kidd, but to be honest I was thinking how humiliating it must have been for him to be so easily manhandled by a physician. He paused, then took my hand and gave a cursory shake. All was not right between us still.

I decided to join Kidd for a drink in the hope that whisky would do what stubborn pride could not. It was then that we heard the first shots fired. We stopped and listened. It was coming from above. There were shouts and a few more shots. Kidd pushed past Father Hammett and ran the steps to the top deck, the rest of us close behind.

The scene was one of chaos, men grappling, swords clashing, a fire lit on a pile of ropes. I pushed to the front, ready for anything, not knowing who or what this was about. I thought I recognized some of the men from the fishing village, then I spotted her awkwardly struggling to get over the gunwale, dagger clenched between her teeth, auburn hair flying, and I had to laugh.

"Stop! Everyone, stop fighting!" I shouted as loudly as I could.

Father Hammett and Captain Kidd joined in the chorus, and in a few minutes the fighting ceased as the attackers could plainly see the situation was not what they'd expected.

"Malcolm?" An out of breath Elspeth strangely dressed as a boy stared at me, not quite understanding.

"I am fine, believe me. I am fine!" The notion that people would care enough to try to rescue me touched my heart and I picked her up and swung her around like a rag doll, much to her embarrassment, I am sure, but I was elated. I let her down and whispered, "Thank you for trying."

She straightened herself and gave a smiling scowl that only she could manage. "What happened Malcom? Jocki said you were to meet with Mackmain and later you were seen bound and being carried off."

"Aye, that is all true, and I will explain later but suffice to say we have a confession from Mackmain, and he will pay for his misdeeds."

Hammett and Kidd joined us and exchanged greetings with Elspeth. Then she looked about and got to work. "Some have been injured. Help me treat them, will you?"

* * *

Fortunately, no one was seriously injured, and everyone was thanked and promised rewards for services rendered. We were standing by the rope ladder waiting our turn to be rowed ashore.

"I need to get back to Edinburgh, as soon as..." I was thinking out loud and Father Hammett heard me.

"Och! I neglected to mention we have already sent a letter to your father recommending he ignore any requests from Mackmain, and I assured him you were safe."

"I see, how thoughtful, and what if I wasn't safe?" I still had issues bubbling just below the surface.

"We assumed you would be." Hammett looked uncomfortable and I had no wish to torture him.

"It turned out well. That is all that matters. However, Mackmain is still at large and once he finds I'm not captive, and he'll receive no ransom...I must protect my father." I was trying to think what must be done when Kidd spoke up.

"I can offer my men to help you in Edinburgh, should you need them." He was still touching his jaw constantly and I knew it must be very sore, so I poked Elspeth and whispered. "He needs pain medication." She nodded and dug in her bag for a sachet of herbs, then tucked it in Kidd's waistcoat and leaned close to him and whispered something.

"I have men in Edinburgh, but thank you for the kind offer." I was feeling more charitable now and with Father Hammett's wise counsel could see that the result was worth the sacrifice of my hurt feelings. I smiled and said sincerely, "I truly thank you for what you've done. I am in your debt, sir."

Kidd winced then said. "I trust you will remember your debt when it comes time to protect us from the English."

So that is what all this was about, I thought, as I helped Elspeth into the rowboat. In a few minutes, we reached the dock and she turned to face me. "Malcolm, please promise me this will be the last of it."

I thought a moment. "I cannot. Not while Mackmain is loose. The task is not complete. There are few Town Guards left and I am not sure I trust them with this."

She just sighed heavily and gave me a disapproving look. "I will take you home then. Gracie is tied beside the tavern."

"I don't feel like going home. There is nothing there for me. Take me to the tavern."

"Do you not think you have been in enough trouble for one day? I will not take you to the tavern!" She took my hand. "Come home with me for supper and I may have a surprise for you."

She gave her best version of a wink that made me smile. I didn't know what she had planned but it had to be better than my empty home.

On the way, she explained how she and Jocki had mobilized the fishing village and how proud she was of them all and how frightened she was when she was climbing the ladder up the *Silver Fin*. I wholeheartedly agreed and chuckled at the image of her dressed as a boy with that dagger between the teeth. I tied Gracie at the foot of the path to her cottage, got her some water and feed, then followed Elspeth to the door, steeling myself for whatever prank she'd planned.

She opened the door and called Scathach, who obediently padded over and gave us a welcoming snuffle, tail wagging all the while. "I think Scathach and Henry were married in Edinburgh." Elspeth said with a hint of merriment in her voice. I didn't follow her meaning, so she pointed at the dog's obviously broadening belly.

"Oh, for Heaven's sake!" I roared with laughter and we both knelt and gave the pregnant dog extra hugs.

TWENTY-TWO

Elspeth - Gifts

Self-pity is tiring. A few hours with my book and I was bored with the emotions that kept poking determined fingers into my cloud of misery. I could not remember anything I had seen or read. I closed the worn volume, returned it to the shelf, called Scathach and went for a walk. I was behaving like a love-struck lass, but I was not in love with Aidan. I had tried to be. Why not? He was a lovely man, but in truth, he was just a man whose talent and ingenuity intrigued me. We had much in common, but then, so did Sir Ross and I...and Malcolm. I was being what Malcolm would deprecate as "female and foolish". It was my own fault. I had made much of nothing. Aidan had never indicated that he wished to be more than a friend. And he would still be that. Life was not simple. The coward that lived in me wanted to leave for Skye at once, but I would not listen. Spence's murder must be solved before I could return to my childhood home in good conscience. My inquiries would begin with Aidan's list of people who used gold leaf. I turned resolutely toward the frame-maker's shop, Scathach padding along beside me.

What I knew of the murder filled my thoughts. I was ashamed to admit how much I disliked Spence. Had my feelings blinded me to the point that I had overlooked something? The scene in the laundry yard was as freshly vivid as it was the day it happened. I could still smell the blood and feces and death from the autopsy. My stomach lurched.

Spence had been a large, well trained warrior. He would not have been subdued easily. His killer had to have been his equal. There were few in Torrport who could have strangled him. Or, perhaps that was why there were two of them? The wool merchant heard three voices, one that might have been a lad or a woman. Aggie the laundress? Most assuredly not. But who wanted Spence dead, and why? The Jacobites, the smugglers, someone he diced with or played cards with and cheated? That made me think of the Captain of the *Silver Fin*, and what about Gilly? He had beaten her so severely she miscarried. Not that she wanted the babe, but who knows what had been in her mind? And then there was his wife, Rachel. Spence was a philanderer. She certainly had reason enough.

I needed to meet with Malcolm. He had returned and walked into his home to find Jocki and me devouring a warm pie I had brought down to the boy, and smiled his way into sharing it. Jocki had already told me he had seen him at the docks earlier. I wondered what could be so important there? He was thinner, but only two faint scars from the experiment showed on his handsome face. He looked exhausted. I had not the heart to bring up the murder, but I would have to do so soon.

* * *

I found myself standing in front of the frame-maker's. Like many others, Jean-Bernard Barbier had fled to England from France after the Revocation of the *Edict of Nantes*. I stared at the sign hanging over his shop, a marvel of paint and gilt decorated with a shell center, acanthus fan corners and crested at the top with a cabochon topped by a cluster of flowers secured with a ribbon. It was exquisitely crafted, and completely covered with gold leaf. Upon entering the low beamed room, I was transported to a world made of picture frames, mirrors, snuff boxes, cases for clocks and small ornamental pieces of unknown stuffs. Nearly all gleamed with gold, and most were covered thickly with intricate designs of strapwork, foliage, garlands and swags. Here and there a grotesque peeped out from an allegorical scene destined to decorate some expensive commission. A movement in one corner became a petite, neatly dressed, and very young woman. Behind her a huge man was seated at a worktable beneath a window. He stopped painting, his outsized hands making the delicate paint brush look slightly ridiculous. He had been painting graceful golden veins on raised green leaves surrounding a frame and looked at me questioningly.

"How may I help thee?" The woman's voice was a lyrical softly accented English.

"I have come to ask some questions for the Laird." I made my own voice calm and friendly. "We are pursuing the murder of Sir Spence. May I ask if you knew him?"

The woman looked at her husband, who responded in a carefully dispassionate tone. "We knew him. He was a customer. I made a frame for his wife. Tis there. He was not happy with it." He pointed to a small exquisitely painted frame hanging from a beam. "He felt his coin and patronage entitled him to...more than the frame. I disagreed. We did not deal after that." His wife's face bloomed with color and she kept her eyes steadfastly on the floor.

"I see," I said, slowly, comprehending. "Thank you." I looked around the shop again, taking in the surfeit of gold. "Your work is most striking, sir. I see you use much gilding. Where do you find the gold leaf you need?"

The wool merchant had obviously been bragging of his find, for the frame maker understood the reason behind my question immediately. His lips twisted into a slight bitter smile. "I purchase it from the blacksmith, as do most, lady."

I ploughed on. "And, do you remember where you were on the night Sir Spence was murdered?"

His wife spoke hurriedly. "He was with me, my lady. I do so swear to that." He said nothing, but touched her arm gently and gave me a wry look. He twisted back to his work, dismissing me. His wife moved purposely to the door, her slender back stiff with resentment, and held it open for me. I thanked them both and moved to leave. They would vouch for each other, which left no way of disproving either one.

As I reached the threshold her husband's low voice stopped me. "I did not kill him, lady. But I cannot say with truth that I regret his passing." I nodded without turning, and left.

* * *

Sir Ross was next. His medical use of gold leaf was a common practice. Many physicians prescribed edible gold for pain and sore limbs. I used it in my own preparations. He was my patient, but what did I really know about him? He and Gregor had not lived long in Torrport. Sir Ross was obviously wealthy with a sharp sense of business. His shipments were eagerly welcomed by the merchants, with their often-exotic cargos from ports spanning the world, including those of the Dutch, French and Russians. Probably in his late thirties or early forties, he was still quite attractive. He read and spoke several languages fluently, was highly intelligent, articulate and possessed of a droll sense of humor. I liked him.

Gregor answered the door, his dark beard was freshly trimmed. The black clothing, austere and immaculate as usual, did not quite disguise the aura of danger about him, or the width of his shoulders or the size of his hands. I studied his face. It revealed only a calm courtesy. After a swift appraising glance, he bowed me into the house. Sir Ross was standing in front of the large bookcase at the back of the room staring at the contents. He too, was dressed faultlessly, as though ready for a morning call, and the room smelled pleasantly of some exotic incense or potpourri. Not even the faintest whiff of his recent affliction remained. He smiled warmly and came toward me with outstretched hands lifting one of mine; he bent over and directed a light kiss just above the surface of my skin. I could feel his warm breath and the softness of his beard as it brushed against my fingers. "Well come, Lady Elspeth. Tis

290

unexpected but fortuitous. You have been much in my thoughts. The Laird has told us that you will be returning to Skye soon. I am quite devastated." He placed his hand affectedly over his heart and smiled, but his gaze was intent.

"Tis true." In return, I gave him my most disarming smile. "But mayhap I shall return, sir. Who can know what the Fates have decided. I have promised Laird MacLeod that I would return as soon as I have put my life here in some order. There are patients to see and arrange for, and Laird MacDuff has asked Sir Malcolm and me to investigate the murder of Sir Spence."

Gregor displayed no reaction to my words, but a flicker of something showed for an instant in Sir Ross's eyes, before he smiled at me. "And how may I help you, my lady?"

"He was a friend of yours, was he not? Can you tell me a bit more about him?"

"As I have told you, Lady Elspeth, He was only an... acquaintance." He looked at me appraisingly. "What more shall I tell you? Sir Spence was for hire. Gold was his master. One dares not befriend such. I have known of him for many years. He was a mercenary for the Tsar, and, as such, known in the Russian court. A most useful man at times. There was some unpleasantness over a woman, I think, and he returned to Scotland to become Second for Laird MacDuff at much the same time we arrived."

Directness and honesty were best when speaking with Sir Ross. "And was he being useful on the night he was murdered?" I challenged. A grim little smile played about Sir Ross's mouth. "Not at all useful, my lady. And lest you be curious, I was here all evening examining a new shipment of furs, was I not, Gregor?"

Gregor, in the act of setting down a heavy tea tray, paused. "It is as you say, my lord." It was a reprise of the frame-maker and his wife. One might suspect a lie but be unable to prove it so.

As Gregor's large hands deftly moved the delicate porcelain bowls to the table I had a sudden recollection of them around Sir Ross's neck. "No." I breathed, remembering the scars on his arms. Had some of them been caused by Spence's vain struggle to free himself? Gregor had the strength to hold him. I looked in his eyes, trying to see past the flat darkness, and spoke without thinking. "Why would you kill him?"

He went still. "I beg your pardon, lady?" His voice was tranquil and without inflection but the sense of menace I felt was so compelling that I took one involuntary step back before I could control my reactions. We stood there staring at each other until Sir Ross's composed voice shattered the moment.

"Come now, Lady Elspeth. Surely you cannot seriously believe that? I have told you that Gregor was with me when Sir Spence met his unfortunate end. I will swear to that." His voice held a dangerous commanding edge I had not heard him use before. I was not certain whether it was directed at me or at Gregor, but we both reacted to it like subaltern recruits.

I pulled myself together and looked at Sir Ross. "I...see," I said slowly. A feeling of great sadness enveloped me. Disappointment? I did not want this. The room had become suffocating. I needed to leave quickly before I was ill. My face must have reflected my feelings. Malcolm says I would be a terrible card player, but then he really knows little of me.

Sir Ross cocked his head to one side and his voice became the gentle one I knew. "Come see the furs," he cajoled. "There is one the exact color of your hair. I must show you. And have some tea. This is a new blend just arrived yesterday." Chills shivered across my skin, and I refused both the offer of fur and refreshment, leaving before I could retch on the expensive Persian carpet. Neither of them tried to stop me.

Minutes later, walking along the narrow stone road leading to the path toward the cottage, I had the terrible feeling that I had lost something that had become precious to me.

* * *

I arrived back at the cottage to find Julianne and the bairn in the big chair before the fire. My painful thoughts were consigned to a hidden place in my mind. Jocki was there too, stirring up the coals to heat the kettle. Julianne had come to beg some honey and beeswax from our hives. Scathach was resting her massive head on Julianne's knee and exchanging stares with the bairn in her lap. Julianne stroked the dog. "She has grown bigger. The food in Edinburgh, I suppose."

"Or Henry," I said. She looked down and laughed, finally noticing that Scathach's increase in size was primarily around her belly.

"Aye. Remember your promise. I get one of her pups. We want one to raise with the bairn." She flushed. "Elspeth. There is something I want to share with you. The Tsar, the babe's father, I mean, will soon break our handfasting." She looked up and hastened to add, "Please, do not be upset. I knew this was how it would be from the beginning, but I wanted the babe acknowledged, to have no stain on his name. In Russia, the Tsar has ruled that a handfasting may be broken by either person, at will. He will soon announce the end of ours in his country, although he will provide generously for our bairn's future, so there is no need to fret. I am grateful for that, and truly I no longer love him. I am not certain that I ever did in a lasting way. The Imperial Court is like a bright feverish dream or part of a bewitching romantic fable. Now the tale is told." She inhaled deeply. "But I have this precious gift to keep." She pulled the babe to her and kissed the soft dark curls on the top of his head. "Is he not worth any price? See this?" She touched a small dark spot on the babe's right cheek. "His father has marked him."

"Tis only a birthmark, Julianne, and may fade as he grows." I touched the bairn's wee hand. He grasped my thumb strongly with his tiny fingers, gurgled, and burrowed into my heart. I did not ask her about Aidan.

After Julianne left, I cleaned the cottage thoroughly, taking pleasure in the comforting effect it had on me. Scrubbing floors on my knees permitted me to pray fervently as well.

* * *

Margaret had asked that I come to her, so I bathed, put on clean clothing, packed a basket with a new cheese wrapped in waxed linen, and made my way to the castle. The guard knocked on the door to Lady Margaret's solar, and I found her with Rachel, their heads together over a basket of the colored silks that Sir Ross imported. Margaret was blooming. Comelier than I had ever seen her. She arose, smiling and came toward me. Rachel stayed as she was, her face turned away, quietly arranging the silks by color. Unlike her mistress, she looked pale and ill.

"Lady Elspeth! I have a new cartoon." She pointed to a colored drawing over her tapestry loom which she would copy. I made appropriate sounds of appreciation. It was a complicated and elegant design that would bear the stamp of her formidable skill at the loom. "Tis lovely, Lady Margaret. You wished to see me?" She had the grace to blush. "Aye, tis vain I know, but I wished to ask if there is anything I can do to avoid the lines of childbirth on my belly? I have often heard that after childbirth women become...unattractive to their husbands. Please tell me what I can do?"

I smiled and thought it premature to worry so, but decided encouragement was in order. "I have some salve to apply to your belly, lady. Use it every morning and evening. It will help. Use it on your breasts, too. Let us see how you are doing."

She had heeded Malcolm's instructions. She smelled clean, a faint pleasing odor of scented soap on her skin. Odors rouse memories. "Lady Margaret" I said slowly. "Where did you get your soap? It is most distinctive."

"Tis my own make, with my own perfumes in it. I have done so since I was but a girl of thirteen, and my mother insisted that every woman should have her own personal scent, one that is associated with her. She took me to the perfumers and I chose a blend that I have used since. Tis a mixture of rosemary and orange oil...a bit of vanilla, and a few other things. I scented several bookmarks and a handkerchief for my husband. He says they bring me to him when he is away." She smiled secretly. "Would you like a ball of it? I share it with those that do like it. If you place it in a chest with clothing, it freshens them and keeps the vermin away. Tis the rosemary."

Rachel had gone still. Lady Margaret chattered happily on, but I no longer heard her words. The soap in Sir Spence's mouth had smelled much like Lady Margaret's soap. Rachel, Spence's wife, had access to it. But then, Lady Margaret said she "often shared it", so that might mean nothing. "I should be most pleased to have it, Lady Margaret." I wanted to compare it with the piece we found in Sir Spence's mouth, just to be certain I was not imagining the similarity. She sent Rachel to fetch one of the balls. The woman wrapped it in a square of silk, and gave it to me. I took my leave. When I returned to the cottage I pulled the small gob of soap we had removed from Spence's mouth from the earthenware pot where it was secured, and bent over to sniff it and the ball Rachel provided. They were the same.

* * *

Delay would not help. I went to the smithy. Aidan was polishing a flat circle of metal, and I stood quietly at the door, watching him work, until he came to a good stopping place. The covered contraption I had seen was gone. He was focused on his work, but I knew he was aware of me. After a moment, he straightened, rotated his shoulders to relax them and turned to face me. He was good to look at and I felt a selfish twinge of regret for the loss of my foolish dream, but only for a moment. His smile was warm, but I could sense the wariness in him. "Lady Elspeth, have you come with another commission for me...perhaps my own head?"

"Nay, though I doubt not that you could create it. Perhaps we can discuss the instrument you and the Tsar are working on? I wish truth between us, Aidan. We have become friends and I would have it to remain so."

He regarded me thoughtfully. "I consider you so, but there are other loyalties that must be honored as well. I can say only that I have known the Tsar for many years, and that what we are working on together is, like your metal boot, a project I am helping him with."

My breath hitched, and I fear my voice rose. "Aidan, the things you have created for me are for bettering lives. Can you say the same for what you are making for him? I know well enough what I saw, and if it works as I believe it is intended, it will allow one person to kill many in a few seconds. Is that beneficial?"

Aidan sighed. "That would depend on who is wielding it, and why, would it not? Would you prefer an enemy have it first?"

He was right, of course. Someone else would soon see the potential of such a weapon. "Very well." I could not refute his words. I lowered my voice and changed course. "Aidan, Laird MacDuff has asked that Malcolm and I investigate the murder of Sir Spence. Do you know of anyone with reason to wish him dead?"

There was a long brooding pause before he answered. "Lady, he was an evil man, a mercenary who could be purchased to do anyone's bidding. A man without honor. I should imagine there are many who wished him ill. In Russia, he took pleasure from the violence he inflicted on those who ran afoul of his temper, and many here have felt his brutality."

It was true. I wanted to ask him where he was on the night Spence was murdered, but I could not. Instead I asked him about his relationship with Julianne. He answered me honestly.

"I have loved her since she was a small bairn following me about and pestering me with questions. Her family went to France, and we lost touch for a while. But later, we met again when both our fathers went to Russia to work for the Tsar. Mine was not invited to court as often. Julianne was much favored because of her beauty and charm. You know the rest. When she returned to stay with Laird MacDuff, I followed, at the request of the Tsar." I must have looked startled for he continued. "Ironic is it not? He wished me to guard her. There are those in Russia who would not be pleased if she had a son. The Tsar guards his own. I am not the only one who came to Torrport because of Julianne." He turned away. "It has been...very testing, but I think it ends."

I remembered what Julianne had told me, and had not the heart to say more. I left him, my mind filled with yet more questions and answers. Once home I wrote down what I had learned and the conclusions I had drawn on my rounds as clearly as I could. I sanded the pages of closely written black script and folded them into a pocket inside my cloak. I would give them to Malcolm when we met for lunch.

* * *

I was restless, so I decided to work in the garden and was on my knees applying compost when Jocki came running up the path. "Lady Elspeth!" He was shouting, his voice wavering and breaking between the words as young boys do when filled with alarm. "They took Sir Malcolm! We has...have to get im. He were...was tied up...and they hurt him. I saw im. I were hiding an watching! Twas the Captain. They took im aboard the *Silver Fin*! I seen im...We has to hurry!"

His lessons in proper English dissolved in his distress. Putting my hand on his heaving chest, I tried to calm him. "Jocki, are you sure it was Captain Kidd? They are friends. He would not betray Malcolm."

Jocki was frantic. "I tell ye, Lady. Twas im! An...an that other un, Mackmain. Sir Malcolm, he went to meet im...an give me a coin and tool me to go 'ome, but I follered im. Rowed meself out to the ship, I did, in me wee currach. An I seen it all." He was shaking.

"All right, it will be all right. Shhh... Let me think." I needed to change clothes and get my weapons. "This is what I want you to do. Go to the tavern and tell your father I ask his help. He told me I could depend on him after I took care of Leana, so he will come. Tell him I need armed men to help rescue Sir Malcolm from the *Silver Fin*. I will be right behind you, as quickly as I can change into more...umm...useful clothing." I winked at him and he managed a small smile at my comment before he vanished down the path to the village. Within minutes I had tucked my hair inside "Tam Morrison's" dirty cap, and the rest of me into the boys clothing that turned me into him. It hung even looser since my time in Edinburgh. I added a knapsack with medical supplies, and was soon trying to outrun the midges in my race to the village.

MacTavish was waiting behind the tavern, surrounded by a motley crew of unlikely looking saviours. It pleased me to know that Malcolm had such friends here, and that his skills were respected. The men looked dangerous and not one seemed surprised when "Tam" appeared, leading me to conclude that my "Tam" identity was both known and accepted by the people of the village. So much for anonymity. I would sort that later. MacTavish looked at me for orders, but I had none. What I wanted was simple: to rescue Malcolm. MacTavish and his cohorts would know better than I how it should be accomplished. He nodded and turned to the men. They murmured softly among themselves for a moment, then three broke away and faded silently into the darkness. The rest checked their weapons. Most had belaying pins as well as knives. A few had pistols. Within moments three dark wooden boats glided quietly toward us over the water. We divided ourselves among the boats, stepping cautiously over grappling lines in the bottom. I realized that this sort of adventure was not new to most of the men. The large wooden oars dipped soundlessly into the inky water as we pulled away from the docks and toward the ship. No one spoke. Sound carries easily over water. We made it across the open water to the shelter of the *Silver Fin's* hull without raising an alarm. Unless they looked straight down over the side, we were now invisible to those on the ship. The men holding the grappling irons looked at each other, and at some signal I did not see, tossed them in unison over the rails onto the deck and began scrambling up the knotted ropes attached to them. The noise drew running footsteps, but the first of our group had already gained the deck and I could hear steel and wood striking flesh. "Tam's" hat flew off as I pulled myself up to follow, my knife in my teeth so I could grasp the rope easily. It was a scene of absolute bedlam as MacTavish's men struggled with the pirates and first blood spattered the deck, and a few heads. I was trying to slip past the melee to find Malcolm, when I heard a loud incredulous laugh and a familiar voice shouting "Stop! Everyone, stop fighting!" It was Malcolm.

Other voices joined his...and the men reluctantly began to back away from each other. I recognized the voices of Father Hammett and Captain Kidd, with some astonishment. Jocki had just butted Captain Kidd in the belly, and he was looking ruefully down at the boy. "Stop, lad. Tis over." Malcolm put a gentling hand on Jocki's shoulder, and he shuddered once and sat down hard on the wooden planks, his face buried in his hands. Malcolm was still laughing as he assured his rescuers of his wellbeing. Many of the "gentlemen" were friendly with the villagers, and there were some sheepish looks and apologies as things calmed down.

I gave Malcolm a withering glance and began to see to the men. Several had been injured, but none seriously. Jocki picked himself up, stared suspiciously at Captain Kidd, and came to help me. The men from the tavern had acquitted themselves well. The smugglers had more injuries than the villagers. Captain Kidd ordered a barrel of rum tapped, and soon both groups had melded into that strange ritual camaraderie that men enjoy after battles. I saw MacTavish tip his cup to the Captain, who returned the gesture. When I had finished my rounds of those who needed care, Malcolm came quietly to my side and put his cloak around me. I was grateful, since the men had studiously avoided looking at my legs and buttocks immodestly revealed by the pants. I had made them uncomfortable. Malcolm secured the silver clasp of the cloak around my neck, and gently kissed my sweaty forehead. "Thank you, Elspeth." He reached down and ruffled Jocki's hair which caused the boy to redden with pleasure. MacTavish appeared at my side, and with two of his men, rowed me back to the village and saw me safely home. I thanked him profusely, but he just smiled and repeated that he was my man, and would always be. I let Scathach out, stripped off my useless disguise, bathed and fell into bed. It had been a very long day. I did, however, bolt the door.

* * *

The next morning, I was awakened by a soft but insistent knock and a low whine from Scathach who was standing at the door. I wrapped myself in my arisaid and unlocked the door to find Julianne and the babe. She was carrying a small elaborate cask, and looked pale and stricken.

"Julianne? Come in, what has happened? Are you well, the babe?"

"No...no...nothing is wrong. It is just...The Tsar left this." She held up the cask helplessly. "I needed to talk to someone. I don't know what to do." She put the bairn in the basket by the fire, which would soon be too small to hold him, and Scathach settled down next to it in her usual place, nose nuzzling the rim, great paws on either side.

Julianne held out the cask again, folding my hands around it and pushing it toward me as though she wished to rid herself of it. "Look! What shall I do with this?" She sounded confused and frightened. I took the cask and opened it. A folded paper with a broken seal of red wax and ribbon covered its contents. I lifted the letter out and almost dropped both. The small chest was filled with loose gem stones, and small velvet pouches. A fortune in jewels flashed erratically in the morning light. I understood her panic at once. The contents could probably buy a small kingdom.

Everything would have to be assessed and arrangements made for safekeeping. She motioned to the letter. "Read it, Elspeth, please." It was from the Tsar.

I skimmed over the personal parts and concentrated on the portions that affected Julianne and the bairn. The Tsar asked after his son and said that the contents of the chest were to be used to support Julianne and the babe. He would publicly announce their handfasting at an end in Russia. She was now free to marry another. He said that he would always care for her and the bairn, but that he must have an heir that would be accepted by his people, and his first duty was to his country. He wished her well and said that he would ever be at her service if she needed anything. There was nothing about returning, or seeing the bairn again. It was clearly a letter of goodbye colored with the gilt of guilt. I refolded it neatly, placed it back into the cask and closed the lid. A small golden key hung from a silk tassel affixed to the lock. I placed it in the keyhole, turned it, and placed the cask in her lap.

"Julianne, you must think of this as a gift from God. I suggest you talk to Aidan." I smiled at her expression. "I know you care for each other. He is a good man, and has contacts who can help evaluate the contents of the cask. If I were in your place, I would keep the gift secret. Hide the cask or give it to someone to keep for you, and sell but a few of the gems at a time, quietly, as needed. Think about what you want for the babe's future, and for yourself. Wait a few months to get some perspective on all that has happened. Perhaps both of you should see Father Hammett together?

She lifted her eyes from the box in her lap, then ran her hands gently over it, perhaps seeking any remnants of his touch. Her lips parted on a long sighing breath. "Aye. I will go to Aidan."

I stirred up the hearth to warm the kettle. "We will have tea."   I went to my room and dressed. By the time I returned Julianne was holding the bairn again, the cask laid carelessly aside for the real treasure of her babe.

TWENTY-THREE

Malcolm - Drowning

I returned to Edinburgh as quickly as I could, but Mackmain had already delivered the ransom note to Father. He and Archie were having a war council, with Father pacing back and forth behind his desk, grumbling, with Archie fussing attentively.

"He dares threaten us like this? Does he think we are common merchants?" Father threw his quill pen on the desk, spattering ink drops. He was quite livid.

"Father?" I couldn't help but smile.

"Malcolm? My son, is that you?" He squinted at me, eyes glistening. "In the name of all that is Holy! What is this about? I get a warning from your priest, then a ransom note, then you stroll in like naught is amiss."

"Ah, well, I can explain." I took a few steps closer and watched with amusement as Archie unsuccessfully tried to place a wool shawl on him.

"And what about this?" He picked my pony tail off his desk and shook it at me like a talisman.

"Oh that! Father, please come and sit by the fire and I will explain everything. You will be pleased, I assure you." He protested as Archie guided him to his chair and wrapped him in a warm shawl. I was overjoyed to be home with him, and for a change the bearer of good news. Archie brought us tea, and I explained how it was I lost my hair but gained a confession that could convict Mackmain.

"Father, this letter has his confession as witnessed by Father Hammett Robertson, Captain Kidd and several sailors. For obvious reasons, Kidd is reluctant to testify, but I believe the others will do so." I handed the letter to Father and he read it through, then smiled as he reached the end.

"Well done son, a very clever plan indeed."

"To be truthful, it was not my plan, but Captain Kidd's. I was merely the goat...err...bait." I corrected.

"Perhaps, but you showed courage and determination, didn't you?"

"Thank you, Father. Is this enough for the Magistrate?"

"It should be. I will have it in his hands today, then I expect he will issue an order for the arrest of Mackmain, to bring him in for questioning at least. The Magistrate is an honourable man. He will faithfully follow the law."

"I am sure he is, but who will find and arrest him? There are few Town Guards left and many are compromised through association."

"You must leave this to the Magistrate and the Lord Provost. They will decide what to do." Father must have known what I was thinking because he added. "You have done your part, leave the rest to us and return to your work as a physician."

But I couldn't let it go. "Listen, please Father. Mackmain doesn't know I am not captive on the *Silver Fin*, nor does he know he will soon have an arrest order against him. This, right now, is the perfect time to find and capture him, when he is unawares." Archie was standing by after pouring our tea, but I could sense he was listening more closely than usual.

Father thought a moment, then said. "Good point. It will take a few days to issue the order and gather men to find him."

"By then he could be long gone," Archie interjected and we both looked at him in surprise.

"Archie is right, especially once he discovers I am not captive and there will be no ransom. At that point, there will be no reason for him to stay in Edinburgh with an arrest order hanging over his head." I didn't want to leave here without Father's support, but neither did I want Mackmain to avoid justice.

"Malcolm, I don't want you going after Mackmain alone, if that is what you are thinking. He is too dangerous and has resources beyond your understanding."

"Sir William, if I may?" It was Archie again.

"What is it, Archibald?"

"Thank you, sir. I could accompany Sir Malcolm."

"I was thinking the same, Archibald. George is unavailable, re-equipping the regiment. So, it is on you this time."

I know he was being the protective father, but his assumption of my inability to take on Mackmain rankled. Still, I would not be unappreciative. Accepting their offer was the prudent course. "Archie's help will be welcome, Father, and I have others too."

"Archibald. I want you to promise me that if the situation is untenable, you will pull my son out, and Malcolm, I want you to follow Archibald's lead if there is to be conflict. Do you understand?" We both said "Aye". There was no point arguing.

Then Father continued. "And let me remind you two, we want Mackmain alive. We have plans for him."

"Plans?"

"Malcolm, the last thing we need right now during this damned war is a scandal involving a former senior officer of the regiment and Captain of the Town Guards. It would be highly demoralizing."

This came at me sideways. "Father, are you suggesting we set aside justice because of the war?"

"I most certainly am not! Mackmain will receive justice, but perhaps not the kind meted out in times of peace. We must consider the common good."

"I don't understand."

Father sighed heavily. "Oh, alright. I suppose you should know. We have a secret mission that is ideal for him. He is fluent in French, and knows the right people, and if they believe his story, he may gain entry. If Mackmain accepts this mission, it will mean almost certain death for him."

"If he does not?"

"Then almost certain, becomes certain." A grim smile formed briefly on Father's pocked face.

I noticed Archie trying to hold back speaking. "Father, are you saying that if Mackmain accepts this mission, he could escape justice?"

"That is the inducement. If he succeeds and escapes, he will be free, and we will pay a one-way passage to a colony of his choice. If he succeeds and perishes, he will die a lauded hero. If he fails and lives, we will hunt him down and kill him."

"I see." I was greatly conflicted over this, with my heart wanting vengeance and mind able to see the clear benefits of using Mackmain.

"And don't bother asking about the details of the mission, suffice to say that if successful it could bring the war to a quicker conclusion."

"Aye, Father. I will do my best to deliver Mackmain into the hands of the Magistrate."

"That is my wish, now let us accomplish this as a united family." Strangely, he looked at Archie when he said that, but the moment passed quickly and then the three of us went over the ransom note. Father was to leave a letter under the empty flower pot at the front door by the end of the day stating whether he was willing to pay the ransom. We decided Father would agree to pay, but on condition that he see me alive and well. Our objective was to buy time until we could locate Mackmain.

"It's not likely Mackmain will retrieve the letter himself. He'll probably use local boys to grab it and run. We must be equally prepared to track them without being noticed. I have some ideas for that and but a few hours to put them in place."

"Nothing dangerous, Malcolm. Edinburgh is bad enough without street fighting with one such as Mackmain."

"I will be careful. I want this over and done too. Archie, stay with Father for now. I don't need you yet and God knows what Mackmain might try. Can't have Father unprotected through this."

"I've some mates from the regiment that can guard Sir William while we deal with him," Archie suggested.

I looked to Father for approval. "Aye, Archibald, I will pay your friends from the regiment."

"As good as done, sir." Archie bowed with a smile. This seemed to please him for some reason. "Sir Malcolm, just come get me when Mackmain is found and we'll bring him to speedy justice."

"Indeed, we will Archie." I clapped him on the shoulder, but I was concerned about this much zeal coming from a normally taciturn man. Father started preparing the letter for Mackmain and I departed wondering if I was becoming overly suspicious. Archie was a good man to have on our side, and I should be thankful.

* * *

I stopped in to see Mrs. Simpson and Henry, the latter easy enough to find parked by the fire in the kitchen. I pulled up a chair and Henry flopped his big head on my lap for a well-deserved fondle and scratch. I was immersed in my dog grooming when Mrs. Simpson returned from shopping with a chunk of meat wrapped in cloth and a sack of assorted vegetables. She gave a cheery greeting and I noticed with amusement that Henry was much more interested in her food purchases than in my need for him.

I watched as she put everything in the pantry, Henry helping, of course. "I miss you in Torrport, you know."

"Aww, how kind of you to say, Malcolm." She took a cutting board and knife and placed it on the table.

"How are things here?"

Her mind seemed to be elsewhere, and she looked at me as though I'd spoken for the first time. "Alright, I guess."

"You would tell me if there was a problem, wouldn't you?"

"I, I...Och, Malcolm." She suddenly sobbed. "It is Archibald. I don't know what is wrong with him lately."

"What of him?"

"He has been acting strangely...sullen...aloof...more so than usual, I mean. He won't discuss it."

"I see. Has he mentioned someone called Mackmain?"

"Nay, but I do think it has to do with the regiment. Overheard him speaking to some of his old army mates. One said it was time for retribution." She came over and knelt beside me, Henry following close behind, then she took my hand and pressed it to her cheek. "Malcolm, please watch out for Archibald."

I heaved a sigh. "I will Mrs. Simpson, I will. And you can help too, Henry." I patted them both on the head and we all laughed, even Henry, I think, meanwhile I hoped Archie wasn't going to end up being a liability or break her heart.

* * *

It was all too easy to travel around Edinburgh incognito these days. Most men had taken to wearing long cloaks with hoods, scarves wrapped around the face and neck and leather gloves, all to protect against contact with smallpox. I borrowed one of Father's black cloaks and added enough of the rest, so I would not be readily identified. Mrs. Simpson filled my pockets with edibles and I was off, but soon discovered I was overdressed for this surprisingly warm day. Within minutes I'd stowed the scarves and gloves and opened the cloak, and could only wish no one recognized me anytime soon.

Our plan was thus. We would use the messages between Father and Mackmain to locate him, then move in for the capture. First, I needed some inconspicuous boys for tracking. I immediately thought of the ones who'd mugged me a few weeks back. They lived nearby and should be easy enough to find.

I stopped at their alley and leaned against the corner wall to look. There were fewer this time, at least those I could see. I readied my pistol and pushed back my cloak for easy access to sword and dagger. As I entered, there was a whistle, then another in response, and at once all were alerted and watched me intently as I walked toward them.

"Who would like to earn some coin, legally this time?"

I could see the eyes of a few betray others hiding in the shadows. I would not let them get too close. The cute boy with the mop of sandy hair they'd used as lure was there and looking like he wanted to flee. A cocky older boy strode toward me. My right hand went reflexively to my pistol. That stopped him, for now. "I have a job for all of you and it pays well. Interested?"

"We don't betray our mates, and you'll not get your coin back, mister." The voice came from a darkened doorway and when he came forward I could see he was the one who'd held the pistol to my head. This time he was armed only with those threatening dead eyes.

"Hear me out. This has nothing to do with what happened before." I chuckled, to let them know I was not here for revenge.

"Then speak," the boy with dead eyes commanded.

I decided to trust them, at least somewhat. "It is about Mackmain, former Captain of the Town Guards. He's wanted by the Magistrate and we need to find him. Can you help?"

I listened as the boys discussed it. It seems Mackmain wasn't one of their favourites either.

There developed a consensus that it could be fun and profitable, so the boy in charge asked, "How much will ye pay and what do we 'ave to do?"

I explained that we needed a group of boys to follow whoever picked up a letter from under Father's flowerpot. The letter would be taken to Mackmain and I needed his location, and it all had to be done discreetly.

"A silver coin for everyone who helps. Will you do it?" They all nodded eagerly, no doubt imagining what they would do with the silver coin. "One more thing. If anyone has ideas of betraying us, think again. Those who help Mackmain, will be hunted down with him. Understand?" That brought silence. "Will you do this for Scotland and the Queen?"

"Nay, but we will do it for the coin, won't we boys?" There were nods and mutters of agreement and now I knew how to control them.

I was reasonably certain the boys would do their part, but just in case, I needed an alternative. We only had a few days and Mackmain could yet escape if we didn't play this perfectly. The two ways most people used to leave the city were by carriage and by ship through the port at Leith. Father's townhouse was on Forrester's Wynd, a few blocks from Parliament and the Courts, and Mackmain lived not far away on Kinlock's Close, both just off Lawn Market, a major thoroughfare. I needed first to find out if he had a horse and if it looked like he was getting ready to flee.

The city was starting to come back to life, with more vendors and people in the streets and even a few carriages for hire. I didn't much like skulking about, not exactly my style, nor did I want to advertise my presence, just yet. So, I did my best to blend in, stuck to the shadows and avoided conversation. I soon found Mackmain's house, or rather the building where he lived. The ground floor was a bakery with a door on the side leading to a staircase to the upper floors. The building was several stories of Tudor beam and stucco with a typical overhang on the second floor facing the alley.

I pushed open the door and listened. There was little to hear, but the smells of cooking and humanity mingled to make a predictable miasma. Often rich and poor and those in-between, lived in the same building sharing stairs if not floors. The walls of the stairwell and halls were badly stained with soot and unidentified liquid leaks. Usually the apartments were much better maintained than the common areas, but if Mackmain was wealthy from bribes, he certainly wasn't showing it off living here.

I silently made my way up, looking for some sign that Mackmain made his lair here. On the third floor, an old highland woman, wrapped in frayed tartan, was rocking and knitting by the hall window at the far end. She called to me. *"Sir, if ye ur lookin' fur Captain Mackmain. He is awa'."*

I didn't come closer and continued to obscure my face. "I have something for him. Do you know when he'll be back?"

"*Nay. he jist said he'd be awa' fur a while an' tae keep an yak it.*"

"Did he take his horse?"

Her wheezy laugh was followed by some coughs, then she said, "*Nowhaur tae pit a cuddie in th' city, is thaur?*"

"I suppose not." I responded carefully. So, he didn't have a horse. That narrowed it down. If he was going to leave Edinburgh, it would likely be by carriage or ship and I needed both watched.

I nodded to her. "Thank you, lady."

"*When th' Captain returns, fa shaa Ah say was lookin' fur heem?*" She'd put down her knitting and was leaning forward.

"Tell him if he needs a berth, to see me at the Sand Bar Pub in Leith in two days."

The old woman chuckled. "*Ach, Ah kent he was gettin' ready tae lae.*"

It was good to know he was preparing to leave. I waved to her and left, planning my next stop, the stagecoach to Glasgow that ran three times a week from the coaching inn. It was a combination of stable and inn that featured the worst aspects of both, including the smell of manure never far from the dining room, at no extra charge. Nonetheless it was full of patrons trying to get to and from the cities and points in between. I'd treated the stable–boy's sister and sought him out. He was lounging on a barrel smoking a pipe. "How's your family?" I asked.

"We'll bide, doctor." He blew out a large cloud of smoke and tamped his pipe.

"And your sister? Is her smallpox waning?"

"*Och, she is a terrible secht, but th' pocks ur startin' tae slag aff.*"

"Then as long as the fever doesn't return, she's in the clear."

"*Ah expect sae, doctor. Noo if thaur is naethin' further, Ah main water th' horses.*"

"There is one thing, before you go. We are looking for a man called Mackmain. He is wanted by the Magistrate and may try to leave the city on the stagecoach."

He tapped his pipe on his boot, then smiled. "*Ah ken Mackmain. He is a huir uv a bad cheil.*"

"He is a bad one indeed. If you see him, let me know right away, and there will be a coin in it for you."

"*Ah willnae tak' yer coin doctor. Ye saved mah sister.*"

"Then we'll be even." I tipped my hat to the young highlander.

* * *

Thankfully, the carriages were running again to Leith and I arrived at the Sand Bar Pub in time for a hearty meat pie and ale lunch and a chance to consult the pub owner, Calum Duncan. Leith had taken the brunt of the damage from the smallpox epidemic, and the few businesses still functioning were struggling. The pub was nearly empty, and it was lunch.

"Doctor Forrester, good to see you, but I hope you're not here with more unpleasant news."

I chuckled. "This time the news is good. The smallpox is burning itself out and people are starting to return to Edinburgh."

"Aye, I have noticed a few ships landing this week, and they say more to follow."

Calum joined me at the booth near the counter, then shouted to the girl. "The good doctor will have the usual, on the house."

I smiled. "I will pay for the pie and ale, Calum, but I do have a favour to ask."

"That being?"

I told him all about Mackmain, that he might try to book passage on a ship, and could he put out the word around the docks, so forth.

"I will, doctor. We don't need men like that, do we?"

"He'll be brought to justice," I said confidently.

Epidemics, famines and wars change how we see the world. We end up craving peace, security and good government, and have little patience for those who offer the antithesis. But when times are good, we are drawn to adventure and risk, and laugh at the exploits of bad men like Mackmain. Humans are a perverse lot, but right now, Mackmain was completely out of step with the times.

I enjoyed my lunch and Calum's company, assured that Mackmain would be spotted if he tried to leave Edinburgh. What we could do about it was another question, but I headed back to the city feeling I'd done all I could for now and the next step was Mackmain's.

* * *

The hypnotic rumble of the carriage wheels had almost put me to sleep by the time I got back. It was mid-afternoon, and it wasn't likely Mackmain or his messenger would retrieve the letter until the concealing darkness of night, so I decided to drop by McLaren's infirmary on my way home. The sunshine was beating down full-force and I was drenched in sweat by the time I crossed the infirmary threshold into its welcoming shade and cool. I was greeted not by the chaos of the past weeks, but by the pleasant scene of a bard playing his harp and reciting rhymes of better times, an appreciated diversion for the few remaining smallpox patients. McLaren was treating someone, so I had a chance to speak privately with Gwen, for the first time...since. I well-remembered the beauty of her former self, and to be honest she was looking dreadful, but I could tell by her demeanor that she was on the mend.

306

"Malcolm, I am glad you've come. I have news!" A spark of her old radiant smile flashed across her face.

I hugged her gently and whispered, "Wonderful to see you are doing so well. Now tell me your news."

"Angus has proposed we marry, and I have accepted!" She giggled. "Is that not wild!"

I was hoping something would happen, but honestly, I was astonished. It had only been days. "That's wonderful, Gwen! Congratulations to you both. You'll not find a finer man in all of Scotland." I blathered, but truly wished them well. The resiliency of the human spirit never ceases to amaze.

"I am very happy, despite my current situation." She grimaced. "I am well-aware of how ugly I am. But dear Angus loves me as I am, and I love him too. That is enough, isn't it?"

"Love is all that's important in this world, and I'm certain Angus will treasure you. Be faithful and surround him with love and he'll be the best of husbands."

"I know, Malcolm, and I am glad I have your approval. It means more than you know, and I have more news."

"More?"

"Yes, more. It is Mackmain. He is up to something again. My sources say he is going to come into a lot of money soon and intends to leave Edinburgh."

I wasn't sure how much I should share with Gwen. The situation was in flux and I didn't want information getting out, just yet. "That is very interesting. Well I hope we've seen the last of him, if that's true. I'm trying to avoid all that for now, so please don't tell anyone I'm in Edinburgh."

"I understand, Malcolm. Well, I don't really. At this point, I don't care about the past or Mackmain. He and his friends can go to hell, as far as I am concerned." That last part was uttered with such venom in her voice that I knew she still did care about the past, and it made me even more determined to bring this affair to a proper end.

"Keep her away from Mackmain!" McLaren had found us. "She might kill him, and I don't want his death on her hands." He was grinning, but I knew he was dead serious.

"I have no doubt of what she is capable!" We all laughed, then Angus and I embraced, and I offered congratulations along with a quip about babies on the way. I noticed them exchange furtive glances, then Gwen blushed. I was delighted.

* * *

The walk home gave me time to review our preparations. I wanted my life back and Mackmain out of it, and with some luck both could be accomplished within a few days.

As I rounded the corner to Forrester's Wynd, I was surprised to see the boys sitting on the front step. It was far too early.

"What is it?" I asked the older boy who rose to meet me.

"We've completed our task an want to be paid, sir," he said seriously.

I looked at the four of them, then back to the older boy. "You'll receive your coin, but first tell me what happened and where Mackmain went?"

The older boy explained that the letter was taken late afternoon by a boy they knew, who delivered it to Mackmain, but a few blocks away near the Parliament. The boy waited while Mackmain read the letter, then gave the boy another letter. Then they split up. The boy brought the second letter back here and Mackmain walked to the carriage that goes to the port at Leith.

I thought a moment. "Did you see him get on the carriage to Leith?"

The older boy turned to one of the others who nodded and said, "Aye, he did."

"Are you sure no one saw you following?"

"We're careful and knows the ways hereabouts, sir."

"You've done well, then." I opened my pouch and gave each one a silver coin.

"If Mackmain is captured, come back and I'll give you another coin, but if there's been any treachery on your part..." I scowled at them. They understood.

Henry was bouncing around at the entrance, sensing a hunt was about to start, his ancient blood responding instinctively. Behind him, Mrs. Simpson stood wringing her hands and looking distraught. "I...I've never seen Archie like this. Malcolm, please don't go. Let Mackmain go. Tis not worth the risking of you both."

I patted her shoulder on the way by. "This is men's work. Make us some food and drink to take." I was brusque but had no time for anything but the task at hand. Archie and Father were in the study, both armed and ready for war. Father was all in black, with sword and pistols and angry pocked face looking more like an evil pirate than a Scottish Lord.

"We'll take the fight to them...That damned Mackmain! Never liked him." Father was gripping the handle of his sword, ready to draw and slash.

"Father, what did Mackmain's letter say?"

"Read it yourself!" He reached over and slid it across the desk. It was brief and to the point, like the last one. It said to meet at the second-to-last stone warehouse at the main docks at Leith at four-o-clock in the morning. Come alone with the coin to get your son.

I looked up at Archie. "We'll go. Are you ready and are your friends coming to guard Father?

"Aye, I be ready, and they should be here soon," he said with a fierce tone.

Father interrupted. "I am in no need of a guard. I will lead this attack. Archibald, you are my second and you must protect my son."

I sighed inwardly. I suspected this might happen. "Father, you are in no condition for battle. You are still weakened by smallpox. Archie and I will handle this." I hoped he could see the common sense of it. He looked formidable but in his weakened state, he would be nothing but a liability. Of course, I couldn't tell him that.

His face looked ready to explode. "I am not useless! God damn it!"

I could feel his frustration. It is not easy to let go. "Father, we need you here to work with the Magistrate. Make sure the order for his arrest is made. There may be others in the Town Guard involved too. This work needs you here. Archie and I can deal with Mackmain. Please, Father."

He folded his arms, glaring at me, not wanting to give in and appear weak, so I appealed to Archie. "What do you think? Can we take Mackmain, the two of us?"

Archie stood at attention. He may not say much, but I knew Father trusted his opinion. "Mackmain is cunning as a fox, but he's few supporters now. If he's alone or with a few, we can take him, unless he knows Sir Malcolm is free and has set a trap."

"Then it may be best to wait and gather a force to attack," Father mused.

"He likely will be gone by then. It will be for naught," I countered, and Archie nodded in agreement.

"If I may, sir?"

"Go ahead, Archibald," Father said impatiently.

"If we go early and hide in the warehouse, we can read the situation and act as best befits. If we can take him, we will, if not..." Archie shrugged, but I had the feeling there was much more on his mind than he was saying.

"I fully agree with Archie. We'll bring Mackmain in if we can." We both waited for father's blessing.

"Archie, bring my son home alive." It was decided.

* * *

We found the warehouse and a good place to conceal ourselves to wait. There'd been no carriages running and it had been a long walk loaded down with weapons and provisions. On the way, we'd stopped by the Sand Bar Pub to see if there were any reports of Mackmain and his men. There'd been naught but a rumour of someone prominent seeking a berth on the next ship out. This from a friend of the port master. On that basis, we decided to pay the port master's office a visit. It was close to midnight and few were about.

"Can you force the door, Archie," I whispered.

"Nay, don't have to, it's open." We walked right in.

"Then the log book should be over here." I'd remembered from my previous visit.

Archie lit a small torch as I fumbled for the black book on the desk. We both leaned close. It was a ledger of ship and captain's names along with arrival and departure dates and cargo. It was already open, and it was apparent there were few ships in port. Only one due to leave this morning. The *Chantilly*, bound for Amsterdam.

"Well, I'll be damned!" I blurted, and Archie gave me a questioning look.

"Same ship that brought smallpox," I whispered.

"Is there a connection?"

"Likely not. Just odd, is all."

"At least now we know where to look if we lose Mackmain."

"We have what we need. Let's find the warehouse and get in place before Mackmain arrives."

* * *

Our discovery at the port master's office had been a few hours ago and we'd taken turns napping, eating, and observing, with only the night watchman coming by on the dock every hour to relieve the boredom. The warehouse itself was mostly empty, with crates stacked on one side and bales on the other. From the smells, the crates contained salt fish and the bales raw wool. Combined with the pervasive odour of rotting jetsam, it was not a pleasant place to linger. There were two double doors facing the dock and an open hatch in the floor between them, near the front. The hatch had a wooden crane and metal winch with pulleys and ropes to haul cargo up and down from waiting boats below. There was just enough light from the dock lanterns outside for us to see it all dimly, once our eyes adapted.

I reckoned it was getting on three now. No sign of Mackmain and I was starting to cramp, crouching too long on the wood floor. I could see Archie shifting from one leg to the other and noticed a grimace as he did so. Our plan was to wait until Mackmain and his group arrived. If there were too many, we would bolt for the door. If we could, we would confront them, with Archie preventing escape and me attacking Mackmain. We'd jammed the far doors, to make it difficult to escape. The only easy way in or out was the double doors on our side of the warehouse. The confrontation would be fast and brutal with surprise giving us the edge.

I leaned close to Archie and whispered, "Ready?"

He grunted, and I took that as an affirmative.

This close I could see the outline of his face. It looked cruel, grim, and I thought back to his eagerness to take on Mackmain and wondered if there was a reason beyond wanting to serve Father. There was no time for introspection, I just wanted this over quickly and again rehearsed the steps once they arrived and hoped it would go as planned.

Then I heard a hushed voice from outside, then another responding. Neither were Mackmain, then a creak of the door opening slowly and light from a torch entering before them.

"Take your position on either side, boys. I'll stand back here by the winch."

That was unmistakably Mackmain's voice!

I peered out between the bales. There were two men and Mackmain. The men had torches. All three were wearing heavy dark cloaks and were well armed. We could do this. I poked Archie and nodded. He nodded back. We'd agree that as soon as they closed the door, we would attack. We waited, with shallow deep breaths, trying not to make a sound.

"We can make our escape down there. I see the boat is ready." Mackmain was looking down the hatch, his sword already out, as one of his men took up position and the other started closing the door.

"Keep it open a crack, John. If you see Forrester coming with men, whistle and we'll leave."

That was his plan then. He'd rob Father if he could and make his escape to the *Chantilly* under cover of darkness using the rowboat beneath the warehouse. Very clever indeed.

The creaking of the door closing stopped. It was time. We were but a few feet from them. I rose and drew my cutlass and dagger. Mackmain looked up, startled.

"Waiting for someone?" I asked then threw myself on Mackmain getting in a good slash that caught him on his sword arm. Then he almost stabbed me with an unexpected dagger thrust from his other hand.

We were eye to eye now and his fleeting look of astonishment quickly transformed to hatred. "You again! You are going to die this time, boy." He growled then slashed viciously with his cutlass.

Out of the corner of my eye I could see that Archie had quickly disabled one of the men by the door and was hacking at the other. The second man was putting up a better defense having dropped his torch and pulled a pistol and sword. I'd easily warded off the cutlass strike and Mackmain and I were dancing around the hatch and crane rigging, each trying for advantage. I grabbed the rope and pulley and swung it at him, ready to slash him as he jumped out of the way. Instead, he leapt across the hatch at me, gouging my forearm with his dagger. The pain stung, and I swore and pushed him back and he almost toppled down the hatch, and in that half-second of imbalance when his arms were open, I charged and knocked the cutlass out of his hand. It was all but over now.

Then there was a booming crack from a pistol and I turned to look. Archie appeared to be hit, and his assailant was coming for the kill. I yelled, "Archie, look out!" then flung my dagger at the man, clipping him on the side of the face. I turned back to Mackmain just in time to prevent a dagger thrust to my gut by grabbing his hand by the wrist. We were nose-to-nose now, and all I could do was pound Mackmain on the side of the head with the butt of my cutlass as his free hand was trying to push me back. He looked stunned, so I dropped my cutlass and grabbed his other wrist to subdue him. He was very strong. I looked in his fierce eyes as I did weeks ago in the Guard House and was overcome by that intense feeling of hatred again. I wailed, then bashed my forehead into his face, once then again and again. He was screaming in agony, my strength seemed to increase as I pounded him, blood gushing from us both as we grappled precariously beside the open hatch. Then I pulled to one side and tripped him, and we tumbled to the floor.

"I have you now, you bastard!" I was on top of him pinning his wrists. Then I heard a loud moan, and fearing the worst glanced up to see Archie covered in blood and standing over the man who was writhing on the floor with Archie's sword embedded in his gut. Archie pulled his pistol and came rapidly toward us.

"I have him Archie," I gasped, almost out of breath. Archie didn't stop. Instead he raised his pistol and pointed it toward us. "No, Archie. It's done!" I let go of Mackmain's wrist nearest Archie and raised my arm to stop him. He had that look about him I'd seen once before, when he'd shot that man in the back in front of McLaren's infirmary, that look of a cold-blooded executioner.

"Nay. It is not done, but it will be now!" he said all too calmly, then I saw his finger tighten on the trigger. Mackmain must have seen it too because he grunted and pushed me off and tried to roll away. The blast was blinding, and I felt Mackmain lurch and slide into the open hatch with me still hanging on, one hand gripping his wrist. I couldn't let go. Not now, not when I'd finally beaten him.

Mackmain pulled me down after him and were locked together pirouetting in mid air. I hit the boat first, the back of my head clipping something hard, then the full weight of Mackmain slammed into me. He tried to get off. I was only part way in the boat, dazed and gasping, but still hanging on to him. He punched me once or more and was trying to break free. I had to get out of range or it would be over soon, so I grabbed the front of his cloak with my free hand and pulled him toward me; but that tilted the boat and we instantly rolled into the water.

It was a frightening shock, all cold, dark, disorienting. I'd automatically held my breath before we'd submerged, but it was not enough. I knew I only had seconds, so I released the hold on his cloak, tried to reach for the boat. Nothing. He was jerking his arm trying to break free, but I would not let go.

My lungs were searing, my free arm thrashing, trying to find a hold. I thought, is this how it would end, my life forfeit, because I wouldn't let go? Will Father think me the fool or the hero? I knew I didn't want to die, not because of this arsehole, anyway. I had to let go of Mackmain, and of my hatred that had lead me to the brink and over. I tried to release my grip, but my hand was seized stiff on his wrist. I panicked and yanked wildly and forced it off. I was free, but near breaking point now. I looked up for the surface, arms flailing to rise, but my cloak was like a sea anchor holding me in place. I thought I saw a glimmer of light, or was it imagined? Then I felt a kick, or something strike my upraised arm. Was it Mackmain? Was he safe and I the one to die instead? I felt near the surface. I had to take a breath and end the agony. This must be the surface, surely. It must be safe to take a breath now. I open my mouth and gasped. My lungs filled...with water. Mother forgive me. In seconds, all went black.

TWENTY-FOUR

Elspeth - Resolution

Scathach lifted her massive head, ears pricked, gold eyes turned to the door. She stood, padded over, and quietly placed herself before it. Friends then. I had heard nothing, but we were going to have guests. There was no knock. The door simply opened none too gently, and Janet and Cawdie swept into the room bringing a draught of cool air and the unmistakable aura of perfect pleasure. She glowed like a beacon and he exuded masculine satisfaction. I found myself pulled into Janet's arms and crushed to breathlessness, Cawdie, as usual, standing back, alert behind his deliberately bovine face. He did reach down to stroke Scathach, who pressed herself against both in welcome, the sweep of her tail endangering everything within its reach. Of course, the bairn was in Janet's arms within moments. Julianne surrendered him with a smile. Janet lifted him to Cawdie who touched the babe's face with a huge finger, and flicked a look at Janet that caused her to color most becomingly. Everyone was laughing and speaking at once...and the din was welcome. The cottage had been too quiet. Things settled, and we began to weave ourselves into each other's lives again. Janet asked about the Tsar, and Julianne told her he had returned to Russia.

Cawdie left us to our chatter. After he had been away from home, he had a habit I found endearing. I had first seen him do it in Skye. He would take a beaker of ale, and walk around to make certain everything was as he had last seen it. It was his touchstone. Even small changes were noted. The cask of jewels lay in his path where Julianne had left it earlier, his gaze lingered on it several moments before he moved on. I could sense the questions in his mind. Julianne could explain it. Perhaps he and Janet would have some practical ideas about what to do with the contents.

Janet held the bairn and babbled to him in that private language women and babes speak. Unexpectedly she handed him to me, clasped her hands in her lap, and said softly, "Elspeth, I wish to handfast with Cawdie." She hurriedly added, "Nothing will change. Everything will stay as it is. In Edinburgh, I nearly lost him. I want to be with him, Elspeth, while we can. You are not to worry. We will take care of everything. All we ask is your blessing."

"Oh, Janet." Tears filled my eyes. "Of course, you have my blessing, and anything else I can give you! I am so pleased and happy for you both. Malcolm told me this would happen." I looked at Julianne who was crying too. Women do that at the mention of handfasting...and all three of us began talking at once. Cawdie fled. The coward. Malcolm and I had to meet with the Laird, so I told Julianne to tell Janet and Cawdie about the Tsar's gift, embraced Janet again. and slipped away.

✳ ✳ ✳

Malcolm met me in the vendor's alley near the castle. We needed to discuss what we wanted to say or accomplish. I had made a fair copy of the report, and planned to give it to the Laird, without comment. He could read it, make of it what he would, then ask questions. Malcolm was not convinced that was the best way, so I told him to do as he felt best. He would, anyway. At the castle, we were shown immediately to the Laird's chamber. Malcolm walked ahead of me with that arrogant and assured swagger he had. I followed meekly enough behind him, half fearing we would both be tossed out as soon as the Laird read the report. We found him at his desk. When he saw us, he closed the ledger he was working on, pushed it to one side, and ordered his steward to leave.

"Come in you two."

I took a deep breath, stepped from behind Malcolm's reassuring bulk and diffidently placed the copy of our report in front of him.

"You asked us to prepare a report about the death of Sir Spence. Tis here, with the list of suspects and our conclusions."

Malcolm interrupted. "I think it might be best addressed if we go over it with you, sir." He removed his own copy of the account from an inner pocket of his jacket and consulted it. Laird MacDuff leaned back in his chair and waited, his fingers beating a tattoo on the satiny surface of the desk.

Malcolm referred to the page in his hand. "This is what we know. We were called to the laundry by one Aggie Scrogie, Torrport laundress, daughter of the local tavern keeper. When questioned, she said she had come to start the fires for her laundry at about seven in the morning. She found the victim kneeling over one of the wash tubs that was filled with bluing, his face submerged. According to her account, she pulled him out, realized that he was not breathing and began to scream. Her mother, roused by the cries, sent her for Lady Elspeth, who returned to the laundry with her but was unable to revive the man. He was identified as John Spence, your Second in Command. Lady Elspeth sent for me immediately and we examined the body. He had been dead for several hours. Rigor mortis had set in, and his body retained the kneeling position in which he had been found. His head and collar were wet. The rest of his clothing dry. There were bruises and signs of injury on his face and neck and post mortem lividity on his face, forehead and lower legs, consistent with the death. There were no obvious fatal wounds. He may have been drowned or killed before being deliberately arranged at the tub. There was coin in his belt, and he wore two rings. We found no sign of the silver pistols he always carried. They may have been stolen."

Malcolm paused. The Laird regarded us irritably, tapping the point of his quill pen on the desk. It would have to be re-sharpened.

"May we sit?" The Laird sighed with resignation. "Forgive my lack of courtesy. Please, do so." Malcolm moved two chairs nearer the desk and we sat.

He continued. "We sent for you. You asked us to investigate. On your authority, we performed an autopsy and determined that death had resulted from strangulation. There was no water in the lungs, no other internal injuries to the body. He had blood and scrapings of flesh beneath his nails, so his murderer likely was marked. We also found the remains of a ball of soap in his mouth. It had to have been deliberately placed there after his death by his murderer or murderers."

Malcolm looked down at the paper again and cleared his throat. "There are witnesses. The wool merchant, James Allen, told us that he was awake and heard angry voices coming from beside the tavern. He thinks there were two, perhaps three. One was Spence. The other may have been a woman. There was some shouting.

"Did he see anyone?" the Laird interrupted and leaned forward, pinning Malcolm with hard eyes.

"Not then. He says he saw shadows thrown by the torches, but nothing recognisable. His window looks down into the alley, not the tavern yard, so shadows and sounds are all that he was able to see and hear from there. But it piqued his curiosity, so he went to the side door and cracked it open a bit to get a better look. He saw a figure running toward the castle. It was cloaked so he did not see the face, but he had the impression it was slight, and could have been either a man or woman.

The Laird laid back in his chair. "Go on."

"No one else admits seeing anything, but the mercer also heard an altercation. He has a fondness for the drink, and his wife had banished him from her bed. He was sleeping in his small stand behind the warehouse, rolled in woolens on a pallet under a table. It is known he often does so when he and his goodwife are at odds. He said voices awakened him, followed by the sound of blows, and scuffling. Fearing to get involved, he pulled more cloth over himself and sought to remain unseen. There were more furious words, then silence."

The Laird looked at them. "That's all you have? A man who saw shadows and heard men talking, and one drunken sot that cowered beneath his wares and merely heard voices?"

I bit my lip, and let Malcolm deal with the scepticism. My stomach tumbled to my feet. The Laird was not the least interested in hearing what we had to say. Malcolm continued as though the Laird had not spoken. "Moreover, the mercer picked up fragments of gold leaf in the alley, which he gave to Lady Elspeth. He said they fell from the running figure which in his drunken state, he thought was a fairy. Gold leaf is not common in Torrport, but several residents and craftsmen use it. Elspeth discovered that the local supplier was Aidan Buchanan, the blacksmith. Aidan gave her a list of those who had purchased it from him and she questioned each one. We have a prepared a list of possible suspects for you, based on relevant factors."

Malcolm looked up, studied the Laird with a small frown and went on. "It could have been much longer if we included all who wished him ill. Your Second was not much favored. According to those who knew him, he could be paid to turn a blind eye to questionable cargo or activities. He was suspected of cheating at cards, liked the drink and women too much and became brutal when drunk or angered. Many we questioned had reason to wish him ill and were not unhappy about his demise.

The first suspect Elspeth interviewed was the Torrport frame-maker Jean-Bernard Barbier. Apparently your Second went to him to have a gift made for his latest convenient. Spence felt his exalted patronage entitled him make free with the frame maker's goodwife. Barbier took great exception to his pretensions and refused to serve him. That and the gold leaf were clues pointing to the frame-maker. He is certainly large and strong enough to have killed Spence, but we do not feel that the insult to his goodwife was enough motivation. Harriet Barbier is a very beautiful woman and I am sure the frame-maker has dealt with unwanted admiration of her before. Spence was simply another conceited customer. Harriet Barbier swore that her husband had not left the house on the night of the murder, but that would be expected in any case. They are known as quiet hard-working people not given to causing trouble."

He moved on. "Gilly Fletcher. It is common knowledge that she was Spence's favorite and that he was not happy when she became pregnant. When she rebuffed his public groping at the tavern, he beat her so badly she lost the babe. I doubt if she wanted it, but his treatment of her may have warranted retaliation. As a woman, she might not be able to do it personally, but she had many friends in the fishing village, and there were those who would not have hesitated to help her rid the world of Spence. She might well have had a part in the murder. She was working the night of the murder, and saw Spence go upstairs with a new lass at the tavern. She said he had on his pistols then. However, my Laird, you have dismissed Gilly previously, as an unlikely suspect, and there does not appear to be a connection with the gold leaf found by the mercer. We defer to your opinion.

Aidan Buchanan is our next suspect. Aidan beats gold to make gold leaf, so would logically have fragments of it on his clothing; however, he is far to large to have been the one seen by the wool merchant and mercer. As far as we know, Aidan had no reason to harm Spence, although he would certainly be able to physically do so, and Aidan has an alibi. Daniel Gow, his assistant, says they were tending a sick horse together that night.

Malcolm turned the page. "Sir Ross Campbell."

At this, the Laird straightened. "Sir Ross? Are you both quite mad?"

I found my voice. "Sir Ross is on our list because of his purchase of gold leaf which he uses as both affectation and medication. He and Gregor often worked with Spence on...projects of mutual interest." I stole a look at Malcolm, remembering our night in the cave. Should I have mentioned that?

The Laird gritted out. "What possible motive can you ascribe to Sir Ross? He certainly knew Spence, but only as my agent on occasion. Ross is a friend and has been quite helpful in my dealings with... some of our...visitors and the Tsar. I fear you have both lost sight of your purpose and are chasing chimeras."

Malcolm retorted. "Perhaps, but Elspeth suspects that his shipping activities include smuggling a bit more than exotic goods. She thinks it's quite possible that he's receiving and dispatching messages from France via some of his passengers and the small French fashion dolls he collects with some regularity. Ross says that he and Gregor did not leave the house on the night of the murder, but that could be questioned. It is true that there is no discernable motive unless Spence cheated him in some fashion. Still, something is awry there, and if he is passing information to the French, that is treason. However-much we suspect there may be motive, it is unlikely Ross was the one who strangled Spence. He has been ill lately, and would probably not have had the strength to over-power Spence, unless there is something we have missed." MacDuff glared at us and clamped his lips together.

Malcolm looked down again. "Rachel Espy, Spence's wife, is of interest. She had more than enough motive to want him dead. It was humiliating to have him cheating on her so blatantly at every opportunity. Gilly was his convenient and not adverse to bragging about it." He paused. "Elspeth suspects that Rachel poisoned Julianne."

"God's Bones!" the Laird exploded. "Are ye daft? Rachel has no reason to want Lady Julianne dead!"

I found my tongue again and answered him. "Not that we are aware of, sir. Perhaps jealousy? But she had opportunity. I believe she gave Lady Julianne marchpane that had been mixed with arsenic when she visited Lady Margaret on the eve she delivered the babe. Twas the only thing Julianne remembers eating that they did not share. Neither Lady Margaret nor Rachel like marchpane, although Rachel commonly makes it for the castle kitchen and uses gold leaf to decorate it! I am aware that Rachel could not have killed Spence by herself, but, like Gilly, she could have easily hired an assassin. The fishing village is filled with those who would take a life for pay without a qualm. During the autopsy, we found remnants of a scented soap ball in his mouth. I identified the soap ball as one that Rachel helps Lady Margaret make. It was placed in his mouth quite deliberately, after he was dead, viciously and with purpose to my mind, a woman's trick. Mayhap the soap was a comment on his lies? Who can say? But she had access to the gold leaf and the soap. I believe the "youth's" voice that both the wool merchant and the mercer heard was that of Rachel, arguing with her husband. I also believe it was Rachel that was seen running past the wool merchant and mercer on her way back to the castle, and that she may have inadvertently dropped a flake of gold leaf. She lives here at the castle, and could easily have slipped out without anyone knowing."

The Laird looked at Malcolm. "Malcolm, do you believe this whiffle-waffle"? He sounded hard-pressed.

"I am keeping an open mind, sir." Malcolm started again. "Gregor Volkof is the last name on the list. He knew Spence in Russia. As Sir Ross's servant, he worked closely with Spence in Torrport and in the fishing village. Elspeth and I have reason to know they both associated with the *gentlemen*, as they are sometimes called, or more precisely *smugglers*, and had a mutual dislike and distrust of each other." He glanced at the Laird, who was staring fixedly at him.

"When Elspeth was called to treat Gregor for the pox, he was feverish, raving about killing someone. At that time, she saw scratches on his arms that could have been made by Spence's struggles to free himself. We can see no apparent motive for him to kill Spence unless Rachel enlisted his help and paid him. There also is the common link of Russia between Lady Julianne, Gregor and Spence, although we do not know if that is relevant. Despite that, based on the autopsy, evidence found at the scene of the murder, eye-witness accounts, and interviews, we believe Spence likely was killed by Sir Ross's man, Gregor, most probably at the behest of Rachel, but possibly on orders from his employer, Sir Ross." Malcolm looked up at the Laird expectantly.

"Hold, the both of you!" Laird MacDuff leaned back, held up his hand and exchanged one of those expressions men use with each other, then exhaled slowly. "I should have expected this. I underestimated you. The report is well done. My congratulations. And you are right about Gregor, if not about everything." He shifted uneasily in his chair. "But I cannot, more rather, will not, use your report." He stood up and began to pace. I sat dumbly, too shocked to respond. "Your findings are correct on most points, and indeed, had you come to me yesterday morn, I might have moved on your conclusions, with perhaps undesired results. But, sometime after noon, a shipment belonging to Sir Ross arrived, bringing a package for Julianne and a letter for me, from the Tsar. The tidings it brought cast a whole new light on what has been happening here, and the murder." He stopped, frowning, then resumed. "It seems that our Spence was in the hire of the Tsar's sister, Sophia, who has several times attempted to overthrow him. Despite being confined to a cell in the Novodevichy Convent, she has support among the old Russian guard who seek to reinstate her, and a long reach extended further by gold. I was told she has come very close to killing the Tsar twice. So, he fears her with good cause. When Julianne found herself with child, Sophia thought that if the babe was a son, he could be a danger to her plans. So, she plotted to have Julianne assassinated. That attempt was foiled but made it obvious that Julianne could not safely remain in Russia. The Tsar sent her here, but..." He paused again. "...but knowing Sophia, he also sent three people to guard her. Sir Ross, Gregor, and Aidan."

I was dazed. "But what about Sir Spence? He was your man."

MacDuff grimaced. "I believed he was. He came to me with a tale of recuperating after being injured in Russia, and brought a letter from one of his commanding officers. I took it as truth. I needed well trained men, and he was that. He made a place for himself here, and as you know, my wife's servant handfasted with him. Spence was good at what he did, and excellent at training the men. He was invaluable to me and my interest in providing...discreet transportation...for certain travelers and cargos. Unfortunately, he also had a weakness for women and the drink."

Laird MacDuff studied us. "But it turns out he was a hired assassin, sent here specifically to rid Sophia of the threat she fancied she saw in Julianne and the babe. Julianne was no more than his latest assignment. You know well she almost died and very nearly lost her bairn. Indeed, at the time I thought she had, and felt twas for the best. Then she told me the babe was alive, and that set the cat among the pigeons!" He stopped pacing and stood in front of us. "The Tsar told me in his letter that he ordered Sir Ross to have Spence killed, before he could try again to kill Julianne and the babe. I am sure Spence was the one who poisoned her when she was here."

So, it was not Rachel who had hired Gregor, but the Tsar, through Ross. I had been so certain. I still did not see how Spence could have poisoned Julianne, but I was clearly in error. What could I say to that? Where lay right and wrong? I looked at Malcolm. He brushed an invisible speck of dirt from his breeches and spoke quietly. "I see your problem, sir. And what of Sir Ross?"

The Laird grunted. "He has friends in high places, in many countries. A net he spreads wide and to good effect. There are those who find his services valuable beyond all things. He is, therefore, quite literally, untouchable. Not that I would blame him for Spence's murder." His face was hard. "I would have done it myself had I known. Therefore, I cannot, and will not, arrest him or his servant."

Malcolm nodded. "Understood." He looked at me. "Elspeth?"

I struggled to make my thoughts fit this new reality.

"I think," MacDuff said gently, "too much is at stake here to let the death of one murderer by another become important. Sir Ross has assured me that he takes full responsibility for Spence's demise and will deal with any repercussions. Spence's wife, Rachel, will be cared for. Margaret is attached to her, and needs her more than ever now. As for Julianne, the Tsar told me he has made it known in Russia that he has released her from their handfasting. He hopes that Sofia will think that means he has no intention of ever recognising his son, but he will make certain that Julianne will always be protected, nevertheless. Aidan will continue to guard her and the bairn. That is all I can say. Spence's death will be listed as death by misadventure." He picked up our report, hesitated fleetingly, and consigned it to the hungry flames in the fireplace before turning back to us.

"Give me your copies." We did, and they followed his into the fire.

"I hope that you will accept that this is how it must be."

We had little choice, and left quietly.

* * *

With the Laird's *solution* of the murder, there was no longer any reason to delay my return to Skye. The MacLeod was unhappy enough with me. After some rumblings in Skye about my "unnatural powers", he wanted me where he could protect me. Witchcraft is a crime punishable by death, although the trials were no longer under the jurisdiction of the Church, but the ordinary courts. There had been few trials for witchcraft in the highlands, but Mull and Renfrew were close enough to cause concern. Accusations were taken seriously. The fates of Janet Cornfoot and Thomas Brown, accused by a malicious teenaged boy, were proof of that. The fear for our good name and my personal safety was the reason the MacLeod gave me, but he also brought me a letter from my Aunt Rhona. I am sure he knew its contents, even though the seal had not been broken. Her words cut through me like a knife in my belly. She said she had something that I needed to see, and that it was possible my sister, Erika, still lived! How could that be? I closed my eyes and relived the memory of the last time I had seen her. They had called me, saying she was dying. She lay ravaged with smallpox, no longer possessed of the beauty I had selfishly envied her, the pustules so thick they often touched, and the purple blue eyes swollen shut. She was lost in a deep unmoving coma. I too was ill, but the disease had been less severe with me and I was already recovering. Ranuff stood stiffly by her bed, eyes red from lack of sleep and weeping. The boy we had both loved since we were children had become a fine-looking man, and he had chosen her. One of his hands clutched hers as though he was willing his strength into her failing body. I could feel his desperation.

She could not hear me, and he would not wish to. I reached over, smoothed back a sweat soaked curl from her forehead, and let my fingers rest on her cheek, telling her of my deep unspoken love without words. Had I imagined the tremor in her eyelids as I did so? I kissed her gently, and left them. In the morning, I was told that she had died in the night, and Ranuff had insisted on taking her body to his lands for burial. No one stopped him. He loved her. If they could not be together in life, then they would be so in death. I had never questioned what happened. But now my aunt's letter had given me reason to wonder. It was time to go home.

* * *

I found Cawdie in the stalls, and asked him to bring me the black leather Italian trunk. He made no comment, but when he returned with it, Janet was with him. She stood there, her arms folded. "And when are we leaving?"

"We? Janet, you and Cawdie are not going with me. You have a new life together. Your handfasting will be soon. I am going alone. There is no reason you must go. All will be well. Stay here and take care of the cottage and the animals. I will return when I have dealt with whatever needs doing."

"*Nae, lassie. whaur ye gang, we gang.*" Cawdie growled, his own great arms crossed over his chest. "'*at is th' way it is. We ur pledged tae ye. Ye gang nowhaur withit us until heel freezes o-er.*"   Janet pressed her body to his and they faced me together...two stubborn Scots that could not be swayed. Thank the gods! I was weak with relief.

There was much to be done before we left. Cawdie and Janet decided to wait and be handfasted in Skye where their old friends could attend. They seemed pleased by that. Julianne and Aidan had spoken to Father Hammett, and were going to be married in the kirk. They would wait at least six months for all the furor and gossip to die down, so it would not be announced for some months. The chest from the Tsar had been hidden in the kirk. Only Father Hammet, Aidan and Julianne knew where. They would use the contents only as needed. Aidan wanted nothing to do with the fortune. He planned to build a new home next to the smithy, but wanted a place for them until it was finished. His spartan quarters over the smithy would not do. I would offer the cottage in return for keeping it free of vandals and vermin. He and Jocki could tend and use the animals and herb garden as well. I hoped to return in time for their wedding.

I needed to tell Laird MacDuff I was leaving. Malcolm would be the only physician in Torrport. He would have to deal with the women, and several were pregnant. He would not particularly like it, but he would be good at it. While I was worrying over this and making lists of what we needed for the journey there was a soft tap at the door. Janet opened it, and from the timbre of her voice, I knew it was someone she did not know well or disliked. It was Rachel.

She asked diffidently if she could see me. I stood hastily. "Rachel? Is Lady Margaret well?" My first thought was for the babe. Older women often have trouble carrying.

She peered past Janet to me. "No, my Lady, tis nothing like that. May I ask the favor of a bit of your time?" Her voice was shaky but resolute, trembling from a curiously sensual mouth. Bluish crescents underlined apprehensive eyes in her pasty face, as though she had not been sleeping well.

"Of course. Janet, will you prepare us some tea." I looked again at Rachel. She must have lost a stone, for her clothes drooped limply about her body. "And some of that seed cake and honey." I smiled at Rachel. "It may not be as pretty as your confections, but it is delicious. Janet is well known for her baking." The woman grew even whiter. "Rachel?" I feared she would faint, and hastily led her to the chair by the fire. Scathach moved aside and watched us. "Rachel, what is it? How can I help you? Are you ill. Tell me."

"Yea, Lady." She spoke with an effort, and was shaking uncontrollably. Suddenly words flooded from her. "Yea...my lady. I am not well. Ill with my own guilt, hatred, and stupidity. Tis too much to live with. I cannot bear it. I thought to kill meself, but then I went to Sir Ross because he knows...he knows everything. Gregor is his man. He told me I had nothing to worry about, but should come to you and tell you." She looked at me beseechingly, her eyes filled with pain. "It was me, me! I am a murderer. I almost killed Lady Julianne and her babe. And helped kill my husband John. At least, I did not try to stop them. I wanted him dead. I was a fool. I thought he loved me, when he was just using me. Please, lady, believe me. I did not know the marchpane was poisoned. I swear it."

I must have made some sound for she stopped and looked at me helplessly, tears streaming down her face and dripping from the point of her chin.

"What? What are you saying Rachel? What poison, and who are you talking about?" But I knew.

She caught her breath, looked away, and rambled on as though I had not spoken. "He came to the kitchen...and said he would help me, that his hands were stronger than mine and faster...so he mixed the paste for me that day, the almonds and honey and...and it seems something else...that would kill her." The words spilled from her faster and faster. "I vow, lady, I did not know. But when I heard she was sick and almost died, then I remembered. I remembered his hands, and the powdered white sugar, or something, he kept adding to the paste. He said Lady Julianne would love it. And that I should bring any that was left back and give it to him for his men. Lady Margaret does not like the taste of almonds, nor do I. I did as he told me...and then...and then she almost died...he lied so, Lady Elspeth. I wanted to believe him...but so many things, other women. He even asked me for a ball of the soap Lady Margaret and I made. Told me he wanted the soap to remind him of me when we could not be together, and then gave it to his convenient. I smelled it on her in the tavern when we were there. She leaned over him and rubbed her breasts against his arm. Right before me! Did he think me such a leadenpate I would not know the scent?"

She inhaled and slumped back in her chair, exhausted, eyes closed, still speaking but more slowly. "I thought he was going to see her that night. I followed him. With a ball of the soap in my pocket to confront him. I caught up with him in the yard behind the tavern. He was furious that I was spying on him. My temper made me brave, and I told him I knew he was meeting his convenient, and that I knew what he had caused me to do to Lady Julianne, and that I had kept several pieces of the marchpane sweetmeats he had poisoned, and threatened to give them to the Laird. He was enraged, called me terrible things, and hit me so hard that I stumbled and fell. He was kicking me when Gregor stepped out of the shadows and stopped him." She paused and took another deep breath.

"I do not know how Gregor came to be there, but I was grateful. They argued. I just lay there only half aware of what was going on. But I did hear John call Gregor a traitor. My head was still ringing, it was hard to understand. Gregor said something about Lady Julianne and someone named Sophia, then Gregor just put his hands around John's neck and held him until he stopped moving. John was a big man, and fought him, but Gregor was the stronger. May God forgive me, I was glad. I pushed myself up just as Gregor dropped John. He made a strange sound as he hit the stones, like a cough, but he I knew he was dead. Gregor looked at me almost apologetically.

Gregor carried John to the laundry, so his body would not be found until we had time to get home. The filled tub was sitting there. I was not thinking clearly, but I thought his soul should be washed clean, so I asked Gregor to put him there on his knees. I pushed the ball of soap into his lying mouth to clean his lying tongue, and his head fell into the water. I left it there, so he would take it to Hell with him. I took his silver pistols. They cost dearly. Then we left." She sighed tiredly. "That is all. I must ask forgiveness from you and Lady Julianne, and...and the babe. I never wanted to harm them, I swear. Only God can forgive me for not helping my husband."

I felt as though I needed a bath after being awash in the chaotic visions of her words.

Janet had been listening, and brought over the tea when Rachel's outburst ceased. Rachel looked calmer now, as though she had been eased of a great burden. Her tale had helped me as well. I am not certain, but I think I murmured something about the mercy of God to his imperfect children, and forgiving oneself, and tried to get her to eat and drink a little. She needed to talk to Julianne. Their lives would touch over many years to come. She promised she would, and said that knowing she might have caused the death of Lady Julianne and the wee bairn tortured her still. She left looking slightly better than she had when she arrived. I, on the other hand, felt as limp as wet laundry before starching. The pattern was increasingly clear, and ugly. We had suspected Rachel as an accomplice in her husband's murder. Was she telling the truth? Or part of it? Her vivid confession was very disturbing, and I badly needed to erase the images from my head.

* * *

After grubbing in the garden for several hours, I felt better. My willow wood trug basket was filled with fresh herbs and garlic. I noticed that one of my old leather gloves had a finger that needed stitching. I stood, shook my skirts, rubbed ineffectually at the stains and dirt, pushed back damp curls that had escaped my braids, turned, and stumbled into an unmoving wall of warm wool. Two hands grasped my arms and kept me from falling backward. I looked up into the amused eyes of Sir Ross. I flushed, wondering how long he had been standing there watching.

He released me at once. "Lady Elspeth. Janet told me you were in the garden. Forgive me for startling you. Shall I return another time?"

I was chagrined but it was too late to make myself presentable. I thought idly, as I noted Sir Ross's fastidious dress, that the fistula must have been especially humiliating to him. Removing my filthy gloves, I laid them in the trug. "Shall we sit out here? It is peaceful and private, and I like the mixed smells of earth and herbs and flowers. Tis soothing." I plucked a white rose from the bush near the bench, picked a spring of rosemary and one of mint from the trug, and offered the small bouquet to him.

He looked down at it, and accepted it gravely. "I think you know why I am here. I understand Rachel came to see you earlier? Perhaps you will wish your posy returned after we have spoken."

"Perhaps. I will grant you that it was unsettling. I have never thought you guilty of deceit, Sir Gregor, yes, but you? That is more difficult for me to understand."

His face altered slightly. Sometime during the past weeks, it had become more refined, almost gaunt, but his eyes were steady on mine. "I make no excuses for my actions." He gazed down at the posy again, the combined odors were stronger from being grasped tightly. "The hands holding this token are as bloody as Gregor's. It was my order that killed Spence. Gregor only did as I commanded him."

"As Sir Spence did as he was commanded?"

"Yes." Something feral burned in his eyes for a moment. He did not elaborate.

"Men see things so differently that I have oft wondered if we are the same species. I suppose we all do as we feel we must." I absently pulled a loose thread from my sleeve and the seam parted. Yet another repair. The conversation with Rachel lay like lead in my belly, so I simply asked.

"Gregor had arranged to meet Spence at the tavern that morning. That Rachel followed him was an unexpected complication. Gregor would have waited for a better time had Spence not begun beating her. He regrets that deeply."

"Yes, I can see that he would." The last piece had fallen into place. I finished destroying the sleeve and patted the remains into place. "You know I am leaving soon?"

"Indeed. The Laird told me. When will you go?

"As soon as I can arrange transportation. Cawdie and Janet will be attending me."

"I see. I have prepared something for you". He reached into his jacket and removed a thick envelope. It was not sealed. "You may do with it as you see fit. It is a letter of reference for you that might be of use in securing permission to practice as a physician. I will gladly appear for you as well. You have only to ask." He turned away for a moment, then faced me again, his countenance more unguarded than I had ever seen it. "Lady Elspeth, I would have you take with you the knowledge that I am your friend. This is not an appropriate time for me to say more, but I pray you will find it in your heart to forgive me and think of me kindlier after some time has passed." He lifted my hand from my lap and kissed it lightly. "Be aware that I am your servant, and will ever be. You have but to call and I will come to you." Before I could answer he rose and strode away, the posy still gripped tightly in his hand, its fragrance faintly discernable in the still air, fading as he left.

* * *

Transportation had to be arranged for us, and for Scathach. Fortunately, the road to Glasgow was well traveled, although lurching along it in a stagecoach would be agonizing. I thought fleetingly of traveling as "Tam Morrison" so I could ride horseback, but I would never be permitted to do so. At least I could afford for all of us to sit inside instead of in the large open basket attached to the back or on the roof with the luggage. Those who had to do so were subject to the vagaries of weather and the constant threat of highwaymen. There was seating for eight inside the coach. I would purchase all the tickets for us. It was patently obvious that Janet, Cawdie, Scathach and I counted as eight. I called Scathach and walked to the smithy to purchase the tickets and find out what time we needed to be there. Aidan was shoeing a pretty bay mare when I arrived, so I went into his little shop to see what he had that might be useful as gifts for our return to Skye. A copy of The *Edinburgh Courant* lay on the table. The increasing popularity and influence of these small sheets caused concern in some political circles, but I relished the advertisements. A notice on the back page was of interest.

"That the Famous Loozengees for curing the Cold, Stopping and pains in the Breast, the Kinkhost: are to be sold by George Anderson at the foot of the Fifth Mercator, and at George Moubray's Shop, posit to the Main-Guard. Price 8p the box."

I speculated on their contents. Maybe Malcolm could bring me a package of them for comparison? Mine had decoctions of several herbs and honey, boiled to hardness.

Aidan came in, wiping his hands on his leather apron, his smile welcoming but watchful. Ross must have warned him. Honesty again. "Sir, Aidan..." I stopped. What could I say? It was not my place to judge others. I had sworn never to harm, but might not circumstance tempt me to hire someone to do it in my stead? I sighed and began again. "Aidan, let there be only truth between us. I know about Gregor and Spence, and Rachel came by too. I understand about you and Julianne. Can we not be on good terms?" I smiled ruefully. "Julianne and the bairn have come to mean much to me. Mayhap I should be thanking you."

"No...no... Never that." His voice was rough. "I have loved Julianne as long as I can remember, and I shall love the babe because he is part of her. In truth, if Spence were not already dead, I would kill him myself."

I knew he would guard Julianne with his life. He halted. "Lady, I would do the same if anyone dared harm you." His words wrapped around me. With them we slipped almost back into our old relationship. We were friends. Time would smooth the rest.

We discussed the tickets for the stagecoach. It would have to be two days hence so that the other stops could be advised not to sell more inside vouchers for that day. Arrangements for passage to Skye would have to wait until we reached the Port of Glasgow. I bought the tickets and reduced his shop stock by a silver cup, three brooches and a pomander on a chain for my aunt.

I offered him the use of the cottage in exchange for its care while I was away. He accepted eagerly, and was soon describing the new house he would build for Julianne and the bairn. The plans were drawn, and he was looking for the right materials. I suspected it would be the grandest home in Torrport. A tiny twinge of longing and envy surfaced, but it was soon suppressed in the satisfaction of helping suggest better ways to build his dream. The new box sash windows would be the first in Torrport. He had already made a mold for the lead weights used in the windows and showed me the first one he had made. It resembled nothing so much as a cudgel with a large eye on one end.

* * *

I spent the next day seeing patients and letting them know I was leaving. The poorer ones accepted the news stoically. It was not quite fair to Malcolm, but I encouraged them to go to him if they needed help.

I stopped by the bakery to see Una and the bairn. Malcolm had asked me to find a wet nurse for her babe, while he tried a new medicine for her diabetes, and I had done so. Martha, one of Aggie's laundry women, had been delivered of her child at about the same time as Una. She was a large, clean, comfortable woman who was delighted to share the bounty of her breasts with Una's babe in return for her daily bread. Both bairns looked round and rosy. Una was as pale and fragile as her spun sugar decorations. I told them I was leaving for a while, but that I hoped to return, and they both gratified me with expressions of dismay. I would miss the life I had made here.

One happenstance relieved my guilt about leaving somewhat. I had returned to the frame-maker's shop to purchase a wee looking-glass. His goodwife was speaking quietly with an immensely pregnant woman. She gave her a small bottle and patted her hand comfortingly. After the expectant mother left, she showed me several small, lovely mirrors, and I chose one. Evidently the conclusion about the murder of Spence had spread, for she was much more responsive. While she was wrapping the mirror, I drew her out. She shyly disclosed that she had been a midwife in France! At this point, her care was limited to the Huguenot women who had sought refuge here. Many spoke only French, and kept to themselves. She knew I was also a midwife and we tested each other cautiously until we were both satisfied with the extent of our mutual knowledge. I told her about some of my patients and asked if she would be interested in seeing them. She was. We parted with shared satisfaction and the beginnings of friendship. I could hardly wait to tell Malcolm. She could be of great assistance to him. Margaret would like her, too. A woman who understood French fashions as well as the more intimate feminine concerns? A perfect blend.

The last thing on my list was Jocki. He had taken to reading and numbers like a fish to water. I hoped that Malcolm would keep him occupied and encourage his learning. A chest filled with salves and herbs that I though Malcolm could use was ready. I put a note about Harriet and Jocki in it and closed it. Cawdie would take it to Malcolm's office when he delivered the soap I was sending to Aggie. I would personally deliver the fabric I had purchased in Edinburgh to Molly MacTavish. I would miss Leana, and all of them. I spared a moment to indulge in a wee dram of sadness, then finished packing and took the roll of material and walked to the fishing village.

* * *

At dawn the next morning, we bundled what we were taking into a cart, gave the cottage a last sweep and dust, and told a tearful Jocki to remember to take care of the cow and the garden. He was to share with his mother and anyone else who might need it. I looked around for the last time...placed the short letter I had written Malcolm on the table, and left, closing the door softly.

Even at that hour the smithy yard was bustling with organized confusion. Aidan came out to help us. He and Cawdie put our bundles and chests on top of the stagecoach, and the small bags of essentials inside. Lady Margaret had sent Rachel with a basket of cheeses, bread and fruit to break our fast. Thankfully, there were no sweetmeats.

It was time to leave. I found myself looking around for something...someone. Janet and Scathach were already inside the coach and I had started to follow them when five horsemen cantered into the yard. All were dressed in black, and astride black horses. They carried themselves like warriors. Here and there, a flash of silver reflected off sheathed weapons in the watery golden morning light. At night, they would be invisible. The fifth horseman dismounted and came toward us. It was Gregor. He stood before me and bowed deeply, his face expressing nothing, as usual. My eyes went involuntarily to his hands, imagining them around Spence's throat, lifting him, taking his life. I shuddered slightly in revulsion at the vision. His expression did not change, but I realized that he knew exactly what I was thinking. For the barest moment, I felt a flicker of exquisite pain and terrible sadness coming from him. Then it was gone.

"Sir Ross has sent me to wish you God Speed. The four men are outriders who will accompany you to Glasgow." He bowed, rather more stiffly this time, and walked away, leaving me frozen to the spot. The outriders took their positions around the carriage.

Cawdie nodded approvingly to them, awoke me from my trance with a light touch of his big hand and helped me into the stagecoach. He raised his arm in a salute to Aidan and climbed in. The coach listed slightly then balanced as he settled, his big feet carefully positioned to avoid ours. Scathach whined and attempted to insert her massive pregnant self between us on the seat. Janet pushed her firmly to the floor, where she sighed in resignation, bumped against our legs circling to find exactly the right spot, and flopped. The driver blew his horn, wrapped the reins around his hammy fist, and bellowed at the man holding the horses to "give em their 'eds." We were away.

Thank God, we had all the seats.

TWENTY-FIVE

Malcolm - Aftershocks

Edinburgh, Scotland.

"Tell me again. What happened after Archibald dragged you out of the water?" Father stared at me with that look of disapproval designed to whither the most stalwart soul.

"You should be addressing that question to Archie. I know little more than I've already told you. I awoke in the rowboat puking up sea water. I was in a lot of pain."

We were around the kitchen table, several hours after my confrontation with Mackmain, being grilled by Father. McLean had already come by to sew up the gash on my forearm and the flap of skin and hair gouged from the back of my head. My lungs were much abused, and I was still coughing up bits of jetsam. Aside from that, I was sore but glad to have escaped death by drowning, an experience I won't soon forget.

Mackmain had double-crossed Captain Kidd by trying to grab the ransom for himself. Made sense. Had he followed through with their original plan, he would've been at the mercy of Kidd, well-outnumbered at Torrport. No honour among thieves. Kidd should've known, but perhaps he did, and it mattered naught. In the end, once Mackmain saw I wasn't captive, he must've realized he had only one option: kill me and flee.

"Was there no sign of Mackmain, then?"

"Naught but the cloak Archie found floating under the dock at daybreak. I believe Mackmain was still alive when I let go of him." Archie was saying little, sitting shirtless with bandaged ribs and filling his face with porridge. I didn't tell Father that the reason I ended up in the water was because Archie had shot Mackmain. I'd subdued Mackmain and could have brought him in but for that. Instead, I was having to play the incompetent to save Archie from Father's wrath. I still wasn't certain why he shot Mackmain beyond what he'd told me later, that it was for someone in the regiment. It was even more worrisome because this was the second time Archie exceeded orders. Was that Father's intent? It was hard to know. There is the spoken and then there is the implied in relationships.

Archie finished eating and spoke up. "Ah think he's dead. Couldn't survive in that water, could he? He's at the bottom. Fish feed, he is, sure as I'm sitting here."

Father smiled approvingly. "You are probably right Archibald, but we have no body, no proof. As a result, the order for his arrest will remain in place until this is resolved. The area needs to be searched carefully this week."

I countered. "It was dark. If he could hold his breath longer than me, he could have surfaced after I let go and found a boat nearby; there were several of them around. From there, he could have made his way to the *Chantilly*."

"I say he's dead, and we searched for hours after sunrise, me and the dockworkers. Found naught but the cloak." Archie was adamant, and I was wondering why. He'd fired at a range of no more than six feet. Did he hit Mackmain, or not? At the time, I was facing Archie and the flash from the pistol temporarily blinded me, then I was immediately pulled into the hatch and down. It seemed unlikely that Mackmain could have put up such a struggle, then escaped after being shot, but then it would have depended on many factors.

"Did you check the *Chantilly*?" Father asked again, perhaps hoping for a better answer this time.

"She'd sailed with the morning tide," I repeated.

"Yes, yes," Father said, annoyed with me. "I knew I should have lead this expedition. It was a good thing Archibald was there, at my insistence, I might add."

"Aye Father, I'm glad Archie was there to save me again." I looked at both older men and wondered which of them was the more delusional. The thing is that Archie had not even tried to correct my version of the story, and now I had this paranoid thought worming into my brain that perhaps he'd set this up with Mackmain. It was the perfect escape, with or without ransom money. I knew I wasn't thinking clearly though, having just enough of McLean's laudanum to dull the pain and impair the mind. For now, Mackmain would have to live in that ether of uncertainty until he was proven alive or dead. Whatever the result, I was glad to be rid of him, and deep in my flawed heart I knew that if I ran into him again I'd kill him without regret, and consequences be damned.

✳ ✳ ✳

I set aside concerns about Archie and his role in the Mackmain affair, but I knew at some point they must be addressed, at least to assuage my suspicious mind. For now, I was content to rest and let Mrs. Simpson fuss over me and fill my belly with all sorts of delectable foods. She seemed to think me in need of fattening, a thought I found amusing in my weakened state.

I knew his voice as soon as he entered. It was John Beaton, as jovial as ever and wanting to see *Prince Malcolm*, as he mockingly referred to me in a voice annoyingly cheerful.

"Ah, there you are, lazy sod!" He entered my bedroom encumbered with a large package and even larger grin. One was not allowed to be sad in his presence, his cherub countenance radiating universal happiness and good-will. "This is for you. Get dressed, we must be there within the hour."

He had me stumped, but I was caught in the power of his presence. "Mmm. And where is it we are going?" I sat up in bed. My forearm and head throbbed with pain in unison.

"Young's memorial, of course. Did no one tell you?" He looked at me curiously.

"Mmm. I've been busy."

"Ah. Well just in case you didn't bring a black waistcoat, he is one of mine. May not fit perfectly, but..." He unwrapped it ferociously, paper scraps raining in all directions, then held it up to me while I put on a fresh shirt, and trousers. His waistcoat didn't fit me, too much tummy, providing further proof for Mrs. Simpson of my need of fattening; but with black shoes and tricorn hat, I looked decent enough to pass inspection and we set off on foot to Saint Giles' High Kirk a few blocks distant. As we were walking, Beaton mentioned that these memorial services had become common recently because of the smallpox epidemic and rapid disposal of bodies in common graves. It didn't give people time for a proper send off, so the wealthy and prominent victims were given memorials later in lieu of funerals.

After the Bishop's War for control of the Church of Scotland in the last century, Saint Giles' was partitioned, based on congregation. It had become a mutilated, shared space that pleased few. Young's service was on the Presbyterian side, and it was full when we arrived. Evidently, Young had many thankful patients. Beaton and I were ushered to seats near the front reserved for family and close friends. Through the service, I sat meditating, letting the words and music flow without really listening. Instead I closed my eyes and remembered Young. Images, one after the other and things he'd said. He was a truly remarkable man, and if anyone had the right to be called a holy martyr, it would be him. Of course, he would have mocked the suggestion. We all admired him, those of us in medicine, anyway. He was the natural leader of our generation of physicians trying to modernize medicine using science, and will not be forgotten anytime soon.

Beaton poked me. "Were you asleep?" he whispered.

"No. Communing with Young."

"Time to go." Beaton offered to help me up and I took it for once, remembering the advice to let others support me.

* * *

It was time to go home, but first I needed to resolve one remaining issue. I informed Mrs. Simpson I'd be back before dark and set out for McLaren's infirmary. It was quiet when I arrived. The clutter from the smallpox epidemic had been cleared away and the place scrubbed clean. McLaren wasn't there so I left a note and headed back to the street, toward McLean's surgery. The city was becoming busy again. People were out sweeping, repairing, replacing. Everyone was wanting a return to normalcy, to put these past weeks behind them. We all wanted to forget. Remembering is too painful sometimes, isn't it, but some things must not be forgotten, not ever.

McLean was consulting a patient. I had some business to discuss and wanted to thank him for everything he'd done. He'd been a valuable ally and friend.

"Malcolm. I haven't much time today. Lots of people coming back to Edinburgh and with complaints they preferred not to have treated by the village hag." He laughed heartily and extended his hand.

"Then I'm glad your practice is flourishing. It's well-deserved."

"Thank you for saying so, but I am so short-staffed now I've been wishing for fewer patients, not more." He grimaced. I knew how he felt. It was feast or famine, the life of a doctor.

"I'll make it brief, so you can get on with your day. I'm going to rally our experiment group and try to formally present our findings. Do you have any suggestions?"

"Mhm. Well from my perspective it was a success. The procedure is straightforward. Needs some fine-tuning, but that can be done as we learn more. I am sure the College of Surgeons will accept it, with a bit more proof. In any case I have a good supply of dried scabs for future experiments."

"That's what I wanted to hear. Thank you. Cameron has the full report and you are welcome to use it. We need support from both Colleges."

"Aye, indeed we do, and I will do my part if there is any chance we can defeat smallpox."

"I'm glad we can count on you. One last thing. Thank you again for what you did for us, but I hope next time our experiment doesn't include combat." I chuckled.

"Och, but I quite enjoyed that part!" We both laughed, and I knew then that there was a part of me that enjoyed it too. It was my guilty secret and perhaps his too.

My last stop was at Young's, or shall I say Beaton's infirmary now. John was not in either, so I left a note for him with an invite to meet tomorrow at nine in the morning at McLaren's. It was time to formally present our findings."

* * *

Back at Father's I could hear them in his bedroom. "It still fits."

Archie was helping Father dress in his court robes. "Isn't it a little soon for that, Father?" I said teasing him.

"It has been far too long, Malcolm." He replied in that gruff way he has. I knew he was right and I was very pleased to see him wanting to go back to work.

"Half-days to start, Father."

"I am not an idiot, you know, and besides, you are not my doctor. In fact, the esteemed doctor McLaren gave permission, just yesterday." He puffed out his chest adjusting the front of the gown.

"Then who am I to disagree?" Father seemed in good spirits, so I took the plunge. "Umm, Father I need what you have on Turnbull."

Father's smile turned down. "Why?"

"We intend to formally present our research findings tomorrow and need all the leverage we can muster. Turnbull can be very stubborn, even when clearly wrong."

Father turned back to face the mirror, adjusting his cravat. "I'll not have you deposing him. Men like that are more valuable in-place and controlled."

"I understand, Father. I have no intention of doing that, unless there is no choice."

"Then be sure you don't provoke a situation where you think you have no choice."

I sighed. Father knew me so well, didn't he? "I'll do my best. Now please tell me what you have on Turnbull."

"I suppose it is time to show that arrogant weasel who is master. Now how do I look?"

* * *

There was only a name and address on the scrap of paper Father handed me. The address was on a lane a few blocks away, not far from the one where I'd met the boys who'd robbed me. Father just said, "Ask her about Turnbull."

The building was one of those that'd been partly burned in the great fire a few years back. There'd been attempts to repair it, but the results were uneven, to be charitable. I stepped over the refuse at the door and made my way up the rotting staircase, trying not to touch anything. I knocked on the second door on the fourth floor, as instructed. There was a scraping sound, then a weak "Way'd ye want?" from the other side of the door.

"I'm looking for Lady Wilson. Tis Doctor Malcolm Forrester." I listened for the response. Instead the door opened abruptly, and I found myself looking in the dead eyes of the boy who'd robbed me and helped us track Mackmain.

"Mam is dressing," he said and stepped aside to let me enter. The place was a hovel, whisky bottles on the floor, an unmade bed in the corner, dirty pots on the cooker. It told a story. I had a closer look at the boy. He was mid teens, big, raw-boned, already very intimidating.

"Lady Wilson is your mother?"

"Aye. Father left us years ago." He said that with a sneer of defiance.

"If this is about my Leslie, you can clear out," she said on entering, still flicking things off her dress. She was one of those fair middle-aged women that once were considered beautiful and now found themselves on the cusp of aging badly, and in denial about it.

"Your son did us a service and was well-rewarded. I'm here to see you. It's about Turnbull." I waited for her reaction, but it was Leslie who spoke first.

"He'll feel mah blade if he hurts mah mammy again."

I believed him.

"Shush. None of that now Leslie. Doctor, why are you asking about Turnbull?"

I explained briefly, about the smallpox experiment and Turnbull's opposition to it, then asked for her help.

"Doctor, I had no choice after my cursed husband left. Had a boy to feed, didn't I?"

"I understand. Not here to judge."

She nodded, then continued. "It was easy money, but for the men like him who like to hurt us. We have no choice you see. The brothel owns our contract and insists we service even the likes of him." She looked away, perhaps embarrassed by the memories and having to speak of it in front of her son.

"Not anymore mammy. Ah will see to it," Leslie blurted.

"Lady Wilson, men like Turnbull must be opposed. Help us and I promise to find an apprenticeship for your son. It's the best I can do to help you both." They looked at each other. I could tell my offer wasn't what they'd expected, but they seemed interested.

"What do we have to do, then?" It was Leslie who decided for them.

* * *

We all met next morning at McLaren's, Beaton, McLean, Cameron, and me plus a few others. Gwen was there too, enjoying her new role as infirmary manager and fiancé. I apologized to her about Mackmain. She seemed uninterested and I spoke too much of it. People are resilient, an admirable trait that at times comes off as cold hearted.

After a brief consult, we agreed to go as a united group to present our findings and offer recommendations. I'd already sent a boy to Turnbull's letting him know we'd be coming at eleven.

"It should've been Young presenting today," I said. "I will do it, but this is the last time. This group must find a new leader. I'm needed in Torrport." They understood. "Now let's go over what we need to present."

It didn't take long. At the end, Beaton said. "How are we going to deal with the old man?"

"I have a guest that I'll use if it comes to that," I replied.

"I do as well," Beaton added with a wily smile, and I cocked my head waiting for him to explain. "If needed," he expanded without giving anything away.

"Alright, we have a few surprises then, if Turnbull is uncooperative. We must not underestimate him though."

"Easier said," mumbled McLaren.

We arrived just before eleven. On the way, I'd stopped by to pick up Leslie, and when we arrived I noticed Beaton's fiancé, Gillian Findlay waiting in a carriage parked nearby. Even Gwen had come with McLaren. If nothing else, we had supporters.

We were standing outside Turnbull's home uneasily chatting about the steamy weather and waiting for Cameron to show up with the official report. "Wait here til I call," I said to Leslie. He nodded and sat on the step. Cameron arrived panting and grumbling about the delay. I turned him in the right direction and lead the way in. Fraser was at the reception desk and knew better than to play games with us. Instead he immediately scurried to his master, then returned a minute later to hold the door open.

Turnbull was pacing before the fire, a serious scowl on his lined face. There were several additional chairs set-out. He bade us be seated. No warm welcome this time. This could be war, if not played well. I sat nearest his favourite chair, wanting to be right in his face. The others sat warily as though expecting a trap. Would the Town Guards burst in and arrest us, or would the chairs have hidden weapons to stab us? It was that kind of atmosphere.

Turnbull remained standing, pacing, hovering menacingly. He really was too old to intimidate any of us physically, but the psychological war had begun.

"Thank you for seeing us on short-notice. We have the report and recommendations for your support," I began, controlling my tone.

"I have agreed to meet, not support you," He snapped back.

"It is a beginning." I looked straight in his eyes briefly then glanced back at Cameron. "Please give the report, Sir."

Cameron went through it, exactly as planned. Turnbull continued pacing. It was hard to know from his passive expression if he was listening or planning his next move.

After Cameron finished, I summarized. "In the experiment, it was clearly shown that inoculation with aged scabs can induce immunity. No one who'd received the treatment, subsequently contracted full-blown smallpox." I looked around the room. "Do we all agree?" There was agreement.

"Too small a sample, and the test subjects were all physicians and could have encountered smallpox previously. Your so-called proof is not valid." He looked down at us with his best condescending glower.

"I agree. This was but a start. More research is needed, on a wider range of patients. That is our first recommendation."

"It is too dangerous! It is irresponsible to put patients at risk like that. I cannot support it."

"Hear us out, please!" I would not be rebuffed so easily this time.

He folded his arms and sneered. "Go on then, if you must."

I knew at that point he was not prepared to support us, and his mind would not be changed without significant inducement, but we'd agreed to present all our results and recommendations. "We recommend that an expedition be funded to travel to Asia, to study techniques and observe results first-hand." Turnbull just rolled his eyes. I smiled, then signalled to Gwen to fetch Leslie.

"Our final recommendation is to use the techniques we learned in a series of experiments to determine best methods." I finished then stood to face him. "Do you support our results and recommendations, Sir?" He was about to tell us to go to hell or worse when Gwen returned with Leslie.

"Who...?" Turnbull clearly was startled.

"May I present Leslie Wilson, good son of your mistress, Lady Wilson, the one you abuse on a regular basis." There was a gasp from Gwen and I think I heard Leslie mumble a threat.

"I have done nothing illegal, I assure you," Turnbull exclaimed. I think it was beginning to dawn on him what this was about. He intended to stonewall us and now this.

"I agree Sir Turnbull, your behaviour is not illegal, but would you like your wife to know about it, or the wider community?" I took a step closer and now we were nose-to-nose.

"Are you threatening me, Sir?" Turnbull had that look of frightened indecision about him. Would he fight or flee?

"Indeed, I am. For the good of the community, I might add."

Then I saw his shoulders sink, and I gently pushed him to sit in the empty chair behind him. "You will not oppose research to find scientific cures, in future, will you?" I gazed down at him knowing this was my chance to end this now.

He turned his head away and muttered. "I will not stop you."

I didn't have his full support and chances are he would find another way to impede us. It was a small victory, but not enough. I was at a loss.

"Gentlemen!" All eyes turned to see Gillian Findlay enter dressed strikingly in shimmering black with white lace at the right places. "Ah Lady Gwen." She walked over, and they embraced. "I hope I am not too late?" She joined me and smiled mischievously. I wasn't sure what would come next. "My fiancé John Beaton asked me to attend. I am so pleased to meet you Doctor Turnbull." She held out her white-gloved hand and he took it tentatively and bowed. Then she turned her head to Beaton. "Did you tell them?"

"Nay." Beaton shook his head.

"Ah, then shall I?" We all waited.

"It is timely," Beaton answered.

Gillian smiled broadly. "I am so pleased to be able to do this! As some of you may know, my family owns the Findlay Shipyards, one of the area's largest employers. We care about our people. When they are sick, our business suffers. When they die, a part of us dies too. These epidemics hurt us all, and if we can help bring an end..." She looked from one to the other of us. She had our attention now. "Mother and I have decided to provide a generous endowment to be used to find ways to cure these terrible diseases."

I looked at her incredulously, then to Beaton. He winked. All I could say was: "Brava!" and applauded. She received a standing ovation. Even Turnbull seemed slightly thawed.

Lady Findlay smiled graciously then bade us be seated. "And we must not forget our most important leader and ally, Professor Turnbull. We also have decided to fund a position of Chair of Medical Research, with the first recipient being Professor Turnbull!" I choked on that one, and started to object when she clarified. "Of course, the physicians and College must work together, or I am afraid we will not be able to continue our support." She stared at Turnbull and he nodded in assent. This was one impressive woman.

"We all thank you Lady Findlay. I'm certain your support will save many lives. It's what we all want, isn't it?" There were smiles and thanks from everyone but Turnbull, who I'm sure was trying to find solid ground in this new firmament. "Let me summarize. We all agree to support these smallpox results and recommendations and do further research under the direction of the College lead by the esteemed Professor Turnbull." Everyone agreed, including for the first time Turnbull.

We left elated. I was a bit sceptical, but then Turnbull could take credit for positive results and disavow negative ones, all-the-while taking Gillian's money. It could be the solution we sought.

Beaton waved me over. "I hope that settles it Mal."

"I hope so too, and that was quite a surprise you two pulled!"

Beaton's face glowed and he turned to Gillian and gushed. "She is wonderful, isn't she?"

"Indeed. We must toast our benefactress at the earliest." I could sense something new between them, those unspoken looks and touches at every opportunity. Could they be in love?

"All is well with you both?" I hated prying, but had to know.

"Good, Mal, and you?" he responded automatically.

"John, don't be coy with your friend. Malcolm, John would want you to know we are going to be married! The date is set, and you are invited, of course." Gillian looked at Beaton who was turning a lovely shade of rosy pink.

"Ah, that explains his excessively cheerful mood lately." I laughed at his discomfiture.

"You two are the perfect couple, and I wish you both all the best. We shook hands and promised to stay in touch, then I grabbed Leslie and brought him over to meet McLean. "If you're looking for an apprentice, this lad deserves a chance. He is intelligent and brave." McLean looked him over quickly.

"Can't promise anything, but come over early and we can talk. Here is my address, I hope you can read." Leslie was grinning proudly as I left him. It was time to pack.

* * *

I rode on the roof of the carriage back to Torrport, not out of necessity, but desire. It was one of those perfect days when there is nothing on earth better than filling lungs with fresh air and feeling the calming sun on your face. I saw with new eyes that day, with eyes of appreciation and thanks for such a beautiful world. The hours on the carriage also gave time to reflect. The past weeks had been very hard, on my body especially. I daydreamed about lounging on a cushion at the coffee house reading the news and sipping bitter brew. A well-deserved respite, surely? I also thought of my friends and all we'd experienced, and longed for another convivial meal of delicious food and hearty laughter. Was I asking too much? I realized I wanted a return to a simpler life, to be a good doctor, to have friends, and yes perhaps even a wife and children. My mind flitted dreamily from desire to desire as the carriage bounced along the rutted road, then drifted to more serious thoughts. What had been accomplished? Was it worth it? I wasn't sure. Ultimately, I suppose it will only be known in the distant future, and maybe not even then. Actions have consequences, good and bad, and not always as intended. I, more than most have experienced that fearsome bite of reality.

The carriage came to a rattling stop in front of the stables, the horses lathered and in need of water. I was elated to be home, to my Torrport. I never imagined I would feel this way about this scruffy town. I stood and filled my lungs with salty sea air, then jumped down with my bag. Oddly, Jocki was there to meet me. He was holding a burlap bag under his arm and waving. "Welcome back, doctor!" He said enthusiastically. I was suspicious. What was up now?

"Your locum is gone and Lady Elspeth..." He started chattering much too quickly.

"I'm starving, Jocki. I hope you bought some food." I looked curiously at him then saw the bag wriggle.

"Been expecting you." He grinned as we walked the short blocks to home.

I opened the door and cast my gaze from side to side. All was in good order. "Thanks for keeping an eye on things." I said sincerely while removing my cloak. Out of the corner of my eye, I saw Jocki place the bag on the floor gently. The bag moved again, and I thought I heard a weak mewing sound from within. "What do you have in there?" He was kneeling beside it now and lifting the opening.

"Ah found him yesterday, alone and on the rocks."

A tiny orange and white head poked out of the bag followed closely by a demanding "Mew!"

I laughed. "A kitten!" I bent down for a closer look. The kitten bravely strode over to meet me.

"Can we keep him? We need a good rat catcher."

"Mhm," I said as the kitten rubbed his scent on my leg.

"I will take good care of him. Please, doctor."

I needed no further convincing. "Then we shall call him Rocky."

Jocki lifted the kitten to his face and said, "Hear that Tiger, you have a new name!"

"Don't feed him too much or he'll be of no use for catching rats."

Jocki shook his head. "Oh no, sir. I shall take the best care of him."

I unpacked, then Jocki and I shared a simple meal of bread, cheese and ale. It was good to be home.

✳ ✳ ✳

Andrew and Elspeth had left me a pile of patient reports to review. I spend the rest of the day going over them and deciding which ones needed a follow-up visit. I also had to see Laird MacDuff. I relished the idea of getting back to work without distraction and drama. But first I needed to reward my best colleague, Elspeth. I took out a fresh sheet of paper and penned a letter of commendation and support that she could use in her quest to become a recognised physician. I knew from experience she was as good as any. Sadly, the College would not accept women, but perhaps there were other ways, and I would not obstruct her. I folded the letter and sealed it, then walked to the stable to get Gracie and the gig.

The early evening air released the heat of day and we took our time making our way along familiar streets, stopping to chat with friends and patients. There is a sense of belonging, isn't there? Every heart needs a happy home, and I'd found mine. I stopped at the wine shop and picked up a few bottles to share then tied Gracie at the bottom of the hill leading to Elspeth's cottage. There were only a few thin clouds in the sky and the sun was filling the flowers around her door with a rich palette of light. I smiled in anticipation and knocked. The door swung open.

I poked my head it and said "Hello". The room was dark and there were no sounds.

My eyes adjusted enough to notice the room was empty but for a few bits of basic furnishings. What had happened? I could see a piece of paper on the kitchen table held in place by a knife. I opened it, then went outside to see better.

It read,

"My Dear Friend. We are on our way back to Skye. I regret that we must take our leave before you return, but tis for the best. Fare thee well, and pray for me. Elspeth."

I read it again to be sure I understood. It was clear enough. My heart sank. I came to celebrate, and now this. Selfish me. We were becoming such good friends and now they've gone. I almost wept. The letter slipped from my fingers as I looked toward the town then to the fishing village. "They need me," I muttered, eyes glistening. Gracie was munching a tuft of grass as I walked past her and climbed aboard. "Let's go Gracie, we have work to do."

The End

EPILOGUE

Elspeth – Skye, Autumn 1705

It was a cell. The opulence of the furnishings could not hide that. A small child sat quietly on a soft sheepskin rug in front of the large stone hearth. Firelight licked along the curving strands of gold and red curls tumbling over her shoulders. I thought I had made no sound, but her head turned sharply toward me. "Mother?"

The purple blue of her eyes fixed on my face. It was a moment before I realized she was blind.

Malcolm – Autumn 1705

The crew said it was the remnants of a storm making the round-trip from the Americas. We'd past the Point of Sleat on Skye heading for the narrows at Kylerhea, when the storm caught us. We could do nothing but try to hold in place, sails and sea-anchor down, and pray we weren't pushed on the rocks and drowned. My stomach had long since emptied, and with memories of my near drowning at Leith all too fresh in mind, I again opened the soggy letter from Elspeth. She wrote: *I need you...*

HISTORICAL NOTES

This is a work of fiction built on a framework of history. It takes place Spring. 1705 in Scotland.   Part of the story occurs in Edinburgh and part in the imaginary town of Torrport approximately where the fetching village of Aberdour is located on the Firth of Forth. Queen Anne occupied the throne of both England and Scotland. Scotland had its own parliament, but the English and some Scots wanted to unite England with Scotland, Wales and Northern Ireland to form Great Britain, with one parliament for all. Meanwhile the followers of James Francis Edward Stuart "The Old Pretender" and his followers called "Jacobites" were working to overthrow Protestant Queen Anne and reinstate the Catholic Stuart line on the English and Scottish thrones. It was a politically unstable time.

Tsar Peter the Great of Russia had visited England a few years earlier to learn ship building skills to help modernize his navy and merchant fleet. It also is known that he employed many Jacobite Scots as tradesmen, advisors and   leaders of his military. The Jacobites tried to elicit his help in reinstating the Old Pretender back on the throne of Scotland and England. It is unlikely that Tsar Peter came to Scotland. That part is fiction.   However, what would have happened had the Tsar fathered a child with a Scottish lass in his court? We explore that idea in one of the main plots involving the poisoning of Julianne and the murder of Captain Spence, and investigated by Elspeth MacLeod with Malcolm Forrester's help.

The smallpox plot is also speculation. We know that in 1700 Sir Martin Lister reported to the Royal Society in London that a method for conferring immunity to smallpox was known in Asia. Yet no action was taken for another hundred years and after millions of deaths. Meanwhile, the foundations of the scientific method that involved systematic observation, measurement, and experimentation had been laid in the previous century. There was considerable debate whether it was better than traditional methods. There also were concerns that this new scientific method was not compatible with Church teachings and that diseases like smallpox were tests or punishments sent by God. The lead protagonist in this plot, Malcolm Forrester, newly trained on the Continent in the scientific method, pushes the limits in his quest to solve the greatest medical problem of his age. This unfortunately did not happen in history, but it might have.

The book was written as the result of online discussions between the authors about our common Scottish heritage. Bettyanne's father was a Bethea, a sept of the MacLeod clan, while Albert's mother is of the Forrester clan. We used some clan characters and histories of the period interspersed with fictional characters. For example, Sir William Forrester and his son George are drawn from history, but there was no son named Malcolm. The Beaton sept (Bethea in the southern USA), was well known for their abundance of physicians, and we used that in writing Elspeth's character and her cousin John Beaton. Many of the other characters were inspired by real men and women in history facing situations typical of the age.

We consulted a great many primary and secondary sources while writing this book and tried to stay within the bounds of reality while creating an entertaining story. The most difficult part was getting into the minds of the people. There was a much in common with today's world, but significant differences. Life was more tenuous than today, with violence, poverty and disease common. That must have affected beliefs and thoughts in a world much less secular and stable than ours. But it is from historical characters like the courageous Elspeth and swashbuckling Malcolm that our modern world was built. We salute them.

CAST OF CHARACTERS

Allen, James: Wool merchant and patient
Beaton, John: Physician, Edinburgh and friend of Malcolm Forrester
Buchanan, Aidan: Blacksmith and metalsmith in Torrport
Barbier, Jean-Bernard: Frame maker
Cameron: Edinburgh Advocate
Campbell, Ross: Middle aged merchant in Torrport
Duncan, Calum: Owner of the Sand Bar Pub
Spence, Rachel: Lady Margaret's handmaid
Fletcher, Gilly: Barmaid and convenient at MacTavish Tavern
Forrester, George: Older brother of Malcom serving as an officer in the military
Forrester, Malcolm: Physician of Torrport and son of William Forrester
Forrester, William: Judge, father of Malcolm and George Forrester
Fowler, Archibald: William Forrester's servant
Fraser: Turnbull's assistant
Gow, Daniel: blacksmith's assistant and horse rental
Gwen: Malcolm Forrester's lover
Henry: Malcolm's dog
Kidd, William, Jr., Captain: Smuggler
Liddell: Edinburgh Physician
MacCool, Molly: village seamstress
MacDuff, Douglass: Laird of Torrport
MacDuff, Margaret: Laird MacDuff's wife
MacLeod, Cawdie: Former warrior, protector of Elspeth
MacLeod, Elspeth: Healer in Torrport and cousin of John Beaton
Mackmain, Donald, Captain of the Edinburgh Town Guard
MacTavish, Molly: Wife of MacTavish and mother of Jocki
MacTavish, Jocki: Son of MacTavish the tavernkeeper

MacTavish, Leana: Daughter of Molly and MacTavish, sister of Jocki
MacTavish: Tavernkeeper in the fishing village
McLaren, Angus: Edinburgh Physician
McLean, Alistair: Edinburgh Surgeon
Mitchell, Andrew: Torrport locum Physician
Morrison, Julianne: Relative of Laird MacDuff
Morrison, Tam: Elspeth as a boy
Robertson, Hammet: Reverend in Torrport
Ross, Janet: Companion of Elspeth MacLeod
Scathach – Elspeth's dog
Scrogie, Aggie: Torrport laundress
Scrogie, Alexander: the tavernkeeper's son
Scrogie, Danyell: Tavernkeeper
Scrogie, Wynda : Wife of the Torrport tavernkeeper
Spence, John, Captain: MacDuff's Second
Turnbull, Robert: Edinburgh Physician and Head of the College of Physicians
Volkof, Gregor: Sir Ross Campbell's manservant
Young: Edinburgh Physician

ACKNOWLEDGEMENT

Our thanks are extended to family and friends who tolerated our madness in writing this book. We especially appreciate those who bravely read those early chapters and offered helpful advice, and Tom Vowler who provided expert editing.

ABOUT THE AUTHORS

Albert Anthony Marsolais

Albert is a retired scientist and businessman who worked in the field of genetics and biotechnology. He lives in Ontario, Canada with his wife Laurel.

Bettyanne Bethea Twigg

Bettyanne is a curator and objects conservator who specializes in antique dolls and toys. She and her husband Homer live in the mountains of Maryland, with their dog, Pepper and sundry feral cats.

www.ingramcontent.com/pod-product-compliance
Lightning Source LLC
Chambersburg PA
CBHW051605100726
47898CB00001B/232